About the Authors

Michelle Douglas h[...] since 2007, and be[...] world. She's a suck[...] have a secret stash of choco[...] and [...] how to laugh. She lives in Newcastle Australia wi[...] own romantic hero, a house full of dust and books, and an eclectic collection of sixties and seventies vinyl. She loves to hear from readers and can be contacted via her website www.michelle-douglas.com

Rebecca Winters lives in Salt Lake City, Utah. With canyons and high alpine meadows full of wildflowers, she never runs out of places to explore. They, plus her favourite holiday spots in Europe, often end up as backgrounds for her romance novels because writing is her passion, along with her family and church. Rebecca loves to hear from readers. If you wish to e-mail her, please visit her website at: www.cleanromances.net

Stacy Connelly dreamed of publishing books since she was a kid writing about a girl and her horse. Eventually, boys made it onto the page as she discovered a love of romance and the promise of happily-ever-after. In 2008, that dream came true when she sold All She Wants for Christmas to Mills & Boon. When she is not lost in the land of make-believe, Stacy lives in Arizona with her two spoiled dogs.

Wedding Belles

Wedding Belles: The Billion Dollar Bride

MICHELLE DOUGLAS

REBECCA WINTERS

STACY CONNELLY

MILLS & BOON

First Published in Great Britain 2021
By Mills & Boon, an imprint of HarperCollins*Publishers*, Ltd
1 London Bridge Street, London, SE1 9GF

www.harpercollins.co.uk

HarperCollins*Publishers*
1st Floor, Watermarque Building,
Ringsend Road, Dublin 4, Ireland

WEDDING BELLES: THE BILLION DOLLAR BRIDE
© 2021 Harlequin Books S.A.

An Unlikely Bride for the Billionaire © 2016 Michelle Douglas
The Billionaire Who Saw Her Beauty © 2016 Rebecca Winters
How to Be a Blissful Bride © 2018 by Stacy Cornell

ISBN: 978-0-263-30260-8

MIX
Paper from
responsible sources
FSC™ C007454

This book is produced from independently certified FSC™ paper
to ensure responsible forest management.

For more information visit: www.harpercollins.co.uk/green

Printed and bound in Spain
by CPI, Barcelona

AN UNLIKELY BRIDE FOR THE BILLIONAIRE

MICHELLE DOUGLAS

To Amber and Anthony, and Jessica and Tim,
who are raising the next generation of heroes
and heroines with grace and style...
and a splendid sense of fun!

CHAPTER ONE

'BUT—' MIA STARED, aghast, at Gordon Coulter '—that's not my job!' She was a trainee field officer, not a trainee event manager.

Her stomach performed a slow, sickening somersault at the spiteful smile that touched his lips. Gordon was the council administrator in charge of Newcastle's parks and wildlife—her boss's boss and a petty bureaucrat to boot. Plum Pines Reserve fell under his control. And he'd made no secret of the fact that he'd love to get rid of her—that he was simply waiting for her to mess up so he could do exactly that.

She did her best to moderate her voice. 'I'm in charge of the weed extermination project that's to start on the eastern boundary. Veronica—' the reserve's ranger '—insists it's vital we get that underway as soon as possible. We're supposed to be starting today.'

'Which is why I've handed that project over to Simon.'

Every muscle stiffened in protest, but Mia bit back the objections pressing against the back of her throat. She'd worked ridiculously hard on fine-tuning that project, had gathered together an enthusiastic band of volunteers who didn't care one jot about her background. More exciting still, she and Veronica had planned to take a full botanical inventory of the area—a comprehensive project that had filled Mia with enthusiasm. And now she was to have no part in it.

'This isn't up for debate, Mia.'

Gordon pursed his lips, lifting himself up to his full paunchy height of five feet ten inches. If it was supposed to make him look impressive, it failed. It only drew her attention to the damp half-moons at the armpits of his business shirt.

'You have to understand that teamwork is vital in an area as poorly funded as ours. If you're refusing to assist the administrative team in their hour of need then perhaps this isn't the right organisation for you.'

She wanted to know where Nora was. She wanted to know why Simon hadn't been given *this* job instead of her.

'The Fairweathers will be here at any moment, so if you *are* refusing to assist…'

'Of course I'm not refusing.' She tried to keep her voice level. She couldn't afford to lose this job. 'I'm surprised you'd trust me with such an important assignment, that's all.'

His eyes narrowed. 'If you screw this up, Maydew, you'll be out on your ear.'

She didn't doubt that for a moment.

'Naturally Nora will take over once she returns.' His lips tightened. 'She assures me you're the only one who can possibly deputise in her stead.'

She bit back a sigh. Nora wanted her on the events team, claiming she was wasted as a field officer. Mia had plans, though, and they didn't involve being part of the events team.

Where was Nora?

She didn't ask. She refused to give Gordon the satisfaction of telling her it was none of her business. She'd ring Nora later and make sure she was okay.

The receptionist knocked on the office door. It was Nora's office, but Gordon co-opted it whenever he decided to work from Plum Pines rather than his office at Council Chambers.

'Mr Coulter? Mr Fairweather is here.'

'Send him in.'

Mia moved to the side of the desk—she hadn't been in-
ited to sit—fighting the urge to move to the back of the

om, where she'd be able to remain as unobtrusive as pos-
ble.

'Mr Fairweather, it's delightful to meet you!' Gordon
moved forward, arm outstretched, greasy smile in place.

Mia repressed a shudder.

And then she glanced at Dylan Fairweather—and had to
blink, momentarily dazzled by so much golden...*golden-
ness*. Dear Lord, the papers did Dylan Fairweather no justice whatsoever. Not that Mia spent much time reading the
society pages, but even *she*—hermit that she was—knew
that Dylan Fairweather was considered one of Australia's
bright young things. Earlier in the year he'd been named one
of Australia's Top Twenty Eligible Bachelors.

If steal-your-breath sex appeal was one of the criteria
then Dylan Fairweather had that in spades! Too-long dark
gold hair and sexy designer stubble coupled with a golden
tan had Mia's fingers curling into her palms. At six feet two
he towered over Gordon, his pale blue business shirt and
sand-coloured chinos achieving a casual elegance Gordon
had no hope of matching.

Nor did his clothes hide the breadth of his shoulders or
the latent strength of powerful thighs. All that power and
flaxen golden brilliance should have made him look terrifying—like a prowling lion. But it didn't. He looked...he
looked like a prince out of a fairytale.

Mia tried to tear her gaze away, but couldn't. Never, in
all of her twenty-five years, had she been in the presence of
someone so physically perfect.. She remembered one of the
women in prison describing how she'd felt when she'd first
laid eyes on Vincent van Gogh's painting *The Starry Night*.
That was how Mia felt now.

Swallowing, she shook herself, appalled at the way her
heart raced, at the craving that clawed at her belly. Pulling
in a breath, she reminded herself that she wasn't some primitive savage, controlled by greed and impetuous impulses.
Not any more.

When Gordon had said she'd be taking care of the Fairweathers today, she'd been expecting a blushing bride an. her aunt, maybe an attendant or two. She hadn't been expecting the bride's *brother*.

His pleasantries with Gordon exchanged, he turned to her and offered his hand with an easy, 'Dylan Fairweather.'

She took it automatically, appreciating the just-firm-enough grip and almost melting under the unexpected warmth of his smile.

You're not the melting type.

'Mia Maydew. It's nice to meet you. Carla is taking a call. She should only be a moment.'

'That's no problem at all.' Gordon ushered Dylan to a chair, frowning at Mia over his head.

Dear God! Had her paralysing preoccupation been evident for all to see? Heat climbed into her face. Brilliant. Just brilliant.

Gordon took his chair. He still didn't invite Mia to sit. 'Unfortunately Nora can't join us today. She sends her apologies. She was involved in a car accident on her way to work this morning.'

Mia couldn't prevent her involuntary intake of breath, or the way her hand flew to her abdomen, just below her breasts, to counter the way her stomach jumped. Startlingly brilliant blue eyes surveyed her for a moment, and while the brilliant colour might have the ability to distract a mere mortal, Mia sensed the shrewdness behind them.

Dylan Fairweather shifted ever so slightly on his chair. 'I hope she's okay.'

'Yes, yes, she's fine, but her car is apparently a write-off. I insisted she go to the hospital for a thorough examination, though.'

Mia closed her eyes briefly and let out a breath.

'Wise,' agreed Dylan—*Mr Fairweather*.

'In her stead—as a temporary measure, you understand—you'll have Mia here to run you through wedding options.

Anything you'd like to know—ask her. Anything you'd like to see—she'll show it to you. I promise that nothing will be too much trouble.'

Easy for him to say.

She straightened. It wasn't the Fairweathers' fault that Gordon had thrust her into the role of Assistant Events Manager. She'd helped Nora out before with weddings and corporate events. She'd do everything she could to answer the Fairweathers' questions and help Carla plan the wedding of her dreams.

'If you'd like to take it from here, Mia?'

'Certainly.' She forced a noncommittal smile to her face. 'If you'd just hand me the Fairweather file from the top drawer of the desk, I'll take Mr Fairweather through to the meeting room.'

She was tempted to laugh at the disgruntled expression that flitted across Gordon's face. Had he really thought she didn't know about the file? She'd helped Nora compile parts of it earlier in the week. Did he hate her so much that he'd risk a lucrative account, not to mention some seriously good publicity, to undermine her? The thought killed any urge to smile.

She had to counsel herself to take the file calmly, before leading Dylan Fairweather out of the office to the meeting room. Her pulse skittered and perspiration gathered at her nape. She preferred working with animals to people. Better yet, she liked working with plants. With over one hundred and seventy hectares of natural bushland to its name, it should have been relatively easy to avoid human contact at Plum Pines Reserve.

'Can I get you tea or coffee…maybe some water?' She gestured for Dylan to take a chair at the table, doing what she could to stop her fingers from shaking. This account had excited Nora enormously and, Gordon aside, Mia wanted to do her best for her boss.

From across the table Dylan eyed her closely, a frown in

his eyes, although his lips remained curved upwards in a pleasant smile. 'I think a carafe of water and three glasses would be an excellent idea.'

He thought *she* needed a drink of water? Dear Lord. She scurried away to fetch it. Did her nerves show that badly? She usually came across as a difficult study. She took a couple of deep breaths to compose herself before returning to the meeting room.

'Nora is a friend of yours?' he asked when she was seated, taking charge of the carafe and pouring a glass of water before pushing it across the table to her.

It hit her then that he'd misread her nerves as worry for the other woman. She hesitated. Would Nora consider Mia a friend? 'Nora is a close colleague. I like her a lot.'

'The news of her accident was a shock?'

She wasn't used to anyone being interested in her reactions. 'It was. I'm relieved it's not too serious.' When he continued to stare at her—which did nothing to slow her heart-rate—she forced her lips upwards. 'I'll call her later to check if there's anything she needs. It's kind of you to be so concerned. Now, let me show you the material Nora and I have gathered in relation to Ms Fairweather's wedding.'

'Please—you must call us Carla and Dylan.'

Must she? There was a certain protection afforded by the formality of Mr and Ms.

The customer is always right.

She bit back a sigh. If that were the case…

'Dylan.' She tested the name on her tongue. It emerged without any effort at all and tasted like her favourite brand of dark chocolate—flavoured with a bite of sea salt. His smile was her reward, making her forget the rest of her sentence.

'See…it wasn't so hard, was it—Mia?'

He made her name sound like a song.

He smiled. 'I can see why Carla requested you work on her wedding'

She opened her mouth and then closed it, blinking. 'I

think you've mistaken me for someone else. I'm afraid don't know your sister, Mr Fair—uh… Dylan.'

He stared across at her, but in the end he merely nodded and let it go without challenge. It was as if someone had cut a string and released her.

She glanced down at the folder in an effort to collect herself. 'Do you know…?' She cleared her throat. 'Do you know where Carla would like the ceremony to take place?'

He glanced towards the door, as if hoping his sister would magically appear. 'Beside some lily pond. It's apparently where she and Thierry met.'

Right. Mia jotted a note down on her pad.

Blue eyes twinkled across the table at her when she looked up at him again. 'Aren't you going to gush about how romantic that is?'

Should she? Was gushing part of the job description?

He laughed as if he'd read that thought in her face, pointing a lean tanned finger at her. 'You, Ms Maydew, are *not* a romantic.'

He stared at her as if he knew her. It was utterly disconcerting. She had no intention of letting him know that, though.

She pointed her pen back at him. 'I *am*, however, an excellent worker.'

'Perfect.' His grin widened. 'You'll at least provide a port of sanity amid all the craziness.'

That made her lips twitch. She'd watched TV programs about Bridezillas. Was that what they had on their hands with Carla?

'Hallelujah!' He raised his hands heavenwards.

'What?'

'I finally managed to get a proper smile out of you.'

She stared at him, nonplussed. Why should he care one way or the other whether she smiled or not? Was smiling also part of the job description?

Darn it—it probably was! Give her animals and plants any day.

She forced her lips to curve upwards.

'Oh, dear me, no! On a scale of one to ten, that's not even going to score you a three.' He donned a mock commentator's voice. *'And Mia's smile has only scored a two point one from the Romanian judge!'*

She had to choke back a laugh.

He leant his elbows on the table. There was the whole width of the table between them, but somehow he seemed to bridge that distance without any effort at all. Maybe it was a combination of his height and breadth? She could make out the tiny laughter lines that fanned out from his eyes. She suspected Dylan laughed a lot. She noted the dusky eyelashes…ridiculously long and tipped with gold…and the firm fullness of his bottom lip. She'd bet he kissed a lot too. A pulse started up in the centre of her chest.

'I suspect, Mia Maydew, it'd be really something to make you laugh.'

She couldn't explain why, but she found herself jerking back as if he'd just propositioned her.

To cover her confusion, she folded her arms and narrowed her eyes. 'I have your number, Dylan Fairweather.' She used his full name in the same way he'd used hers. 'You're an incorrigible flirt. I suspect you can't help yourself.'

He raised his hands. 'Guilty as charged! But it's flirting without intent…just a bit of frivolous nonsense.'

His smile made her stomach tumble. 'Then why…?'

'Because it's fun.' His grin widened and she swore he had the devil in his eyes. 'Aren't you going to flirt back?'

She couldn't help it. She laughed.

Thank heavens! The woman *could* laugh.

Dylan sat back and let out a breath when the rather plain and schoolmistressy Mia momentarily transformed from uptight and ordinary-looking to mischievous imp. His gaze lingered on her mouth. He hadn't noticed how wide and generous it was earlier.

Since he'd witnessed her shock at learning of Nora's accident, and sensed her nerves at being thrust into the role of wedding co-ordinator, he'd wanted to put her at ease. Putting people at ease was his stock in trade. Mia might call it flirting, but it was nothing more than a bit of harmless fun designed to make her laugh and loosen up. And it had half worked—she'd laughed.

Having now seen Mia smile for real, though, he could see that she was neither plain nor schoolmistressy. It was just an attitude she cultivated. Interesting…

Nora had been ecstatic yesterday when he'd mentioned that they'd like Mia as part of their wedding team. Nora mightn't have known it, but she'd unwittingly supplied a glowing character reference for Mia. He sat back, resisting the urge to rub his eyes. He wanted everything associated with this wedding to be a joy for Carla. He meant to ensure it went without a hitch.

If only he could be certain the damn wedding should go ahead!

The walls of the glassed-in meeting room pressed in on him. He wanted to be outside and in the fresh air. *Now!* He wanted to be away from the fresh juniper berry scent of the woman opposite. It had his mind turning to black ski runs in St Moritz, with the wind tearing at his hair and the cold making him feel alive. Which was ridiculous. While he might be on leave, this was no holiday. Besides, if there'd been less frivolity in his life recently Carla might never have become embroiled with a man like Thierry.

Carla's happiness—that was what he had to focus on. 'Is the lily pond far? Can you show it to me?'

'You want to see the lily pond *now*?'

'Yes.'

'What about your sister?'

'She's on the phone to her intended. She could be hours. I'll text her so she'll know where to find us.'

Dutifully he pulled out his phone.

Mia taking me to lily pond. Meet there.

He held it out for her to see and then hit 'send'.

Without another word Mia led him out into the warm summer sunshine and he filled his lungs with eucalypt-scented air. The small office block sat on the edge of a rectangle of lush lawn that had to be at least two football fields long. Covered picnic tables marched down each of its sides, shaded by a variety of gum trees, plum pines and bottle-brush trees. The red blossoms of the bottlebrushes had attracted a flock of rainbow lorikeets which descended in a noisy colourful rush.

A peacock strutted through the nearest picnic shelter, checking for crumbs and leftovers, while a bush turkey raked through a nearby pile of leaves. All around the air was filled with birdcalls and the scent of warmed native grasses. Groups of people had gathered around the picnic tables and on blankets on the grass. He could hear children's laughter from the playground he glimpsed through the trees.

'This place is popular.'

She gestured that they should take a path to the left. 'It is.'

Her dark brown hair, pulled back into a severe ponytail, gleamed rich and russet in the bright light. She didn't wear a scrap of make-up. Not that she needed to. She had a perfect peaches and cream complexion that he hadn't appreciated under the strip lighting of the office.

He pulled his mind back to the matter at hand. 'Can we book the entire reserve for the wedding?'

'I'm afraid not. Plum Pines is a public park. What we *can* do, though, is rope off the area where your event is being held to keep the general public out.'

'Hmm...' He'd have to rethink the security firm he'd ini-

tially considered hiring. The wedding security would b
bigger job than he'd originally thought.

She glanced up, her gaze sharp. 'Is that going to be a
problem?'

'Not if I hire a good security firm.'

'Let me know if you'd like any recommendations.' She
led him across a bridge spanning a large pond. 'Officially
the park is open from seven a.m. to seven p.m.'

He stared out at the expanse of water, noting several black
swans sitting on the edge of the far bank. 'Is this the lily
pond?'

'No, it's the duck pond.'

He glanced down into the water and blinked when a tortoise poked its small head out of the water. 'That...' He
halted to point. 'That was...'

She glanced over the railing. 'A Common Longneck Tortoise. The pond is full of them.'

Hands on hips, he completed a full circle, taking in the
surroundings. Plum Pines was undeniably pretty, and the
native forest rising up all around them undeniably grand.
He'd visited some of the most exotic places the world had to
offer and yet he'd somehow missed experiencing what was
in his own backyard.

'I can't believe we're in the middle of the second largest
city in New South Wales. It feels as if we're in the middle
of the bush.'

'Yes, we're very privileged.'

That was a rote reply if he'd ever heard one—trotted out
for the benefit of visitors. What did Mia really think of the
place? Did she love it or loathe it? Her lips were pursed into
a prim line that had him itching to make her smile again.

'You'll need to apply to the council for an event licence
that'll allow the wedding to extend beyond those hours.
There shouldn't be any issue with that, though.'

She moved off again, with her no-nonsense stride, and

...er another glance at where the tortoise had disappeared ...e set off after her.

'Have you had any weddings that *haven't* extended beyond seven p.m.?' All of the weddings he'd ever attended had kicked on into the wee small hours.

'There's been a trend for morning weddings with lunchtime receptions. So, yes.'

She was so serious. And literal. He found himself starting to laugh.

She glanced at him, a frown crinkling her forehead. 'What's so funny?'

'You're not so good at small talk, are you?'

Her face fell and she stuttered to a halt. 'You want small talk?'

That made him laugh again. 'How do you enforce the seven p.m. closing time?'

'We close the gates to the car parks. There's a hefty fine involved to have the gates opened. Our people, along with your security firm, will have a list of your guests' number plates so they can come and go as they please.'

'Right.'

'And, as Plum Pines is in the middle of suburbia, we don't get much foot traffic or many homeless people looking for a place to put up for the night.'

That was something, he supposed.

She consulted her notepad. 'Do you know how many guests the bride and groom are planning to invite?'

'Carla informs me that she wants "a small and intimate affair".'

That frown crinkled her brow again. 'Do you happen to know what your sister's idea of "small" might be?'

'I wouldn't have a clue.' He had no idea if Thierry came from a large family or not. The other man had closed up like a clam when Dylan had asked him about them. 'I can't say that I know what she means by "intimate" either.'

Mia nodded. 'I think we can guess that fairly accurately—it probably includes fairy lights strung all around the marquee and surrounding trees, white linen tablecloths with centrepieces involving ivy and candles, vintage china and a string quartet.'

'You don't sound like you approve.'

She swung to face him. 'Mr Fair— Dylan. It's not for me to approve or disapprove. It's Plum Pines' job to help Carla plan the wedding she wants.'

'But—' He broke off.

'What were you going to say?'

He read the thought that flashed through her eyes—*Gordon Coulter promised nothing would be too much trouble.*

'Dylan, I'll do my best to deliver whatever is needed.'

Her moss-green eyes stared back at him, earnest and steady, and he found himself needing to pull a breath of air into cramped lungs. 'I need you to be as committed to this wedding as Carla.'

'I'm committed—I can promise you that.' Her teeth worried at her bottom lip. 'But that's not what you meant, is it? You want me to be exuberant and…and bouncy.'

He winced, realising how absurd that sounded when uttered out loud. He just wanted to see her smile again. *That* was what this was all about—and it was pure nonsense on his part.

He rubbed his hand across his nape. 'I think of weddings and I think of joy and excitement and…and *joy.*'

He wanted Carla's life filled with joy—not just her wedding. A fist tightened about his chest. If Thierry hurt her he'd—

Mia moved into his field of vision, making him blink. 'There's a lot of behind-the-scenes work that needs doing to make a wedding successful.' She pointed her pen at him. 'Joy and excitement are all well and good, but I figure my job is to keep a level head.'

A level head? That was exactly what he needed.

'Don't you believe someone can be quietly enthusiastic?' she asked.

'Of course they can. I'm sorry.' He grimaced. 'It's the bride who's supposed to go loopy, right? Not her brother.'

One of those rare smiles peeped out, making his heart thump.

'You're excited for her.' Too soon she sobered again. 'I'm naturally quiet. It doesn't mean I'm not invested.'

'Whereas I'm naturally gregarious.' It was what made him so good at his job. 'I sometimes forget that not everyone else is.'

'Do you still want to see the lily pond?'

'Yes, please.' He spoke as gravely as she did. 'My seeing the lily pond is not dependent on you being exuberant.'

He could have sworn that her lips twitched—for the briefest of moments. It sent a rush of something warm and sweet surging through his veins. He was glad he'd had a chance to meet her on his own. Carla had spoken of her often enough to make his ears prick up. It had been a long time since Carla had made a new female friend.

The question he needed to answer now, though—was Carla more than just a job to Mia? He'd give his right arm for Carla to have a girlfriend with whom to plan her wedding. And whatever the two of them dreamed up—schemed up—he'd make happen.

When he glanced back he found Mia staring at a point beyond him. He swung around to see an emu enclosure... and an emu sitting on the ground in the dirt. He glanced back to find her chewing her lip. 'Is that emu okay?' They *did* sit down, right?

She hesitated. 'Do you mind...?' She gestured towards the fence.

'Not at all.'

'Hey, Charlie—come on, boy!' Mia rattled the fence and the emu turned to stare, but when he didn't otherwise move she pulled out her phone. 'Janis? It's Mia. Charlie is looking decidedly under the weather. Can you send someone out to check on him?' Her lips pressed together as she listened to the person at the other end. 'He's sitting down and not responding to my calls.' She listened some more. 'But—'

She huffed out a breath and he could see her mentally counting to five.

'Right. If that's the best you can do.' She snapped the phone shut and shoved it back into her pocket.

'You're worried about him?'

One slim shoulder lifted. 'Charlie's been hand-raised. He's a social bird. Normally he'd be over here, begging for a treat. Everyone who works here is fond of him.'

Dylan glanced across at the emu. 'You want to go and give him the once over?'

She glanced around, as if to check that no one had overheard him. 'Would you mind?'

'Not at all.'

'It should only take me a moment. I just want to make sure he doesn't have something caught around his legs. Discarded plastic bags are the bane of our existence—they seem to blow in from everywhere.'

'I don't mind at all.'

Besides, he wanted her full attention once Carla arrived. He wanted her focussed on wedding preparations—not worrying about Charlie the Emu.

She moved towards a gate in the fence and unlocked it with a key she fished out from one of the many pockets of her khaki cargo pants.

She glanced back at him apologetically. 'I have to ask you to remain on this side of the fence. It's actually against the law for me to take you in with me.'

'Believe me, I'm happy to stay on this side of the fence, but...' he glanced across at Charlie '...that emu is huge. What if he attacks you?'

He couldn't in all conscious just stand here and do nothing.

'He won't hurt me. I promise.'

'In that case I promise to stay on this side of the fence.'

Nevertheless, he found his heart pounding a little too hard as she slipped into the enclosure and made her way towards the giant bird. She ran a soothing hand down its neck, not in the least intimidated by its size. He reminded himself that she was trained to deal with these animals, but he didn't take his eyes from her.

Slipping her arms beneath the bird, she lifted it to its knees, and Dylan could see something wrapped tight around its ankles. The poor bird was completely tangled! He watched in admiration as she deftly unwound it, shoving the remnants into her pocket. The entire time she crooned soothingly to the emu, telling him what a good boy he was and how pretty he was. Charlie leaned into her as much as he could, trusting her completely.

Finally she placed her arms beneath him with a cheery, 'Up we come, Charlie.'

The emu gave a kind of strangled *beep* before a stream of something green and vicious-looking shot out of the back of him, splattering all over the front of Mia's shirt. Only then did the bird struggle fully to its feet and race off towards a water trough. Mia stumbled backwards, a comical look of surprise on her face. She turned towards Dylan, utterly crestfallen and…and covered in bird poop.

Dylan clapped a hand over his mouth to hold back a shout of laughter. *Don't laugh*! An awful lot of women he knew would have simply burst into tears. If he laughed and then she cried he'd have to comfort her…and then he'd end up with bird poop all over *him* too.

Mia didn't cry. She pushed her shoulders back and squelched back over to the gate in the fence with as much dignity as she could muster. Still, even *she* had to find it difficult to maintain a sense of dignity when she was covered in bird poop.

She lifted her chin, as if reading that thought in his face. 'As you can see, Charlie left me a little present for my pains.'

He swallowed, schooling his features. 'You did a very good deed, Mia.'

'The thing is, when an emu gets stressed, the stress can result in...' she glanced down at herself, her nose wrinkling '...diarrhoea.'

'God, I'm *so* glad those birds can't fly!'

The heartfelt words shot out of him, and Mia's lips started to twitch as if the funny side of the situation had finally hit her.

Dylan couldn't hold back his laughter any longer. 'I'm sorry, Mia. You deserve better, but the look on your face when it happened... It was priceless!'

She grinned, tentatively touching the front of her shirt. 'That rotten bird! Here I am, supposedly trying to impress you and your sister with our marvellous facilities...and now you're going to live in fear of projectile diarrhoea from the native animals!'

The sudden image that came to his mind made him roar until he was doubled over. Mia threw her head back and laughed right alongside him. She laughed with an uninhibited gusto that transformed her completely. He'd glimpsed the mischievous imp earlier, but now she seemed to come alive—as if her mirth had broken some dam wall—as if she were a desert suddenly blooming with wildflowers.

Dylan's heart surged against his ribs and for a moment all he could do was stare. 'You should do that more often, you know. Laugh. You're beautiful when you laugh.'

She glanced up at him, the laughter dying on her lips. Something in the air shimmered between them, making them both blink. Her gaze lowered momentarily to his lips, before she turned beetroot-red. Swinging away, she stumbled across to the tap that stood by the gate in the fence.

Heat pulsed through him. So...the serious Mia wasn't immune to his charms after all?

The next moment he silently swore. *Damn!* He deserved a giant kick to the seat of his pants. She'd accused him of flirting earlier—but he hadn't meant to give her the wrong impression. He didn't want her thinking anything could happen between them. All flirtation and teasing on his part was entirely without intent.

She knelt at the tap and scrubbed at her shirt with a piece of rag. She must keep a veritable tool shed of handiness in those cargo pants of hers.

He watched in silence as she washed the worst of the mess from her shirt. 'I have a handkerchief if you need it.'

'Thank you, but I think this is the best I'm going to manage until I can change my shirt. Shall we continue on to the lily pond?'

'Yes, please.'

She gestured towards the path. 'Do you mind if I ring the office to give them an update on Charlie?'

'Not at all.'

And just like that they withdrew back into reserved professionalism. But something new pounded through Dylan—a curiosity that hadn't been there before. What an intriguing paradox Mia was proving to be...a fascinating enigma.

Which you don't have time for.

With a sigh, he pushed thoughts of Mia from his mind and forced his attention back to the impending wedding. He had to focus on what really mattered. He couldn't let Carla down—not when she needed him.

CHAPTER TWO

THEY REACHED THE lily pond two minutes later. The moment Dylan clapped eyes on the enchanting glade he understood why Carla had fallen in love with it. True to its name, large green lily pads decorated a small but picturesque body of oval water. Native trees and shrubs curved around three of its sides. The fourth side opened out to a large circle of green lawn.

Mia pointed to that now. 'This area is large enough for our medium-sized marquee, which holds sixty guests comfortably. That leaves the area behind for the caterers to set up their tents and vans for the food.'

Carla chose that moment to come rushing up—which was just as well, as Dylan had found himself suddenly in danger of getting caught up on the way Mia's wet shirt clung to her chest.

Carla grinned at Mia—'Surprise!'—before taking Dylan's arm and jumping from one foot to the other. 'Isn't this just the most perfect spot?'

He glanced down at her—at her smile made radiant with her newfound happiness. 'It's lovely,' he agreed, resolve solidifying in his gut. This wedding had come out of left field, taking him completely by surprise. But if this was what Carla truly wanted, he meant to create the perfect wedding for her. 'Where's Thierry?'

A cloud passed across her face. 'Something's come up. He can't make it.'

That was the problem. Thierry. Dylan didn't like the man.

His sister had suffered enough misery in her life, and Dylan had every intention of protecting her from further heartache.

Carla moved towards Mia. 'Please tell me you're not cross with me.'

'So…you're not really Carly Smith, frequent visitor and keen student of environmentalism?'

Carla shook her head.

Mia glanced down at her notepad. 'With your background, I imagine you need to be careful with your privacy.'

Carla winced. 'Please tell me you don't hate me. You've been so kind. I love shadowing you when you're on duty for the wildlife displays. You never talk down to me or treat me like I'm stupid. Oh!' she added in a rush. 'And just so you know, I really *do* have a keen interest in the environment and conservation.'

Mia smiled. 'Of course I don't hate you.'

That smile made Dylan's skin tighten. When she smiled she wasn't plain. And when she laughed she was beautiful.

He pushed those thoughts away. They had no bearing on anything. Her smile told him what he needed to know—Mia genuinely liked his sister. *That* was what mattered.

'Right.' Mia consulted her notepad. 'I want to hear every tiny detail you have planned for this wedding.'

'Hasn't Dylan told you *anything*?'

Mia glanced at him. 'We didn't want to start without you.'

That was unexpectedly diplomatic.

He stood back while the pair started discussing wedding preparations, jumping from one topic to the next as if it made utterly logical sense to do so. He watched them and then shook his head. Had he really thought Carla needed exuberance from Mia? Thank heaven Mia had seen the wisdom in not trying to fake it. He silently blessed her tact in not asking where Mia's maid of honour or bridesmaids or any female relative might be too.

Carla didn't have anyone but him.

And now Thierry.

And Mia in the short term.

He crossed his fingers and prayed that Thierry would finally give Carla all that she needed...and all that she deserved.

Mia spent two hours with Carla and Dylan, though Dylan rarely spoke now Carla was there. She told herself she was glad. She told herself that she didn't miss his teasing.

Except she did. A little.

Which told her that the way she'd chosen to live her life had a few flaws in it.

Still, even if he had wanted to speak it would have been difficult for him to get a word in, with Carla jumping from topic to topic in a fever of enthusiasm.

She was so different from Carly Smith, the wide-eyed visitor to the park that Mia had taken under her wing. She took in the heightened colour in Carla's cheeks, the way her eyes glittered, how she could barely keep still, and nodded. Love was *exactly* like that and Mia wanted no part of it *ever again*.

Carla spoke at a hundred miles an hour. She cooed about the colour scheme she wanted—pink, of course—and the table decorations she'd seen in a magazine, as well as the cake she'd fallen in love with. She rattled off guest numbers and seating arrangements in one breath and told her about the world-class photographer she was hoping to book in the next. Oh, and then there was the string quartet that was apparently *'divine'*.

She bounced from favours and bouquets to napkins and place settings along with a million other things that Mia hastily jotted down, but the one thing she didn't mention was the bridal party. At one point Mia opened her mouth t ask, but behind his sister's back Dylan surreptitiously shook his head and Mia closed it again.

Maybe Carla hadn't decided on her attendants yet. Mia suspected that the politics surrounding bridesmaid hierarchy could be fraught. Especially for a big society wedding.

Only it wasn't going to be big. It was going to be a very select and exclusive group of fifty guests. Which might mean that Carla didn't want a large bridal party.

Every now and again, though, Carla would falter. She'd glance at her brother and without fail Dylan would step in and smooth whatever wrinkle had brought Carla up short, and then off she would go again.

Beneath Carla's manic excitement Mia sensed a lurking vulnerability, and she couldn't prevent a sense of protectiveness from welling through her. She'd warmed to Carly—Carla—the moment she'd met her. For all her natural warmth and enthusiasm she had seemed a little lost, and it had soothed something inside Mia to chat to her about the programmes Plum Pines ran, to talk to her about the animals and their daily routines.

As a rule, Mia did her best *not* to warm towards people. She did her best not to let them warm towards her either. But to remain coolly professional and aloof with Carla—the way she'd tried to be with Dylan—somehow seemed akin to kicking a puppy.

While many of her work colleagues thought her a cold and unfeeling witch, Mia *didn't* kick puppies. She didn't kick anyone. Except herself—mentally—on a regular basis.

'Can I come back with Thierry tomorrow and go over all this again?'

Why hadn't the groom-to-be been here *today*?

'Yes, of course.'

Hopefully tomorrow Nora would be back to take over and Mia would be safely ensconced on the reserve's eastern boundary, communing with weeds.

Carla glanced at her watch. 'I promised Thierry I'd meet

him for lunch. I have to run.' She turned to her brother. 'Dylan…?' Her voice held a note of warning.

He raised his hands, palms outwards. 'I'll sort everything—I promise. Mia and I will go back to the office and thrash it all out.'

Mia's chest clenched. Thrash what out? She didn't have the authority to thrash *anything* out.

She must have looked crestfallen, because Dylan laughed. 'Buck up, Mia. It'll be fun.' He waggled his eyebrows.

Mia rolled her eyes, but she couldn't crush the anticipation that flitted through her.

'I'll buy you a cup of coffee and a blueberry muffin.'

His grin could melt an ice queen.

Lucky, then, that she was made of sterner stuff than ice.

'You'll do no such thing.' She stowed her notepad in her back pocket as they headed back towards the main concourse. 'Gordon Coulter would be scandalised. All refreshments will be courtesy of Plum Pines.'

During the last two hours they'd moved from the lily pond back to the office, to pore over brochures, and then outside again to a vacant picnic table, where Carla had declared she wanted to drink in the serenity. Now, with many grateful thanks, Carla moved towards the car park while Mia led Dylan to the Pine Plum's café.

He grinned at the cashier, and Mia didn't blame the woman for blinking as if she'd been temporarily blinded.

'We'll have two large cappuccinos and two of those.' He pointed at the cupcakes sitting beneath a large glass dome before Mia had a chance to speak.

'You mean to eat two cupcakes and drink two mugs of coffee?' She tried to keep the acerbity out of her voice.

'No.' He spoke slowly as if to a child. 'One coffee and one cake are yours.'

Mia glanced at the cashier. 'Make that one large cappuccino, one pot of tea and *one* cupcake, thank you. It's to on Nora's events account.'

Without further ado she led him to a table with an outlook over the duck pond.

'You're not hungry?' he asked.

She was ravenous, but she'd brought her lunch to work, expecting to be stranded on the eastern boundary, and she hated waste. 'I'm not hungry,' she said. It was easier than explaining that in Gordon Coulter's eyes the events account didn't extend to buying her any food. 'Besides, I don't have much of a sweet tooth.'

She frowned, unsure why she'd added that last bit.

For a moment he looked as if he were waging an internal battle with himself, but then he folded his arms on the table and leaned towards her, his eyes dancing. 'Are you telling me, Mia...?'

She swallowed at the way he crooned her name, as if it were the sweetest of sweet things.

'...that you don't like cake?'

He said it with wide eyes, as if the very idea was scandalous. He was teasing her again. She resisted the almost alien urge to tease him back.

'I didn't say I didn't like it. It's just not something I ever find myself craving.'

His mouth kinked at one corner. Mia did her best to look away.

'Now I have to discover what it is you *do* crave.'

How could he make that sound so suggestive?

'Cheesecake? Ice cream?'

She narrowed her eyes. 'Why do I get the feeling you're trying to find something to use as a bribe?'

'Chocolate?'

Oh. He had her there. 'Chocolate is in a class of its own.'

He laughed, and something inside her shifted. *No shifting!* She had to remain on her guard around this man. He'd called her beautiful and something in her world had tilted. She had no intention of letting that happen again.

'You made my sister very happy today. From the bottom of my heart, thank you.'

It was the last thing she'd expected him to say. 'I... I was just doing my job.'

'It was more than that, and we both know it.'

She didn't want it to be more. This was just a job like any other. 'Naturally Carla is excited. I enjoyed discussing her plans with her.'

To her surprise, she realised she was speaking nothing less than the truth.

Their order was set in front of them. When the waitress left Dylan broke off a piece of cupcake, generously topped with frosting, and held it out to her. 'Would you like a taste?'

Unbidden, hunger roared through her. For the briefest of moments she was tempted to open her mouth and let him feed her the morsel. Her throat dried and her stomach churned. On the table, her hands clenched to fists.

She choked out a, 'No, thank you,' before busying herself with her tea.

Why now? Why should a man have such an effect on her *now*? In the last ten months she'd been asked out on dates... the occasional volunteer had tried to flirt with her...but nothing had pierced her armour.

None of them looked like Dylan Fairweather.

True. But was she really so shallow that someone's looks could have such an impact?

When she glanced back up she saw Gordon Coulter, glaring at her from the café's doorway. Had he seen Dylan offer her the bite of cake? *Great. Just great.*

She shuffled her mantel of professionalism back around her. 'Now, you better tell me what it is you promised Carla you'd sort out. It sounded ominous.'

He popped the piece of cake into his mouth and closed his eyes in bliss as he chewed. 'You have no idea what you're missing.'

And she needed to keep it that way.

She tried to stop her gaze lingering on his mouth.

His eyes sprang open, alive with mischief. 'I bet you love honey sandwiches made with the softest of fresh white bread.'

She had to bite her inner lip to stop herself from laughing. 'Honey makes my teeth ache.'

The man was irrepressible, and it occurred to her that it wasn't his startling looks that spoke to her but his childish sense of fun.

'Ha! But I nearly succeeded in making you laugh again.'

She didn't laugh, but she did smile. It was impossible not to.

Mia didn't do fun. Maybe that was a mistake too. Maybe she needed to let a little fun into her life and then someone like Dylan wouldn't rock her foundations so roundly.

He made as if to punch the air in victory. 'You should do that more often. It's not good for you to be so serious all the time.'

His words made her pull back. She knew he was only teasing, but he had no idea what was good for her.

She pulled her notepad from her pocket and flipped it open to a new page. 'Will you *please* tell me what it is you promised Carla you'd take care of?'

He surveyed her as he took a huge bite of cake. She tried not to fidget under that oddly penetrating gaze.

'Don't you ever let your hair down just a little?'

'This is my job. And this—' she gestured around '—is my place of employment. I have a responsibility to my employer to not "let my hair down" on the job.' She tapped her pen against the notepad. 'I think it's probably worth mentioning that you aren't my employer's only wedding account either.'

She spoke gently, but hoped he sensed the thread of steel beneath her words. There also were cages that needed cleaning, animals that needed feeding and logbooks to fill out. They weren't all going to get magically done while Dylan lingered over coffee and cake.

And it didn't matter how much he might temporarily fill her with an insane desire to kick back and take the rest of the day off—that wasn't going to happen.

'Ouch.' He said it with a good-natured grin. 'But you're right. Carla and I have taken up enough of your time for one day. Especially as we'll be back tomorrow.'

He was coming too? She tried to ignore the way her heart hitched.

'Mia, do you know what line of work I'm in?'

Even she, who'd spent most of her adult life living under a rock, knew what Dylan Fairweather did for a living. 'You created and run Fairweather Event Enterprises.' More widely known as Fairweather Events or FWE. Dylan had made his name bringing some of the world's most famous, not to mention *notorious*, rock acts to Australia.

Under his direction, Dylan's company had produced concerts of such spectacular proportions they'd gone down in rock history. His concerts had become a yardstick for all those following.

FWE had been in charge of last year's sensationally successful charity benefit held in Madison Square Garden in New York. He was regularly hired by royalty to oversee national anniversary celebrations, and by celebrities for their private birthday parties and gala events. Dylan Fairweather was a name with a capital N.

'The thing is…' He shuffled towards her, his expression intent now rather than teasing. 'I know that Plum Pines has its own events team, but *I* want to be the person running this particular show.'

Very slowly, she swallowed. 'By *"this particular show"*, I take it you're referring to Carla's wedding?'

He nodded.

Her heart thumped. Nora would be disappointed.

'I want to do this for Carla,' he continued, fully in earnest now. 'The only thing I can give her that's of any worth is my time. You have to understand it's not that I don't trust the Plum Pines staff, it's that I want to give my sister something that'll actually *mean* something to her—something she can cherish forever.'

Mia almost melted on the spot. To have someone who cared about you so much that they'd go to such lengths… That was—

'Mia?'

She started. 'I'm afraid I don't have the kind of clout to authorise an arrangement like that. But I'll present your case to Nora and Mr Coulter. Please be assured they'll do everything they can to accommodate your and Carla's wishes.' She bit her lip. 'They may have some additional questions that they'd like to ask you.' Questions *she* lacked the expertise and foresight to ask.

He immediately slid his business card across the table to her. 'They can contact me at any time.'

She picked it up. It was a simple card on good-quality bond, with embossed lettering in dark blue—a deeper and less interesting shade than his eyes.

He slid another card across the table to her. 'Would you write down your number for me, Mia?'

She dutifully wrote down the Plum Pines office number, along with Nora's work number.

He glanced at it and his lips pursed. 'I was hoping for *your* number.'

Her hand shook as she reached for her tea. 'Why?'

'Because I think you could be an ally. You, I believe, approve of my plan to be Carla's wedding co-ordinator.'

She hesitated. 'I think it's a lovely idea.' Surely it couldn't hurt to admit that much? 'But I think you ought to know that I have very little influence here.'

'I think you're selling yourself short.'

'If you want to speak to me directly, ring the office and ask them to page me.' She couldn't believe she'd told him to do that, but she couldn't find it in herself to regret the offer either.

For a moment she thought he'd press the matter. Instead he stood and held out his hand. 'Until tomorrow, then, Mia.'

She stood too and shook it, eager to be away from him. 'Goodbye, Dylan.'

She didn't tell him that in all likelihood she wouldn't see him tomorrow. Funny how suddenly the eastern boundary didn't seem as exciting a prospect as it had earlier in the day.

She'd barely settled down in the meeting room with the office laptop, to type up her copious notes for Nora, when the receptionist tapped on the glass door.

'Mr Coulter wants to see you, Mia.'

To grill her about how things had gone with the Fair-weathers, no doubt. She'd have rather discussed it all with Nora first, but she couldn't very well refuse to speak to him.

Taking a deep breath, she knocked on his door, only entering when he bellowed, 'Come in.'

She left the door ajar. She didn't fully trust Gordon Coulter. 'You wanted to see me?'

'Yes.'

He didn't invite her to sit. The smile he sent her chased ice down her spine.

'It's my very great pleasure to inform you, Ms Maydew, that you're fired. Effective immediately.'

The room spun. Mia's chest cramped. She couldn't lose this job. It was all that she had. Her fingers went cold. She *needed* this job!

'You're terminating my contract? But...*why?*'

Dylan stood on the threshold of Gordon Coulter's office, his head rocking back at the words he heard emerging from the other side of the door.

Gordon Coulter was *firing* Mia?

'Your behaviour with Dylan Fairweather today was scandalous and utterly inappropriate. You're not here to make sexual advances towards our clients. You're here to perform your duties as efficiently and as capably as possible—a duty that's obviously beyond you and your bitch-on-heat morals.'

Darkness threatened the edges of Dylan's vision. Mia hadn't made one inappropriate advance towards him—not one! His hands curled into fists. A pity the same couldn't be said for him towards her. He hadn't been able to resist flirting with her in the café—just a little bit. He hadn't been able to resist making her laugh again.

This was *his* fault. How could he have been so careless as to put her in this position?

Gordon continued to wax lyrical on a list of Mia's imaginary faults and Dylan's insides coiled up, tight and lethal. Gordon Coulter was a pompous ass!

'But even if I was prepared to overlook all that,' Gordon continued, his tone clearly saying that he had no intention of doing so, 'I refuse to disregard the fact that when you entered the emu enclosure you put the safety of a member of the public at risk.'

No way, buddy!

Dylan backed up two steps and then propelled himself forward with a cheery, 'Knock-knock!' before bursting into the office.

Two sets of eyes swung to him. Mia's face was ashen. Guilt plunged through him like a serrated-edge knife.

You're nothing but a trust fund baby without substance or significance.

As true as that might be, it meant that he knew how to act entitled and high-handed. He used that to his advantage now, striding into the room as if he owned it and everything inside it.

'You moved very quickly to bring my proposal to the attention of your superiors, Mia. I can't tell you how much I appreciate it.'

He took a seat across from Gordon, making himself completely at home.

'I hope you realise what a gem you have here, Gordon.'

He pulled Mia down to the seat beside him. How *dared* Gordon leave her standing like some recalcitrant child deserving of punishment and castigation? 'Have you finished telling Gordon about my proposal, Mia?'

'Um…no, not yet.'

She swallowed and he saw how valiantly she hauled her composure back into place. *Atta girl*!

'I'm afraid I haven't had a chance.'

'Oh, before I forget—' Dylan turned back to Gordon '—my sister and I will be returning tomorrow with Thierry. If he approves our plans, and if you accept my proposal, then we'll be booking Plum Pines as Carla and Thierry's wedding venue.'

Dollar signs all but flashed in Gordon's eyes. 'That's splendid news!'

'Carla has requested that Mia be available for tomorrow's meeting. I'm sure that won't be a problem.'

'Well, I—'

'Now to my proposal…' he continued, making it obvious that he took Gordon's agreement for granted. He saw Mia bite her lip, as if to hold back a laugh. The tightness in his chest eased a fraction.

'While I understand that Plum Pines has a talented and capable events team, I want to be completely in charge of Carla's wedding preparations—bringing in my own people, et cetera. I understand this isn't how Plum Pines normally operates, but if I promise to acquire all the necessary licenses and, as a show of gratitude, donate…say…a hundred thousand dollars to the Plum Pines Nature Fund, I was hoping you might make an exception.'

Gordon's fleshy mouth dropped open. He hauled it back into place. 'I'm sure we can find a way to accommodate such a reasonable request from such a generous benefactor.'

Dylan rubbed his hands together. 'Excellent.'

Gordon Coulter was ridiculously transparent. Rumour had it he was planning to run for mayor next year. A dona tion as sizable as Dylan's would be a real feather in his cap. Dylan just hoped the good people of Newcastle were smart enough not to elect such a small-minded bully to office.

He made a note to donate a large sum to Gordon's opponent's campaign.

'If there's any further way we can assist you, don't hesitate to ask. We're here to provide you with the very best service we can.'

'Well, now that you mention it... Carla would like Mia as her official liaison between FWE and Plum Pines.'

Gordon's face darkened. 'Mia doesn't have the necessary training. We can provide you with a far better level of service than that, and—'

'It's non-negotiable, I'm afraid.' He spoke calmly. 'If there's no Mia there'll be no Fairweather wedding at Plum Pines—and, sadly, no hundred-thousand-dollar donation.'

It was as simple as that, and Gordon could take it or leave it. If he refused to let Mia act as liaison then Dylan would whisk her away from Plum Pines and find a position for her in his own organisation. He was always on the lookout for good people.

In fact, poaching her was a damn fine plan.

Gordon wouldn't pass on it, though. Dylan knew his type too well.

'If you're happy with Mia's limited experience...' he began, in that pompous fashion.

'Supremely so.'

'I'll have to insist that she consult with Nora closely,' he blustered, in an attempt to save face.

'Absolutely.'

Gordon swallowed a few times, his jowls quivering. 'In that case I'll raise no objections.'

Dylan leant back in his chair. 'Excellent.'

Mia leaned forward in hers, her dark gaze skewering Gordon to the spot. 'And our earlier conversation...?'

His mouth opened and closed before he shuffled upright

in his seat. 'In the light of these…new developments, any further action will be suspended—pending your on-the-job performance from here on in.'

Very slowly she leaned back. Dylan silently took in the way her fingers opened and closed around each other. Eventually she nodded. 'Very well.'

Dylan stood. 'I understand you're a busy man, Gordon, so I won't take up any more of your valuable time. Mia…' He turned to her and she shot to her feet. 'I forgot to give you Carla's mobile number. You're going to need it. I'm afraid she'll be leaving you messages day and night.'

'That won't be an issue,' Gordon inserted. 'Mia understands that here at Plum Pines our clients are our priority. She'll be at your sister's beck and call twenty-four-seven.'

Dylan barely restrained himself from reciting the 'Maximum Ordinary Hours of Employment' section of the *New South Wales Industrial Relations Act*. Instead he gestured for Mia to precede him out through the door.

'Lead me to your trusty notepad.'

He closed the door behind them and Mia didn't speak until they were safely ensconced in the meeting room.

She swung to him. 'You did that on purpose, didn't you? You overheard him trying to fire me so you jumped in and saved my job.'

His chest expanded at the way she looked at him—as if he'd ridden in and saved the day.

She pressed a hand to her chest. 'I think I just fell a little bit in love with you.'

She was the strangest mix of seriousness and generosity he'd ever come across. And totally adorable to boot.

He leaned towards her, but she took a step backwards.

'Sorry, I shouldn't have said that. It was a stupid thing to say. I only meant I was grateful—*very* grateful—for coming to my defence like you did.'

'You're welcome. Gordon is a pompous ass.'

'A pompous ass who has the power to terminate my train-eeship whenever he sees fit.'

'He'd need to show good cause in the Industrial Relations Court. Don't you forget that. In fact—' he widened his stance '—why don't you forget Gordon and Plum Pines and come and work for *me*?'

The beginnings of a smile touched her lips. It made his pulse beat that little bit harder.

'I don't believe I have enough...*exuberance* for your line of work, Dylan.'

'I was wrong about that. You're perfect.'

'No, I'm not!' Her voice came out tart. Too tart.

He frowned. 'I meant that your work ethic is perfect. Your customer service skills are impeccable.' That was *all* he'd meant.

She swallowed before gesturing for him to take a seat. 'If you want me working so closely with you and Carla then there's something you need to know about me.'

He sat in the chair at the head of the table. 'I know all I need to know.'

She fixed him with that compelling gaze of hers, but for the life of him he couldn't read her expression. She took the chair immediately to his left, gripping her hands together until her knuckles turned white.

'I'd rather be the one to tell you than for you to hear it from other sources.'

He straightened. What on earth...? 'I'm listening.'

He watched the compulsive bob of her throat as she swallowed. Her hands gripped each other so tightly he was sure she'd cut off the blood supply to her fingers if she weren't careful.

'Ten months ago I was released from jail after serving a ree-year prison sentence for committing fraud. I think it's fair that you know I'm an ex-convict.'

CHAPTER THREE

MIA WAITED WITH a growing sense of dread for Dylan's face to close and for him to turn away.

His open-mouthed shock rang through her like a blow, but his face didn't close. He didn't turn away.

His frown did deepen, though, and she could read the thoughts racing behind the vivid blue of his eyes.

'No,' she said, holding his gaze. 'I wasn't wrongfully convicted, there were no mitigating circumstances.' She swallowed. 'Unless you want to count the fact that I was young and stupid.'

And utterly in thrall to Johnnie Peters. So in love she'd have done anything he'd asked of her. So in love she *had* done anything he'd asked of her.

'You're not going to tell me any more than that?'

Curiosity sharpened his gaze, but it wasn't the kind of avid, voyeuristic curiosity that made her want to crawl under a rock. It held a warmth and sympathy that almost undid her.

Swallowing again, she shook her head. 'It's sordid and unpleasant and it's in the past. According to the justice system, I've paid my debt to society. I won't ever steal again. I'll never break the law again. But I understand that in ligh' of these circumstances my word isn't worth much. I'll co pletely understand if you'd prefer to deal with Nora than with me.'

He didn't say anything.

'You don't need to worry about my job. You've done enough to ensure I won't be fired...at least, not this week.' She'd aimed for levity, but it fell flat.

He lifted his chin. 'I meant what I said—come and work for me.'

She realised now what she'd known on a subconscious level after only ten minutes in his company—Dylan Fairweather was a good man.

'I appreciate the offer, I really do, but besides the fact that you don't know me—'

'I know you have a good work ethic. If the way you've treated Carla is anything to go by, where clients are concerned nothing is too much trouble for you. They're valuable assets in an employee.'

'According to Gordon I have a problem with authority.'

He grinned, and leaned in so close she could smell the nutmeg warmth of his skin. 'That's something we have in common, then.'

How was it possible for him to make her laugh when they were having such a serious conversation? She sobered, recalling her earlier impulsive, *I think I just fell a little bit in love with you.* She should never have said it. Instinct warned her that Dylan could wreak havoc on her heart if she let him.

She couldn't let him. She wasn't giving *any* man that kind of power over her again.

She pulled in a breath. 'I was fortunate to be awarded this traineeship. The opportunity was given to me in good faith and I feel honour-bound to make the most of it.'

'Admirable.'

It wasn't admirable at all. She needed a job—a way to earn a living. For the two-year tenure of her traineeship ~~'~~e'd be in paid employment. Maybe at the end of that time ~~'~~d have proved herself worthy and someone would take ~~'~~ce on employing her. She needed a way to support ~~ ~~After what she'd done she couldn't ask the welfare support her.

'Do you have a passion for conservation?'

'Conservation is an important issue.'

'That's not the same thing,' he pointed out.

Passion was dangerous. She'd done all she could to excise it from her life. Besides, busying herself with weed extermination programmes, soil erosion projects, and koala breeding strategies—plants, dirt and animals—meant she had minimal contact with people.

And as far as she was concerned that was a *very* good thing.

'Here.' He pulled a chocolate bar from his pocket. 'This is the real reason I came back to the office.'

Frowning, she took it, careful not to touch him as she did so.

'You said chocolate belonged in a class of its own and…'

He shrugged, looking a little bit embarrassed, and something inside her started to melt.

No melting!

'I wanted to thank you for your patience with both Carla and me today.'

'It's—'

'I know—it's your job, Mia.'

Dear Lord, the way he said her name…

'But good work should always be acknowledged. And…' An irrepressible smile gathered at the corner of his mouth. 'I fear more of the same will be asked of you tomorrow.'

It took a moment for his words to sink in. 'You mean…?'

'I mean we want *you*, Mia. Not Nora. I want everything associated with this wedding to be a joy for Carla. She likes you. And that's rarer than you might think.' He suddenly frowned. 'How much will taking charge of this affect your traineeship? Will I be creating a problem for you there?'

He was giving her an out. If she wanted one. *If*.

She pulled in a breath. 'The wedding is nine months away, right?'

He nodded.

Being Carla's liaison wouldn't be a full-time job. Very slowly she nodded too. 'That leaves me plenty of time to continue with my fieldwork and studies.'

If it weren't for Dylan she wouldn't have a job right now *or* a chance to finish her traineeship. She owed him. *Bigtime.* She made a resolution then and there to do all she could to make Carla's wedding a spectacular success.

Her gaze rested on the chocolate bar he'd handed to her earlier. She suddenly realised how she could tacitly thank him right now. Without giving herself time to think, she ripped off the wrapper and bit into it.

'I'm ravenous. And this is *so* good.'

As she'd known he would, he grinned in delight that his gift had given her pleasure. She closed her eyes to savour the soft milky creaminess, and when she opened them again she found his gaze fastened on her lips, the blue of his eyes deepening and darkening, and her stomach pitched.

She set the chocolate to the table and wiped damp palms down her trousers. 'I... This is probably a stupid thing to raise...'

He folded his arms. 'Out with it.'

'I don't believe you have any interest in me beyond that of any employer, but after what Gordon just accused me of...'

She couldn't meet his eyes. The thing was, Gordon had recognised what she'd so desperately wanted to keep hidden—that she found Dylan attractive. *Very* attractive. He'd woken something inside her that she desperately wanted to put back to sleep.

'I just want to make it clear that I'm not in the market for a relationship. *Any* kind of relationship—hot and heavy or fun and flirty.'

She read derision in his eyes. But before she could dissolve into a puddle of embarrassment at his feet she realised the derision was aimed at himself—not at her.

'No relationships? Noted.' He rolled his shoulders. 'Mia, I have a tendency to flirt—it's a result of the circles I move in—but it doesn't mean anything. It's just supposed to be a bit of harmless fun. My clients like to feel important and, as *they* are important to me, I like to make them feel valued. I plan celebrations, parties, and it's my job to make the entire process as enjoyable as possible. So charm and a sense of fun have become second nature to me. If I've given you the wrong impression...'

'Oh, no, you haven't!'

'For what it's worth, I'm not in the market for a relationship at the moment either.'

She glanced up.

Why not?

That's no concern of yours.

Humour flitted through his eyes. 'But what about friendship? Do you have anything against that?'

That made her smile. People like Dylan didn't become friends with people like her. Once the wedding was over she'd never see him again.

'I have nothing whatsoever against friendship.' She'd sworn never again to steal or cheat. A little white lie, though, didn't count. Did it...?

Thierry Geroux, Carla's fiancé, was as dark and scowling as Carla and Dylan were golden and gregarious. Mia couldn't help but wonder what on earth Carla saw in him.

She pushed that thought away. It was none of her business.

As if he sensed the direction of her thoughts, Thierry turned his scowl on her. She wanted to tell him not to bother—that his scowls didn't frighten *her*...she'd been scowled at by professionals. She didn't, of course. She just sent him one of the bland smiles she'd become so adept at.

'Do you have any questions, Mr Geroux?' He'd barely spoken two words in the last hour.

'No.'

'None?' Dylan double-checked, a frown creasing his brow.

'Stop bouncing,' Thierry said in irritation to Carla, who

clung to his arm, shifting her weight from one leg to the other.

'But, Thierry, it's so *exciting*!'

Nevertheless she stopped bouncing.

Thierry turned to Dylan. 'Carla is to have the wedding she wants. As you're the events expert, I'm sure you have that under control.'

He ignored Mia completely. Which suited Mia just fine.

Dylan turned back to Mia. 'There could be quite a gap between the end of the wedding ceremony and the start of the reception, while Carla and Thierry have photographs taken.'

Mia nodded. 'It;s often the case. With it being late spring there'll still be plenty of light left. I can organise a tour of the wildlife exhibits for those who are interested.'

'Oh!' Carla jumped up and down. 'Could we do that now?'

'Absolutely.'

The exhibits—a system of aviaries and enclosures—were sympathetically set into the natural landscape. A wooden walkway meandered through the arrangement at mid-tree height. This meant visitors could view many of the birds at eye level, practically commune with the rock wallabies sunning themselves on their craggy hillside, and look down on the wombats, echidnas and goannas in their pens.

At the heart of the wildlife walk—and the jewel in its crown—was the koala house. Set up like an enormous tree house, the wooden structure was covered on three sides to weatherproof it for visitors, with an arena opening out below full of native flora and an artfully designed pond.

The entire complex was enclosed in a huge aviary. A visitor could glance up into the trees to view the variety of colourful parrots, or along the rafters of the tree house to see the napping tawny frogmouths. Below were a myriad of walking birds, along with the occasional wallaby and echidna. But at eye-level were the koalas on their specially designed poles, where fresh eucalyptus leaves were placed daily. No wire or special glass separated man from beast—only a wooden railing and a ten-foot drop into the enclosure below.

'I *love* this place,' Carla breathed as they entered.

'This is really something,' Dylan murmured in Mia's ear. His breath fanned the hair at her temples and awareness skidded up her spine. 'It's a special place,' she agreed, moving away—needing to put some distance between them.

When they'd looked their fill, she led them back outside to a series of small nocturnal houses—the first of which was the snake house.

Carla gave a shudder. 'No matter how much I try, I don't like snakes.'

They didn't bother Mia, but she nodded. 'We don't have to linger. We can move straight on to the amphibian house and then the possum house.'

'C'mon, Thierry.'

Carla tugged on his arm, evidently eager to leave, but he disengaged her hand. 'You go ahead. I find snakes fascinating.'

Finally the man showed some interest—*hallelujah!*

Thierry glanced at her. 'Mia might be kind enough to stay behind with me and answer some questions?'

The snakes might not bother her, but Mia loathed the caged darkness of the nocturnal houses, hating the way they made her feel trapped. She didn't betray any of that by so much of a flicker of her eyelids, though.

'I'd be happy to answer any questions.'

Dylan caught her eye and gestured that he and Carla would move on, and she nodded to let him know that she and Thierry would catch up.

She moved to stand beside Thierry, nodding at the slender green snake with the bright yellow throat that he currently surveyed. 'That's a tree snake. It's—'

'I can read.'

She sucked in a breath. Was he being deliberately rude?

She lifted her chin. He might be hard work, but she was used to hard work.

'They're very common,' she continued, 'but rarely seen as they're so shy. They seldom bite. Their main form of defence is to give off a rather dreadful odour when threatened.'

Mia was convinced there was a metaphor for life trapped in there somewhere.

'*You* give off a bad smell too.'

Thierry moved so quickly that before she knew what he was doing he had her trapped between the wall and a glass display unit—the olive python on the other side didn't stir.

'Dylan told us about your background—that you're nothing but a common little thief with a criminal record.'

The sudden sense of confinement had her heart leaping into her throat before surging back into her chest to thump off the walls of her ribs.

'When I was in jail—' with a supreme effort she kept her voice utterly devoid of emotion '—I learned a lot about self-defence and how to hurt someone. If you don't take two steps back within the next three seconds you're going to find yourself on your back in a screaming mess of pain.'

He waited the full three seconds, but he did move away. Mia tried to stop her shoulders from sagging as she dragged a grateful breath into her lungs.

He stabbed a finger at her. 'I don't like you.'

And that should matter to me because...? She bit the words back. She'd had a lot of practice at swallowing sarcastic rejoinders. She'd made it a policy long ago not to inflame a situation if she could help it.

'Carla and Dylan are too trusting by half—but you won't find *me* so gullible.'

Giving a person the benefit of the doubt did *not* make Dylan gullible.

'You're not a fit person for Carla to know. You stay away from her, you hear? If you don't I'll cause trouble for you... and that's a promise.'

'Is everything okay here?'

A strip of sunlight slashed through the darkness as Dylan came back through the doors. The doors were merely thick flaps of overlapping black rubber that kept the sun out. A few threads of light backlit him, haloing his head and shading his face. Mia didn't need to see his face to sense the tension rippling through him.

Without another word Thierry snapped away and moved through the rubber panels, his footsteps loud on the wooden walkway as he strode off.

'Are you okay?'

Dylan's concern, absurdly, made her want to cry in a way that Thierry's threats hadn't.

'Yes, of course.' She turned and gestured to the snakes. 'Just so you know: a reptile encounter can be arranged for the wedding guests too, if anyone's interested. Though it has to be said it's not to everyone's taste.'

Dylan took Mia's arm and led her back out into the sunshine, wincing at her pallor.

Her colour started to return after a few deep breaths and he found the rapid beat of his heart slowed in direct proportion.

'I heard the last part of what Thierry said to you.'

He hadn't liked the way Thierry had asked Mia to stay behind. It was why he'd doubled back—to make sure everything was okay.

'It's not the first time someone has taken exception to my past, Dylan, and I expect it won't be the last.'

Her revelation yesterday had shocked him—*prison!*—but he'd have had to be blind not to see how much she regretted that part of her life. He'd sensed her sincerity in wanting to create a new, honest life for herself. She'd paid dearly for whatever mistakes lay in her past. As far as he was concerned she should be allowed to get on with things in peace.

Thierry's threat, the utter contempt in his voice...

Dylan's hands clenched. It had been a long time since he'd wanted to knock someone to the ground. He'd wanted to deck Thierry, though. He'd wanted to beat the man black and blue.

He dragged a hand down his face. It had only been the thought of who'd pay for his actions—Mia—that had stopped him.

You didn't even think of Carla!

Mia stared up at him, her gaze steady. 'Don't blame Thierry. He only has Carla's welfare in mind.'

'It doesn't excuse his behaviour.' A scowl scuffed through him. 'The man's a bully and a jerk. What the hell does Carla see in him?'

She gestured that they should continue along the path towards the amphibian house. 'Don't you know?'

He didn't have a single clue.

'Haven't the two of you talked about him?'

Not really. But to say as much would only reveal what a poor excuse for a brother he'd been to Carla these last twelve months.

He glanced across at Mia and found that she'd paled again, but before he could ask her if she was okay she'd plunged into the darkness of the amphibian house. Was she worried about running into Thierry again?

He plunged right in after her.

'Do you want to linger?'

He couldn't have said how he knew, but he sensed the tension coiling through her. 'No.'

She led them back outside and gulped in a couple of breaths. She stilled when she realised how closely he watched her.

He reached out to stop her from moving on. 'What's wrong?'

She glanced away. 'What makes you think anything's wrong?'

When she turned back, he just shrugged.

Her shoulders sagged. 'I'd rather nobody else knew this.'

Silently, he crossed his heart.

She looked away again. 'I don't like the nocturnal houses. They make me feel claustrophobic and closed in.

They were like being in jail!

He had to stiffen his legs to stop himself from pitching over.

'I'm fine out here on the walkways, where we're above or beside the enclosures and aviaries, but the nocturnal houses are necessarily dark…and warm. The air feels too close.'

She finished with a deprecating little shrug that broke his heart a little bit.

In the next moment he was gripped with an avid need to know everything about her—were her parents still alive? How had they treated her when she was a child? What made her happy? What did she really want from life? What frightened her right down to her bones? What did she do in her spare time? What made her purr?

That last thought snapped him back. He had no right to ask such questions. He shouldn't even be considering them. What he should be doing was working out if Carla was about to make the biggest mistake of her life. *That* was what he should be focussed on.

'What about when you're down below?' he found himself asking anyway. 'When you have to go into the cages to clean them out…to feed the animals?'

He saw the answer in her eyes before she drew that damn veil down over them again.

'It's okay. It's just another part of the job.'

Liar. He didn't call her on it. It was none of his business. But it begged the question—why was Mia working in a place like this when enclosed spaces all but made her hyperventilate?

They found Carla and Thierry waiting for them beside the kangaroo enclosure.

The moment she saw Mia, Carla grabbed her arm. 'I want to become a volunteer!'

Mia smiled as if she couldn't help it 'Volunteers are always welcome at Plum Pines.'

Her tone held no awkwardness and Dylan's shoulders unhitched a couple of notches. Thierry's strictures hadn't constrained the warmth she showed to Carla, and he gave silent thanks for it.

Thierry pulled Mia back to his side, gently but inexorably. 'Stop manhandling the staff, Carla.'

Dylan lifted himself up to his full height. 'That's an insufferably snobbish thing to say, Thierry.'

Carla's face fell and he immediately regretted uttering the words within her earshot.

Thierry glared back at him. '*You* might be happy consorting with criminals, Dylan, but you'll have to excuse me for being less enthused.'

'Ex.' Mia's voice cut through the tension, forcing all eyes to turn to her. 'I'm an *ex*-criminal, Mr Geroux. Naturally, I don't expect you to trust me, but you can rest assured that if my employers have no qualms about either my conduct or my ability to perform the tasks required of me, then you need have no worries on that head either.'

'We *don't* have qualms!' Carla jumped in, staring at Thierry as if a simple glare would force him to agree with her.

Thierry merely shrugged. 'Is volunteering such a good idea? You could catch something...get bitten...and didn't you notice the frightful stench coming from the possums?'

'Oh, I hadn't thought about the practicalities...'

She glanced at Mia uncertainly and Dylan wanted to throw his head back and howl.

'You'd need to be up to date with your tetanus shots. All the information is on the Plum Pines website, and I can give you some brochures if you like. You can think about

it for a bit, and call the volunteer co-ordinator if you have
any questions.'

Thierry scowled at her, but she met his gaze calmly.
'Maybe it's something the two of you could do together.'

Carla clapped her hands, evidently delighted with the
idea.

Thierry glanced at his watch with an abrupt, 'We have
to go.' He said goodbye to Dylan, ignoring Mia completely,
before leading Carla away.

'An absolute charmer,' Dylan muttered under his breath.

Mia had to have heard him, but she didn't say anything,
turning instead to a kangaroo waiting on the other side of
the fence and feeding it some titbit she'd fished from her
pocket. He glanced back at Carla and a sickening cramp
stretched through his stomach—along with a growing sense
of foreboding.

Mia nudged him, and then held out a handful of what
looked like puffed wheat. 'Would you like to feed the kangaroo?'

With a sense of wonder, he took it and fed the kangaroo.
He even managed to run his fingers through the fur of the
kangaroo's neck. The tightness in him eased.

'Do you have anything pressing you need to attend to in
the next couple of hours?'

She shook her head. 'Nora has instructed me to give you
all the time and assistance you need. Later this afternoon, if
I'm free, she's going to run through some things that I probably need to know—help me create a checklist.'

'Will you meet me at the lily pond in fifteen minutes?'

She blinked, but nodded without hesitation. 'Yes, of
course.'

Mia was sitting at the picnic table waiting for him—her notepad at the ready—when he arrived with his bag of goodies.

If he hadn't been so worried about Carla's situation he'd

have laughed at the look on her face when he pulled forth sandwiches, chocolate bars and sodas.

'This is a working lunch, Mia, not some dastardly plot to seduce you.'

Pink flushed her cheeks. 'I never considered anything else for a moment.'

To be fair, she probably hadn't. She'd made it clear where she stood yesterday. When he'd gone back over her words it had struck him that she really *hadn't* thought him interested in her. She'd just been setting boundaries. And if that boundary-setting hadn't been for his benefit, then it had to have been for hers. Which was interesting.

He took the seat beside her rather than the one opposite.

Why was Mia so determined to remain aloof?

He didn't want her aloof.

He wanted her help.

He took her notepad and pen and put them in his pocket. 'You won't need those.' He pushed the stack of sandwiches, a can of soda and a couple of chocolate bars towards her. 'Eat up while I talk.'

She fixed him with those moss-green eyes, but after a moment gave a shrug and reached for the topmost sandwich. She didn't even check to see what it was.

He gestured to the stack. 'I didn't know what you'd like so I got a variety.' He'd grabbed enough to feed a small army, but he'd wanted to make sure he bought something she liked.

She shrugged again. 'I'm not fussy. I'll eat pretty much anything.'

He had a sudden vision of her in prison, eating prison food, and promptly lost his appetite.'

'Dylan?'

He snapped his attention back. 'Sorry, I'm a bit distracted.'

She bit into her sandwich and chewed, simply waiting for him to speak. It occurred to him that if he wanted her help he was going to have to be honest with her.

A weight pressed down on him. Yesterday afternoon she'd looked at him with such gratitude and admiration—as if he were a superhero. Nobody had ever looked at him like that. He didn't want to lose it so quickly.

Not even for Carla's sake?

He straightened. He'd do anything for Carla.

He opened his can of soft drink and took a long swallow before setting it back down. 'I'm ashamed to admit this, but over the last twelve months I've neglected Carla shamefully. She and Thierry have only been dating six months, and the news of their engagement came as a shock. This will probably sound ridiculously big brotherly, but... I'm worried she's making a mistake.'

Mia stared at him for a moment. 'You and Carla seem very close.'

'We are.'

'So why haven't you spent much time together recently?'

How much of the truth did he have to tell her?

He scrubbed a hand through his hair. 'There's an older family member who I have...difficulties with. It's impossible to avoid him when I'm in Australia, and I've wanted to avoid a falling out, so...'

'So you've spent a lot of time overseas instead?'

'Rather than putting up with said family member, I flitted off to organise parties. There was a Turkish sultan's sixtieth birthday party, and then a twenty-fifth wedding anniversary celebration for a couple of members of the British aristocracy. I did some corporate work on the Italian Grand Prix. Oh, and there was a red carpet film premiere that I did just for fun.'

She blinked, as if he'd just spoken in a foreign language. In some ways he supposed he had.

'So there you have it—I'm a coward.'

He lifted his arms and let them drop, waiting for her eyes to darken with scorn. She just stared back at him and waited for him to continue, her gaze not wavering.

He swallowed. 'I came home for Carla's birthday...and for two days over Christmas.' It hadn't been enough! 'That's when she announced her engagement. That's when I realised I'd spent too long away.'

But Carla had finally seemed so settled...so happy. She'd refused to come and work for FWE, preferring to focus on her charity work. Nothing had rung alarm bells for him... until he'd met Thierry.

Mia didn't say anything, but he could tell from her eyes how intently she listened.

'When I heard what he said to you in the reptile house I wanted to knock him to the ground.'

She halted mid-chew, before swallowing. 'I'm very glad you didn't.'

It had only been the thought that Gordon would somehow bring the blame back to her and she'd lose her job that had stilled his hand.

'What he said to you...' His hand clenched and unclenched convulsively around his can of drink. 'I'm sorry you were put into a position where you were forced to listen to that.'

'It's not your responsibility to apologise on behalf of other people, Dylan.'

Maybe not, but it *felt* like his fault. If he'd taken the time to get to know Thierry better before now...

She reached out and placed a sandwich in front of him. 'And you need to remember that just because he dislikes *me*, and my background, it doesn't necessarily make him a bad person.'

Dylan was far from sure about that.

'Even if I didn't have a criminal record, there's no law that says Thierry has to *like* me.'

'Mia, it's not the fact that he doesn't like you or even that he was rude to you that worries me. What disturbs me is the fact that he threatened you.'

'I can take care of myself.'

She said the words quietly and he didn't doubt her. He wished she didn't *have* to take care of herself. He wished she was surrounded by an army of people who'd take care of her. He sensed that wasn't the case, and suddenly he wanted to buy her a hundred chocolate bars… But what good would that do?

No substance, Dylan Fairweather. You don't have an ounce of substance.

The words roared through him. He pulled air in through his nose and let it out through his mouth—once, twice.

'I have less confidence,' he said finally, 'in Carla's ability to take care of herself.' He met Mia's dark-eyed gaze. 'What if he talks to *her* the way he spoke to you? What if he threatens *her* in the same way he threatened you?'

CHAPTER FOUR

DYLAN COULDN'T KNOW it, but each word raised a welt on Mia's soul. The thought of a woman as lovely as Carla, as open and kind as she was, being controlled and manipulated, possibly even abused, by a man claiming to love her…

It made her stomach burn acid.

It made her want to run away at a hundred miles an hour in the other direction.

She recalled how Thierry had trapped her against the wall in the reptile house and her temples started to throb.

She set her sandwich down before she mangled it. 'Have you seen anything to give you cause for concern before now?'

Those laughing lips of his, his shoulders, and even the laughter lines fanning out from his eyes—all drooped. Her heart burned for him. She wanted to reach out and cover his hand, to offer him whatever comfort she could.

Don't be an idiot.

Dylan might be all golden flirtatious charm, but it didn't mean he'd want someone like *her* touching him. She chafed her left forearm, digging her fingers into the muscle to try and loosen the tension that coiled her tight. She wasn't qualified to offer advice about family or relationships, but even *she* could see what he needed to do.

'Can't…?' She swallowed to counter a suddenly dry roat. 'Can't you talk to Carla and share your concerns?'

'And say what? *Carla, I think the man you're about to marry is a complete and utter jerk*?' He gave a harsh laugh. 'She'd translate that as me forcing her to choose between her brother and her fiancé.'

From the look on his face, it was evident he didn't think she'd choose him. She thought back to the way Carla had clung to Thierry's arm and realised Dylan might have a point.

'How about something a little less confrontational?' She reached for a can of soda, needing something to do with her hands. 'Something like… *Carla, Thierry strikes me as a bit moody. Are you sure he treats you well?*'

He gave a frustrated shake of his head. 'She'd still read it as me criticising her choice. I'd have to go to great lengths to make it as clear as possible that I'm not making her choose between me and Thierry, but the fact of the matter is—regardless of what I discover—I have no power to stop this wedding unless it's what Carla wants. And if she *does* marry him and he *is* cruel to her… I want her to feel she's able to turn to me without feeling constrained because I warned her off him.'

His logic made sense, in a roundabout way, but it still left her feeling uneasy. 'You know, you don't have a lot to go on, here. One incident isn't necessarily indicative of the man. Perhaps you need to make a concerted effort to get to know him better.'

'I mean to. I'm already on it.' Her surprise must have shown, because he added. 'It doesn't take fifteen minutes to buy a few sandwiches, Mia. I made a couple of phone calls before meeting you here.'

She frowned, not really knowing what that meant. 'Did you find out anything?'

'Not yet.'

And then she realised exactly what he'd done. 'You hired a private investigator?'

'Yep.'

'Don't you think that's a little extreme?'

'Not when my sister's happiness and perhaps her physical well-being is at stake.'

She recalled Thierry's latent physical threat to her and thought Dylan might have a point. Still…

'I want to ask for your assistance, Mia.'

'Mine?' she squeaked. What on earth did he think *she* could do?

'I want you to befriend Carla. She might confide in you—especially as Thierry has made it clear that he doesn't like you.'

Had he gone mad? 'Dylan, I can be as friendly towards Carla as it's possible to be.' She'd already resolved to do so. 'But when we get right down to it I'm just one of the many people helping to organise her wedding. We don't exactly move in the same social circles.'

'I've thought about that too. And I've come up with a solution.'

She had a premonition that she wasn't going to like what came next.

He leaned towards her. 'If Carla thought that we were dating—'

'*No!*' She shot so far away from him she was in danger of falling off the bench.

He continued to survey her, seeming not put off in the least by her vehemence. He unwrapped a chocolate bar and bit into it. 'Why not?'

She wanted to tell him to eat a sandwich first—put something proper into his stomach—but it wasn't her place…and it was utterly beside the point.

'Because I don't date!'

'It wouldn't be *real* dating,' he said patiently. 'It'd be pretend dating.'

She slapped a hand to her chest. 'I work hard to keep a low profile. I don't need my past coming back and biting me more often than it already does. I have a plan for my life,

Dylan—to finish my field officer training and find work in a national park. Somewhere rural—' *remote* '—and quiet, where I can train towards becoming a ranger. All I want is a quiet life so I can live peacefully and stay out of trouble. Dating you *won't* help me achieve that. You live your life up among the stars. You're high-profile.' She pointed to herself. 'Low-profile. Can you see how that's not going to work?'

He tapped a finger against his mouth. 'It's a valid point.'

He leaned towards her, his lips pressed into a firm, persuasive line. It took an effort not to let her attention become distracted by those lips.

'What if I promise to keep your name out of the papers?'

'How? Australia's golden-boy bachelor slumming it with an ex-jailbird? *That* story's too juicy to keep under wraps.'

Heaven only knew what Gordon Coulter would do with a headline like that.

'I've learned over the years how to be *very* discreet. I swear to you that nobody will suspect a thing.'

'Will Thierry be discreet too?' she asked, unable to hide the scorn threading her voice as she recalled his threat to make trouble for her.

'You leave Thierry to me.'

With pleasure.

Dylan pushed his shoulders back, a steely light gleaming in his eyes, and she had to swallow. The golden charmer had gone—had been replaced by someone bigger, harder…and far more intimidating. Beneath his laughing, charismatic allure, she sensed that Dylan had a warrior's heart.

His nostrils flared. 'I'll make sure he doesn't touch you.'

She couldn't have said why, but she believed him—implicitly. Her heart started to thud too hard, too fast. 'Dylan, surely you'd be better off concocting this kind of scheme with one of Carla's friends? They'd—'

'She doesn't have any. Not close. Not any more.'

Why ever not?

His face turned to stone, but his eyes flashed fire. 'Two years ago Carla's boyfriend ran off with her best friend.'

Mia closed her eyes.

'Carla went into a deep depression and pushed all her friends away. She's never been the sort of person to have a lot of close friends—a large social circle, perhaps, but only one or two people she'd consider close—and...'

'And it was all a mess after such a betrayal,' she finished for him, reading it in his face and wanting to spare him the necessity of having to say it out loud. 'Loyalties were divided and some fences never mended.'

He nodded.

She leapt up, needing to work off the agitation coursing through her. 'Dylan, I...'

'What?'

She swung back to him. 'I don't know how we can pull off something like that—pretending to date—convincingly.'

She sat again, feeling like a goose for striding around and revealing her agitation. When she glanced across at him the expression in his eyes made her stomach flip-flop. In one smooth motion he slid across until they were almost touching. He smelt fresh and clean, like sun-warmed cotton sheets, and her every sense went on high alert.

He touched the backs of his fingers to her cheek and she sucked in a breath, shocked at her need to lean into the contact. Oh, this was madness!

'Dylan, I—'

His thumb pressed against her mouth, halting her words. Then he traced the line of her bottom lip and a pulse thumped to life inside her. She couldn't stop her lip from softening beneath his touch, or her mouth from parting ever so slightly so she could draw the scent of him into her lungs.

'I don't think you realise how lovely you are.'

Somewhere nearby a peacock honked. Something splashed in the lily pond. But all Mia could focus on was the man in front of her, staring down at her as if…as if she were a cream bun he'd like to devour…slowly and deliciously.

It shocked her to realise that in that moment she wanted nothing more than to *be* a cream bun.

Dangerous.

The word whispered through her. Some part of her mind registered it, but she was utterly incapable of moving away and breaking the spell Dylan had woven around them.

'Sweet and lovely Mia.'

The low, warm promise in his voice made her breath catch.

'I think we're going to have exactly the opposite problem. I think if we're not careful we could be in danger of being *too* convincing…we could be in danger of convincing ourselves that a lie should become the truth.'

A fire fanned through her. Yesterday, when he'd flirted with her, hadn't it just been out of habit? Had he meant it? He found her attractive?

'Dylan…' His name whispered from her. She didn't mean it to.

His eyes darkened at whatever he saw in her face. 'I dreamed of you last night.'

Dangerous.

The word whispered through her again.

But it didn't feel dangerous. It felt *right* to be whispering secrets to each other.

His thumb swept along the fullness of her bottom lip again, pulling against it to explore the damp moistness inside, sensitising it almost beyond bearing. Unable to help herself, she flicked out her tongue to taste him.

'Mia…' He groaned out her name as if it came from some deep, hidden place.

His head moved towards her, his lips aiming to replace his thumb, and her soul suddenly soared.

Dangerous.

Dangerous and glorious. This man had mesmerised her from the moment she'd first laid eyes on him and—

Mesmerised...?

Dangerous!

With a half-sob Mia fisted her hands in his shirt, but didn't have the strength to push him away. She dropped her chin, ensuring that his kiss landed on her brow instead of her lips.

She felt rather than heard him sigh.

After three hard beats of her heart she let him go. In another two he slid back along the bench away from her.

'As I said, I don't think being convincing will be a problem. However much you might deny it, something burns between us—something that could be so much more than a spark if we'd let it.'

It would be foolish to deny it now.

'Why do you have a no-dating rule?' he asked.

His words pulled her back. With an effort, she found her voice. 'It keeps me out of trouble.'

He remained silent, as if waiting for more, but Mia refused to add anything else.

'Maybe one day you'll share your reasoning with me, but until then I fully mean to respect your rules, Mia.'

He did? She finally glanced up at him.

The faintest of smiles touched his lips. 'And, unlike you, I'm more than happy to share my reasons. One—' he held up a finger '—if I don't respect your no-dating rule I suspect I have no hope of winning your co-operation where Carla's concerned.'

Self-interest? At least that was honest.

He held up a second finger. 'And, two, it seems to me you already have enough people in your life who don't respect your wishes. I don't mean to become one of their number.'

Despite her best efforts, some of the ice around her heart cracked.

He stared at her for a long moment, his mouth turning

grim. 'I fancied myself in love once, but when things got tough the girl in question couldn't hack it. She left. Next time I fall in love it'll be with a woman who can cope with the rough as well as the smooth.'

His nostrils flared, his eyes darkening, and Mia wondered if he'd gone back to that time when the girl in question had broken his heart. She wanted to reach out and touch his hand, pull him back to the present.

She dragged her hands into her lap. 'I'm sorry, Dylan.'

He shook himself. 'It's true that I'm attracted to you, but you've just pointed out how very differently we want to live our lives—high-profile, low-profile. In the real world, that continual push and pull would make us miserable.'

Mia had to look away, but she nodded to let him know that she agreed. It didn't stop her heart from shrivelling to the size of a gum nut.

'Your no-dating rule obviously rules out a fling?'

'It does.' Anything else would be a disaster.

'So these are our ground rules. With those firmly in place we shouldn't have any misunderstandings or false hopes, right? We just need to remember the reasons why we're not dating at the moment, why we're not looking for a relationship, and that'll keep us safe.'

She guessed so.

He drummed his fingers on the picnic table. 'It occurs to me that I haven't given you much incentive to help me out. I'm a selfish brute.'

His consideration for Carla proved that was a lie.

'I've no intention of taking advantage of you. I'm fully prepared to pay you for your time.'

She flinched at his words, throwing an arm up to ward them off. 'I don't want your *money*, Dylan.'

What kind of person did he think she was?

A thief!

She dragged in a breath. 'I went to jail for fraud. Do you think I'd accept money under dubious circumstances again?'

He swore at whatever he saw in her face. 'I'm sorry—that was incredibly insensitive. I didn't mean I thought you could be bought. I just meant it's perfectly reasonable for you to be financially compensated for your time.'

'No.'

'It doesn't have to be dubious. I'd have a contract drawn up so there wasn't a hint of illegality about it.'

His earnestness made the earlier sting fade, but... 'Tell that to the judge.'

He looked stricken for a moment—until he realised she was joking.

'No money changes hands between us,' she said.

He looked as if he wanted to keep arguing with her, but finally he nodded. 'Okay.'

She let out a pent-up breath.

'So, Mia, what I need to know is...what do *you* want? You help me. I help you.'

He'd already saved her job. She hated to admit it, but that made her beholden to him. She rubbed her forehead. Besides, if Carla was in danger of being controlled, dominated, bullied... She swallowed, remembering Johnnie Peters and all he'd convinced her to do. She remembered how she'd sold her soul to a man who'd used her for his own ends and then thrown her away. If Carla were in danger, this would be a way for Mia to start making amends—finding redemption—for the mistakes of the past.

The thought made her stomach churn. She didn't want to do this.

What? You think redemption is easy? You think it's supposed to be a picnic? It should be hard. You should suffer.

She brushed a hand across her eyes, utterly weary with herself.

'What do you want, Mia.'

She wanted to keep her job. Yesterday she'd have trusted him with that piece of information. Today— She glanced across at him. Today she wasn't convinced that he wouldn't use it against her as a weapon to force her co-operation.

Who are you kidding? You already know you're going to help him. No force necessary.

But it would be unwise of her to forget that beneath the smiling charm Dylan had a warrior's heart. And warriors could be utterly ruthless.

She forced her mind off Dylan and to her own situation. He'd ensured her job was safe for the moment...and for the next nine months until Carla's wedding took place. She'd have less than six months left on her traineeship then. Surely she could avoid Gordon's notice in that time? Hopefully he'd be busy with council elections.

If Carla's wedding takes place.

'There has to be something you want,' Dylan persisted, pushing a chocolate bar across to her.

What *did* she want? One thing came immediately to mind.

She picked up the bar of chocolate and twirled it around. 'Carla's wedding is going to be a big deal, right?'

'A huge deal. If it goes ahead.'

She glanced at him. 'If Thierry does turn out to be your worst nightmare, but Carla still insists on marrying him, will you still go ahead and give her the wedding she's always dreamed of?'

A muscle worked in his jaw. 'Yes.'

She couldn't explain why, but that eased some of the tightness in her shoulders. She stared down at the chocolate bar. 'So—considering this low profile of mine—when you and your people start distributing press releases and giving media interviews about the wedding, I'd like you to give the credit to Plum Pines and Nora and FWE without mentioning my name at all.'

His brows drew down over his eyes. 'But that's unfair! Credit should go where it's due. Being associated with Carla's wedding could open doors for you.'

Or it could bring her past and the scandal to the front pages of the gossip rags. 'You asked me what I wanted. I'm simply telling you.'

He swung back to scowl at the lily pond. 'I don't like it. It goes against the grain. But if it's what you really want, then consider it done.'

She closed her eyes. 'Thank you.'

'But now you have to tell me something else that you want, because I *truly* feel as if I'm taking utter advantage of you.'

She glanced up to find him glaring at her. For some reason his outrage made her want to smile.

'What do I want?' she shrugged. 'I want to be out on the eastern boundary, helping with the weed eradication programme.'

Dylan stared at Mia and his heart thumped at the wistful expression that flitted across her face. He had a feeling that she didn't have a whole lot of fun in her life. Not if weed extermination topped the list of her wants.

If she agreed to his fake dating plan he resolved to make sure she had fun too. It would be the least he could do. There might be a lot of things he wasn't good at, but when it came to fun he was a grandmaster.

He rose. 'Okay, let's go and do that, then.'

'We?' She choked on her surprise.

He sat again, suddenly unsure. 'You'd prefer to go on your own?'

'Oh, it's not that. I… It's just…'

He could almost see the thoughts racing across her face. *It's hard work, dirty work, menial work.* 'You don't think I'm up to it, do you?'

'It's not that either—although it *is* hard work.' She leaned towards him, a frown in her eyes. 'Dylan, you run a world-class entertainment company. I'm quite sure you have better things to do with your time. I expect you're a very busy man.'

He shook his head. 'I'm on leave.' He'd taken it the moment Carla had announced her engagement. 'I have capable staff.'

And he couldn't think of anything he'd rather do at the moment than lighten Mia's load.

Inspiration hit him. 'Listen to this for a plan. If I become a volunteer here that might encourage Carla to become a volunteer too. If you get to work with her and build up a friendship then the fake dating stuff will be easier.'

Her frown cleared. 'There might even be no need for fake dating stuff.'

Maybe. Maybe not. He couldn't explain it, but the thought of fake dating Mia fired him to life in a way nothing else had in a long time. He'd relish the chance to find out what really make her tick.

'We need a cover story.' He rubbed his hands together. 'I can tell Carla that you piqued my interest—hence the reason I became a volunteer—and then we worked together, discovered we liked each other…and things have gone on from there.'

She screwed up her nose. 'I guess that *could* work…'

He grinned at her. 'Of course it'll work.'

She suddenly thrust out her jaw. 'I'm not going to spy on Carla for you.'

'I'm not asking you to. I'm asking you to become her friend.'

'If this works—if Carla decides she wants to be friends—then I mean to be a proper friend to her. And if that clashes with your agenda—'

He reached over and seized her hand, brought her wrist to his lips. Her eyes widened and her pulse jumped beneath his touch. A growing hunger roared through him. He wanted to put his tongue against that pulse point and kiss his way along her arm until he reached her mouth.

As if she'd read that thought in his face she reclai

her hand. He forced himself to focus on the conversation, rather than her intriguing scent.

'I'm asking nothing more than that you be Carla's friend.'

The way her gaze darted away betrayed her assumed composure. 'That's okay, then. As long as we're on the same page.'

'The same page' meant no fling, no relationship…no kissing. He had to keep things simple between them. There was too much at stake.

'Definitely on the same page,' he assured her.

Starting something with Mia was out of the question. She wouldn't last the distance any more than Caitlin had. His whole way of life was anathema to her.

A fist reached inside his gut and squeezed. Caitlin had left him at the absolute lowest point in his life. The devastation of losing his parents *and* her had… It had almost annihilated him. The shock of it still rebounded in his soul. The only thing that had kept him going was Carla, and the knowledge that she'd needed him. He'd found his feet. Eventually. He wasn't going to have them cut out from under him again by repeating the same mistakes.

He turned to find Mia halfway through a sentence.

'… I mean, we can give you overalls, but that's not going to really help, is it?'

She was worried he'd ruin his *clothes*? 'I have my workout gear in the car.'

She folded her arms. 'Along with a four-hundred-dollar pair of trainers, no doubt? I don't want to be held responsible for wrecking *those*.'

He had no idea how much his trainers had cost. But she was probably right. 'Couldn't you rustle me up a pair of boots?'

She gave a reluctant shrug. 'Maybe. Are you sure you want to do this?'

'Absolutely.'

'We'll need to register you as a volunteer. There'll be

forms to fill out and signatures required to ensure you're covered by the Plum Pines insurance.'

The more she tried to put him off, the more determined he became.

He rose with a decisive clap of his hands. 'Then let's get to it.'

She rose too, shaking her head. 'Don't say you weren't warned.

'What's going on here?' Gordon boomed, coming into the office just as Dylan emerged from the change room wearing the overalls and boots that Mia had found for him.

She sat nearby, already dressed for an afternoon of hard work.

She shot to her feet. 'Dylan—'

'Mr Fairweather,' Gordon corrected with a pointed glare.

'Dylan,' Dylan confirmed, deciding it would be just as satisfying to punch Gordon on the end of his bulbous nose as it would Thierry. He glanced at Mia and wondered when he'd become so bloodthirsty. 'I've decided to register as a volunteer.' He shoved his shoulders back. 'I want to see first-hand what my hundred-thousand-dollar donation will be subsidising.'

Gordon's jowls worked for a moment. 'It's very gener-ous of you to give both your money *and* your time to Plum Pines...'

Behind Gordon's back, Mia gestured that they should leave. Dylan shrugged himself into full supercilious mode and deigned to nod in the other man's direction.

'Good afternoon, Gordon.'

'Good afternoon, Mr Fairweather.'

Dylan didn't invite Gordon to call him by his Christian name—just strode out through the door that Mia held ope for him.

Behind him he heard Gordon mutter to the recep'

ist, 'Bloody trust fund babies,' before the door closed behind them.

Mia grinned as she strode along beside him. 'I think he likes you.'

He glanced at her grin and then threw his head back and roared.

'What on earth…?'

The moment Dylan rounded the side of their family home—affectionately dubbed 'The Palace'—Carla shot to her feet. Behind her a vista of blue sea and blue sky stretched to the horizon. It was a view he never tired of.

'Dylan, what on *earth* have you been doing? You're so… dirty! Filthy dirty. *Obscenely* dirty.'

He grinned. 'I signed up as a volunteer at Plum Pines. That was an inspired idea of yours, by the way. The place is amazing.'

She started to laugh, settling back into the plump cushions of the outdoor sofa. 'I have a feeling it's a certain Plum Pines employee rather than a newfound enthusiasm for conservation that has you *truly* inspired.'

He sobered. *What on earth…?* That was supposed to come as a surprise.

He managed a shrug. 'I like her.'

'I can tell.'

How could she tell?

She couldn't tell!

Romance had addled Carla's brain, that was all. She wanted everyone travelling on the same delirious cloud as she. It made her see romance where none existed. But he could work that to his advantage.

'I'm not sure she likes me.'

'And you think by becoming a volunteer it'll make her ook upon you with a friendlier eye?'

'Along with my newfound enthusiasm for weed eradi-
on.'

Carla laughed—a delightful sound that gladdened his heart. There'd been a time when he'd wondered if he'd ever hear her laugh again.

'She won't take any of your nonsense, you know.'

He eyed his sister carefully. 'Would it bug you if I asked her out?'

'Not at all.' She studied her fingernails. 'If you'll promise me one thing.'

'Name it.'

'That you won't judge Thierry too harshly based on today's events. He wasn't at his best. He's very different from us, Dylan, but I love him.' She turned a pleading gaze on him. 'Please?'

He bit back a sigh. 'Okay.'

'Thank you!'

He widened his stance. 'But I want to get to know him better before you two tie the knot.'

'That can be arranged.' Her smile widened. 'We can double date!'

Perfect.

'Perhaps,' he said, not wanting to appear too eager to share Mia with anyone else. 'Are you going to let him talk you out of volunteering?'

'Not a chance.' She laughed. 'I'm signing up first thing tomorrow.'

CHAPTER FIVE

MIA STARED INTO the mirror and rubbed a hand across her chest in an effort to soothe her racing heart.

You look fine.

Dylan had assured her that tonight's date—*fake*date—was casual, not dressy. They were meeting Carla and Thierry at some trendy burger joint for dinner and then going on to a movie.

She really needed to go shopping for some new clothes. She'd not bothered much with her appearance since getting out of jail. She'd avoided pretty things, bright colours, shunning anything that might draw attention.

She glanced back at the mirror. Her jeans and pale blue linen shirt were appropriately casual, if somewhat bland. The outfit wouldn't embarrass her. More to the point, it wouldn't embarrass Dylan. On impulse she threaded a pair of silver hoops through her ears.

For the last five days Dylan had spent every morning at Plum Pines, helping her dig out weeds. And for the entire time he'd remained unfailingly cheerful and good-natured. He'd never once made her feel as if he was counting down the hours until he'd met his side of the bargain.

He continued to flirt outrageously—not just with her but with all the other female volunteers too. It made her feel safe.

She shook her head at that thought. She had to remain vigi- make sure she didn't become too comfortable around him.

She swung away from the mirror, tired of her reflection. The fact remained that she had limited wardrobe options and this was the best that she could muster. Brooding about it was pointless. Besides, she had more important things to worry about.

Like what on earth was she going to add to the conversation tonight?

She strode into her tiny living room and dropped to the sofa. She needed to come up with five topics of conversation. She glanced at the clock. *Fast!* Dylan would be here to collect her in fifteen minutes. She chewed on her bottom lip. No matter how much she might want to, she couldn't sit through dinner without saying anything. That wouldn't be keeping her end of the deal.

Dear God! What to talk about, though? *Think!*

A knock sounded on the door.

Her gaze flew to the clock. He was early. And she hadn't come up with even one topic of conversation!

Dylan hated to admit it, but he couldn't wait to catch a glimpse of Mia out of uniform. Not that he had anything against her uniform, but there was only so much khaki cotton twill a man could take.

In some deep hidden part of himself lurked a male fantasy he should no doubt be ashamed of, but... He'd love for Mia to answer the door in a short skirt and sky-high heels. *So predictable!* He had a feeling, though, that Mia probably didn't own either.

Still, he'd make do with jeans and a nice pair of ballet flats. That would be nice. Normal. And maybe away from work she'd start to relax some of that fierce guard of hers.

He knocked again and the door flew open. He smiled. *Bingo!* She wore jeans and ballet flats. With the added bonus of surprisingly jaunty earrings that drew attention to the da glossiness of her hair. He'd not seen her with her hair d before. He had an insane urge to reach out and run his hand through it, to see if it were as soft and silky as it promised.

He curved his hand into a fist and kept it by his side. He'd meant to greet her with his typical over-the-top gallantry— kiss her hand, twirl her around and tell her she looked good enough to eat—except the expression in her eyes stopped him.

He made no move to open the screen door, just met her gaze through its mesh. 'What's wrong?'

Puffing out a sigh, she pushed the door open and gestured him in. 'You're early.'

'If you haven't finished getting ready I'm happy to wait. You look great, by the way.' He didn't want her thinking that he thought she didn't *look* ready. He didn't want her stressing about her appearance at all.

'No, I'm ready. I just... I don't do this, you know?'

'Date? Yes, so you said. It's not a date, Mia.'

Her living room was small. In fact the whole cottage was tiny. She'd told him earlier in the week that she rented one of the Plum Pines workers' cottages. There was a row of three of them on the south side of the reserve. From what he could tell, she ate, breathed and slept Plum Pines. He glanced around. Which seemed odd when she'd clearly taken few pains to make her cottage cosy and comfortable.

'Are you sure about this plan, Dylan?'

He turned back, frowning at her unease. 'What are you worried about?'

One slim shoulder lifted. 'That I'll embarrass you.' She gestured for him to take a seat on the sofa. She planted herself on a hard wooden chair at the little dining table pressed hard up against one wall.

She moistened her lips and he realised she wore a pale mocha-coloured lipstick. Desire arrowed straight to his ~roin. Gritting his teeth, he did his best to ignore it. For ~'y's sake, he'd warned himself off her—that should have ~ that!

He gritted his teeth harder. Apparently not. But, while he might find her attractive, he didn't have to act like a teenager. He needed to put her at her ease—not crank up the tension further.

'I can't imagine how you think you'll embarrass me.'

'I'm… I'm not much of a talker, but I know I need to keep up my share of the conversation tonight.'

His heart stilled before surging against the walls of his ribs.

She lifted her hands, only to let them drop back to her lap. 'I've been trying to come up with five fool-proof topics of conversation so that…' She shrugged again. 'So that I'm pulling my weight.'

In that moment he wanted nothing more than to tug her into his arms and hug her. He had a feeling that would be the last thing she'd want. He contented himself with leaning towards her instead. She wore a soft floral scent and he pulled it as far into his lungs as he could.

'I don't expect you to become a sudden chatterbox. It's not who you are. I don't want you to change. I like you just the way you are. So does Carla.'

Was she worried that the better they got to know her the less they'd like her? The thought disturbed him.

'It's just…you and Carla are so bubbly and fun. I should hate to put a dampener on that.'

She thought he was *fun*? A smile tugged through him. 'You mean Carla and I are noisy chatterboxes who dominate the conversation and won't let anyone else get a word in edgewise.'

Her eyes widened. 'I did *not* say that!'

He burst out laughing. After a moment she rolled her eyes, resting back in her seat.

'You must've worked out by now that Carla and I love an audience.'

She gave a non-committal, 'Hmm…'

'And you have to remember Thierry will be there, and no one could accuse call *him* of liveliness.'

'I'm not sure I want to be compared to Thierry.'

He tried a different tack. 'How did the school group go this afternoon?'

Her face lit up. 'They had a great time. It's so funny to watch them the first time they touch a snake or a lizard.'

He picked up the book sitting on her coffee table—a recent autobiography of a famous comedian. 'Good?'

'Yes, very. She's as funny on the page as she is on the television.'

He set the book back down. 'Did you hear about that prank the engineering students at the university pulled with the garden gnomes?'

She sent him an odd look. 'I saw the photos in the paper. It was rather cheeky…but funny.'

'What's a dish you've always meant to cook but never have?'

Her frown deepened. 'Um…veal scaloppini.'

'I couldn't help noticing that these cottages don't have any off-street parking.'

Her eyes narrowed. 'And…?'

'And I didn't see a car parked out the front, which leads me to conclude that you don't have a car.'

She folded her arms. 'That's correct.'

'Are you planning to get one?'

'Maybe.'

'When?'

Her forehead creased. 'What is this, Dylan? Twenty Questions?'

'There you go. There's your five topics of conversation, should you need them—a funny incident at work, a book recommendation, a local news story, does anyone have a recipe for veal scaloppini they'd recommend, and I'm thinking of getting a small to medium-sized hatchback—what would I get?'

She pushed her hair back behind her ears, all but glaring at him, before folding her arms again. 'How do you know I want a hatchback?'

'You're young and you don't have kids, which means you don't have to settle for a station wagon yet.'

She unfolded her arms, but then didn't seem to know what to do with them. She settled on clasping them in her lap. And then she smiled—*really* smiled—and it lit her up from the inside out. Her dark eyes danced and he felt a kick inside that should have felled him.

'Five topics of conversation—just like that.' She snapped her fingers. 'You managed it effortlessly. How can you make it so easy?'

'Probably the same way you can identify the difference between a bush orchid and a noxious weed.' He grinned, referencing an incident earlier in the week when he'd set about eradicating the wrong plant.

She continued to stare at him as if he were amazing, and he had the disconcerting feeling that he could bask in that admiration forever. He shrugged. 'Practice. In my line of work I have to talk to a lot of people. Though, if the truth be told, the sad fact is that I have a talent for frivolity and nonsense.'

'Good conversation is neither frivolous nor nonsensical.'

He waggled his eyebrows. 'It should be if you're doing it right.'

She didn't laugh. She met his gaze, her face sober. 'It's not nonsense to put someone at ease.'

His gut clenched up all over again. If he continued to put her at her ease would she eventually let him kiss her?

He stiffened. He and Mia were *not* going to kiss. They weren't going to do anything except find out if Thierry deserved Carla. Full stop.

This was nothing more than a case of opposites attracting He and Mia were too different—too mismatched—to ma¹ things work in the long term. And he refused to do anything to hurt her in the short term. She'd been through enough.

By the end of dinner Dylan could cheerfully have strangled Thierry. The only contributions he'd made to the conversation had been negative, except when Carla had won a grudging concession that his gourmet burger was *'okay'*.

Mia, for all her worry, had been a delightful dinner companion. And nobody had needed to ask her if *her* burger was good. The expression on her face after she'd taken her first bite had made him grin.

Thierry had scowled.

From what Dylan could tell, scowling was Thierry's default setting.

When a lull had occurred in the conversation Mia had mentioned the book she was reading and asked if anyone else had read it.

Thierry had ignored the question.

Carla had invited Mia to join her book group.

Mia had kept her expression interested, but in her lap her fingernails had dug into her palms, creating half-moons in her flesh that he'd wanted to massage away.

She'd swallowed. 'Are you sure I'd be welcome?'

'All are welcome! We meet at the library on the first Wednesday of the month.'

'Well…thank you. It sounds like fun.' And she'd promised to read the following month's book.

Dylan had wanted to hug her. He hadn't known that asking her to befriend Carla, and the specific details involved, would be so difficult for her. The thing was, friendship didn't seem to be an issue at all. He sensed that both women genuinely liked each other. But going out and mixing with people was obviously a challenge for Mia.

He couldn't help thinking, though, that locking herself away and hiding from the world wasn't the right thing to do. He'd taken his cue from her, however, and gone out of his way to invite Thierry for a game of golf. Thierry had declined, saying he didn't play the game. Dylan had then tried inviting him out on his yacht, but Thierry had declined that too, saying he was too busy with work at the moment.

His heart had sunk when Carla had avoided his gaze. What on earth did she *see* in the man?

Now dinner was over, and they were finally seated in the cinema—Mia on one side of him and Carla and then Thierry on the other—Dylan let out a sigh of relief, no longer obligated to attempt small talk with his sister's fiancé.

It wasn't until the cinema darkened, though, that he suddenly remembered Mia's thin-lipped, pale-faced reaction to the nocturnal houses. *Damn it!* Did the cinema have the same effect?

He touched her arm and she started.

'Is being here uncomfortable for you? Is it like the nocturnal houses?' He kept his voice low so no one could overhear.

'No, it's fine. High ceiling...and it's cool. Those things make a difference.' Her eyes gleamed in the dim light. 'Actually, I'm really looking forward to the film.'

It made him wonder when had been the last time *he'd* relished an outing as simple as this one. Reaching over, he took her hand. When she stiffened, he leaned closer to whisper, 'It's just for show.'

It wasn't, though. He held her hand because he wanted to. He leaned in closer because he wanted to breathe in that subtle floral scent she wore.

When the movie started her hand finally relaxed in his as if she'd forgotten it was there. For the next ninety minutes Dylan experienced the romantic comedy tactilely— entirely through Mia's reactions. They weren't reactions visible in her face, but evident only via her hand in his— in the twitches, squeezes, sudden letting go, in her hand's tension and relief. He sat there spellbound as Mia worried for and cheered on the romantic leads. All of it rendered for him through her fingers.

What miracle allowed him to read the language of her hand so fluently? His heart surged against his ribs. He had to be careful not to let his fascination with this woman grow. *Very* careful. Nothing good could come of it.

When Dylan pulled up outside the front of Mia's cottage at the end of the evening she didn't invite him in.

She shook her head when he reached for his door handle. 'You don't need to walk me to my door.'

But what if he wanted to?

This isn't a real date.

He nodded. 'Right.'

She undid her seat belt. 'I just wanted to say…' She swung back, and even in the dark he could see the wariness in her eyes. 'I did have a nice time tonight, Dylan. Thank you.'

'I'm not after thanks. I want to apologise. For Thierry. Again.'

She shook her head. 'Not your place.'

He clocked the exact moment when she gave in to her curiosity.

'But why in particular this time?'

There'd been an excruciatingly awkward moment at dinner. Carla had asked Mia what the last film she'd been to see had been, and Mia had paled. Thierry had pounced with a narrow-eyed sneer.

'It might be more pertinent to ask, *When was the last time you went to the movies?*'

Dylan's gut had churned and an ugly heat had flushed through him.

Mia had answered with a quiet, 'It'll be over four years since I've been to see a movie.'

And the reason why—the fact she'd been in jail—had pulsed in all the spaces between them.

Dylan couldn't imagine Mia in prison—he couldn't make it make sense. But then he recalled her Spartan cottage and wondered if she'd actually left prison at all.

He rubbed a hand across his chest, trying to dislodge the hard ball that had settled there. 'Thierry went out of his way to make sure everyone remembered *why* you'd not been to see a film in so long.'

She glanced down at her hands. 'Dylan—'

'It wasn't only rude, it was unkind.' How could Carla marry someone like that?

Mia rubbed her hands down the front of her jeans. Finally she glanced at him. 'No matter how much you try to ignore it or justify it, the fact I've been in prison is not a small issue.'

He reached out to cup her face. 'Mia, you're more than your past. You're more than the mistakes that landed you in jail.'

Her bottom lip trembled. The pain that flashed through her eyes speared straight into his gut.

She reached up and with a squeeze removed his hand. 'It's kind of you to say that, but it's not what it feels like. It feels huge. It was a defining moment in my life. I completely understand why other people take issue with it.'

With that she slipped out of the car and strode up to her front door.

Dylan waited until she was safely ensconced inside and the veranda light was switched off with an unambiguous 'the night is over' conviction. With a sigh he didn't understand, he turned the car towards home.

Mia set her sandwich down and unclipped her ringing phone. 'Mia Maydew.'

'Mia, it's Dylan and I have brilliant news.'

The sound of his voice made her pulse gallop. She swallowed and did her best to sound cool and professional. 'Which is…?'

'I have an appointment with Felipe Fellini—the photographer Carla's been so hot for.'

That made her brows lift. She hadn't thought the guy did

weddings or celebrity functions any more. Still, the Fair-weathers had a lot of clout.

'She must be over the moon.'

'I haven't mentioned it to her yet. He's agreed to a meeting—nothing more. I don't want to get her hopes up until it's official.'

Dylan was certainly going above and beyond where Carla's wedding was concerned. Especially when he wasn't even convinced that it would go ahead.

Correction—he wasn't convinced that the groom was worthy of the bride. That was an entirely different matter.

'Mia, are you still there?"

'Yes. I… That's great news.' She tried to gush, but she wasn't much of a one for gushing. 'I'm very impressed.'

'Liar.' He laughed. 'You couldn't care less.'

'I want Carla's wedding to be perfect.' And she didn't care how surly, bad-tempered or humourless Thierry happened to be. With her whole heart she hoped he treated Carla with respect, that he made her happy…that he did indeed deserve her.

'That I *do* believe. The thing is, Felipe wants to meet at Plum Pines this afternoon—two o'clock, if possible. He's only in Newcastle for a couple of days, and his decision on whether or not to take the job apparently depends on the potential locations Plum Pines offers for wedding shots. He wants to start with the lily pond.'

In other words he wanted *her* to be available at two this afternoon to take Felipe around.

'That won't be a problem.'

She'd finished supervising the weed eradication programme last week. She was in the process of helping Veronica create an action plan for a particularly inaccessible area on the northern boundary. That, along with path maintenance, was what her week consisted of.

'Are you on your lunchbreak?'

She traced a finger along the wooden edge of the picnic table. 'I am.'

'Excellent! That means we can chat.'

She stared up into the eucalypt canopy above and shook her head. Dylan *always* wanted to chat. The sooner he got back to FWE and his usual work the better. He wasn't the kind of guy who liked sitting around and twiddling his thumbs, and she had a feeling Carla's wedding wouldn't have his full attention until he'd passed judgement on Thierry.

She suspected he rang her just to 'chat' in an effort to remove the sting of Thierry's incivility. Which was totally unnecessary. Only she didn't know how to say so without sounding ungracious.

'What are you having for lunch?'

She was having what she always had. 'A sandwich.'

'What's in it?'

She lifted the top slice of bread. 'Egg and lettuce. Why is this important?' Nevertheless, she found herself suppressing a smile.

'Are you having chocolate once you finish your *delicious* sandwich?'

She choked back a laugh. 'I refuse to have chocolate with *every* meal. I have a banana.'

'But you're missing a food group! You have carbohydrate, protein, a fruit and a vegetable, but no dairy. Chocolate is dairy. It makes for a rounded meal, Mia.'

She couldn't help but laugh. 'I'll see you at two, Dylan.'

She hung her phone back on her belt, a frown building through her. In the last fortnight Dylan had developed the habit of calling her a couple of times a week—always during her lunchbreak. Some days he didn't mention the wedding at all. She sometimes thought his sole reason for calling was simply to make her laugh. But why would he do that?

Was it really all for Carla's benefit?

Do you think he's doing it for your benefit? Do you really think he could be interested in you?

It was a ludicrous notion—utter wishful thinking. They'd set their ground rules. Dylan wasn't any more interested in a relationship than she was, and a fling was out of the question. But the wisdom of that reasoning didn't dissipate the heat building between them. It didn't quash the thrill that raced through her whenever she heard his voice. It didn't stop her from looking forward to seeing him this afternoon.

She bit into her sandwich. Since when had the prospect of a meeting become more attractive than tromping along solitary paths with loppers and a pair of secateurs?

She had to be careful around Dylan. *Very* careful. She couldn't go falling for his charm. Never again would she be a man's sap, his puppet. Not even one as alluring and attractive as Dylan. She'd sworn never to travel that particular path again.

Couldn't you just kiss him once anyway? Just to see?

The illicit thought came out of left field. She stiffened. No, she could not!

No *way* was she kissing Dylan. Any kissing was absolutely and utterly out of the question. That way led to the slippery slope of lost good intentions and foolish, deceitful dreams. She wasn't descending that slope again. She had no intention of falling into the pit that crouched at its bottom.

So...that's a no, then?

A definite no!

She wrapped up what was left of her sandwich and tossed it into a nearby bin. A glance at her watch told her she could manage an hour's worth of path maintenance before she had to get back to meet with Dylan and his photographer. Wrestling with overgrown native flora sounded exactly what she needed.

Neither the exercise nor Mia's resolution to resist Dylan's appeal stopped her every sense from firing to life the moment she clapped eyes on him that afternoon. It made her want to groan in despair.

No despair! She'd only need despair if she gave in to her attraction—if she handed her heart to him on a platter and became his willing slave. The attraction part of the equation was utterly normal. She'd defy *any* woman to look at Dylan and not appreciate him as the handsomest beast she'd ever laid eyes on.

Not that he *was* a beast. Not when he moved towards her, hand outstretched, a smile of delight on his face at seeing her. Then he was an utter sweetheart.

She couldn't stop herself from smiling back.

It's polite to smile.

Polite or not, she couldn't help it.

He kissed her cheek, his warm male scent raising gooseflesh on her arms.

'Mia…' He ushered her towards the other man. 'I'd like you to meet Felipe Fellini.'

She shook the photographer's hand. 'I've heard a lot about you, Mr Fellini.'

'Yes, yes, it is inevitable. Now *this*…' He gestured to encompass the lily pond and its surrounds. 'You must tell me that you have something better, something more original for me to work with than this.'

He strutted through the area in a coat embroidered with wild, colourful poppies, flinging his arms out in exaggerated disappointment while speaking in an affected American-Italian accent.

Mia stared at him, utterly flummoxed. Never, in all of her twenty-five years, had she ever come across someone like Felipe Fellini!

She moistened her lips. 'I…uh…you don't like it?'

'Ugh, darling! You *do*? I mean, *look* at it!' He pointed at the pond, the grass, a tree.

Behind Felipe's back, Dylan started to laugh silently. Mia had to choke back her answering mirth. 'I… I can't say as I've ever really thought about it.'

He swatted a hand in her direction. 'That's because you're

not an *artiste*. My sensitivities are honed to within an inch of their lives, darling.'

It should have been dismissive, but the words held a friendly edge and she suddenly realised he was having the time of his life.

She planted her hands on her hips. 'What's wrong with it?'

'It's a cliché. An utter cliché.'

'But isn't that what a wedding is all about?'

The question slipped out before she could censor it. She wished it back the moment both men spun to face her—Felipe with his hands up to cover his mouth as if utterly scandalised, Dylan contemplating her with those deep blue eyes, his delectable lips pursed.

'Dylan, *darling*, it appears I've met a creature I never thought existed—a truly unromantic woman.'

Dylan folded his arms, nudging the other man with his shoulder. 'I saw her first.'

Felipe spluttered with laughter. 'Darling, I'm not a ladies' man—but if I were…you'd be in trouble. I'd have her eating out of my hand in no time.'

Mia started to laugh. She couldn't help it. Felipe, it appeared, enjoyed flirting and games every bit as much as Dylan.

'Come along, you unromantic girl.' Felipe draped an arm across her shoulders with a smirk in Dylan's direction. 'Show me something worthy of my talents.'

Dylan fell in behind them with a good-natured grin. Mia led them to the utility she'd parked further down the track. One hundred and eighty hectares was a lot of ground to cover. They wouldn't manage it all on foot before dark.

Felipe discounted the first two spots Mia showed him—a forest glade of wattle, with low overhanging branches, and a pocket of rainforest complete with a tiny trickling stream.

'Clichéd?' she asked.

'Totally.'

'You don't know what you want, but you'll know it when you see it, right?'

Dylan's chuckle from the back seat filled the interior of the car, warming Mia's fingers and toes.

'I'll have none of your cheek, thank you, Dylan Fairweather. You, sir, are an uncultured and coarse Philistine.' He sniffed. 'I understand you have a *Gilmore* on your wall.'

For a moment Dylan's eyes met Mia's in the rear-vision mirror. 'You're welcome to come and admire it any time you like, Felipe.'

'Pah!'

At Mia's raised eyebrow, Dylan added, 'Jason Gilmore— like Felipe, here—is a world-class photographer.'

Felipe gave a disbelieving snort and Mia found herself grinning, Dylan and Felipe's high spirits momentarily rubbing off onto her.

'I've never heard of Jason Gilmore, but I've heard of Felipe. So I'm not sure this Mr Gilmore can be all that good. He certainly can't be in the same class as Felipe.'

Felipe reached out and clasped the hand she had on the steering wheel, pressing his other to his heart. 'I *love* this girl.'

In the next instant he almost gave her a heart attack.

'Stop!' he screeched.

She slammed on the brakes, and even though they weren't going fast gravel still kicked up around them from the unsealed road. Before she could ask Felipe what was wrong, he was out of the car and moving with remarkable agility through the neighbouring strip of bush.

She glanced at Dylan in wordless enquiry.

He shook his head. 'I have no idea. But I suspect we should follow him.'

'This!' Felipe declared when they reached him.

Mia stared. 'It's a fallen tree.'

He seized her by the shoulders and propelled her to the tree, ordered her to straddle it. Next he forced Dylan to straddle it as well, facing her. Mia straightened and folded her arms, frowning at the photographer.

'Why do you frown at me?' He glared at Dylan. 'Why does she frown at me? Make her stop.'

'Uh... Mia...?'

'I can see that *you*—' she pointed a finger at Felipe '—will have no regard for Carla's dress.'

'*Pah!* This is art. If Carla wants art then she will need to make sacrifices. Now, do as I say and lean in towards each other.'

Whipping out his camera, he motioned with his hands for them to move closer together.

He heaved an exaggerated sigh. 'As if you're about to kiss. Mia, darling, I know you don't have a romantic bone in your delightful body, but you have a pulse, and you have to admit that your fellow model is very pretty. I need to capture the light and the landscape. Art is *work*.'

She glanced at Dylan to see if he'd taken Felipe's 'pretty' remark as a slight on his masculinity. She found him grinning.

He winked at her. 'You heard what the man said.' And then he puckered up in such an exaggerated way that any threat inherent in the situation was immediately removed. She puckered up too.

With the odd, 'Tsk!' as if in disapproval of their antics, Felipe set about taking photographs.

The flash made Mia wince.

'Headache?' Dylan asked.

'I just don't like having my photo taken.' The last time a flash had gone off in her face had been when she'd been led from the courthouse...in handcuffs. It wasn't a memory she relished.

As if he could sense her ambivalence, Dylan leapt to his feet.

'Darling!' Felipe spluttered. 'I—'

'You'll have to make do with just me as a model, Master Fellini. Run!' he muttered out of the corner of his mouth to Mia.

So she did. She shot to her feet and all but sprinted away, to stand behind and to one side of Felipe, in amongst the bracken fern.

She watched the two men's antics with growing enjoyment. Felipe barked out orders and Dylan promptly, if somewhat exaggeratedly, carried them out. He flirted with the camera without a scrap of self-consciousness. Felipe, in turn, flirted outrageously back.

Double entendres flew through the air until Mia found herself doubled up with laughter. It was just so much *fun* watching Dylan!

Without warning, Felipe turned and snapped a shot of her.

She blinked, sobering in an instant.

Dylan was immediately puffed up, all protective.

Felipe beamed as he stared down at his camera. 'Perfect!'

CHAPTER SIX

MIA SWALLOWED. 'WHAT do you mean, *perfect*?'

He gestured her over. 'Come and see.'

She didn't want to see. She wanted to run away to hack and slash hiking trails, to fill in potholes and be away from people with their unspoken questions and flashing cameras.

Dylan's not like that.

Dylan was the worst of the lot!

She forced reluctant feet over to where Felipe stood with his camera held out to her. Dylan moved across too, and she sensed the tension in his shoulders, in the set of his spine.

'You said you just wanted to test the light—to get a sense of scale and a feel for the locations, figure out how to make them work for you.'

'Darling, I'm an *artiste*. My mind, my eyes, my brain... they're always searching for the perfect shot.'

She went to take the camera from him, but he shook his head.

'Just look.'

She leaned in to look at the display on the screen. Her gut clenched up tight at what she saw.

Dylan leaned over her right shoulder. 'Holy cow...'

In the photograph, Mia stood knee-high in bracken fern, bent at the waist with her head thrown back, her mouth wide with laughter and her eyes crinkled and dancing. The entire picture rippled with laughter. She didn't know how Felipe had managed it, but when she stared at the photo she could feel delight wrap around her and lift her up.

He'd made her look beautiful.

She swallowed and straightened, bumping into Dylan. She moved away with a murmured apology.

'You see what I mean?' Felipe demanded. 'The picture is perfect.'

Her temples started to throb. 'It's a lie.'

'Art doesn't lie, darling.'

She was aware of how closely Dylan watched her, of how darkly his eyes throbbed as they moved between the image of her on the camera and the flesh and blood her. She found him just as disturbing as Felipe's photograph.

'Will you sign a release form, darling, allowing me to use that photograph in my next exhibition? This is *precisely* what I need.'

Her mouth dried. She had a plan. That plan was to remain in the background. *This* wasn't remaining in the background.

Her hands curled into fists. 'No.'

Felipe switched the cameral off with a sniff. 'That photograph could be the centrepiece of my next exhibition. And, darling, I don't actually *need* your permission. I was only being polite. This is a public place. As such, I'm free to take photographs of anything I please.'

Instinct told her that pleading with him would do no good. Her stomach started to churn.

'How much would a photograph like that sell for?'

She'd been aware of Dylan growing taller and sterner beside her. She glanced up and realised he'd transformed into full warrior mode. A pulse started up in her throat, and a vicarious thrill took hold of her veins even as she bit back a groan.

Felipe waved him away. 'It's impossible to put a price on a photograph like that. I have no intention of selling it.'

'Sell it to me *now*.'

Dylan named a sum that had her stomach lurching.

'No!' She swung round to him and shook her head. 'Don't even think about it. That's a ludicrous amount of money for a stupid photograph.'

He planted his hands on his hips. 'It's obvious you don't want it shown in a public exhibition. Let me buy it.'

She folded her arms to hide how much her hands shook. 'I don't want it hanging on your wall either.'

Why would he pay such a huge sum for a photograph of her anyway?

Because he cares?

She pushed that thought away. She didn't want him to care. She hadn't asked him to care!

As if he'd read that thought in her face, Dylan thrust out his jaw, his eyes glittering. 'Felipe, sell me the photo.'

She stabbed a finger at the photographer. 'You'll do nothing of the sort.'

Felipe turned to Dylan, hands raised. 'You heard what the lady said, darling.'

Dylan glowered—first at her and then at the photographer. 'Okay, let me make myself crystal-clear. If that photograph is ever displayed publicly I'll bring the biggest lawsuit you've ever seen crashing down on your head.'

Felipe merely smiled. 'The publicity will be delicious!'

Mia grabbed Dylan's arm and shook it, but her agitation barely seemed to register. It was as useless as rattling iron bars.

'You will do absolutely nothing of the sort!' she said.

His brows drew down low over his eyes, his entire mien darkening. 'Why not?'

'Because you don't own me. You don't get to make decisions for me.' She swung to Felipe. '*You* don't own me either. In a just world you wouldn't get to make such a decision either.'

Nobody said anything for a moment.

'Mia, darling…'

She didn't want to hear Felipe's excuses and justifications.

She turned towards the car. 'I thought art was supposed to make the world a better place, not a worse one. I think it's time we headed back.'

'*Darling!*'

She turned to find Felipe removing the memory card from the camera. He took her hand and closed her fingers over it. 'It's yours. I'm sorry.'

Relief almost made her stagger. 'Thank you,' she whispered, slipping it into her top pocket and fastening the button. She tried to lighten the mood. 'I expect for an *artiste* like yourself great photos are a dime a dozen.'

'No, darling, they're not,' he said, climbing into the car.

All the while she was aware of the brooding way Dylan watched her, of the stiff movements of his body, betraying…*anger*? It made her heart drum hard against her ribs.

'That photograph is truly unique, but I could not exhibit it without your blessing. I do not wish anyone to feel diminished by my art.'

She nodded. Felipe was a good man. So was Dylan. She was surrounded by people she didn't deserve.

'But if you should have a change of heart…ever change your mind…' He slipped a business card into her hand.

She nodded. 'You'll be the first to know.'

She didn't add that a change of heart was highly unlikely. She had a feeling he already knew that.

She glanced in the rear-vision mirror to find Dylan staring at her, his gaze dark and brooding. She had no idea what he was thinking…or what he must think of *her*. Her pulse sped up again. Did he hate her after what she'd said?

She didn't want him to hate her.

She had a feeling, though, that it would be better for both of them if he did.

Dylan showed up at her cottage that night.

Without a word she ushered him in, wondering at her own lack of surprise at seeing him.

'I wanted to discuss what happened this afternoon,' he said without preamble.

'I don't see that there's much to discuss.' She turned towards the kitchen. 'Can I get you something to drink—tea or coffee? I have some light beer if you'd rather.'

'No, thank you.'

Good. They could keep this quick, then. She grabbed some water for herself and motioned him to the sofa, taking a seat at the table.

Dylan didn't sit. He stood in the middle of the room, arms folded, and glared at her.

She heaved a sigh. 'I'm sorry, Dylan, but I'm not a mind-reader. What exactly did you want to discuss?'

'I didn't appreciate your implication this afternoon that I was trying to own you. I simply felt responsible for putting you in a situation that had obviously made you uncomfortable. I set about fixing the situation. I don't see how that can be seen as trying to control you.'

She stared into her glass of water. 'I appreciate your intentions were good, but it doesn't change the fact that you didn't ask me my opinion first.'

'There wasn't time!' He flung an arm out. 'Where people like Felipe are concerned it's best to come at them hard and fast.'

'And what if I told you that your solutions were more horrifying to me than the initial problem?'

'Were they?'

'Yes.'

He widened his stance. 'Why?'

She stood then too, pressing her hands to her stomach. 'Ever since I got out of jail I've had one objective—to keep a low profile, to keep out of trouble. A lawsuit would create a hundred times more furore than an anonymous photograph in some exhibition.'

He straightened, his height almost intimidating. Not that

it frightened her. She sensed that frightening her was the last thing he wanted.

'Are you concerned that someone from your past will track you down?'

'No.' And she wasn't. That was all done with.

His hands went to his hips. 'Look, I understand your dismay at the thought of publicity, but what on earth was wrong with *me* buying the photograph?'

'I'm already beholden enough to you!'

'It's my money. I can do as I please with it.'

'Not on my watch, you can't. Not when you're spending that money solely for my benefit.'

He stared at her with unflinching eyes. 'You'd rather have let that picture go public then be beholden to me?'

She met his gaze. 'Yes.'

He wheeled away from her. When he swung back his eyes were blazing.

Before he could rail at her about ingratitude and stubbornness, she fired a question back at him. 'If Felipe had sold you that photograph, would you have given it to me?'

He stilled. His chin lowered several notches. 'I'd have promised to keep it safe.'

They both knew it wasn't the same thing. She could feel her lips twist. 'So, in the end, it was Felipe who did what I truly wanted after all.'

A tic started up in his jaw. 'This is the thanks I get for trying to help you?'

She refused to wither under his glare. 'You weren't trying to help me. What you're angry about is missing your chance to buy that picture.'

He moved in closer. 'And that scares the pants off of you, doesn't it?'

Bullseye.

She refused to let her fear show. 'I've told you where I stand on relationships and romance. I don't know how I can make it any plainer, but offering such a ludicrous sum for a photo of me leads me to suspect that you haven't heard me.'

'Some women would've found the gesture romantic.'

Exactly.

'Not me.'

He shoved his hands in his pockets and strode around the room. Mia did her absolute best not to notice the way the muscles of his shoulders rippled beneath the thin cotton of his business shirt, or how his powerful strides ate up the space in her tiny living room. He quivered like a big cat, agitated and undecided whether to pounce or not.

She knew exactly how to soothe him. If she went to him, put her arms around his neck and pressed her length against his, he'd gather her in his arms and they'd lose themselves to the pleasure they could bring each other.

The pulse at her throat pounded. She gripped her hands together. It wouldn't help. It might be possible to do 'uncomplicated' when it came to a fling, but refused to risk it.

If only that knowledge could cool the stampede of her blood!

He swung around. 'You might have your heart under lock and key, Mia, but you have no right to command mine.'

He wasn't promising her his heart. Heat gathered behind her eyes. He wasn't promising anything more than a quick roll in the hay, and they both knew it.

'You're forgetting the ground rules. We promised!'

'Just because I wanted that photo it doesn't mean I want *you.*'

But they both knew he desired her in the most primitive way a man could want a woman. And they both knew she desired him back. They were balancing too narrowly on a knife-edge here, and she couldn't let them fall.

She clamped her hands to her elbows. Wrapped up in his attraction for her were feelings of pity, a desire to make things better, and perhaps a little anger. It was an explosive combination in a man like Dylan—a nurturer with the heart of a warrior. He knew as well as she did that they could never fit into each other's lives. But hard experience had taught her that the heart didn't always choose what was good for it.

He leaned in so close his breath fanned her cheek. 'Did you destroy the photo?'

She wanted to say that she had.

No lying. No stealing.

She pulled in a ragged breath. 'No.'

'You *will* give it to me, you know.'

She shook her head. 'I have no need of your money.'

He ran the backs of his fingers down her cheek, making her shiver. 'I didn't say anything about buying it from you, Mia. I meant that eventually you'll give it to me as a gift.'

She wanted to tell him to go to hell, but his hand snaked behind her head and he pulled her mouth close to his own and the words dried in her throat.

Dear Lord, he was going to kiss her!

'The girl in that photograph is the woman you're meant to be. I know it and you know it.'

He was wrong! She didn't deserve to be that girl. She deserved nothing more than the chance to live her life in peace.

His breath fanned across her lips, addling her brain. She should step away, but she remained, quivering beneath his touch, hardly knowing what she wished for.

He pressed a kiss to the corner of her mouth. Her eyes fluttered closed as she turned towards him...

And then she found herself released.

'You want me as much as I want you.'

Her heart thudded in her ears. She had to reach out and steady herself against a chair.

'I don't know why the thought of being happy scares you.'

Disappointment and confusion battled with relief and her common sense, and it took a moment for his words to sink in. She pushed her shoulders back, but didn't lift her chin in challenge. She didn't want him to take chin-lifting as an invitation to kiss her.

'I am happy.'

Easing back from him, she seized her glass of water and took several steps away.

'Liar.'

He said the word softly, almost like a caress. He had a point. The thing was, she didn't need happiness. She just needed to stay on track.

She kept her back to him. 'I don't mean this to sound harsh, Dylan, but my happiness is not dependent on my sleeping with you.'

'I'm not talking about myself, here, Mia, or my ability to make you happy. I'm removing myself from the equation.'

'How convenient.'

'I think you're just as imprisoned now as you were when you were in jail.'

She spun around at that, water sloshing over the side of her glass. 'If you believe that, then it just goes to show how naïve you are.'

He blinked and then nodded. 'I'm sorry, I didn't mean that to sound glib.'

She didn't say anything. She just wanted him gone.

'Was it really so awful?'

She closed her eyes at the soft question. 'Yes.' She forced her eyes open again. 'I am *never* going back. And happiness is a small price to pay.'

His eyes throbbed at her words.

'I think it's time you left, Dylan.'

He stared at her for a long moment, but finally he nodded. 'Are you still okay for Saturday?'

For reasons known only to himself, Dylan had booked her and Carla in for a day of beauty treatments at a local spa. In the evening Mia, and presumably Thierry, were to dine with the Fairweathers at their coastal mansion.

Despite her curiosity about Dylan's home, she wasn't looking forward to either event. But she'd promised.

'Yes, of course.'

'Carla and I will collect you at ten.'

'I'll be ready.'

She'd need to go shopping before then. She had a feeling that she owned nothing appropriate for dinner at the Fairweather estate.

'You're very tense.'

Mia did her best to relax beneath the masseuse's hands, but found it almost impossible. She'd been poked and prodded, scrubbed and wrapped, and waxed and tweezed to within an inch of her life.

People did this for *fun*?

What she'd really like was to ask the masseuse to hand her a bathrobe, find her a cup of tea and leave her alone to soak up the glorious view on the other side of the picture window.

The spa was located on the sixth floor of an upmarket beachside hotel that boasted a sweeping view of Newcastle beach. It would be a relief and a joy to spend half an hour contemplating gold sands and blue seas.

'It's probably because of all the hard physical work she does,' Carla said from the massage table beside Mia's, her voice sounding like nothing more than a blissed-out sigh. 'Isn't this a gorgeous treat, Mia?'

'Gorgeous,' she murmured back. She might have made a no-lying promise, but in this instance the lie was lily-white. She had no intention of dampening Carla's enjoyment. That had been the one good thing about all this—spending time with Carla.

So Mia didn't ask for a bathrobe and a cup of tea. She gritted her teeth instead and endured a further forty minutes of kneading, pummelling and rubbing down.

'Change of plan,' Carla announced, waving her phone in the air as she and Mia moved towards Dylan in the hotel bar.

Mia swallowed and nodded in his direction, not able to meet his eye, glad to have Carla there as a buffer.

He turned on his bar stool. 'Change of plan?'

Mia glance up to find him staring straight at her. All she could do was shrug. She had no idea what Carla's change of plan entailed.

Meeting his gaze made her mouth go dry. Looking at him had the oddest effect on her. She should look away. If she could, perhaps she would. Instead, she gazed at him hungrily. He wore a pair of sand-coloured cargo shorts and... and a Hawaiian shirt that should have made him look silly, but didn't.

It made him look... She swallowed again. He looked like a Hollywood heartthrob, and as he raised the beer he nursed to his lips, a searing hunger burned a trail through her.

'Yes.' Carla finished texting before popping her phone into her handbag. 'Thierry's coming to collect me.'

He was? Carla was leaving her alone with Dylan?

Ooh...*horrible* plan!

'I've talked Mia into spending not just the evening with us, but the rest of the afternoon as well. So you'll need to take her home to collect her things. Thierry and I will meet you by the pool at four.'

With a perfumed air-kiss, Carla dashed out. Mia didn't know where to look. She glanced at her feet, at the window, at the bar.

'Would you like a drink?'

She glanced at his glass, still three-quarters full, and with a sigh slid onto the bar stool beside his. 'Do you think they'd make me a cup of tea?'

'I'm sure of it. English Breakfast, Earl Grey or Chamomile?'

'Earl Grey, please.'

He ordered the tea and without further ado asked, 'What's wrong?'

Straight to the heart of the matter. It shouldn't surprise her.

'Are you feeling awkward after the words we exchanged on Tuesday evening?'

She wished she could say no, but that lie *wouldn't* be lily-white.

'Aren't you?'

She doubted she'd ever have the power to hurt him, but she *had* disappointed him. She suspected women rarely turned Dylan down.

For heaven's sake, why would they? You must be crazy!

'Mia, you've every right to speak your mind. I might not like what you have to say, but there's no law that says you have to say things with the sole purpose of pleasing me. The only person you need to please is yourself.'

Did he mean that?

'I came on unnecessarily strong. I was upset…and I was prepared to throw our agreed ground rules out of the window.' He dragged a hand down his face. 'I'm sorry. You were right to hold firm.'

Her heart had no right to grow so heavy at his words.

'I know a relationship between us wouldn't work. And you've made it clear that a fling is out of the question.' He wrapped both hands around his beer. 'The thing is, I like you. It's as simple and as complicated as that.'

Her eyes burned.

'I'm sorry.' He grimaced. 'Can we be friends again?'

She managed a nod.

They were quiet while the barmen slid her tea in front of her. When she glanced back to him he sent her a half-grin. 'How did you enjoy the treatments?'

'Oh, I…' She hesitated too long. 'It was lovely.' She scrambled. 'Thank you.'

'You're lying!'

She debated with herself for a moment and then nodded, 'I hated it.'

His brows drew down low over his eyes, fire sparking in their depths. 'Was anybody rude or unpleasant…or worse?'

'No!' Before she could stop herself she reached out and touched his arm, wanting to dispel his dark suspicions. 'Everyone was attentive and professional. I couldn't fault anyone. It was me—not them. I just... I just don't like being touched by people I don't know.'

She closed her eyes and pulled in a breath. He must think her a freak.

When she opened them she found him staring down at her, his lips rueful. 'I'm sorry. It seems I'm constantly forcing you to do things you hate.'

She waved that away. 'It's not important. It's all in a good cause.'

'It does matter.'

'Let's talk about Carla and—'

'No.'

Mia blinked.

'Let me apologise. I'm sorry I took it for granted that you'd enjoy a spa day.'

'The majority of women would.'

'You're not the majority of women.'

That was true, but if she dwelled on that fact for too long she might throw up.

'Apology accepted.'

He sat back and she found she could breathe again. He had the oddest effect on her—she simultaneously wanted to push him away and pull him closer.

Maybe this time it wouldn't be like it was with Johnnie.

Maybe. Maybe not. But even if Dylan were willing she had no intention of finding out. She couldn't risk it.

She pushed those thoughts firmly out of her mind. 'Now, can we talk about Carla?'

He grinned. 'Absolutely.'

Despite her confusion she found herself smiling back. 'That was the one good thing about today. I enjoy spending time with her. She's good company.'

'Did she confide anything in you?'

Mia poured herself some tea and stared down into the dark liquid. 'She's totally in love with Thierry. Even if he *is* all your worst fears rolled into one, I can't see how you'll be able to stop this wedding.'

He dragged a hand down his face and her heart went out to him.

'But on the plus side...'

He glanced up, his eyes keen. 'Yes?'

How to put this delicately...? 'I've had some close experience with women who've been in emotionally and physically abusive relationships.'

His eyes went dark. 'How close?'

She knew what he wanted to know—if *she'd* ever been in an abusive relationship. She sidestepped the unspoken question. 'My father was abusive to my mother.'

'Physically?'

'Not quite.' Though that latent threat had hung over every fraught confrontation. 'But he was emotionally abusive until I don't think she had any sense of self left.'

'I'm sorry.'

'I'm not telling you this so you'll feel sorry for me. I'm telling you because I don't see any of the same signs in Carla that I saw in my mother. Carla is neither meek nor diffident. She's kind and easy-going, and I suspect she's peace-loving, but I wouldn't describe her as submissive or compliant. I don't think she's afraid of Thierry's displeasure.'

'Changes like the ones you describe in your mother— they don't happen overnight. They're the result of years of abuse.'

He had a point.

'There are men out there who prey on emotionally vulnerable women.'

He didn't need to tell *her* that. 'You think Carla is emotionally vulnerable because of what happened between her boyfriend and her best friend?'

He ran a finger through the condensation on his glass of beer. 'It's one of the reasons. She was only sixteen when our parents died. It was a very difficult time for her.'

'I expect it was a difficult time for you too. How old were *you*?'

'Twenty-one.'

Twenty-one and alone with a sixteen-year-old sister. Mia swallowed. 'It must've been devastating for you both. I'm sorry.'

He looked haggard for a moment. 'It was tough for a while.'

Understatement, much?

'And then there's the Fairweather name...'

She shook her head, not knowing what he meant.

'It's hard to know if the people we meet like us for ourselves or whether what they see is the money, the tradition, and the power behind the name.'

'But... That's awful!' To have to go through life like that... 'So that's why Carla didn't tell me who she really was when we first met.'

He nodded. 'I've not been sure of any woman since Caitlin.'

Her mouth went dry. 'The girl who broke your heart?'

'The very one.' He lifted his beer and drank deeply.

Leave it alone!

'You said she couldn't handle it when things got rough. Did she...?' She frowned. 'Did she dump you when you were in the middle of your grief for your parents?'

Pain briefly flashed in his eyes, and she went cold all over when he gave one curt nod.

She had to swallow before she could speak. 'I'm sorry.'

He sent her a self-deprecating half-smile that made her want to cry. 'I was head over heels for her. We'd been dating for two years. I had our lives all mapped out—finish uni, get married, see the world. I thought she was my rock. I wanted to be hers. I thought we were...not perfect—never that—but special.' He shrugged. 'I was a fool.'

The grief in his eyes caught at her. 'You were so young,

Dylan. You couldn't possibly have known she wouldn't last the distance. She probably didn't know either.'

He turned his head, his gaze sharpening. 'The thing is, I know you haven't the slightest interest in my money or my name. Funny, isn't it?'

'Hilarious.' She swallowed, understanding now, in a way she hadn't earlier, how serious he was about not pursuing a relationship. The realisation should have been comforting. 'But we both know we wouldn't fit.'

He stared into his glass. 'Building something worthwhile with someone is more than just being attracted to them.'

'Very true.' She wished her voice would emerge with more strength. 'You need to have shared values...to want the same things from life.'

That wasn't them.

He drained his beer. 'Luckily for us we have our ground rules to keep us on the straight and narrow.'

Her heart thudded hard. 'Amen.'

'Are you ready to go?'

She started to nod and then broke off to fiddle with the collar of her shirt. 'I have a problem.'

'Tell me,' he ordered. 'Fixing problems is my specialty.'

'Carla mentioned swimming and lounging by the pool. But the thing is... I don't have a swimsuit.'

He stared at her, and then he smiled—really smiled. 'That's a problem that's easily remedied.'

CHAPTER SEVEN

WHEN DYLAN PARKED the car at the shopping centre Mia removed her seat belt and turned fully to face him. 'We're not going to do the *Pretty Woman* thing in here, Dylan.'

He knew exactly what she meant and a secret fantasy—or not so secret, in this case—died a quick death.

He didn't argue with her. He'd already forced her into too many situations that she hadn't wanted this week.

He wanted to make her smile. Not frown.

He wanted to make her life a little bit easier. Not harder. And he had been making it harder. He couldn't deny that.

Then walk away now. Leave her be.

The look on her face when Felipe had snapped that photograph of her... It burned through his soul now. He'd wanted to make it up to her. He'd wanted to make things right. Nothing before had ever stung him the way her rejection of his aid had done.

She heaved out a sigh. 'Are we going to have to argue about this?'

He shook his head. 'Tell me exactly what you want to have happen in there.' He nodded towards the shops.

'I want to walk into a budget chain store, select a pair of board shorts and a swim-shirt, and pay for them with my own money. I then want to leave.'

Precise and exact.

'Can I make one small suggestion?'

She stared at him as if she didn't trust him and it occurred to him that he didn't blame her. His heavy-handed attempts to come to her defence last Tuesday hadn't been entirely unselfish. He'd wanted that photo.

He'd taken one look at it and he'd wanted it for himself. He couldn't even explain why!

It was pointless denying his attraction to her, but he had no intention of falling for Mia. It would be a replay of his relationship with Caitlin all over again, and he'd learned his lesson the first time around.

It was just… Mia had got under his skin. He hated the way Thierry treated her. He hated the way Gordon treated her. He chafed at how hard her life was—at the unfairness of it. He wanted her to feel free to laugh the way she had in Felipe's photograph.

It's not your job to make her laugh.

Maybe not, but what harm would it do?

He shook himself, realising the pause in their conversation was in danger of becoming too charged.

'It's just a small suggestion.'

She pursed her lips. He did his best not to focus on their lushness, or the need that surged into his blood, clenching hard and tight about his groin. If he stared at them too long she'd know exactly where his thoughts had strayed, and that would be a disaster. For whatever reason, she was determined to ignore the attraction between them. Today he didn't want to force her to face anything she didn't want to face or do anything she didn't want to do.

'Okay.' She hitched up her chin. 'What's this *small* suggestion?'

Her tone told him it had better be small. Or else. Her 'or else' might be interesting, but he resisted the temptation. Today was about making things easier for her.

'I have it on pretty good authority that swim-shirts can chafe.'

She folded her arms, her lips twisting as if she thought he was spinning her a story.

'So you might want to buy a one-piece suit to wear underneath. And, while shirts are great for avoiding sunburn, they don't protect your face, arms and legs, so you might consider adding sunscreen to your shopping list too. And a hat.'

She smiled, and the noose that had started to tighten about his neck eased. 'I have sunscreen at home. I use it for work. But a new hat might be nice.'

He stared at that smile and then fumbled for the door handle. He needed to get out of the car now or he'd be in danger of kissing her.

'Let's go shopping.'

Mia looked cute in her board shorts and swim-shirt—a combination of blue and pink that set off the warmth of her skin and provided a perfect foil for the dark lustre of her hair. She'd look cute in the modest one-piece that he knew she wore beneath too, and while he'd be lying if he said he didn't care about seeing her in a bikini, a large part of him simply didn't care what she wore. That large part of him just wanted her to relax and be happy.

He glanced across. She reclined on a banana lounger, staring at her toes and smiling.

He moved to the lounger beside hers. 'What are you smiling at?'

Her cheeks went a delicious pink. 'Oh, I...'

He leaned closer, intrigued. ''Fess up.'

Her eyes danced. Not long ago they'd all enjoyed a rousing game of water volleyball in the pool, and it had improved everyone's mood—even Thierry's.

'This is going to sound utterly frivolous, but... I'm admiring my toes.'

He glanced at her toes and she wiggled them at him.

'I haven't had painted toenails since I was fifteen or sixteen...and the pedicurist has made them look so pretty.'

They were a shiny fairy-floss pink...and totally kissable.

'I think I'll sit here and admire them too. They're too cute for words.'

She laughed, and something inside him soared.

'I've had a really nice afternoon, Dylan. I just wanted to say thank you.'

'You're welcome. I'm hoping the fun continues well into the evening.'

She glanced across at Carla and Thierry, sitting at a table on the other side of the pool, a giant umbrella casting them in shade. 'Thierry seems a bit more relaxed today. Maybe pool volleyball is the secret to his soul.'

He found himself strangely reluctant to focus on the other couple's real or imagined issues at the moment. 'Would you like to see the Jason Gilmore?' At her frown he added, 'You remember. The photographer Felipe scoffed at?'

She hesitated, and then gestured out in front of her. 'Can it compete with this?'

He stared out at the view spread before them and then rested his hands back behind his head. 'Nothing can compete with this view.'

And it was all the better too for having Mia's toes in the foreground.

'You have a pool that looks like it belongs in a resort.'

The pool was long enough for laps, curving at one end to form a lagoon, with an island in the middle—a handy spot for resting drinks and nibbles. There was an infinity edge that had utterly bewitched Mia when she'd first seen it.

He nodded. The pool *was* amazing. 'But even better is the view beyond it.'

The Fairweather mansion sat on a headland, and the forest leading down the cliff obscured the beach below, but the Pacific Ocean was spread out before them in all its sapphire glory. Waves crashed against rocky outcrops and the spray lifted up into the air in a spectacular display of the ocean's power. It was elemental, primal and magnificent.

'We're incredibly lucky to live here.'

'You are,' she said, but her voice lacked any resentment. She glanced across at him. 'I suspect you work very hard for your luck.'

He gestured to the pool and the house. 'We inherited this from our parents.'

She gazed at him, her eyes moss-dark. 'And yet I bet you'd give it all up to spend just one more day with them.'

Her words hit him squarely in the secret, private part of himself that he let no one but Carla see. If only he could see his father again and ask his advice about how best to deal with his uncle. If only he could sit down with his mother and ask her how he could best support Carla. To have the chance to simply hug them one more time…share a meal with them…laugh with them. His chest burned with the ache of their absence.

'I'm sorry. I didn't mean to make you sad.'

He pushed himself out of his grief. 'Not sad.'

She shot him a tiny smile. 'You're a dreadful liar, Dylan.'

For some reason that made him laugh. 'I miss them. I don't know what else to say.'

'You don't have to say anything.'

With Mia he felt that might indeed be true.

'Is this photograph of yours in your bedroom?'

He stared at her, and a grin built through him. 'Did you think I was trying to whisk you away under false pretences?'

She pointed a finger at him, her lips twitching. 'I'm on to your tricks. You are *not* to be trusted.'

'Ah, but do you *want* me to be trustworthy?' He seized her finger and kissed it.

She sucked in a breath, her eyes widening, and it was all he could do not to lean across and kiss her for real.

If he kissed her now, she'd run.

And he was starting to realise that he'd do just about anything to make her stay. He had no idea what that meant.

'However, in this instance, madam, I'm being eminently trustworthy. The photo hangs in the formal lounge.'

She glanced at her toes, the view, and then at him. 'In that case I should like to see it.'

He rose, holding out his hand to her. She hesitated for a beat before putting her hand in his and letting him help her to her feet. He laced his fingers through hers, intent on holding on for as long as she'd let him.

'Why do you keep it in the formal lounge rather than the living area?'

'You'll understand when you see it.'

She left her hand in his and it felt like a victory.

The moment Mia clapped eyes on the photograph she understood why Dylan didn't keep it in the more informal living areas. Even distracted as she was by Dylan's touch, his fingers laced casually through hers as if he was used to holding hands with a woman, the power of the photograph beat at her.

In her entire life she'd only ever held hands with three men—her father, when she'd been very small, Johnnie, when she'd been very stupid, and now Dylan.

You're no longer either very young or very stupid.

She wasn't convinced about the latter.

She tugged her hand from his to take a step closer to the picture and he let her go—easily and smoothly.

'It's...awe-inspiring.'

She wasn't sure she'd be able to live with it every day. It was so powerful. She wasn't even sure where the power came from...

On the surface it seemed a simple landscape—a preternaturally still ocean with not a single wave ruffling its surface. In the foreground crouched a grassy headland, with every blade of grass as still as the water—unruffled by even the tiniest of breezes. But storm clouds hung low over the ocean, turning the water a menacing monochrome. Behind the photographer, though, the sun shone fierce, piercing the picture with a powerful light, making each blade of grass stand out in brilliant green relief. The contrast—so odd and so true—held her captive.

'What do you think?'

She had to swallow before she could speak. 'Your Mr Gilmore has caught that exact moment before a storm hits—before the wind rushes through and the clouds cover the sun. It's…it's the deep breath. It's like a duel between light and dark, good and evil.'

He moved to stand beside her. 'I feel that too.'

'And you know that in this instance the dark is going to win…'

'But?'

'But I can't help feeling it's not going to prevail—the dark is only temporary. Once the storm has worn itself out the sun will reign supreme again.'

They stood in silence and stared at it. Mia stiffened.

'It's about grief and hope,' she blurted out, unable to stop herself. 'It makes me feel sad and hopeful, and happy…and incredibly grateful, all at the same time.'

She turned to him and found all her emotions reflected in his face.

He nodded. 'I know.'

'It's the most amazing picture I've ever seen.'

'It's the second most amazing one *I've* seen.'

She'd started to turn towards the photo again, but at his words she turned back with a raised eyebrow. 'You've seen something to top this?'

'That photo Felipe took of you—it made me feel all of that and more.'

It was as if a hand reached out to squeeze her chest, making breathing all but impossible. 'Oh, I…'

She didn't know what to say, and the spell was broken when Carla burst into the room.

'Oh, Dylan!'

It seemed to her that he turned reluctantly. 'What's wrong?'

Carla wrung her hands, making odd noises in her throat, and Dylan's gaze sharpened.

Mia stepped forward to take her hand. 'What is it, Carla?'

Carla grasped her hand in a death grip. 'Oh, Mia, there aren't enough apologies in the world.' Turning to Dylan, she said, 'Uncle Andrew has just arrived.'

Her words seemed to age Dylan by ten years. It didn't take a rocket scientist to work out that there was no love lost between them and their uncle. He must be an utter ogre if his arrival could cause such an expression to darken Carla's eyes. As if…as if she might be *afraid* of the man.

Mia glanced at the photograph that dominated the wall and then pushed her shoulders back, aching to see Carla and Dylan smiling and laughing again.

'So…your uncle is a storm?'

Dylan's gaze speared hers. She sent him a small smile.

'I have a relative like that. I guess we'll just have to weather him.' She winked at Carla. 'Who knows? Maybe Thierry will charm him.'

Carla choked back a laugh.

Dylan glanced at the photo and something in his shoulders unhitched. He reached out and gave Mia a one-armed hug, pressing his lips to her hair. It was friendly and affectionate, not seductive, but it heated her blood all the same.

'Come on, then,' he said. 'Let's go and face the dragon.'

Over dinner Mia discovered that the elder Fairweather was everything she most feared—an intimidating authoritarian with views that were as narrow as they were strong. He was the kind of man who took his privilege for granted, but considered it his God-given duty to ensure that no one else in his family did.

Add to that the fact that Andrew Robert Fairweather was a Federal Court judge—he sent people to jail for a living—and Mia could feel her legs start to shake.

This was the person who'd replaced Carla and Dylan's

parents as role model and guardian? Her stomach rolled in a slow, sickening somersault. For all their trust fund money and fancy education, Mia didn't envy Dylan and Carla one jot. She found her heart going out to them in sympathy.

'It's past time I was introduced to this man you mean to marry, Carla. As you won't bring him to meet me, I've had to resort to descending on you unannounced.'

'You're welcome here any time, Uncle Andrew.' Dylan's smile didn't reach his eyes. 'Your room is always kept ready for you.'

'Humph!' He fixed his gaze on Mia. 'Who are *you*?' he barked.

Three years in prison had taught Mia to hide all visual evidence of fear. It had also taught her to fly beneath the radar. 'I'm Mia. Just a friend of Carla and Dylan's.'

He immediately passed over her to start grilling Thierry.

Thierry, it appeared, ticked every box on the elder Fairweather's list of what was desirable. As a self-made man in the world of finance, Thierry had power, position, and money of his own. They even knew some of the same people.

If Andrew Fairweather had expected Thierry to fawn he'd be sadly disappointed, but for the moment at least he didn't seem to hold that against the younger man.

Their exchange took the heat off the rest of them for a good fifteen minutes. Three sets of shoulders lowered a fraction. Dylan, Carla and Mia even dared to nibble at their thin slices of smoked salmon.

It wasn't until the entrée had been cleared away and a delicious risotto served that Fairweather Senior turned his attention back to his niece and nephew.

'Pray tell, Carla Ann, what are *you* doing with the education you've been so fortunate to have had? Frittering it away like your brother, no doubt?'

Carla glanced at Dylan. The older man had to be joking, right?

'Carla has no need to work for a living,' Thierry inserted

smoothly. 'She's in the fortunate position of being able to help others—a role she takes seriously and one I'm happy to support. Recently she's been busy working on charitable projects, including some important conservation work. I couldn't be more proud of her.'

Wow! Go, Thierry. Mia didn't blame Carla in the least for the look of unabashed adoration that she sent him.

Dylan glanced at Mia and raised an eyebrow. She could only shrug in answer.

'Well, what about *you*?'

His uncle fixed Dylan with a glare that made Mia quail internally. Silence stretched and she searched for something that would help ease the tension that had wrapped around the table.

She forced a forkful of food to her mouth and made an appreciative noise. 'This meal is really lovely. I'd... I'd like to become a better cook.'

Everyone stared at her. Her stomach curdled. She loathed being the centre of attention. She grasped the lifeline Dylan had given her on a previous occasion.

'I've always wanted to make veal scaloppini. I don't suppose anyone has a good recipe for that particular dish, do they?'

It was Thierry, of all people, who answered. 'I have a fool-proof recipe.'

Thierry *cooked*? She shook off her surprise. 'Would you be willing to share it?'

'Yes.'

Andrew Fairweather's face darkened. 'Dylan, I—'

'Maybe I could make it and you could all come to dinner at my place to try it?'

Carla finally got with the programme. 'What a lovely idea, Mia.'

From the corner of her eye Mia could see Mr Fairweather opening his mouth again, his hard gaze burning in Dylan's direction. She set her fork down.

'Maybe we should set a date?'

She couldn't seem to help herself, but she had a feeling she'd say anything to halt the malice she could see sitting on the end of the older man's tongue.

'What about Saturday two weeks from now?' Carla suggested.

'I'm free.' She had no social plans slotted into her calendar at all.

When she glanced at Dylan she found him smiling at her.

'Sounds great. If you're sure?'

Her stomach started to churn. She was very far from sure, but she couldn't back out now. 'If it's a disaster we'll just call out for pizza.'

She'd aimed for light, but even though both Dylan and Carla laughed it occurred to Mia then that nothing could lighten the mood around the table.

'Back to business!' Mr Fairweather boomed. 'Dylan, I want to know what you're working on at the moment.'

All her offer of dinner had done was delay the inevitable. His uncle fired question after question at Dylan—all of them designed to put him on the defensive, all of them designed to make him look small.

A frown built through her. But...*why*?

She glanced from Dylan to his uncle, trying to understand the animosity that crackled between them. Carla said nothing, just stared down at her plate of untouched food. Thierry met her gaze, but there was no help to be had there. His curled lip was directed at *her*, not at Fairweather Senior.

'You were given all of the tools to make something of yourself and you've wasted them,' Andrew Fairweather was saying.

No, he hadn't!

'I'm sorry I've disappointed you, sir.'

No! A hundred times no! Dylan shouldn't apologise to this man. In whose world could Dylan ever be construed as a failure? How could anyone conceivably interpret Dylan's achievements as worthless or lacking in value?

Would *no one* stick up for him?

Fairweather Senior slammed his knife and fork down. 'You could've done something *important*! Instead you've wasted the opportunities presented to you on trivial non-sense. You should be ashamed of yourself. You lack back-bone and brains and you're—'

'You are *so* wrong!' Mia shot to her feet, quailing inside but unable to sit and listen to Dylan being run down like that any longer. 'What Dylan does is neither shallow nor trivial. He brings people's dreams to life. Don't you realise how important that is?'

'Important? He throws *parties* for a living. It's disgrace-ful!'

'You really mean to tell me you can't see the merit in what Dylan does?' Her daring and defiance made her stomach churn, but she couldn't stop herself. She turned to Dylan. 'How long have you had to put up with this?'

'Mia, I—'

She swung back to his uncle. 'Your nephew provides people with memories they can treasure for a lifetime. Dylan doesn't just "throw parties"—he doesn't just light sparklers and eat cake. He creates events that mark milestones in people's lives. He creates events that honour their accomplish-ments. He provides an opportunity for people to celebrate their achievements with their families, their friends and their peers. That's what life is about. It's not trivial or shallow. It's *important*!'

'*Duty* is what's important!'

Mia swallowed and reminded herself that she wasn't on trial here. Regardless of how much she displeased him, Fair-weather Senior couldn't send her to jail simply for disagree-ing with him.

'I agree that working hard and being a useful member of society is important—it's what we should all strive for.

And Dylan does both those things.' She lifted her hands sky-wards. 'Can't you *see* how hard he works? Can't you *see* how talented he is? He has a gift—he's a creator of dreams. And if you can't see the value in that then I pity you.'

She dropped her crisp linen napkin to the table. 'If you'll all excuse me for a moment...?'

She turned and walked out of the dining room. Every-thing started to shake—her hands, her knees...her breath. Letting herself out of a side door, she stumbled down a se-ries of steps and collapsed onto a low retaining wall that stood just beyond the light of the house. Dropping her head to her knees, she felt her shoulders shaking with the sobs she couldn't hold back.

'Shh...'

She found herself lifted and planted in Dylan's lap. His arms moved about her, holding her securely against him. His warm scent surrounded her.

'Why are you crying, Mia? You were magnificent.'

'I scared myself.' She hiccupped through her sobs. 'I... Men like your uncle scare me.'

'Men like that scare everyone. But at the moment I think he's more afraid of you.'

He said it to make her laugh, but she was still too shaken. She lifted her head and scrubbed her fists across her face. Dylan slapped her hands away and dried her face gently with the softest of cotton handkerchiefs.

'Look at me,' he urged gently.

'No.' She stared instead at her hands, but she couldn't prevent herself from leaning into him and taking comfort from his strength and his warmth.

'Why not?'

She pulled in a shaky breath. 'Because I know what I'll see in your face, Dylan, and I don't deserve it.'

'You don't think you deserve admiration and gratitude?'

'I don't.'

'Mia, you—'

'It was a man like your uncle who sentenced me to three years in jail. And he was right to do so. I'd broken the law. I'd taken money that didn't belong to me.'

She hadn't kept it, but that was neither here nor there.

'That's why my uncle scares you?'

She met his gaze then. 'I meant everything I said at the table. Every single word.'

His eyes throbbed into hers. 'I know.'

'But, Dylan, don't you see? All it would've taken was for Thierry to tell your uncle that I'm an ex-convict and that would've instantly negated everything I'd said.'

'Not in my eyes.'

No, not in Dylan's eyes. She reached up and touched his cheek. 'But it would in your uncle's…and most other people's too.'

He turned his head to press a kiss to her hand. She went to pull it away but he pressed his hand on top of it, trapping it between the heat of his hand and the warmth of his face.

'Does it matter what people like my uncle think?'

'Yes.'

'Why?'

'Because it means that whenever I stand up against some injustice, as soon as my background is known my protests have no effect, no impact. In fact it usually makes things worse—as if their association with me taints them. I might as well have kept my mouth shut.'

'You're wrong.'

The intensity of his gaze held her trapped. She couldn't look away.

'After you left just then, Carla announced to the table at large that she was proud of me. It's the very first time she's ever stood up to him.'

Her heart pounded against the walls of her chest. 'Have *you* ever stood up to him?'

'On Carla's account—but never my own.'

She couldn't stop herself from brushing his cheek with her thumb. It turned his eyes dark and slumberous.

Dangerous.

The word whispered through her, but she didn't move away. She liked being this close to Dylan.

'You shouldn't let him treat you the way he does.'

'I realised that tonight for the first time. I've made a lot of excuses for him over the years. He lost his brother, and he and my aunt provided a home for Carla when our parents died.' He shrugged. 'The family tradition of law and politics is important to him, but I had no intention of ever following that path. Letting him rant and rave at me seemed a small price to pay, but...'

'But?' she urged, wanting him to break free from all the belittling and bullying.

'But I hadn't realised until tonight how much I'd let his voice get inside my head. Somewhere over the years I'd unknowingly started to agree with him—started to define myself by his standards. But tonight you stood up and reminded me of why I do what I do. And I felt proud of it.'

She smiled. It came from way down deep inside her.

Dylan stared at her. His gaze lowered to her lips and the colour of his eyes darkened to a deep sapphire. A pulse started up in the centre of her.

'I want to kiss you, Mia.'

Her heart fluttered up into her throat. 'Oh, that would be a very, *very* bad idea.'

'Why?'

A part of her wished he'd just seize her lips with his and be done with talking.

Crazy thought!

'Because...' It was hard to talk with her heart hammering in her throat. 'Because I've made it clear where I stand in relation to romance and relationships.'

'And you think I want more?'

They'd set their ground rules, but...

'Do you?'

'Things change.' He spoke slowly, frowning.

His reply frightened her, and yet she didn't move away.

'I haven't changed.' She'd meant the declaration to sound defiant, but it came out whisper-soft and full of yearning. She couldn't drag her gaze from the firm promise of his lips.

'If you really don't want me to kiss you, I won't.' He trailed his fingers down her throat and along her collarbone. 'I meant to say earlier that I love your dress.'

The change of topic should have thrown her, but she grasped it like a lifeline. 'It's new. I bought it especially.' She hadn't been able to resist the raspberry-coloured linen dress once she'd tried it on.

'For tonight? For me?'

Her eyes met his.

No lying.

'Yes.'

His fingers continued to trail delicious paths of sensation across her skin. 'Are you sure your stance on romance hasn't changed?'

She couldn't look away. 'Positive.'

Liar.

'I still want to kiss you.'

She should move away, put an end to this insanity.

'And I think you want that too.'

Her heart beat so loud she thought he must hear it.

'Would you like me to kiss you, Mia?'

Her pulse thumped. 'I'll own to some curiosity,' she managed.

'Is that a yes?'

She met his gaze and nodded. 'Yes.'

CHAPTER EIGHT

MIA REALISED HER mistake the moment Dylan's mouth claimed hers.

She'd thought his first touch would be gentle, but it wasn't. It was sure and firm and a complete assault on her senses.

Dylan wanted to overwhelm her with sensation—perhaps in punishment for her 'my stance on romance hasn't changed' comment. He wanted to thank her for sticking up for him at the dinner table… And somehow both of those impulses cancelled out the underlying threat in the other and dragged Mia under as if she'd been picked up by a giant wave.

She wound her arms around his neck and held on, waiting for the crash to come as the wave barrelled her along… But it didn't slam her down as she'd feared. Dylan's arms cradled her, holding her safe, and in the end all Mia could do was sink into them.

He nibbled her bottom lip, coaxing her to open to him. And she did. She wanted to hesitate, to hold back, but she couldn't. His tongue laved her inner lips and something inside her unfurled. His tongue coaxed hers to dance and something inside her sparked to life, filling her veins with heat and her soul with joy.

Dylan deepened the kiss, kissing her so thoroughly and with such intensity that his name was wrenched from her throat.

He lifted his head for a moment, his eyes glittering, and she suddenly realised that the flirtatious charmer had been stripped away to reveal the warrior beneath. And every potent ruthless sinew of his being was focussed wholly on *her*.

It should have made her afraid.

But she wasn't afraid of him. All she had to do was tell him to stop. And she knew that he would.

One corner of his mouth lifted, as if he'd read that thought in her face. 'You think I'm going to give you a chance to *think*, Mia?'

Her heart thumped. 'Dylan, sex won't make a scrap of difference. I—'

The force of his kiss pushed her head back. One of his hands traced the length of her—slowly, lazily—and Mia couldn't help but kiss him back with just as much force, hunger ravaging her body.

She wanted this man.

If she couldn't have him she thought she might die.

And then his hand was beneath the skirt of her dress... and her hands were where they shouldn't be...

And somewhere nearby a door slammed.

Mia stiffened and pulled her hands to her lap. Dylan tugged her skirt down and put his arms around her, holding her close, just as Carla came around the side of the house.

She pulled up short when she saw them. 'I hope I'm not interrupting anything.'

Dylan laughed, the rumble vibrating through Mia's body in a delicious wave of sensation. 'Of course you're interrupting something.'

Carla waved that away. 'I wanted to let you know that Uncle Andrew has left. He's decided to stay at his club in town before heading back to Sydney tomorrow.'

Mia gripped her hands together. 'I'm sorry. I had no right to cause such a scene—'

'You were wonderful! I wish...' Carla hauled in a breath.

'I wish I'd had the gumption to say something like that to him years ago.'

'Carla,' Dylan began, 'you—'

'No.' She fixed him with a glare. 'You've always stuck up for me. I should've done the same for you.'

She turned to Mia. Mia tried to remove herself from Dylan's lap, but he held her there fast.

'The thing is,' Carla said, thankfully unaware of Mia's agitation, 'I've always been so terribly afraid of him. But tonight when you said you pitied him I realised you were right. And…' she shrugged '…now I find I'm not as afraid.'

Dylan frowned. Mia had to fight the urge to smooth his brow.

'I don't want you to be afraid of anyone,' he said.

Mia knew he meant Thierry.

Carla waved that away. 'I just wanted to make sure the two of you were okay. And to let you know the coast is clear.'

'We're fine.'

'And you, Mia?' Carla checked despite her brother's assurance.

'I'm fine too.'

'Carmen—' she was the Fairweathers' housekeeper '—is making ice cream sundaes.'

'We'll be along in five minutes.'

'Don't let him sweet-talk you into anything you're not ready for, Mia.'

'Cross my heart,' Mia promised, but that reminded her that Carla knew her brother's reputation. It reminded her that Dylan had a lot of experience with women while she had very little experience with men.'

Carla sent them a cheeky grin. 'But I *will* say the two of you do look cute together.'

Mia had to fight the urge to drop her face to her hands and weep. How could she have let things go this far?

Carla disappeared and Mia tried once again to rise from Dylan's lap, but his arms tightened about her.

'Do you really mean to ignore that kiss?'

His hand splayed against her hip, as if to urge her to feel what he was feeling.

'That kiss was amazing...intense.' His face darkened. 'It was a whole lot more than just a kiss and you know it.'

Her heart thumped. If she let them, his words could weave a spell about her. She couldn't let that happen.

'Yes,' she said. And then, so he knew what she was referring to, she added, 'Yes, I *do* mean to ignore that kiss.'

Her words made him flinch. Heat gathered behind her eyes and her throat started to ache.

'To punish yourself?' The question was scratched out of him—a raw rasp.

'No.' She refused to let the tears building behind her eyes to fall. 'To save myself.'

'I don't understand.'

The throb in his voice had her closing her eyes. 'And I hope to God you never do.'

This time when she tried to get up he let her.

Dylan watched Mia walk away and his heart pounded against the walls of his ribs. He wanted her with a savagery that frightened him.

He couldn't recall wanting Caitlin like this.

He couldn't recall wanting any woman with this kind of hunger!

He wanted to shred their ground rules to pieces—tear them up and burn them. He wanted Mia in his bed.

But do you want her in your heart?

The roaring inside him screeched to a halt. He swallowed. *No.*

But you're prepared to seduce her? To make things harder for her.

He shot to his feet. He wouldn't make them harder! He'd make sure she enjoyed every moment of their time together.

He'd make her laugh and he'd lavish her with gifts. He'd give her anything she wanted.

Except the quiet life she craves.

He whirled around, hands fisted. She was wrong about that. She should be living life to the full—not hiding herself in the shadows. She should be living her life like the woman in Felipe's photograph—full of joy and laughter. If only he could get her to see that.

If only...

He stilled. If he managed that, then maybe she'd rip up those ground rules herself and welcome some fun—some pleasure—into her life. It was worth a shot.

Thrusting out his jaw, he moved towards the house.

Mia sat at a picnic table, listlessly feeding a peacock what looked to be part of her usual lunchtime sandwich, and something in Dylan's chest tightened. It was four days since their kiss and she looked pale and tired. She looked the way he felt. It didn't give him the slightest sense of satisfaction or triumph.

He wanted her. His lips tightened. And she wanted him.

She had another think coming if she thought he'd give up. He wanted to know what she'd meant by saving herself, and he had every intention of finding out. Once he knew, he'd be able to develop a game plan for knocking down those walls of hers.

She half turned, as if she'd sensed his presence, dropping her sandwich when their gazes collided. The peacock immediately pounced on it.

Dylan forced his legs forward. 'It's just as well I brought these or you'd go hungry.' He dropped a couple of chocolate bars to the table before taking the seat opposite. 'How are you, Mia?'

'I'm okay.' She reached for one of the chocolate bars but didn't unwrap it, worry lurking in the depths of her eyes. 'How are *you*?'

He'd meant to tell her that he couldn't sleep at night for thinking of her. Instead he shot her a grin and winked. 'I'll be a whole lot better once I've eaten this.'

He seized the second chocolate bar and was rewarded when her shoulders unhitched a fraction.

'I'm glad you dropped by today,' she said.

He stared at her. For a moment he felt like punching the air. He didn't push her, though. He'd let her tell him why in her own time.

'Carla asked me to give you this.' He pulled a piece of paper from his pocket. 'It's Thierry's veal scaloppini recipe.'

'Why didn't she give it to me herself?'

He shrugged, hoping he hadn't given himself away. 'She said she was busy.' And he'd latched on to any excuse to see Mia. 'Maybe she thought I'd see you first.'

'Are you busy? There's something I'd like you to see.'

'I'm free as a bird.' Even if he hadn't been he'd have cancelled any appointment for her.

'Good. Come with me.'

She led him along a narrow track through dense native forest. Everything was hushed and serene. He marvelled anew that such a place existed in the middle of the city. Mia didn't talk and he was content to follow behind, admiring the dark lustre of her hair and the innate grace of her hips.

After ten minutes she slowed. Turning to him, she put a finger to her lips and then held down the branch of a Bottlebrush tree, gesturing for him to look.

He glanced at her, wondering what on earth she'd brought him here to see. He turned to survey the view and sucked in a breath. Moving closer, he held the branch for himself while Mia moved off to one side.

She'd brought him via a circuitous route to the far side of the lily pond. Just in front of him—no more than twenty yards away—stretched out on a picnic blanket, were Carla and Thierry. Carla's head was in Thierry's lap and he was idly combing his fingers through her hair. She laughed up at him at something he'd said.

Dylan's heart started to thump. He stared from his sister's face to her fiancé's face and back again. Eventually Mia's fingers wrapped about the top of his arm and she pulled him away. Pressing her finger to her lips again, she led him along a different path until they emerged into a rocky clearing. She sat on a boulder and stared at him with pursed lips.

He fell down onto a neighbouring rock, his mind racing. Finally he glanced across at her. 'I have *never* seen Carla that happy.'

She nodded, as if the sight of that much happiness had awed her.

'How did you know they were there?'

'I accidentally stumbled across them on Monday. I noticed Thierry's car in the car park a little while ago and figured they'd be there again today.'

'She's totally in love with him...and...and completely *happy*.'

'Did you notice the way he looked at her?'

He had. An ache stretched behind his eyes. 'He looked at her as if she were the most precious person on earth.' His shot to his feet and paced up and down for a bit before swinging back to Mia. 'A man who looks at a woman like that is never going to hurt her. He's going to do everything in his power to protect her, to cherish her...to make her happy.'

Mia nodded.

He started to pace again. Seeing Carla and Thierry together like that, so unguarded, it should put his mind at rest...

He collapsed back on his rock and Mia reached out to clasp his hand briefly. 'Dylan, you're not losing Carla. You're gaining a brother-in-law.'

'But he's such an unpleasant man!'

She sat back. 'I suspect the more you get to know him, the better you'll come to like him.'

Could she be right?

'I also think...'

He glanced up, suddenly on guard. There was something too tight in her voice, which was at odds with the casual way she ran her fingers along a tall spike of native grass.

'You also think...?' he prompted.

She rubbed her hand across her throat, not looking at him. 'I think our dating pretence is no longer necessary.'

She told you kissing her would be a bad idea.

He hadn't known it would have her bringing their relationship to such an abrupt halt!

There is no relationship.

But he wanted there to be. Not a relationship, *exactly*, but a relationship of sorts.

He was careful to keep his thoughts hidden. He didn't want to scare her off more than he already had—didn't want her retreating further. He hadn't got where he was today by revealing his hand too soon.

'You're probably right,' he said instead.

She seemed to tense up and then relax in equal measure. He ducked his head to hide his smile. Mia Maydew was one conflicted lady. If she'd just let him help solve that conflict...

'Please tell me you're not going to dump Carla as abruptly?'

Her head shot up. 'Of course I'm not going to dump Carla. Carla and I will be friends for as long as she wants us to be friends.' She folded her arms and glared at him. 'And, Dylan, I hate to point this out, but I'm not dumping *you* either. We were never going out to begin with. We were only pretending.'

'I wasn't pretending when I kissed you. And I don't care how good an actress you are, Mia, I don't think you were pretending either.'

She moistened her lips and swallowed. The pulse at the base of her throat fluttered like a caged thing. A ravaging hunger swept through him. If he kissed her now, here in this quiet, private place where they wouldn't be interrupted...

'Don't even think about it!'

Her eyes flashed fire. So much for not showing his hand. He stared at the ground and pulled in a breath, nodding. 'Sorry, I lost my head for a moment—let it drift to where it shouldn't have gone.'

He shoved his shoulders back and lifted his chin.

'Though if I'm ever fortunate enough to make love with you, Mia, it'll be in place where I'll have the opportunity to show you in every way I know how just how beautiful and desirable I find you. There'll be no rush. And your comfort will be paramount.'

Her eyes grew round.

He leaned in close. 'I've no inclination for a quick roll on spiky grass, where we'd be half eaten by ants and mosquitos or happened upon by unsuspecting hikers. When I make love to you, Mia, I mean for you to be fully focussed on me.'

She swallowed.

He brushed his lips across her ear. 'And when it happens I promise that you will be.'

She leapt away from him, glancing at her watch. 'My lunchbreak is almost up. I have to get back to work.'

He followed her to the main picnic area. It was awash with people enjoying the afternoon sun.

A question pressed against the back of his throat, but he held it in until they were fully surrounded by people. 'Will you give me one more fake date?'

Her hands went to her hips. 'Why?'

It would give him something to work towards. It would give him time to come up with a plan to overcome her objections to an affair.

'I want a chance to grill Thierry in a non-confrontational way, in a place that's not intimidating...and you *did* invite us all to dinner.'

Her shoulders suddenly sagged. 'I did, didn't I?'

She'd only done it to try and keep the peace, to try and head off his uncle's vitriol.

'You can cry off if you want. I can make your excuses easily enough. Nobody will mind.' He didn't want her looking so careworn—not on his account. 'Cooking for guests can be stressful if you haven't done it in a while.' He gave an exaggerated eye-roll. 'And I suspect I've stressed you out enough already.'

Her lips twitched. 'The cooking doesn't worry me. It's only for four—not fourteen.'

'What *does* worry you, then?'

She hesitated. 'My house.'

He couldn't gauge what she meant, but the way her hands twisted together caught at him. 'What's wrong with your house? I know it's small, but none of us are going to care about that.'

'It looks like a prison cell.'

He winced at her bluntness.

'It's bare and uninviting and...and I'm ashamed of it.'

'You've no reason to be ashamed of it. It's clean and functional. Neither Carla nor I care about things like that. And if Thierry does then he's an idiot.'

One slim shoulder lifted. 'I know it shouldn't matter. It's just... I have no talent for making things look nice.' She stared at a copse of trees. 'Maybe I could get a magazine or two, for tips on how to make it look a bit better.'

'I can help you with that.'

She raised an eyebrow, but he waved her scepticism away. 'You don't want a complete makeover. You just want it to look a little cheerier...a bit warmer, right?'

She nodded, but the wariness didn't leave her eyes.

'Look, I'm not an interior designer, but I've had to consult on set designs for concerts and themes for parties. Seriously, we could spruce up your little cottage with nothing more than a few accessories. I swear you'll be amazed at how easy it is.'

She didn't say anything.

'What's your budget?' he asked, so she'd know he wasn't offering to pay for anything, that he wasn't trying to bribe her.

She named a sum that, while small, would easily cover what she needed.

He rubbed his hands together. 'We can work with that.'

Her eyes narrowed. She folded her arms, her fingers drumming against her upper arms. 'What on earth do *you* know about budgets?'

It was a fair question. 'I had a crash course when I started up my company. And I'm given a budget from my clients for every event I take on. If I want to make money I have to stick to it.'

She glanced down at her hands. 'I'm sorry—that was ungracious. Of course you—'

'I'm a trust fund baby, Mia. If I chose I could live in the lap of luxury for the rest of my life without having to lift a finger. You're not the first person to question my credentials.'

She stared up at him, a frown in her eyes. 'You *haven't* chosen to live that way, though.'

He shrugged. 'I wanted something more. I wanted to create something of my own. Besides, the family tradition is not to sit idly back and rest on one's laurels. And as neither law nor politics interested me…'

'You decided to forge your own path?'

'And—as you so succinctly reminded me last Saturday night—I should be proud of that. And I am.'

She nodded.

'So, in return, will you let me help you decorate your cottage? We might not be dating for real, but there's no rule that says we can't be friends, is there?'

She chewed her lip.

Dylan's heart dipped. '*Is* there?'

'I…'

She moistened her lips and a sudden thirst welled inside him.

'I've largely kept to myself since…over the last eleven months.'

Would she *ever* confide the hows and the whys that had landed her in prison? He could search out police reports, court records—and he had no doubt that Thierry had done exactly that—but he didn't want to. He wanted Mia to tell him herself. It was obvious she regretted her crime. And she'd paid her debt to society. But her past still haunted her.

His heart surged against his ribs. 'Do you resent my and Carla's intrusion into your life?'

'No. I… I'd forgotten how nice it is to have friends.'

As those words sank in his mouth dried. 'I'm honoured to be your friend, Mia.' He swallowed. 'Carla would say the same if she were here. Neither of us take our friends for granted.'

'I know. It seems strange, when we're from such different backgrounds, that we can have so much in common.'

He rolled his shoulders in an effort to loosen the tension in them. 'Shall we go shopping, then? On Saturday? To spruce up your cottage?'

'I'm working till midday.'

'I'll call for you at one.'

'Um…'

She hesitated, and he knew it was a big step for her.

'Okay.'

He gave in to the temptation of kissing her cheek. 'I'll see you on Saturday.'

When he reached the end of the path he looked back to find her still watching him. He lifted his hand in farewell. With a visible start she waved back, before disappearing along a path between the office and a picnic table.

His hands clenched. Had anyone ever put her first? Fought for her? Put everything on the line for her?

He knew the answer in his bones—no, they hadn't.

Do you want to be the next person to let her down?

He *wasn't* going to let her down! He was going to show her how to live. When they parted company, she'd be glad they'd met. *That* was his objective.

Mia gazed around her tiny living room and could barely credit the difference a few knick-knacks made. She'd never had a chance to try her hand at decorating before. Her father had maintained a rigid view on what was and wasn't respectable—a line her mother had never crossed—and Mia hadn't even been allowed to put up posters in her room. She'd learned early on that it was easier to submit and keep the peace than to rebel.

When she'd met Johnnie his home had already been beautifully furnished. She'd been in awe of his taste. And in the two years between leaving home and moving in with Johnnie she'd lived such a hand-to-mouth existence there'd been no money left over for decorating the mean little rooms she'd rented.

And then there'd been prison. She'd learned to make do with as little as possible there. She'd left the place with the same attitude, but for the first time she questioned that wisdom. It was true that she didn't want to get too attached to material things—like Johnnie had. But it wasn't a crime to make her living space comfortable. It wasn't a crime to make it welcoming for visitors.

'Earth to Mia?'

She snapped back when a hand was waved in front of her face.

'You were miles away,' Dylan teased. He gestured to the room. 'Do you like it?'

'I love it.'

Shopping with Dylan today had been...*fun*. It had also been a revelation. She'd thought he'd walk through the shops and select the things she needed—like her father and Johnnie would have done. He hadn't, though. He'd asked her opinion every step of the way.

'I love the colour scheme you've chosen.' He planted his hands on his hips and glanced around. 'It makes everything so much lighter in here.'

'The colour scheme was a joint effort. I'd never have known where to start.'

He'd taken her shopping and asked her what colours she liked. She'd eventually settled on a china-blue and a sandy taupe. She now had scatter cushions and throw rugs in those colours on the couch, as well as a tablecloth on the table. New jars in a jaunty blue lined the kitchen counter, a vase and some knick-knacks sat on the mantel, and two beach prints in funky faded frames hung on the walls. A jute rug with a chocolate-coloured border rested beneath the coffee table and a welcome mat sat at the door.

Mia turned a full circle. 'It's made such a difference.' She clasped her hands beneath her chin and let out a long pent-up breath. A breath she felt she'd been holding ever since she'd proffered the dinner invitation. 'I no longer need to feel embarrassed.'

'A vase of fresh flowers here.' Dylan touched a spot on the kitchen counter. 'Maybe a plant on the coffee table or the hall table there, and the room will be perfect.'

Yellow-headed daisies in the kitchen and an African violet on the coffee table. 'I'll get them through the week.'

He grinned at her. 'Even better—it all came in under-budget!'

His delight with himself made her laugh. She watched his face light up with pleasure as he studied the room he'd helped her to transform and her heart started to thud against her ribs.

Friends? She didn't believe in promises and words, but Dylan's actions today had spoken volumes. He'd given her his friendship willingly and generously. He'd treated her like a friend.

Now it was her turn.

CHAPTER NINE

'WITH US COMING in under-budget and all...' Mia's mouth started to dry. 'Well, I was thinking...how about I buy you dinner as a thank-you?'

Dylan swung to her, his eyes alert and watchful...hopeful.

'As a friend,' she added. She didn't want him getting the wrong impression.

'When?'

She strove for a shrug. 'This evening, if you're free.'

'I'm free.' He glanced down at himself. He wore a pair of cargo shorts and a button-down cotton shirt. So did she. 'Can we go somewhere casual?'

'Casual sounds good.' Casual sounded perfect!

'I know—gorgeous evening...end of summer and all that... There's this great pizza place down near the beach. It does takeaway.'

His face lit up and all she could do was stare. When—how?—had he learned to milk enjoyment from every moment?

'When was the last time you had pizza on the beach?'

'I... Never.'

'C'mon, then.' He took her hand and led her to the front door. 'That's an oversight that should be corrected immediately.'

* * *

'See? Didn't I tell you this was an inspired idea?' Dylan claimed a patch of pristine white sand and grinned at her.

Mia bit back a laugh and spread out a towel so he could place the pizza boxes onto it. 'I'll reserve judgement until I've tried the pizza.' She dropped two bottles of water to the towel too, and then turned to survey the view spread out in front of them.

They had another half an hour of light—possibly longer. The water reflected the last of the sun's brilliance in tones of pink, gold and mauve. Barely a breath of breeze ruffled her hair, and the only sounds were the whoosh of the waves rushing up onshore, the cries of the seagulls wheeling overhead and the laughter of a family group picnicking further along the sand. To her left, Newcastle's famous Nobby's Lighthouse sat atop the headland. Straight out in front of her was the Pacific Ocean.

So much space. So much room to breathe.

She pulled in a deep breath before turning to find Dylan watching her. With a self-conscious shrug she sat beside him. But not too close. She kept the pizza boxes between them. 'You couldn't have chosen a better spot. It's wonderful down here.'

'A perfect night for a picnic. Now, try a piece of this pizza."

She took a piece from the proffered box and bit into it. The flavours melted on her tongue and it was all she could do not to groan in appreciation. 'Good...' she murmured. 'Seriously good.'

They munched pizza in silence for a bit. The longer they sat there, the lighter Mia started to feel. Dylan reminded her of all the pleasures—big and small—that the world held. Even after almost eleven months she was still afraid of giving herself over to enjoyment.

'A penny for them.'

His voice broke into her thoughts.

'One moment you were enjoying all of this and the next moment you weren't.'

'Oh!' She swung to him. 'I'm having a lovely time. Truly.'

Her stomach clenched. She'd come here to tell him the truth.

So tell him the truth.

She finished off her piece of pizza and reached for a paper napkin. 'If you want to know the truth, I'm afraid of enjoying it too much.'

'Why?'

She couldn't look at him. 'In case I do something stupid and it's taken away from me again.'

He was silent for a couple of beats. 'You're talking about prison?'

She nodded.

'Is there any reason to believe you'll end up back there?'

Not if she remained vigilant.

'I find it hard to take my liberty for granted.' She grimaced. 'You don't understand how much you take it for granted until it's taken away. Prison is a punishment—it's supposed to be unpleasant. The thought of messing up and ending up back in there...' She shivered. 'So sometimes I find myself lost in a moment of enjoyment and then I remember jail and I wonder... I wonder how I could cope if I found myself back there again.'

He leaned towards her, drenching the air with a hint of smoky nutmeg. It mingled with the scents of ocean and pizza and she couldn't recall relishing anything more in her life. She wanted to close her eyes and memorise that scent, so she could pull it out and appreciate it whenever she needed to.

'Mia, you're a different person now. You won't make the same mistakes again.'

She wasn't convinced—especially on that last point. 'I think you need to know my story.'

'I'd like to know it very much.'

'It's sordid,' she warned.

She couldn't make this pretty for him, no matter how much she might want to. He just shrugged, his eyes not leaving her face. It made her mouth dry.

'Have you really not looked me up?' There'd be newspaper articles and court reports he could access.

'I wanted to hear the story from you—not from some so-called factual report that leaves out the truly relevant facts.'

She had a feeling that should have surprised her, but it didn't. She glanced down at her hands. 'I think I mentioned that my father was a...a difficult man.'

'Emotionally abusive to your mother?'

She nodded, fighting the weariness that wanted to claim her. 'When I was sixteen I finally stood up to him.'

'What happened?'

'He gave me a black eye and kicked me out.'

Dylan's hands fisted.

'I found temporary shelter in a homeless refuge and got work waitressing.'

'School?'

'I couldn't manage school *and* work.' She blew out a breath. 'That's something prison *did* give me—the opportunity to finish my high school education. It's my high school diploma that made me eligible for the traineeship at Plum Pines.'

'Right.'

She couldn't tell what he was thinking so she simply pushed on. 'When I was eighteen I met a man—Johnnie Peters. He was twenty-five and I thought him so worldly. I'd had a couple of boyfriends, you understand, but nothing serious.'

'Until Johnnie?'

'Until Johnnie...' She swallowed the lump that threatened her throat. It settled in her chest to ache with a dull throb. 'He swept me off my feet. I fell hopelessly in love with him.'

A muscle in Dylan's jaw worked. 'Would I be right in suspecting he didn't deserve you?'

She could feel her lips twist. It took all her strength to maintain eye contact with Dylan. 'The key word in my previous sentence was *hopelessly*.' She stared back out to sea. 'I had a lot of counselling when I was in jail. I understand now that there are men out there who target foolish, naïve girls. Which is exactly what I was.'

He reached out to squeeze her hand. 'You were young.'

She pulled her hand from his. 'When something looks too good to be true, it usually is. I knew that then, but I ignored it. He made me feel special, and I wanted to be special.' She gripped her hands together. 'He organised a new job for me—nine to five—where I was trained in office administration. It seemed like a step up. I was ridiculously grateful not to be on my feet all day, like I had been when waitressing.'

When she'd been in prison she'd longed for that waitressing job—aching legs and all. She should have been grateful for what she'd had. Content.

'He moved me into his lovely house and bought me beautiful clothes. He was a stockbroker, and I thought he could have his pick of women. I felt I was the luckiest girl alive.'

'He cut you off from your family and friends...controlled your finances?'

'My family had already cut me off, but...yes.' That was something she'd come to realise during sessions with her counsellor. 'Things seemed perfect for a couple of years. What I didn't realise was that he had a gambling problem.'

'What happened?' he prompted when she remained silent.

'He started asking me to deposit cheques into accounts that weren't in my name and then to withdraw the funds.'

'You gave all the money to him?'

'I gave him everything.' She'd been an idiot. 'Of course it was only a matter of time before I was traced on CCTV.'

'And Johnnie?'

'He was cleverer than I. He was never seen in the vicinity of any of the banks at the time, and he denied all knowledge.'

His mouth grew taut. 'The scumbag fed you to the wolves.'

She turned to him, the ache in her chest growing fierce. 'He was even smarter than that, Dylan. He convinced me to feed *myself* to the wolves. I told the police he was innocent.'

Anger flared in his eyes. 'How long did it take you to realise what he was?'

Her stomach churned. She'd told herself it would be better for Dylan to despise her than it would be for him to love her. A part of her died inside anyway.

'About four months into my sentence…when he hadn't been to see me…when he stopped answering my letters.'

'Then you turned him in to the authorities?'

She shook her head.

'You continued to let him walk all over you?'

She stiffened at the censure in his voice. 'Three things, Dylan. One—I had no proof. Especially not after the testimony I'd given in his favour. Any testimony to the contrary would've simply been written off as the ravings of a disaffected lover. Two—I needed to draw a line under that part of my life and move forward. And three—I deserved my punishment. Nothing was ever going to change that.'

'He *manipulated* you!'

'And I let him. I *knew* what I was doing was wrong. The first time I cashed a cheque he told me it was for his elderly aunt. The second time he said it was a favour for a work colleague. The third time he just asked me to do it for him, said that he was in trouble. I knew then that I was breaking the law, but I did it anyway. He never physically threatened me. I just did it.'

'But I bet the emotional threat of him breaking up with you hung over every request?'

It had. And she hadn't been able to face the thought of losing him. Talk about pathetic! 'I told you it was sordid.'

'Three years seems a long sentence for a first offender.'

She moistened her lips. 'I stole a *lot* of money.'

He stared out to sea and her heart burned at the conflict

reflected in his face. 'You made a bad choice and you've paid for it.' He turned, spearing her with his gaze. 'Would you make the same decision again, given what you know now?'

'Of course not. But we don't get the chance to live our lives over. We just have to find ways to live with our mistakes.'

'Shunning the simple pleasures in life won't help you do that.'

He had a point.

His brows drew down low over his eyes. 'Don't you worry about other young women he might have targeted?'

Her heart started to thump. Trust Dylan to worry about vulnerable women he didn't even know. She glanced down at her hands. 'Fourteen months into my sentence Johnnie attempted an armed hold-up on a security van. He wasn't successful. He was sentenced to fifteen years. I think the foolish young women of the world are safe from him for the moment.'

'Good.'

Neither one of them went back to eating pizza.

'Is that why you let men walk all over you?'

She stiffened. 'I don't let *you* walk all over me.'

His lips twisted, though his eyes remained hard. 'There's hope for me yet, then.'

'No, there's not! I—'

'You've let Gordon, Thierry and Felipe all treat you like you're worthless. Your father and Johnnie both treated you badly. Do you *really* hold yourself so cheaply?'

Her heart surged against her ribs. 'Neither my father nor Johnnie are in my life any more. Thierry doesn't matter to me one jot! Felipe *didn't* take advantage of me. And as for Gordon...'

Dylan folded his arms and raised his eyebrows.

'He has the power to fire me. Keeping my head beneath the parapet where he's concerned is the smartest course of action. It won't be forever.'

'There'll always be Gordons in your life in one form or another. Are you going to turn yourself into a doormat for all of them?'

'If I do it'll be none of your business!'

'Why tell me all of this, then?'

'Because if we're going to be *friends*—' she ground the word out '—eventually the press will find out who I am and my story will come out. And it wouldn't be fair to have the press spring something like that on you without preparing you first.'

He dragged a hand down his face.

'And...'

He stilled. 'And...?'

She didn't want to continue, but she had to. It was the reason she'd started this conversation. 'And I wanted you to understand why I have no intention of ever pursuing another romantic relationship.'

He stared at her, but she couldn't read the expression in his eyes.

'Because you were burned once?'

'Because I don't like who I am when I'm in love. I refuse to become that person again.'

He shot to his feet. 'Are you likening me to this Johnnie Peters?'

She shot to her feet too. 'Of course not!'

He stabbed a finger at her. 'That's *exactly* what you're doing. You're saying that if you let yourself be vulnerable to me, I'll take advantage of you.'

She could feel herself start to shake. 'This is about me, not you!'

'Garbage. I—'

He broke off when a bright flash momentarily blinded both of them. Mia realised two things then—night had fallen...and someone had just snapped their photo.

Without another word, Dylan charged off into the darkness.

Biting back a groan, Mia set off after him.

* * *

Dylan hurled himself at the shape that had emerged in the darkness, bringing the anonymous photographer down.

He tried to clamp down on the rage that had him wanting to tear things apart with his bare hands. He wanted to tear apart the men who'd let Mia down—her father, the despicable Johnnie Peters. He wanted to tear apart her mistaken view of herself as some kind of spineless push-over. He wanted to tear apart her view of *him*! Most of all he wanted to tear himself apart, and he didn't know why.

Don't tear the photographer apart. He's just doing his job.

'Fair go, Fairweather!'

Dylan pushed himself upright as Mia came running up. She shone the torch on her phone on the photographer, confirming Dylan's suspicions. A hard ball lodged in his belly.

'Percy Struthers. What the hell do you think you're doing, sneaking up on me again *now*?'

Percy had created a PR firestorm last year, when Dylan had been in charge of a Turkish sultan's sixtieth birthday celebrations. Percy had released a photo of Dylan and the Sultan's very beautiful youngest daughter, linking them romantically. It had been a lie, of course, but try telling *that* to an enraged Turkish sultan...

Percy Struthers was the grubbiest of the gutter press, and trouble with a capital T.

Mia had broken the law—she'd done wrong and she'd paid the price—but the world was full of immoral, unethical people who lied and cheated. Were *they* sent to jail? Hardly! Some of them were applauded and clapped on the back for it—like tabloid journalists and politicians.

'It's news whenever a new woman turns up in your life—you know that.'

'Give me the camera.'

With a sigh, Percy handed it over.

Dylan stood and indicated for Mia to shine her torch

on the camera. With a flick of his fingers he removed the memory stick.

Percy clambered to his feet, caught the camera when Dylan tossed it back to him. 'It won't stop the story, you know.'

'Without a photograph the story won't gain traction.'

They both knew that.

The photographer gave an ugly laugh. 'But one of us will eventually get a photo—you can't remain on your guard twenty-four-seven.'

Beside him, Mia stiffened. Dylan wanted to throw his head back and howl. This was her worst nightmare, and it was he who'd dragged her into it.

'I know who she is,' Percy continued. 'And I know what she's done.'

Her *absolute* worst nightmare.

'Aren't you afraid she's on the make? That you're simply her latest target?'

He felt rather than saw Mia flinch. A ball of fury lodged in his gut.

Don't rise to the bait. Don't give the pond scum anything. Don't feed the frenzy.

It hit him suddenly how much his name, his position, were black marks against him in Mia's book.

Percy gave another of those ugly laughs. 'An ex-con? *Really*, Dylan? What are you trying to prove? Or have you developed a taste for a bit of rough?'

Dylan reached out and took Mia's hand. 'I think we're done here.'

'Run along, darlin'.' The photographer smirked. 'We all know what you're after.'

And then he called her a name that no man should ever call a woman.

Dylan whirled around, his right hand fisted, and smashed him square on the nose. Blood burst from it as the man reeled backwards to sprawl on the ground. Pain shot up Dylan's arm.

Mia sucked in a breath, and even in the darkness he could see the way her eyes flashed.

Percy cursed. 'You'll pay for that, Fairweather.

Mia tried to tug her hand from Dylan's but he refused to relinquish it. He towed her in the direction of the car instead. He had to get out of here before he did something truly despicable—like beat Percy Struthers to a pulp.

Mia sat in tight-lipped silence all the way home, only unfolding her arms to push herself out of the car once he'd pulled up at the front of her cottage. She slammed it with a force that made him wince.

He had to jog to catch up with her. She didn't hold the front door open for him, letting it fall behind her, meaning he had to catch it. But at least she hadn't slammed it in his face. He told himself that was something.

'You're...uh...cross with me?'

She turned on him, and her eyes flashed with so much anger the hair at her temples seemed to shake with it.

She seized his right hand and glanced down at it. 'Does it hurt?'

'Yes.'

'Good.'

She dropped it as if it burned her. Moving to the freezer, she took out a packet of frozen peas. Grabbing his hand, she slammed it on top of his grazed knuckles. It didn't really hurt any more, but he winced anyway, hoping it would give her more bloodthirsty impulses a measure of satisfaction. And he submitted when she pushed him towards one of her hard wooden chairs—not so hard now they sported pale blue chair pads.

She lifted his left hand and dropped it on top of the peas to hold them in place, then retreated to sit on the sofa and glower at him.

The silence started to saw on his nerves. 'You think I'm an idiot?'

'Totally.'

'He had no right to call you what he did.'

'You are *utterly* infuriating!' Her hands balled into fists. 'What he called me was despicable, but the best thing you could've done was walk away without giving him the satisfaction of reacting.' She shot to her feet and started to pace. 'Oh, but, *no*—you couldn't manage that, could you? No! Your honour demanded reparation for the lady—regardless of how much more difficult you'd be making it for said lady!'

He shifted on the chair. 'I…uh…'

'The story will break in the tabloids, the ugliest accusations will be made, and I'll be hounded by reporters and photographers at work. *Hell!*' She flung her arms out. 'Just wait until Gordon catches wind of this. I'll be out on my ear.' She swung to him, thumping a hand to her chest. 'I *need* to finish this traineeship. I need a decent qualification so I can get a job.'

'I've already told you—come and work for me.'

'I don't *want* to work for you!'

Her rejection stung. He shot to his feet then too. 'That's right—you'd rather bury yourself in some godforsaken place where you can sentence yourself to a life of solitary confinement.'

'That's *my* decision to make.'

He wanted to hurl the peas across the room. Except he didn't want to ruin the pretty new furnishings. He had to settle for dropping them in the sink instead.

He moved back into the middle of the room. 'I have no intention of making light of your experiences with the criminal justice system, but you're letting one experience colour your entire life.' That hard lump of anger in his chest rose up into his throat. 'And I am *not* Johnnie Peters.'

Her entire frame shook. 'I told you—this is about *me*. Not you.' She didn't yell, but her words speared through him as if they'd come at him at great volume. 'You *punched* a man tonight, Dylan. That photographer can have you charged with assault. He'd be within his rights.'

It was true. It had been foolish to react. He couldn't find it in himself to regret it, though.

'And you made *me* an eye witness to the event.'

He swung back to meet her gaze. What he saw there made his heart burn.

'If I were in love with you, and you asked me to lie to the police about what had happened tonight...'

She didn't finish the sentence, but her pallor made his stomach churn.

'You're afraid you'd perjure yourself for me?'

'If I fell in love with you, Dylan, I'm afraid I'd risk everything again.'

He reached out to curl his fingers around her shoulders. 'I would *never* ask that of you.'

She moved away until his hands dropped back to his sides. 'The best way for me to avoid that kind of temptation is to avoid romantic attachments altogether. All I want is a quiet life. It doesn't seem too much to ask. It doesn't seem like such a big sacrifice to make.'

Ice sped through his veins. 'You're mistaken if you think living a half-life isn't a sacrifice. It'll keep you out of jail, it'll keep you out of trouble, but there are worse things than jail.'

She blinked, as if that wasn't a thought that had ever occurred to her.

'Living a life without love is one of them. And here's another thing for you to think about. If I fell in love with *you*—' he pointed a finger at her '—who's to say you wouldn't have the same power over me that Johnnie had over you? Who's to say you wouldn't force me to turn my back on my principles?'

The words spilled from him with an uncanny truth that left him reeling.

Her mouth dropped open.

He forged on, not understanding what was happening to him. 'Do you think I'd lie, steal or perjure myself for you?'

Her hands twisted together. 'You might lie for me…if it wasn't a big lie.'

He widened his stance. 'But the rest?'

She bit her lip and finally shook her head. 'No.'

'What makes you think *you* would, then?'

'My past tells me I'm weak.'

'Do you really think three years in prison—with all the education and counselling you received—hasn't made you stronger?'

She still labelled herself as weak-willed and easy to manipulate. He understood her fear of prison, and her determination never to find herself back behind bars, but she was wrong. She might let people like Gordon push her around, but she was as strong as one of the Plum Pines the reserve was named after.

Behind the dark moss of her eyes he could see her mind racing. He mightn't have convinced her. *Yet.* But he'd given her something to think about.

He snaked his hand behind her head and drew her face close to his.

'What are you doing?' she squeaked.

'I'm giving you something else to think about. Do you *really* want to live without this, Mia?'

He wanted to slam his lips to hers and kiss her with all the pent-up frustration tearing at his soul. He didn't. She'd tensed, ready to resist such an assault. And he didn't want to hurt her. If she'd let him he'd do everything he could to make her happy.

He touched his lips to hers gently, slowly exploring the lush lines of her mouth—savouring her. He poured all of himself into the kiss, wanting to give her as much pleasure as he could.

With a shiver and a sigh she sank against him, her hands fisting in his shirt. At his gentle demand she opened up to him and he felt as if he was home. Murmuring her name, he moved to gather her close—only to find a hand planted on his chest, pushing him away.

'Stop.'

He released her immediately.

Her chest rose and fell as if she'd been running. 'You shouldn't be kissing me.'

He couldn't think of anything he'd rather do.

'What you should be doing is readying yourself for the PR disaster that's about to hit.'

He remained silent until she lifted her gaze to his. 'I promise you won't lose your job.'

She snorted her disbelief. 'Will you please warn Carla too? I think it'd be a good idea if you told her all that I told you tonight.'

'You want Carla to know?'

'It seems only fair.'

'No.' He refused to be a party to her shutting herself off from people. 'If you're truly her friend, Mia, then *you* tell her.'

With that, he spun on his heel and left.

Dylan stumbled down Mia's front steps, feeling as if he'd descended a drop of a thousand feet. He put out a hand to steady himself, but there was nothing to grab on to. He stood there swaying, praying he'd find his balance soon.

What had just happened?

Idiot!

The word screamed over and over in his mind, but he didn't know why.

What was so idiotic about anything he'd done tonight? Mia might think him an idiot for punching Percy Struthers, but the man had deserved it. Given the chance, he'd do it again! And he wasn't an idiot for refusing to be labelled as another Johnnie Peters either.

Pain shot into his jaw from clenching his teeth too hard. He was *nothing* like Johnnie Peters!

He lurched over to his car and flung the door open, but he didn't get in.

He wasn't an idiot for fighting against Mia's mistaken view of herself. She wasn't weak! She was one of the strongest women he knew.

Stronger than Caitlin.

He froze. Where had *that* come from?

But... Mia *was* stronger than Caitlin.

His mouth dried, and his heart was pounding so hard it sent nausea swirling through him. Mia was *exactly* the kind of woman who'd go the distance with a man—who'd take the good times with the bad, who'd weather the storms. Mia wouldn't turn tail and run at the first sign of trouble. If things got tough she'd dig her heels in and wait it out.

Idiot!

It finally hit him why that word kept going round and round in his mind. He collapsed on to the car seat. He'd been telling himself all this time that what he wanted with Mia was an affair, but that was a lie.

He wanted it all. *He loved her.* He wanted a chance to build a life with her.

His vision darkened. He raked his hands through his hair. All this time he'd thought he'd been keeping his heart safe... and yet the whole time he'd been falling in love with her.

His hands clenched about the steering wheel. He would *not* give up! Mia had told his uncle that he, Dylan, made dreams come true. Was there the slightest chance on earth that he could make *her* dreams come true?

If he wanted to win her heart he had to find out.

CHAPTER TEN

THE STORY DIDN'T break on Monday or Tuesday. It didn't break on Wednesday or Thursday either. There wasn't a single item in the newspapers about Dylan, let alone any shady ex-convict women he might be dating.

Not that they *were* dating.

Even if he'd made it clear that he'd like to be.

Mia's wilful heart leapt at the thought, avoiding all her attempts to squash its exuberance.

She'd finally gathered up the courage to ring Carla on Tuesday night. Carla had claimed she didn't care about Mia's history—that she only cared about the kind of person Mia was now. Mia had even believed her.

She hadn't seen Dylan all week. He hadn't dropped by Plum Pines during her lunchbreak. He hadn't rung her for no reason at all other than to talk nonsense until she started to laugh in spite of herself. He hadn't even rung to talk about the wedding.

Despite her best intentions, she missed him.

She didn't just miss him—she *ached* for him.

On Friday morning, when it was barely light, she rushed the one and a half kilometres to the nearest newsagent's to buy a newspaper. Again, nothing.

Saturday dawned—the day of her dinner party—and still no scandal broke. She could hardly imagine what strings

Dylan had pulled to hush up the story. Could she start to breathe more easily?

It didn't make the memory of their encounter with the photographer fade, though. She physically flinched whenever she recalled the moment Dylan had punched the other man. Was he *crazy*? He could have been hauled off in a paddy wagon and thrown in a cell overnight! All because someone had called her a bad name.

Couldn't he see that for the rest of her life there'd be people who'd be happy to call her bad names? What would he do—punch them *all* on the nose?

Dylan deserved better than that.

So do you.

The thought whispered through her and she had to sink down into the nearest chair. Her heart thumped, the pulse in her throat pounded and her temples throbbed.

There are worse things than prison.

Dylan was right.

Shame, sharp and hot, engulfed her. She'd stolen money from people—people who hadn't deserved it. Knowing she was capable of that—living with that knowledge—was the worst thing of all. She'd willingly spend another three years in prison if it would rid her of the taint. But it wouldn't. Nothing would. Saying sorry to the people she'd hurt, doing her jail time, being a model prisoner, having the counselling— none of that had helped.

The only way she could ensure she never did something like that again was to stay away from people as much as she could.

Heat burned the backs of her eyes. She pressed a fist to her mouth. She wanted to believe Dylan—believe that she'd changed, become stronger, that no one could manipulate her now. His face rose up in her mind...a beautiful dream she'd kept telling herself was out of reach. Her every atom yearned towards him.

With a half-sob, she closed her eyes. She couldn't reach for that dream until she was certain she'd changed.

But how could she ever be certain of that?

Mia glanced at the plate of nibbles she'd set on the coffee table—some nice cheese and fancy crackers, along with some fat feta-stuffed olives. Should she add some grapes to the platter?

She clasped and unclasped her hands. She wasn't serving an entrée—just a main and a dessert...and these pre-dinner nibbles.

She peered into the refrigerator to check on the individual crème-brûlées she'd prepared earlier. What if they'd spoiled?

They hadn't.

She glanced at the wine. What if she'd chosen the wrong sort? She knew nothing about wine. The man at the liquor store had been helpful, but still...

What if nobody wanted wine? What if they wanted something she didn't have? She'd stocked up on mineral water and cola. She'd filled umpteen ice cube trays, so there'd be plenty of ice, but... She hadn't thought to buy port. What if someone wanted an after-dinner port? Or sherry!

She twisted her hands together. What if she ruined the veal scaloppini?

We'll call out for pizza.

What if she spilled a whole bottle of wine?

We'll mop it up.

What if—?

Relax.

The voice in her head sounded suspiciously like Dylan's. Funnily enough, it *did* help calm her panic.

It's just a dinner for friends. Nothing to get het up about.

A knock sounded at the front door and her heart immediately leapt into her throat.

They were twenty minutes early!

Does it matter?

Yes. No. She didn't know.

She wiped her palms down her pretty pink summer dress—another extravagant spur-of-the-moment purchase. She'd been making a few of those since she'd met Dylan—not that she could find it in herself to regret them.

Pulling in a breath, she went to answer it. Dylan stared at her from behind the screen. He held a bottle of wine and a bunch of flowers, but she barely noticed them against the intensity of his burning blue eyes.

Swallowing, she unlatched the screen and pushed it open. 'Come in.'

He kissed her cheek—all formality—and handed her the wine and flowers. 'Gifts for the hostess.'

She swallowed again, her senses drenched with the nutmeg scent of him. 'Thank you.'

While he might be physically close, his reserve made him seem a million miles away. Her fingers tightened around the stems of the flowers. She had no idea how to breach that distance. She wasn't even sure she should attempt it.

'I didn't know if you'd come.' She moved behind the kitchen counter to find a vase for the flowers—yellow-headed daisies.

'I'd have let you know if I couldn't make it.'

Of course he would. He had impeccable manners.

She glanced up to find him scrutinising her living room, a frown—small but unmistakable—settling over his features.

She set the vase of flowers on the kitchen bench and walked across. 'What's wrong?' Maybe he hated cheese and olives. She could have sworn he'd eaten them the night she'd dined at the Fairweather mansion.

He gestured to the room. 'Do you mind if I make a few adjustments?'

'Knock yourself out.'

He immediately shifted the cushions out of their perfect alignment and shook out her throw rug before casually draping it across the sofa. He took a decorative rock from the mantel and placed it on the coffee table, pushed the platter of cheese and olives from the centre further towards one end. He moved the vase of fresh flowers she'd bought that morning to the end of the mantel, rather than dead centre, and then pulled a magazine and a book from the magazine rack, all but hidden by the sofa, and placed them on the little table by the door.

'There!' He dusted off his hands. 'Now the place looks lived in.'

Mia blinked. His few simple changes had made a big difference. The room now radiated warmth rather than stiff awkwardness.

Her hands went to her hips. 'How do you even know how to do that?'

He shrugged. 'You just need to relax a bit more, Mia.'

Relaxing around Dylan... Was that even possible?

She swallowed. 'I spoke to Carla through the week.'

'I know. She's talked of little else.'

Mia couldn't work out whether he was pleased about that or not.

'Carla's the reason I'm early. She seemed to think you might need a hand, and that I should be the one to offer it.'

He didn't smile.

She gestured to the room, trying to lighten the mood. 'Obviously she was right.'

He just stared at her, his eyes blue and brooding.

She pressed a hand to her stomach. 'I...uh... I think I have everything under control.' She kicked into hostess mode. 'Can I get you a drink? Beer, wine...soft drink?'

He chose wine. She poured wine for both of them and invited him to help himself to the cheese and olives. They sat there barely talking, barely looking at each other. Mia excused herself and pretended to do something in the kitchen.

They were rescued from their excruciating awkwardness when Carla and Thierry arrived fifteen minutes later.

'Oh, look at your cottage!' Carla gushed, hugging her. 'It's so quaint and pretty.'

Carla's kindness eased some of the burning in Mia's soul, and she could only give thanks that his sister's presence made Dylan a little more sociable. Thierry neither hugged her nor kissed her cheek. Not that she'd expected him to do either. He barely said hello.

The veal scaloppini was a melt-in-the-mouth success. The dinner, however, wasn't. Dylan complimented her on the food, made small talk about nothing of note, and every time Mia glanced at him a knife twisted into her heart. His despondency—his *unhappiness*—was her fault.

She hated it that she'd hurt him. And she didn't know how to make it right. More to the point, she didn't know if she *should* make it right.

Carla's eyes grew increasingly narrow as she glanced from Mia to Dylan. Thierry just continued to survey Mia with his usual and by now familiar suspicion.

She told a funny story about a wombat at Plum Pines but only Carla laughed.

She mentioned that she was considering getting a car and asked if they had any opinions on what she should buy. Thierry said he wasn't interested in cars.

Carla gaped at him. 'Liar!'

'I'm interested in *sports* cars. Mia can't afford one of those.'

'Don't be so rude!'

'No, Thierry's right,' Mia jumped in. 'I'm just after something reliable and economical.'

Dylan then subjected them all to a long, monotonous monologue about the pros and cons of a particular model of hatchback that had their eyes glazing over and Mia wishing she'd never asked the question in the first place.

'What is *wrong* with you two?' Carla finally burst out at the two men. 'I think it's brave of Mia to tell us the full story of her past. I don't care what the two of you think—it doesn't change the way *I* feel about her. She's been a lovely friend to me.'

'Carla, that's really nice of you.' Mia's heart hammered up into her throat. 'But I think you ought to know that Dylan doesn't have an issue with my past either.'

Carla folded her arms, her eyes flashing. 'Then what's the problem? What's wrong with the pair of you?'

'That's none of your business,' Thierry bit out.

'Dylan is my brother. Mia is my friend. Of *course* it's my business.' She turned to Mia. 'Is it because of that incident with the photographer?'

Dylan's hands clenched about his knife and fork. 'Why the hell did you have to tell Carla about that anyway?' he shot at Mia.

An answering anger snapped through her. 'I didn't know it was a state secret. Besides, I thought it only fair that Carla be prepared for the story to break.'

'I told you I'd take care of it!'

'You'll have to excuse my scepticism. I didn't know your reach was both long and powerful enough to stop a story that juicy from making the headlines.'

'There's a lot you don't know about me!'

He glared at her.

She glared back.

'Why did you wait until Tuesday night to tell Carla?'

The question ground out of Thierry, cutting through everything else.

Mia moistened her lips. 'Because I was afraid that once she knew the whole truth she'd despise me.'

Thierry leaned towards her. On her other side she felt Dylan tense.

'She *should* despise you.'

'Thierry!'

Carla's pallor caught at Mia's heart.

'Ignore him. He has a giant chip on his shoulder because his father was in and out of prison all through his childhood.'

Mia's jaw dropped as Thierry's animosity made sudden and perfect sense.

Thierry shot to his feet. 'I told you that in the strictest confidence!'

They all stared after him as he slammed out of the house.

Carla leapt up too, grabbing her handbag. 'I'll call you tomorrow,' she said to Mia, before racing after him.

Mia glanced at Dylan. Did *he* mean to slam out of her cottage as well?

He stared back, his mouth a hard straight line, and she realised he meant to do no such thing.

She swallowed. 'Dessert?'

'Please.'

Before Mia could retrieve the crème-brûlées the cottage phone rang. That phone hardly ever rang.

She lifted the receiver. 'Hello?'

'This is Andrew Fairweather, Ms Maydew—Dylan and Carla's uncle. Perhaps you remember me?'

His tone of voice said, *Of course you remember me.*

'Yes, sir, I do.'

'A disturbing report has reached me claiming that you and my nephew are romantically involved. Well?'

His tone reminded her of her father. Her hands trembled. *You stood up to your father.*

She pushed her shoulders back. 'No comment.'

'I know about your background, young lady!'

Her fingers tightened about the receiver. 'I can't say as I'm surprised.' She glanced at Dylan to find him watching her closely.

'I'm giving you a friendly warning.'

Oh, yes—very friendly.

'Stay away from my nephew and niece or you *will* be sorry.'

'I'll keep that in mind.'

The line went dead. She dropped the receiver to the cradle and made for the kitchen.

'Was that the press?' Dylan demanded.

She set a crème-brûlée in front of him and slid into her seat. 'Have a taste.'

He looked as if he wanted to argue, but he spooned some of the dessert into his mouth and an expression of bliss spread across his face. He swore—just a little swear word—in an expression of wonder, not of alarm or anger. 'This is *amazing*.'

She stared at him, her chest clenching and unclenching, her skin going hot and cold, and something inside her melted so fast she wanted to cry out loud at the shock of it.

She loved him.

She loved him utterly, but she couldn't see how things between them could ever work out.

'Mia?'

She straightened. 'It wasn't the press on the phone, Dylan. It was your uncle.'

Dylan swore—one of the rudest words he knew.

Mia flinched. For all that she'd been to jail, she was no hardened criminal.

'I'm sorry. I shouldn't have said that.

She waved his apology away. 'It doesn't matter.'

It *did* matter. She deserved better. 'He warned you off?'

'Yes.'

He set his spoon down. 'What did he threaten you with?'

Her lips lifted a fraction. 'It wasn't a threat, but a "friendly warning".'

As if that were somehow different! He wished to God he could smile with her, but his sense of humour had deserted him. It had abandoned him when he'd walked away from her last week.

Fear had taken its place. Fear that he would never find a way to win her love.

'And it wasn't specific—just a general warning to stay away from you and Carla or I'd be sorry.'

'Are you going to heed him?'

She picked up her spoon and pressed it gently to the crust of her crème-brûlée until it cracked. 'Surely you and Carla have some say in the matter?'

He stilled. That felt like progress. 'You're not going to buckle under to his bullying?'

'Your uncle reminds me of my father. I stood up to my father and the world didn't come crashing down. Mind you—' her sigh arrowed into his chest '—it didn't do me any good either.'

The smile she sent him made his eyes burn.

'I suspect that if he chooses, your uncle could cause trouble for me.'

'And all you want is a quiet life?'

She lifted her eyes heavenward. 'I *crave* a quiet life.'

Life with him would never be quiet.

She brought her spoon down on top of her dessert again, shattering the toffee crust further. 'But me standing up to your uncle isn't going to be enough for you, Dylan, is it?' She met his gaze, her eyes troubled. 'You want more from me, and I don't know if I can give it to you.'

He straightened *I don't know* was a monumental improvement on *No chance at all.*

'You want our relationship to become physical, and you assure me you can keep that news under wraps from the press. I'm even starting to believe you. But can you promise me—?'

He leaned across and pressed a finger to her lips. 'First things first.' He needed to remove a significant problem before focusing on the reasons behind her softening. 'You think my uncle can cause problems for you at work with Gordon?'

'The thought has crossed my mind.' She stabbed the spoon into her dessert. 'I liked my plan—gain a useful qualification that'll keep me in employment—but I think it's time to say goodbye to it.'

He removed the crème-brûlée from her grasp and placed

it out of reach before she totally mangled it. 'You have a new plan?' Even though he knew it was a long shot, he couldn't help hoping he featured in this Plan B of hers.

'I think I'd better start looking for unskilled work—factory work or waitressing. At a pinch I suppose I could join the fruit-picking circuit.'

A hand reached out and wrung his heart. *'No!'*

Her raised eyebrow told him he had no say in the matter.

'I *won't* leave you worse off than I found you. I *won't* be responsible for that.'

Too late.

The words whispered through him, leaving a bitter aftertaste. 'I promise to do everything in my power to ensure you keep your job at Plum Pines.'

He could see that while she believed the sincerity of his intention she didn't think he'd be able to achieve the desired outcome. She had a point. His uncle held a lot of sway.

He drummed his fingers on the table. 'Right. If that doesn't work… Look, I know you don't want to work for FWE, but you could still do a traineeship with the company.' He drummed his fingers harder as his mind raced. 'I'd put you under one of my managers. You'd hardly see me. Our paths would barely cross.' He'd make sure they didn't if it would help her accept his offer. 'After two years of working for FWE, you could get a job anywhere in the industry. Job security would never be an issue for you again.'

'Dylan, I—'

He held up his hand. 'This is only a fall-back plan, in case you're fired from Plum Pines. I don't want to be responsible for you losing your job. Ever since I've met you, all I've done is cause you trouble.' He started to tick off the list on his fingers. 'Gordon tried to fire you for flirting with me, when I was the one doing the flirting. I introduced you to Thierry, who tried to play the heavy with you. Felipe put you in an untenable position when he snapped that photograph. The press have tried to go to town on you. And now my uncle has threatened you. It's not a list to be proud of.'

She glanced away. When she turned back, her eyes were dark and troubled. 'I fear you're paying for it too, though,' she said.

She was worth any price he had to pay. Which would be fine if he were the one paying the piper and not her. When he looked at the facts baldly, he'd done nothing but cause her trouble.

'That really is quite a list.' For the briefest of moments her eyes twinkled. 'It hasn't been all bad. You've bought me chocolate, and I've had my toenails painted. And I got the opportunity to see some amazing art.'

It was a paltry list in comparison.

She pressed her hands together. 'Most importantly, though, we now know Thierry isn't mistreating Carla.'

That *was* something. He'd never have found that out if it weren't for Mia.

'I've also learned some decorating tips and had the opportunity to cook veal scaloppini. What more could a girl want?'

A whole lot more!

He dragged a hand back through his hair. 'Dinner tonight was truly awful. Not the food,' he added quickly. 'The atmosphere.' And that had mostly been his fault too.

Mia pleated the tablecloth. 'I thought you were sulking.'

He couldn't seem to find any middle ground where she was concerned. 'I've been trying to give you some space, but the effort is killing me.'

As soon as he said it he knew the admission was too much. Mia sat further back in her seat. Further away from him. He had to swallow a groan at the pain that cramped his chest.

Pulling in a breath, he forced himself to focus on the important topic of their conversation. 'Please tell me that if you do lose your job you'll allow FWE to employ you. I can't stand the thought of bringing that much trouble to your door.

I know it means working in events management, rather than in conservation, but once you've gained the qualification you can arrange your working hours so you can study at night for a different qualification if you want. If I'm reading you correctly, it's job security that's really important to you.'

She was silent for several long moments, but eventually something in her shoulders unhitched. 'Okay.'

He stared at her. 'You mean it?'

'I'm really, *really* hoping I don't lose my position at Plum Pines.'

'We'll call that Plan A.'

'But if I do lose it, then, yes... I'd like to accept your offer of a position at FWE. We can call that Plan B'

'You'll trust that I won't try and take advantage of the situation?'

She nodded, and he found that he could smile. If she trusted him that far...

He rubbed his hands together. 'I feel we're making progress.'

'Progress?' The word squeaked out of her. 'How?'

He leaned towards her. 'I want to throw our ground rules out the window, Mia. I thought I only wanted an affair with you—fun, pleasure, satisfaction.'

At each word her eyes widened.

'But I was wrong. I want a whole lot more than that. I want—'

She pressed her fingers to his lips before he could tell her he loved her. Her throat bobbed convulsively. 'You're moving too fast for me.'

He pressed a kiss to her fingers before wrapping her hand in his. 'I'll slow down.'

'Do you even know how to do that?'

'I'll learn.'

Her brow creased. 'Dylan, I can't promise you anything.'

'I know. I might have hope, but I don't have any expectations. I have no right to expect anything from you.'

Dark eyes stared into his. 'You have so much faith in me, and I have so little in myself.'

She had to find that faith or there'd be no chance for them. They both knew that.

Her gaze drifted down to his mouth. Her eyes darkened and her lips parted, as if she couldn't get enough air into her lungs.

'And yet your beauty continues to addle my brain,' she murmured, almost to herself. 'That can't be good.'

An answering desire took hold of him, his stomach muscles tightening and his skin tingling. 'I think it's excellent.'

She moistened her lips, her chest rising and falling. 'Would you like to stay the night?'

For a moment he couldn't breathe. His free hand clenched and then unclenched, before clenching again. 'I would *love* to stay the night, but you told me sex wouldn't make a difference.'

Her mouth opened, but no sound came out.

'Can you promise me that it *will* make a difference, Mia?'

Her gaze slid away and she shook her head.

He pulled in a breath and held strong. 'I want more than crumbs from you. I want everything.'

She looked as if she wanted to run away. 'I'm sorry. That was stupid of me. Especially when I just asked you to slow down.' She rubbed her brow. 'We should bring this evening to a close and you should say goodnight.'

He rose, forcing her to rise too. If he didn't leave soon he'd be in danger of settling for anything, however small. 'It's a hostess's duty to escort her guests to the door.'

She bit back a smile as he pulled her along in his wake. 'You're just angling for a kiss.'

He backed her up against the wall. 'It excites me to know you're burning for me.'

Her breath hitched. 'You promised slow.'

'It's just a kiss, Mia.'

'Nothing is *just* anything with you, Dylan. We both know that.'

'Then tell me to stop.'

Her gaze moved from his eyes to his mouth. 'Just a kiss?'

He grinned down at her and shook his head. 'I mean to leave you *really* burning, Mia.'

Her eyes widened. 'I—'

He covered her mouth with his own, keeping the caress gentle until she relaxed beneath his touch, her lips moving against his, her mouth opening to him... And then, without warning, he deepened the kiss, intensifying it using his lips, tongue, teeth. His hands pressed into the small of her back until her full length was against his. He used every weapon in his armoury to assault her senses.

'Dylan...'

His name was a groan of need on her lips, and it nearly drove him mad. She tangled her hands in his hair, drawing him closer as she tried to crawl into his skin, inflaming him beyond endurance. He pressed her back against the wall, his hands sliding down over her backside, his fingers digging into her buttocks, pulling her up and into him, his need for her a fire in his blood.

She wanted him too. They could have each other and...

He eased away from her. Their eyes locked. He wanted so much more than this from her, but he knew that if she asked him to stay now, he would.

She pulled in a breath, as if reading that thought in his face. With something that sounded like a sob, she planted a hand to his chest and gently pushed him away.

'Go.'

CHAPTER ELEVEN

MIA BARELY SLEPT that night. She gave up trying just before dawn. So when Carla pulled up at the front of the cottage just after six a.m. Mia happened to be sitting on her front step, nursing a mug of coffee.

She stood and opened the front gate, ushered Carla through. Carla trudged up the path and collapsed on to the step, and Mia's heart clenched at the sight of her friend's red-rimmed eyes.

Then she noted the faint blue bruise on Carla's right cheekbone and a hot pit of anger burned in her belly.

She brushed her fingers beneath it, unable to stop her eyes from filling. 'Not Thierry?'

Carla's eyes filled too. 'No. He's a jerk, but not that much of a jerk.'

'Not Dylan.'

It was a statement rather than a question. Dylan would never strike a woman.

Carla gave a short laugh. 'I think he'd rather throw himself off a cliff than hurt a woman.' She glanced at Mia and rolled her eyes. 'I mean *physically* hurt a woman. From what I can tell he's broken his fair share of hearts. The fact you're up so early leads me to believe he's given *you* a sleepless night.'

Mia felt her lips twist. 'In this instance I believe it's safe to say I've returned the favour.'

Carla's attempt at a smile almost broke Mia's heart. She sat down and put her arm around Carla's shoulders. 'Your uncle?'

Carla rested her head against Mia's. 'Yes...' she whispered.

The swine!

They sat like that for a while, letting the early-morning peace seep into their souls.

A sigh eventually shuddered out of Mia. 'He hit you because of me, didn't he? Because you refused to end our friendship. I'm sorry I've caused trouble for you, Carla. You don't deserve it.'

Carla lifted her head. 'He hit me because I refused to obey him—because I'm choosing to live my life the way I see fit. And it's not the first time it's happened.'

Mia called him one of the worst names she could think of.

A giggle shot out of Carla, but she nodded in agreement.

'C'mon.' Mia hauled her to her feet. 'Have you had an *ounce* of sleep?'

Carla shook her head.

She led her inside and pushed her in the direction of the bathroom. 'Go wash your face.' She pulled a soft cotton nightie from a drawer and ordered her to put it on, then pulled the covers back from her bed. 'In.'

'Oh, but...'

'We'll make a game plan after you've had some sleep.'

Carla glanced at the bed. 'A couple of hours *would* be good.' She glanced back at Mia, biting her lip. 'I really, *really* don't want to see either Thierry or Dylan at the moment. I know it's asking a lot of you, Mia, but I just...'

'You want to sort through things at your own pace. That's understandable.'

'I'm tired of men thinking they know what's best for me, telling me what to do.'

'I'll take care of Thierry and Dylan if they show up.'

Carla climbed into the bed.

Mia pulled the covers up to her chin, squeezed her hand briefly. 'Sleep well.'

She fortified herself with more coffee and went to sit back out on the front step to keep guard.

Dylan showed up at nine o'clock.

He looked tired and haggard and her heart went out to him. She forgave him—a little—for her own sleepless night.

He collapsed onto the step beside her. 'I've been looking for her for a couple of hours.' He gestured to Carla's car. 'Thierry rang at seven. I thought she was with him. That's when I realised she was missing. I'm glad she's here.'

Thierry chose that moment to pull up behind Dylan's car.

'She's a grown woman, Dylan. If she chooses to spend the night elsewhere, surely that's her business? Not to mention her prerogative. I'm sure *you* wouldn't appreciate it if she sent out a search party whenever *you* didn't come home.'

He thrust out his jaw. 'She's not answering her phone.'

'Likewise.'

She said it as gently as she could, but Dylan's eyes narrowed, the irises going a deep sapphire.

Thierry charged up the path. 'I want to see her!'

'I'm sure you do.' She kept her voice calm. 'But the fact of the matter is she doesn't want to see either of you at the moment.'

'Me?' Dylan shot to his feet. 'Why doesn't she want to see *me*?'

'I believe the phrase was, "I'm tired of men thinking they know what's best for me."'

Both men's jaws dropped.

Dylan paced.

Thierry just stood there with his hands clenched. He glanced at the door.

'It's locked,' Mia said. 'And if either one of you has the slightest interest in her well-being you won't start banging on the door. She's asleep.'

Dylan halted his pacing. 'You put her to *bed*?'

'I did.'

Thierry rested his hands on his knees, his face grey. 'I don't know what to do. I've been such an idiot.'

Dylan leapt forward and grabbed him by his shirtfront and shook him. 'What the *hell* have you done to her?'

'If I have to get the hose out to cool the pair of you off, I will.'

Those blue eyes swung to her. She read the anger in them—and the indecision.

'Let him go, Dylan. Carla is perfectly aware that the two of you have her best interests at heart, but she's entitled to a time out whenever she needs one. She doesn't have to consult with either of you beforehand.'

Dylan stared into her eyes so intently it felt as if he was scouring her soul. Finally, with a nod, he released Thierry. 'Sorry.'

Thierry straightened his shirt. 'No problem.'

She glanced back at Thierry. 'I don't know what your argument was about last night, but if you're truly sorry—'

'I am!'

'Then I suggest you come up with an honest explanation for why you behaved the way you did, promise to do better in the future, and have a heartfelt and grovelling apology ready.'

His fists opened and closed several times. He nodded hard. 'Right.'

His earnestness almost made her smile. 'Flowers might help too.'

His chin lifted. 'I can come back?'

She knew she wouldn't be able to keep him away indefinitely.

'You can come back at four. I'm not making any promises. It's up to Carla to decide if she wants to see you or not.'

'Right.' He swung away and made for the gate. He halted when he reached it and turned back. 'Thanks.'

With a nod, he was gone.

Had Thierry just *thanked* her? Wow!

Both she and Dylan watched him drive away—Mia from her spot on the step, Dylan from where he stood in wide-legged masculine magnificence on her pocket of front lawn.

As soon as Thierry's car had disappeared, he swung back to face her. 'Okay, you can let me see her now.'

'I'm sorry, Dylan, but the same holds true for you too.'

'You have to be joking!' He stalked across to loom over her. 'You *know* I only have Carla's best interests at heart.'

She stood, using the step to give her a height advantage. 'Has it never occurred to you that all your big brotherly protectiveness—some might call it *over*-protectiveness—could be a *little* stifling?' She uttered 'little' in such a way that he couldn't miss the fact that she meant *a lot.*

He gaped at her. 'It's my job to look out for her.'

'She's an adult. She can look out for herself.'

'Just because your family let you down, it doesn't mean that's the way every family works.'

He spoke the words in a voice so low and controlled it sent ice tiptoeing down her spine.

He held out his hand, palm flat, eyes glittering. 'Give me the key.'

Her heart quailed, because she suddenly realised what a betrayal he would see this as—her keeping him from his sister. She wanted to weep. She'd finally found the one sure way to distance him, and now that she had she didn't want to use it.

Give him the key.

She lifted her chin and forced steel to her spine. 'No.' Planting her hands on her hips, she leaned towards him. 'Carla doesn't want to see you at the moment. Go home, Dylan. Stop being a bully.'

His hands fisted and his entire body started to shake. 'I could take it from you by force.'

She folded her arms and raised an eyebrow. They both knew he wouldn't.

He swore and she flinched. He didn't apologise, but she didn't expect him to.

'A *bully*?' The word ground out of him. 'I can't believe you're lumping me in the same class as Thierry.'

The pain in his words cut at her. 'I *do* put you in the same class as Thierry. Thierry loves Carla—adores her. He'd lay his life down for her. I know you would too. It doesn't change the fact that Carla doesn't want to see either of you for the time being.'

His eyes blazed, but his face turned to stone. He turned and stormed down the path, leaving as she'd ordered him to.

The backs of her eyes burned and her vision blurred. A lump lodged in her throat. Whatever fragile link had bound them together had been severed, and she felt the pain of it deep down inside her. It tore at something she thought might never be fixed.

At the gate, he halted. His shoulders sagged. She hated it that she'd hurt him, but she readied herself for a different form of attack.

He came back, his face sombre, his eyes throbbing. 'I owe you an apology. I just acted like a two-year-old throwing a tantrum because he's been denied what he wants. But I'm worried about Carla.'

'I know.'

He clasped her shoulders. 'Is she okay?'

He stared into her eyes and she realised he meant to trust whatever she told him. Her mouth went dry.

'Mia?'

Her heart thudded, though she couldn't explain why. 'She's upset.'

'With Thierry?'

'I suspect so. But mostly with your uncle.'

Dylan's lips pressed together in a tight line. 'His car was at the house when I got back last night. It was late, so he was already in bed. He left after breakfast. We shared a few home truths. I don't think he'll be back. I told him that if he caused trouble for you at your place of employment you'd come and work for FWE. I don't think your job will be in jeopardy from *that* region, Mia.'

'I... Thank you.'

'I didn't know he'd spoken to Carla.'

It wasn't her place to tell him about his uncle's violence. 'I think that after some sleep, and some lunch and some talking, Carla will be fine. She just needs time to clear her head.'

He squeezed her shoulders and then released her. 'Okay.' He really meant to trust her?

'Thank you for looking after her.'

'She's my friend. Of course I'm going to look out for her.'

His eyes throbbed into her. 'I don't mean to be a bully.'

It took all the strength she had not to reach out and touch his face. 'I know that too.' And he wasn't—not really. 'If you were really a bully you'd have taken the key from me by force.'

'You don't see it, do you?' he said.

A desolation that made her heart catch stretched through his eyes. Her mouth went dry. 'What don't I see?'

'I just harangued you, bullied you, all but emotionally blackmailed you, but you held firm. You chose to do what you thought was right rather than submit to my will. Do you still believe you're weak and easy to manipulate?'

She froze. 'I...'

The yard spun.

'I can't keep doing this, Mia.'

Her gaze speared back to his. 'What do you mean?'

'I love you.'

Her heart stuttered in her chest.

'You *know* I love you. With everything that's inside me. I'd do anything to win your love. But it's not enough, is it? You're still so far away. I lose myself and I get so frustrated... I start to yell and then I turn into a bully.'

'Dylan, I—'

He pressed his fingers to her lips. 'I love you, Mia. I want to have a life with you. But I won't bully you into that. If you ever come to me, I want it to be because you love me too.'

She did love him, but…

Confusion swirled through her and she couldn't make sense of the riot raging through her. The smile he sent her made her want to cry.

He leaned forward and pressed a kiss to her brow. 'Tell Carla if she needs anything to call me.'

She nodded.

He held her gaze for a moment. 'I mean to give you all the space you want, Mia. If you change your mind, you know where to find me.'

Fear clutched at her heart.

With a nod, he turned and strode away. This time he didn't stop at the gate.

Every step that he took away from her increased the ache in her chest tenfold.

Carla slept until noon.

'Did Thierry show up?'

'He did. So did Dylan.'

'What did he say?'

'Dylan said you're to call him if you need anything.'

'What did *Thierry* say?'

Oh. 'The man is half out of his wits with worry for you… and fear that you're going to dump him.'

'Good!'

'I told him to come back at four. I didn't guarantee that you'd see him. But if you really don't want to see him again he'll need to hear it from you.'

Carla bit her lip.

'Can things not be fixed?' Mia asked.

Carla folded her arms. 'I guess that depends on him. He wants to be all strong and solitary and untouchable—but that's *not* how relationships work. It's not how *marriage* works.'

Each and every one of those darts found their mark, although they hadn't been aimed at her.

Mia rubbed a hand across her chest, trying to ease the ache there. 'I believe he's sincere in wanting to make amends.'

'You think I should see him?'

She recalled the absolute happiness on Carla's face when she and Thierry had picnicked. 'I think you should give him a hearing. I think things can be patched up.'

The other woman tried to hide it, but she brightened at Mia's words. 'What about Dylan?'

'I think you should call him.'

'I meant what about *you* and Dylan?'

Oh. She glanced down at her hands. 'I don't know. I need to go somewhere quiet and think.'

'So there's hope?'

She met Carla's gaze. 'I *hope* there's hope.'

After a moment Carla said, 'I'm going to ring Dylan. I want Uncle Andrew charged with assault.'

Mia's head shot up, a fierce gladness gripping her. 'Good for you. Women shouldn't have to put up with violence at the hands of men.'

Carla twisted her hands together. 'It'll create a media circus, though.' She eyed Mia uncertainly. 'And the reason for our argument will come out—which means you'll be spotlighted in the media too.'

'Me?'

Carla reached out and took Mia's hand. 'I know how much you've dreaded the media getting hold of the story that you and Dylan are dating. If the thought of publicity freaks you out that much, I won't go ahead with it.'

Her heart thumped. She waited for dread and fear to fill her, but they didn't. *Why* wasn't she crippled with fear?

The answer came to her in an instant. Ever since she'd

been released from jail she'd thought that scandal and losing her job, losing the chance of the quiet life she craved, were the worst things that could happen to her. She'd been wrong. Watching Dylan walk away this morning—that had been the worst thing.

Very slowly she shook her head. 'It doesn't freak me out. At least, not much.' She met her friend's gaze. 'You have every right to slay your dragons. I'll help in any way I can.'

Carla wrapped her in a hug. 'Thank you.'

At four o'clock Mia let herself into the Plum Pines office. Sunday was one of the busiest days as far as the general public were concerned—lots of barbecues, picnics and viewing of the exhibits. It was a busy day for the volunteers who helped to run the wildlife displays too, but the administration of the reserve was a strictly Monday-to-Friday enterprise. Which meant she'd have the office to herself.

With a heart that pounded too fast, she switched on one of the computers and then pulled Felipe's memory card from her pocket. Swallowing hard, she retrieved the image he'd snapped of her.

It filled the screen. She flinched and had to look away.

It's only a photograph!

She glanced back and tried to study the picture objectively, but after only a few seconds she had to look away again.

Muttering something rude under her breath, she pushed out of her chair and paced across to the far wall. Hauling in a breath, she turned back to the image once more.

Her heart squeezed tight and her eyes filled. Felipe had captured something that attracted and repelled her at the same time. He'd captured something that both soothed and frightened her.

What was it?

In that photo her expression was so unguarded it made her head spin. Was it hope?

She moved back towards the computer monitor to study the image more minutely, biting down on her thumbnail.

Hope was part of it, but…

She reached out and touched the face on the screen.

That smile…

The emotion pulsing through the photograph was *joy*. It was so present she could almost feel the laughter wrap around her.

Joy? She'd spent so long feeling ashamed of herself, so determined not to repeat her mistakes, she'd forgotten. She'd forgotten she had a lot of good inside her too.

Her hands clenched and unclenched. She'd told herself that she couldn't have fun and hope and joy in her life because she didn't deserve them—not after the things she'd done.

But…

She'd made a mistake—a big one—but that mistake didn't have to define the rest of her life unless she let it. Her heart hammered against her ribs. She didn't need to shut herself away. She just needed to choose the right path… the right life.

She fell back into the chair, her cheeks wet. There wasn't a tissue in sight, so she dried her cheeks on the sleeves of her shirt and sniffed rather inelegantly.

'Right, then.'

She might as well start living that life right away.

She seized the phone and punched in a number.

'Felipe Fellini.'

'Felipe, it's Mia.'

'Mia, darling—what can I do for you?'

She told him.

After she'd hung up she pulled in a breath and rang Dylan.

He answered immediately. 'Mia! Is everything okay?'

His caller ID must have given her away.

The sound of his voice made her throat dry and she had to clear it before she could speak. 'Yes.'

'I've spoken to Carla. Are you sure you're all right with the publicity that a suit against Andrew will involve?'

She nodded, and then realised he couldn't see her. 'I'm sure.'

There was a pause. 'That's a surprise.'

She nodded again, more to herself this time. 'Yes.'

'What can I do for you?'

'I was wondering...' She wiped a damp palm down her jeans. 'I was wondering if I could invite you on a date next Saturday night. There's something I want you to see.'

'Has this anything to do with Carla and Thierry?'

'No. It's to do with me.'

'What time would you like me to pick you up?'

Dylan's heart thumped when he knocked on Mia's door. All week he'd alternated between hope and despair. Hope that this was the new beginning with Mia that he craved. Despair that this would be her way of bringing things between them to an end once and for all.

She opened the door. For a moment all he could do was stare. 'You look stunning!'

She wore a scarlet dress with a shimmering satin bodice, fitted beneath her breasts. The skirt fell to her knees in a cloud of chiffon that moved as she walked.

She pushed a strand of hair behind her ear. 'You look very nice yourself.'

He was glad he'd worn a dinner jacket. Especially when her hand fluttered up to her throat, as if the sight of him made it hard for her to breathe. The smile she sent him, though, held a hint of shyness—like a girl on her first date.

This probably *was* her first real date in nearly four years. Tenderness washed over him.

After she'd locked the front door he held out his arm, ridiculously pleased when she placed her hand in the crook of his elbow. 'Your chariot awaits.'

For good or for ill, he had a feeling he'd remember tonight for the rest of his life.

'Where are we going?'

She gave him an inner-city address. He had no idea what was there, but he didn't ask any further questions. He'd let the evening unfold at the pace she chose for it.

Dylan glanced out of the car window. Light spilled from the industrial-sized windows of a warehouse. He opened his mouth to ask Mia if she was sure she had the address right, but closed it again when she lowered her window and waved a card at an attendant standing on the footpath. The attendant directed them to a parking spot in front of the warehouse's huge double doors—the doors were closed except for a smaller door inset into one of them.

He switched off the ignition and turned to her. 'What *is* this?'

'I—' She broke off and hauled in a breath.

That wave of tenderness washed over him again, threatening to crush him. He reached for her hand. 'Are you nervous?'

'A little.'

'Of me?'

'Yes.'

The word whispered out of her and something blossomed in his chest. *Hope.* And it took firm root. 'You don't need to be nervous about me, Mia.'

He was hers. All hers. He didn't tell her out loud that he loved her, but he pressed a kiss to her palm, knowing that if she wanted to see it his love for her would be written all over his face.

Her gaze travelled over him and her breath snagged, her gaze catching on his mouth. Hunger and need chased themselves across her face. An answering hunger roared through him.

'Oh!' Her hand tightened in his. 'You can distract me *so* easily!'

The grin inside him built. 'Excellent.'

'Before you distract me further, I want to show you something. And then I want to talk.'

'And *then* can I distract you?' He waggled his eyebrows.

She gurgled back a laugh. 'Perhaps. If you still want to.'

He'd definitely still want to.

Without another word, he pushed himself out of the car and went around to open her door. She took his arm.

'This—' she gestured to the building in front of them '—is something of a first. Felipe has been prevailed upon to give the people of Newcastle a preview of his up-and-coming Sydney show.'

Dylan's stared at her. 'Who prevailed upon him?'

She moistened her lips. 'Me.'

She had?

Before he could ask what that meant, Felipe came towards them, arms outstretched.

'Darlings!' He kissed them on both cheeks in flamboyant greeting. 'I'm honoured to have you as my guests. Come!'

Dylan's head whirled as Felipe gave them a personal tour of some of the most amazing photographs Dylan had ever seen—his commentary both entertaining and revelatory.

Dylan glanced at Mia. She'd contrived this for *him*? Because she knew he appreciated art and photography? His heart gave a giant kick. Nobody had ever arranged anything so perfect for him in all his life. It had to mean *something*.

'And this, darlings, is the *pièce de résistance*! The jewel in my crown.'

Felipe led them around a screen to an enormous photograph positioned on one of the warehouse's end walls.

Mia!

He took a step towards it and Mia's hand slipped from his arm. It was the photograph of Mia! Her joy, her laughter and her love greeted him from the wall and he almost stopped breathing.

His every muscle tightened. He swung back to her, hands fisted at his sides. He'd lost the ability to be charming. Everything had been stripped away except raw need. 'What does this mean?'

Mia glanced at Felipe, who put a key into her hand.

'Lock up when you're done.'

She nodded her thanks.

It was only then that Dylan realised they were alone in this magnificent space. The show had been for him alone.

Mia didn't speak until the clang of a door informed them that Felipe had left. She moistened her lips. 'Are you cross that I gave Felipe permission to use the photograph in his exhibition?'

'Cross? No.' He glanced at the photo again and searched himself. He didn't feel disappointment either. Only wonder. 'I just want to know what all this means.'

'It means I've finally realised you were right.'

She moved to stand beside him and gestured up at the picture, though he could only look at *her*—the flesh and blood woman.

'That *is* the person I should become. It's...' She met his gaze. 'It's the real me.'

Her admission stunned him.

'I've realised that I deserve to be happy. More to the point, I've realised I *want* to be happy. And I've realised that being a field officer and leading a quiet life *won't* make me happy.'

She glanced at the photo and then at him.

'*You* make me happy, Dylan.'

He stared at her, humbled by the vulnerability in her eyes.

'I... I couldn't be happy until I forgave myself for my past.' Her hands twisted together. 'I know I've hurt you, and I'm so sorry for that. Truly. I'm hoping I haven't hurt you so badly that you can't forgive me. I'm hoping—'

He didn't let her finish. He kissed her instead.

The shock of his assault made her wobble on her heels, but he wrapped an arm about her waist and pulled her close, steadying her. She wrapped her arms around his neck and kissed him back.

When he lifted his head her eyes glittered and her chest rose and fell. And then she smiled, and it was just like the smile in the frame behind her—full of joy and love.

'That felt an awful lot like a you-still-love-me-too kiss.'

He stroked his fingers down her face. 'I will *always* love you.'

She took his face in her hands. 'I promise I will look after your heart and be the best person I can for you.'

He stared into her eyes, humbled all over again. 'Nobody has ever made a more meaningful vow to me. I'll cherish it forever.'

A cheeky smile peeped out. 'Good, because I'm also going to ask you to give me a job. I quit Plum Pines yesterday.'

He gaped. She just grinned back at him, so delighted with herself that he had to laugh.

'I don't want to be a field officer, and I don't want to be an events manager either. I just want you to give me a regular office job so I can put myself through a psychology major at university. I want to be a counsellor.' She lifted her chin. 'I think I have something of value I could offer to people.'

He ran his hands up and down her back, revelling in the way it made her shiver. 'How about I gift you the opportunity for full-time study as a wedding present?'

She went very still and Dylan held his breath.

'You want to *marry* me?' she whispered.

Very gently he took his arms from around her and, gripping both her hands, went down on one knee. 'Beautiful Mia, will you do me the very great honour of becoming my wife?'

Tears shone in her eyes. When she nodded, they spilled onto her cheeks.

He rose and she threw her arms around his neck. 'I can't

think of anything I want more than to spend the rest of my life with you, Dylan.'

He laughed for the sheer joy of it, swinging her around. 'How does November sound? We have a wedding going begging. We might as well use it.'

She eased back. 'What on earth are you talking about? Carla and Thierry have made up and—'

'They flew out to Vegas yesterday.'

She gaped. 'No!'

'So... November is ours if we want it.'

An enormous smile spread across her face. 'It's...perfect!'

He glanced at the photo on the wall and then down at her. 'No, Mia, *you're* perfect.'

She touched his face, her smile radiant. '*We're* perfect. Together.'

He couldn't top that, so he kissed her instead.

EPILOGUE

CARLA AND THIERRY bundled Mia out of the limousine and whisked her straight inside the small marquee that had been set up especially for her benefit—to shield her from the press and allow her a chance to freshen up.

As they'd only driven from her suite at an inner-city hotel with glorious views of the harbour to Plum Pines Reserve—a drive of less than fifteen minutes—she didn't really see what kind of freshening up was required. Unless she was supposed to try and quieten the excited dervishes whirling in her stomach. She had no chance of stilling *those*. She wasn't sure she wanted to.

Perhaps she should try and tame the grin that made her face ache? But she had no hope—nor desire—to do that either.

Carla, stunning in her hot-pink bridesmaid's dress, crouched down to adjust Mia's skirts.

Mia laughed ruefully. 'I went overboard, didn't I? I look like an oversized meringue.'

'You look *gorgeous*.' Carla continued to fluff up the skirts. 'Your dress is *beautiful*.'

The moment Mia had clapped eyes on the confection of raw silk and pearl beading she'd fallen in love with it. Apparently when she had said that she meant to live life to the full rather than hide in the shadows she'd meant it.

She hugged herself. 'It *is* beautiful.'

'I can't wait to see Dylan's face when he sees you.'

Today, nobody could mistake Mia for anything other than what she was—the bride, the centre of attention, the belle of the ball marrying her prince.

Those dervishes whirled faster and faster. Her cheeks ached from smiling. She lifted her chin. She wasn't ashamed of her joy. She wanted to share it with everyone.

She turned to find Thierry surveying her with his now familiar unsmiling gaze.

He nodded. 'You look stunning.'

She wriggled with excitement. 'I *feel* stunning. I'm so happy I think I could float off into the atmosphere.'

For the briefest of moments Thierry smiled, and it tempered the severe lines of his face. When he smiled, she could see why Carla had fallen for him.

She touched his arm. 'Thank you for agreeing to give me away.' He hadn't hesitated when she'd asked. He'd agreed immediately.

'I'm honoured.' One shoulder lifted. 'I'm starting to think I'd do anything you asked of me.'

From behind him, Carla sent her a wink.

Thierry frowned. 'You're sure we're okay?'

She rolled her eyes. 'I swear to God, Thierry, if you apologise to me one more time we're going to fall out.'

He shuffled his feet. 'It's just… I'm really sorry I misjudged you.'

Given his background, and the hardships his father's choices had forced on his family, Mia couldn't blame him for his reservations where she'd been concerned.

'As I misjudged myself, I can hardly blame you for doing the same. But it's all in the past now, and that's where it'll remain. It's time to move on.'

That was her new motto and she'd embraced it with gusto.

She reached out to take Carla and Thierry's hands. 'You're my family now—my sister and brother. I can't tell you how fortunate that makes me feel.'

Carla's eyes filled. Thierry cleared his throat a couple of times.

Mia blinked hard. She would *not* ruin her eye make-up. She wanted to look perfect for Dylan. 'So that's a yes—we're *very* okay.'

On impulse, they all hugged—before Carla tut-tutted and said something about crushing Mia's dress.

Mia laughed at her fussing, but a wave of excitement somersaulted through her. 'Oh, is it time yet? I can't wait—'

The flap of the marquee flew open and Felipe appeared. He clasped his hands beneath his chin when he saw her.

'Radiant!' he pronounced, before whisking a compact from somewhere and touching a powder puff lightly to her nose. He kissed the air above her cheeks. 'Perfect!'

He pulled out his camera and snapped a couple of pictures.

She waggled a finger at him. 'Don't forget—those photos are mine and Dylan's. None are to mysteriously appear in an exhibition.'

'Cross my heart, darling. Besides, your dishy intended is paying me enough to make it worth my while.' He pouted. 'Also, he made me sign some awful form full of lawyer-speak.'

Mia laughed.

'I've been sent to tell you everything is ready.'

'Oh!' She clasped her hands together.

'Nervous, darling?'

'Excited.'

He squeezed her hands. 'I wouldn't have missed this for the world.'

And then he was gone.

Carla handed her a bouquet of pink and white peonies. 'Ready?'

A lump lodged in her throat. All she could do was nod.

Thierry held the flap of the marquee open to reveal the red carpet that would lead her to Dylan. Carla set off down the carpet first. Thierry made Mia wait until Carla was half-way down the makeshift aisle before stepping after her.

Mia was vaguely aware of the beautiful music playing, of the murmurs of appreciation from their wedding guests, but her focus was wholly centred on the man standing at the other end.

His blond hair gleamed golden in the sunlight. His broad shoulders and strong thighs were outlined to perfection in his tuxedo. His heart was in his eyes. He didn't try to hide it from anyone, and she wasn't sure she'd ever seen anything more beautiful in her life.

Awe rose up through her…and more happiness than her body could contain. It spilled from her eyes and onto her cheeks.

He took her hand. His throat bobbed with emotion as he swallowed.

'You're so beautiful you make my eyes water,' she whispered, not caring about her make-up.

He smiled down at her. 'You're so beautiful you make my heart sing.'

The celebrant cleared her throat. 'Ready?'

Mia smiled up at Dylan. 'Yes.'

The service was simple but heartfelt. The reception was the epitome of joy and elegance. Mia felt like a fairytale princess.

After the meal had been eaten, toasts made, the cake cut and the bridal waltz completed, Dylan took her hand and they sneaked outside to stand at the wooden railing overlooking the lily pond. Lights twinkled in the trees, glimmering across the water's surface.

Dylan took her face in his hands and kissed her. A sweet, gentle kiss that promised a lifetime of kisses.

'Happy?' he murmured, easing back.

'More than I ever thought possible.' She smiled up at him before glancing back towards the marquee. 'Has anyone ever told you that you know how to throw a fabulous party?'

'What can I say? I'm gifted.'

She gurgled back a laugh. 'Look.' She pointed to Carla and Thierry dancing. 'They look gorgeous together.'

Dylan snorted. 'Carla should've had a wedding like this! *Elopement?*' He snorted again.

Mia leaned back against him. 'You just love any excuse to throw a party.'

'What's wrong with a party?'

'Absolutely nothing. I adore parties. I'm especially loving this one.'

She bit her lip then, and glanced up at him again.

'Are you sorry your Uncle Andrew isn't here?' The man might be a miserable excuse for a human being but he was still Dylan's uncle.

'Not a bit. I'll be happy if I never clap eyes on him again.'

There hadn't been enough evidence to charge Andrew with assault against Carla, but the scandal hadn't done the older man any favours. Especially since a young intern who worked in his office had made similar allegations against him. He'd been suspended pending an internal inquiry. If found guilty he'd lose his job. His political ambitions would be nothing more than dust.

Mia glanced up into her new husband's face and knew Andrew wouldn't be making trouble for any of them ever again.

Dylan smiled down at her. 'The day I won your heart was the luckiest day of my life.'

She turned in his arms, resting her hands against the warm hard contours of his chest. 'I'm the real winner, Dylan. You made me believe in love again. You showed me the power it had to do good. Whatever happens in the future, I'll never forget that lesson.' She touched her fingers to his face. 'I love you. I'm going to spend the rest of my life making you very, *very* happy.'

She wondered if her face reflected as much love as his did. She hoped so.

'Want to know what would make me happy right now?' he murmured, a wicked light flitting through his eyes. 'A kiss.'

Laughing, she reached up on tiptoe and pressed her lips to his, telling him in a language that needed no words how much she loved him.

* * * * *

THE BILLIONAIRE WHO SAW HER BEAUTY

REBECCA WINTERS

This is for my super-marvellous father,
Dr John Z. Brown, Jr, who was adored by his
many thousands of patients during his long career.
I've praised him before in other books
because he was the best!

CHAPTER ONE

"SIGNOR MONTANARI?"

Rini was just getting in the limo. He looked around in the direction of one of the reporters who'd followed him outside the doors of the fourteenth-century Palazzo Colonna in Rome. Dozens of them had assembled to cover the European Congress of Businessmen.

"A moment of your time, *per favore*—one piece of news I can use for my lead story in *La Repubblica*?"

Why not?

"Since Italy imports almost all of its hydrocarbon demand, a doubling of domestic production would help the country reduce its energy bill. I'm planning to find them in Italy."

"Where?"

"That's my secret for now."

The reporter beamed for having been given a partial scoop. "*Mille grazie, signor.*"

He nodded and closed the door before his driver took him to the heliport for the flight to his mountaintop villa in Positano, on the Amalfi Coast. Now that the two-day September conference covering the economic problems facing Europe was over, Rini was eager to explore his latest project. On Monday he'd be leaving for the coast of Southern Italy, but tonight he had other plans.

Once the helicopter landed on the pad behind his villa, he jumped down and found his housekeeper, Bianca, out by the pool watering the tubs of flowers. She looked up when she saw him.

"Welcome back."

"It's good to be home."

"How's your father?"

"Well as can be expected." Rini had flown to Naples after yesterday's session and spent the night with his *papà*, who seemed to be handling the loss of Rini's mother a little better these days. She'd been the heart of their home and Rini would always miss her happy, optimistic spirit.

"Was the conference beneficial?"

"I'm not sure *beneficial* is the right word. *Chilling* would be more accurate. Europe is in trouble economically, but I'd rather not think about that tonight."

"Do you want dinner?"

"I'd love one of your meals, but I'm meeting Guido tonight. It's his birthday." His best friend from childhood, the son of Leonides Rossano, who owned Rossano shipping lines, had texted him earlier in the day:

The parents are throwing a party for me on the yacht. Please say you can make it. I know you're at a conference, but I need your advice about something serious. By the time you arrive it will be breaking up so we can talk in private.

The message sounded serious, even for Guido, who clearly wasn't in a celebratory mood. He obviously had no plans for the weekend with a woman. His friend was as bad as Rini, who had no plans in that department, either. The two of them made quite a pair, but for entirely different reasons.

Guido was still looking for the right woman who hadn't come along yet. Rini didn't have the same problem. The right woman wasn't out there for him because she wouldn't want him when he had to tell her he was infertile. An old soccer injury he'd suffered in his youth had made it impossible for him to give any woman a child.

The pain of that realization had grown worse with every passing year, increasing his dissatisfaction with his own personal life. Whenever he did meet a woman he cared about, he held back, not allowing the relationship to develop into something deeper. It always came down to his fear she would reject him if she knew the truth.

He'd been denying his deep-seated needs for such a long time, he'd forgotten what real fulfillment was like. Since his sister Valentina—the mother of two children and now ecstatically married—had recently moved out of his villa, his unhappiness had deepened.

She'd lived with him through her whole pregnancy. He'd helped her with the baby when she'd first come home from the hospital. He'd loved every minute of it, but he'd carried a secret pain in his heart because he knew *he'd* never be able to be a birth father. When she'd married Giovanni and moved out, Rini felt the emptiness of the villa. It echoed the emptiness in his soul for what could never be.

Valentina's happiness, not to mention that of his younger brother, Carlo, who enjoyed a wonderful marriage and had a little girl, heightened his awareness that the key element in his life was missing. He envied his brother for being able to give his wife a child. Rini's doctor had told him he was a fool to let that prevent him from falling in love. "The right woman will be able to handle it," he'd reminded him.

Rini didn't believe it as he walked through the villa to his suite and stripped for a shower to get ready. After slipping into his black tuxedo, he reached for the wrapped gift he'd bought for the occasion. Once he'd said goodbye to Bianca, he left for the helicopter. The new hand-tied fishing fly he'd purchased for Guido was reputed to bring results. They often fished the mountain streams for trout. He thought his friend would be pleased.

Twenty minutes later he landed on board the Rossano luxury superyacht moored in the Bay of Naples, reminding him that not everyone was feeling the economic crunch. The yacht boasted seventeen staterooms and all the amenities of a five-star hotel, including a swimming pool and dance floor.

Twilight had descended, lending magic to the spectacular surroundings of one of the most beautiful and photographed bays in the world, with Mount Vesuvius in the background. He told his pilot to come back later and jumped down as Guido strode over to him.

"I've been waiting for you. Saw you on the evening

news. Impressive stuff. I was afraid you wouldn't be able to make it. Thanks for coming."

"As if I'd miss your birthday." He pulled the small package out of his jacket and handed it to him. *"Buon compleanno."*

They gave each other a hug, then walked into the salon-cum-bar for a drink. He opened his present and held up the lure. "Just what I need."

"Good. Let's go fishing next weekend. I'll clear my schedule for next Saturday." Rini had been working himself into the ground and needed a break.

"Perfect." With a smile of satisfaction he put the present in his pocket. With dark blond hair, good-looking Guido could have his pick of any woman. The money behind his family name made him sought after and somewhat cynical, as he feared no woman saw him for himself. Guido was the best friend Rini could ever have had. He hoped the only son of Leonides Rossano would end up one day with a woman worthy enough to win his heart.

Rini's name and wealth made him a target, too. Women came on to him, causing him to question if any of them loved him for himself. Coupled with his problem of infertility, Rini imagined it was possible he'd end up a bachelor for good.

"Was it a nice party?"

"Different. One of the big fashion houses asked Father for permission to film a show on the yacht. You missed the whole thing."

"Sorry about that. The meeting in Rome went longer than anticipated."

Rini followed him down the steps to the deck, where he greeted his friend's parents and family, who made up some of Naples's most elite socialites and were beautifully dressed. Rini was well acquainted with many of them. An orchestra played music and the drinks were flowing.

They moved over to the area where a smorgasbord had been set up. By now he was hungry. After filling his plate, he joined his friend at one of the tables away from the others, where they could eat and talk alone.

"Your text said you wanted advice. What's going on with you?"

Guido started to say something when his father broke in on them. Two attractive women with long hair he hadn't seen before were with him. Rini exchanged a glance with his friend, who looked annoyed at the interruption. They both got to their feet.

"Dea Loti and Daphne Butelli, may I present my son Guido and his best friend, Rinieri Montanari."

"How do you do," Rini said, eyeing both of them.

"You missed their show, Rini," the older man interjected.

"As I indicated earlier, I was unavoidably detained on business."

"Well, you're here now. They have to leave on the tender in a few minutes. Maybe you could give them a dance before they go?"

Guido's father never stopped hoping his son would meet the woman he couldn't live without. Rini knew his friend was upset at being railroaded, but agreed to the request. "It would be our pleasure."

He gravitated toward the woman closest to him, who was dressed in purple. After walking her over to the dance floor, he drew her in his arms. "I've never been to a fashion show before. I'm sorry I missed it."

"I doubt it's the kind of thing the CEO of Montanari's generally does on the weekend." By now Guido was dancing with the other model.

"I understand it's hard work. Did you have a chance to eat yet? We don't have to dance if you're hungry."

"Thank you, but no. I don't want anything. I have to watch my figure."

"Well, your discipline definitely shows."

She flashed him a beguiling smile. "Do you live in Naples?"

"No, but I work here."

It surprised him when her hands slid up his chest and around his neck. "Daphne and I are going to be in Naples one more night because of an afternoon show at the Grand Hotel Parker's, then we have another show in Rome. Perhaps we could get together tomorrow evening for dinner after the show?"

Her eyes stared up at him in unmistakable invitation.

"I'm afraid my plans are indefinite at the moment, but I've certainly enjoyed this dance with you."

She held her smile. "Well, if you straighten them out, call me around seven at the Grand Hotel Vesuvio, where I'm staying, and ask for Signorina Loti." In the next breath she planted a hungry kiss on his lips he hadn't been prepared for. Then she darted away.

Rini went back to the table to wait for Guido. In a few minutes his friend joined him. "Sorry my father did that to us." One eyebrow lifted. "After the kiss she gave you just now, are you going to see her again?"

"No." Her pushy style had put him off. "What about you?"

"Not interested. You know damn well Papà told her you're the most eligible bachelor in Italy, next to me, of course." He said it without mirth.

Rini shook his head.

Guido studied him. "Maybe she decided to try the direct approach to get beneath your armor."

"I'm afraid it didn't work."

An exasperated sigh escaped. "Papà doesn't know when to give up. In fact it's because of him I need to talk to you. I've made a decision to take a year off from the family business to invest in something I really want to do. He won't like it, but I want your opinion. Come on. Let's get a drink in the bar."

Rini followed him, wondering what was on his friend's mind.

After a dive with colleagues that produced no new finds, twenty-eight-year-old Alessandra Caracciolo returned home late Monday afternoon. Bruno Tozzi had left his scuba gear in the cruiser with hers and would come by for it in a day or two. Instinct told her he'd done it on purpose so he'd have an excuse to see her again.

Since their last dive, when Bruno had buddied her, he'd made it no secret that he wanted to be with her all the time, but she didn't have romantic feelings for him. Though she dove with him and their friends for their work, that had to be the extent of their relationship. The next time they were together, she would make it clear she wasn't interested and never could be.

She tied the boat to the dock of her family's private pier. Garbed in flip-flops and a man's long-sleeved shirt that she'd thrown over her blue-and-white polka-dotted bikini, she headed for the Land Rover with her duffel bag.

Once in the car, she drove on sand past the helipad and around to the front of the castle. When she reached it, she would take a shower and wash her hair. Alessandra wore it neck-length because she spent so much time in the water. It dried fast and the natural curl made it easy to take care of.

As she pulled up near the main entrance, she saw a limo parked in the courtyard, making her curious. All vehicles came across the causeway from the mainland at Metaponto, a port town of Basilicata, Italy. But after five o'clock, any visitors were escorted out by staff.

Their family's castle on the tiny island of Posso off the Ionian coast dated back to Queen Joanna of Naples, who ruled in 1343. Besides tourists from Bari and Taranto, who were allowed visits to the castle four hours a day on Tuesdays and Wednesdays with a guide, dignitaries from the world over called on her father, Count Onorato Caracciolo, asking favors because of his influence in the region.

Alessandra got out of the car and hurried inside past the tapestry of the queen hanging on the wall in the huge front foyer. She headed for the grand staircase, eager to make herself scarce until she'd cleaned up.

The moment she reached the first step, a deep male voice called to her. *"Signorina?"*

She whirled around to see a tall, incredibly gorgeous dark-haired man in a charcoal-colored business suit walking toward her, his dark brows furrowed. Still holding the duffel bag in one hand, Alessandra clutched the railing with the other.

He stared at her so strangely. "I thought I was hallucinating, but it *is* you. Since Saturday night you've cut your hair. I don't understand. How did you know I was coming here today? On the yacht you told me you had another show to do in Rome," he murmured.

The way his piercing black-brown eyes played over her face and figure, she knew he had a history with her identical twin, Dea. He was the most striking male Alessandra had ever seen in her life. She found herself envying her beautiful sister for having met him first and couldn't fault her taste. Men had never been able to resist her.

Alessandra cleared her throat. "I'm sorry, *signor*, but I'm not Dea."

Embarrassed to be caught looking so messy and disheveled after her diving trip, she ran up the steps without looking back. Her sister would never allow herself to be seen like this. All the way to the next floor she felt the man's penetrating eyes on her retreating back and bare legs, causing her to tremble.

Had her sister finally met the one she'd been looking for? Dea had always kept their family identity private. Because she was a model, she called herself Dea Loti so no one would know she was the daughter of Count

Caracciolo. For her to divulge her secret to this man meant their relationship must have turned serious, otherwise he wouldn't have known where she lived.

No doubt she'd invited him to come. Did she want the family to meet him? But his scrutiny of Alessandra led her to believe he hadn't looked pleased to see her here. Maybe Dea hadn't told him she had a twin. Alessandra didn't know what to think.

If only she hadn't arrived back from her dive trip until tomorrow, this wouldn't have happened and she wouldn't be haunted by that man's image engraved on her mind. It shocked her to realize that at long last there might be an important man in her sister's life. Alessandra knew her sister's quest had been to find the perfect man while she made the most of her modeling career. Their parents would be overjoyed.

Six years ago she and Dea had gone through a terrible experience involving a man, one Alessandra had hoped to marry. But when he met Dea, he fell for her and followed her to Rome. Their relationship didn't last, but the pain of betrayal had cut Alessandra like a knife and it had taken a long time to recover. Since the falling out with her sister, no man of importance had come into either of their lives.

In the last two years she'd tried to put the past behind her and get back the friendship they'd once shared. Dea came and went from home according to her hectic schedule and their family had enjoyed some good times. Evidently this past summer Dea had found romance after she'd gone back to Rome. Love on a yacht, no less… If that gorgeous man owned it, then he could keep her in the lifestyle she desired.

But for some reason Alessandra had been oddly upset by the encounter in the foyer, unable to understand why. *Except that she really could*… These days her own love life was nonexistent.

Once inside the bedroom, Alessandra plopped the duffel bag on the floor and got out of her clothes. Her mind was still on Dea, whom she hadn't seen for six weeks. Her sister had developed an interest in fashion and modeling at an early age and that hadn't changed.

Alessandra led a different life altogether. She couldn't remember when she didn't have an interest in the archaeology of this region of Italy. The island castle itself was built on an ancient archaeological site. Since college she'd been involved in several multidisciplinary studies in the field of archaeology within a Mediterranean perspective, with particular emphasis on Southern Italy.

Without being able to scuba dive, she could never have achieved her dream to do the necessary underwater work with friends she'd made among the archaeological staff at the University of Catania. Scuba diving wasn't for everyone. Dea couldn't understand her passion for it, but it didn't matter because their parents approved and supported both her and Dea in their individual endeavors.

After a shower and shampoo, she blow-dried her hair, then dressed in pleated tan pants and an ivory-colored linen blouse. With an application of coral frost lipstick, she left the room on khaki wedgies and went in search of her parents. They'd married for love and were very close. Unlike many couples, they did everything together whether it was for business or pleasure. Though Alessandra had never discussed it with Dea, their parents' happy marriage had been the ultimate role model for both sisters.

On the way to their apartment she saw Liona, the wiry housekeeper who'd come to work for them at eighteen and had been with them ever since. She was like another member of the family and ran the large staff with precision.

"If you're looking for your *mamma,* she left for Taranto two days ago to help your aunt, who fell and broke her hip."

"Oh, no! Poor Fulvia."

"She'll be all right, but your mother will probably be gone for a few more days."

"I need to call them."

They started down the staircase together. "I'm glad you're back. You know how your father worries."

Liona was the one who worried about Alessandra. She thought scuba diving was dangerous. Alessandra gave her a hug. "It's good to see you. How's Alfredo?" Liona's cat had been sick.

"The vet says he's getting old and shouldn't go up and down stairs."

"I'll help carry him for you."

"Bless you. Did you have any luck on this last diving trip?"

"I wish."

"Oh, well. Another time. Are you hungry? I'll tell the cook."

"Please don't bother her. I'll find something to eat later. Thanks, Liona."

She hurried toward her father's office, wondering if the male visitor was still with him, then scoffed with impatience because the man was on her mind at all.

"Ciao, Papà."

"Alessandra!" Her grayish blond father stood up from his desk and hugged her. "You were gone too long this time."

"It was only a week."

"We always miss you. Did you have a good time?"

"Yes, even if we didn't find anything of significance." She walked around to sit in one of the leather chairs facing his desk. "I'd much rather know about you and mom. Liona told me Zia Fulvia broke her hip and Mom went to Taranto to help her."

He nodded. "Your aunt will make a full recovery. Your mother could be back tomorrow."

"Oh, good. So tell me what else has been happening while I've been away."

His brows lifted. "Something unexpected. I'm glad you're back so we can talk. More than anyone else I want your input because you have a fine mind."

"I got it from you and Mamma." Her comment produced a chuckle. So maybe her assumption had been right. "It wouldn't have anything to do with the man I saw in the foyer earlier this evening, would it?"

He cocked his head. "Actually it would. When did you see him?"

"I'd just come in the castle when he spoke to me."

"Did he introduce himself to you?"

"No. It wasn't like that. On my way up the staircase he mistook me for Dea before he headed for your office, that's all."

Her father nodded. "I guess I shouldn't be surprised. Her face is everywhere."

"Papà—" She smiled at him. "Are you pretending with me?"

"About what?"

"Was he here because of her?"

The count blinked. "Not that I know of."

"Oh." She needed to keep her thoughts to herself. "Who is he?"

He smiled. "If you didn't live in your world of books and ancient underwater artifacts, you would have recognized him as the CEO of Italy's most powerful engineering dynasty, Rinieri Montanari."

She stirred in the chair. "Of course I recognize the Montanari name. Who wouldn't?" It explained the man's aura of authority.

Her father sat back and touched the tips of his fingers together. "His family has accumulated great wealth. He's the brilliant one driving the company to new heights. A week ago he made an appointment to come and see me about a business proposition."

"That sounds interesting."

"I'll give you a little background. Night before last he was on the news following the European Congress of Businessmen held in Rome. I saw the gleam in his eyes. He said he had secret plans to grow the economy.

Today we talked and arranged for him to come back tomorrow to get into the details."

He'd aroused her curiosity. "What is he after?"

"He'd like to drill for oil on our property."

Alessandra shifted in the chair. "He and dozens of others who've wanted the same thing for the last half century," she muttered. "Since he knows it's not for sale, why is he coming back?"

"This man is different from all the others. He wants to lease the land."

Lease? "Are you considering letting him?"

"I'm thinking about it."

"Wow."

Her father eyed her curiously. "Why do you say that?"

"I thought our property was inviolate."

"Leasing isn't the same thing as selling."

"You're right."

"Alessandra, something's on your mind. Why did you ask if he was here because of Dea? Has your sister confided in you about him?"

"No, Papà. In fact I haven't spoken to her for almost two months."

"Hmm. If he'd met her before, he didn't mention anything about meeting her to me."

"Why would he if he didn't know anything about our family?"

"But what if he does know? It makes me wonder what came first, the chicken or the egg?"

"What do you mean?"

"He might have met Dea before he ever called me."

Alessandra was trying to understand what her father was getting at. "Why is this troubling you so much?"

"I'm your loving *papà*. My daughters were born princesses of the Houses of Taranto and Caracciolo. Because of our family history, you know I've always wanted to protect you from unscrupulous men."

His explanation surprised her. "That sounds like medieval thinking. Papà, you don't honestly think the CEO of Montanari Engineering fits in that category?" *That gorgeous man? The one she'd envied Dea for meeting first?* Alessandra didn't want to believe it. Something about him had impressed her deeply.

"Though we don't use the titles anymore, there are some men who try to calculate the monetary worth of our family. There's nothing they would like more than to acquire your bank accounts and assets more than your love."

Alessandra frowned. "The man comes from his own family dynasty and doesn't need more."

"One would assume as much, but for some men one dynasty isn't enough." His gaze swerved to hers. "I don't want to think it. But if he has targeted Dea to marry her and eventually gain possession of our property, I don't like the thought of it."

She didn't like it, either. Not at all. "Personally I don't believe it." Alessandra didn't want to believe it. Not about that man. Whatever history her sister and Signor Montanari might have together, she didn't want to think about it. To be with a man like him...

Alessandra got to her feet. "Don't let it bother you, Papà. Have you had dinner yet?"

"No."

"I'll bring you something."

"*Grazie*, but I'm not hungry."

"I'm afraid I am. I haven't eaten since I got back. Excuse me while I grab a sandwich. If you want me, I'll be in the library."

Alessandra left the office and headed for the kitchen to find something to eat. Afterward she walked to the castle library on the main floor, the repository of their family history where she could be alone. Years earlier she'd turned one corner of it into her own office, complete with file cabinets and a state-of-the-art computer and printer, plus a large-screen television for viewing the many videos she'd compiled. This had been her inner sanctum for years.

She sat down at the desk and got back to work on the book she was writing about Queen Joanna. Just as she'd settled down to get busy, the phone rang. It was her father.

"Papà?"

"I just wanted to let you know I've got business in Metaponto. The pilot is flying me in a few minutes."

"Do you want company? I'll go with you."

"Not tonight, *piccola*." Her father's endearment for her. When Alessandra was born, she was the younger twin by three minutes and the name *little one* stuck. "I'm sure you're tired after your scuba-diving trip, so you get some sleep and we'll talk in the morning. I could be gone a couple of hours and will probably get back late tonight."

"All right."

While she got back to work she heard her father's helicopter fly away. She kept busy for another hour, then went upstairs to get ready for bed. But when she slid under the covers, she didn't fall asleep right away. Memories of the past with her sister filtered through her mind.

Though their personalities were entirely different, she and Dea had been as close as any two sisters until college, when Francesco had come into Alessandra's life. She'd fallen in love and they talked about getting married. But before they got engaged he met Dea, who was more confident than Alessandra and had already started her modeling career.

Her sister had a beauty and lovability that had drawn guys to her from her teens. By contrast, Alessandra felt rather dull and unexciting. Certainly she wasn't as attractive. But she'd always accepted those truths and never let them affect their friendship. Not until Francesco had laid eyes on Dea. From that moment everything changed. Alessandra felt herself lose him and there wasn't anything she could do about it.

He followed her sister to Rome and she never saw him again. Francesco sent Alessandra a letter explaining he couldn't help falling in love with Dea and hoped she wouldn't hate him too badly. As for Dea, Alessandra didn't see her for two months. When her sister came home, she told Alessandra she was sorry for what had happened. She explained that Francesco had done all the running, and she'd soon found out he was a loser. Alessandra was lucky to be out of the relationship.

The trauma of being betrayed by Francesco and her

sister had completely floored her. It had taken a long time to work past the pain. Though they'd shared sisterly love in the past, from that time on they'd had a troubled relationship and two truths emerged. Alessandra didn't know if she could trust a man again and Dea would always be the beautiful one who usually got the best of Alessandra. People seemed to love her the most.

Alessandra had to live with the knowledge that she was known as the clever one, a scholar with a sense of adventure. She'd thought that by the age of twenty-eight she would have finally gotten past her jealousy of Dea's ability to attract men. But it wasn't true. Otherwise meeting Signor Montanari, who'd met Dea first, wouldn't have disturbed Alessandra so much.

If her father was right, what a sad irony that this man might be using Dea to get what he really wanted, making both sisters appear as poor judges of character. First the chef Alessandra had fallen for who couldn't remain faithful once he'd laid eyes on Dea. Now Signor Montanari, who looked like the embodiment of a woman's dreams. But what if her father learned this man had a secret agenda? The troubling thought kept her tossing and turning all night.

CHAPTER TWO

ON TUESDAY MORNING Alessandra awakened and headed to the bathroom for a quick shower. She dressed in jeans and a blouse. After brushing her hair and applying lipstick, she walked down the hall past the stairs to her parents' apartment wearing her sandals.

She knocked on the door with no result, so she opened it and called out, "Papà?" He was probably in the sitting room drinking coffee while he read his newspapers, but the room was empty. Frowning, she retraced her steps to the staircase and hurried downstairs to the small dining room where the family ate breakfast. Maybe she'd find her father there.

The second she opened the doors, she received a shock. Her sister stood at the antique huntboard pouring herself a cup of coffee.

"Dea! What a surprise! It's good to see you!" She looked beautiful as usual in a stunning blue dress and high heels. Alessandra rushed over to hug her. "Where's Papà?"

"In the office."

"I didn't know you were coming home." She reached for a glass of juice and a roll.

"Neither did I until I got a phone call from him last night."

"You did?" That was news to Alessandra. He must have called her on his way to Metaponto.

Dea's eyes darted to her without warmth. "He told me Rinieri Montanari had come to the castle to do business with him and wanted to know if I had been dating him. He seemed concerned enough that I decided to make a quick trip home to talk to him about it."

"He's always trying to protect us, you know that."

They both sat down at the banquet-size table. "What I'm curious about is how *you* know Rinieri Montanari." The tone of her sister's point-blank question had an edge. There had to be another reason her sister had made a sudden flight home. Alessandra didn't begin to understand what was going on.

"I don't! Didn't Papà tell you? Signor Montanari was in the foyer when I came in from my scuba-diving trip yesterday. As I started up the staircase he called out to me. I had no idea who he was. He thought I was you."

"Did he say anything else?"

"Only that he acted surprised you were here at the castle and commented that you'd cut your hair since he'd been with you on the yacht. He said you'd told him you had another show to do in Rome. I took it that's why he seemed shocked to find you here. I told him I wasn't you, then I went up the staircase. That's it."

Dea sipped her coffee slowly. "So he mentioned the yacht."

"Yes."

She could hear her sister's mind working. "Is that *all* he told you?"

Dea sounded so worried, Alessandra was perplexed. "I swear it."

Her sister's mouth tightened.

"Have you worked this out with Papà?"

She put down her empty cup. "Not yet, but I will when we fly back to Metaponto in a few minutes."

"But you just got here last night!"

"I have to return to Rome for another show. As soon as Papà finishes up business with Signor Montanari, he's flying me to the airport." She checked her watch. "They've been together for the last half hour."

With nothing more forthcoming, Alessandra knew she'd been dismissed and rose to her feet, feeling chilled. "Then I'll say goodbye to you now." She leaned over to kiss her cheek.

Until Alessandra could talk to her father alone, she would have to wait to know what had gone on. Dea was going back to Rome without clarifying anything about her relationship with Rinieri Montanari. In fact she hadn't been this cold to Alessandra in a long time.

She left the dining room without saying anything and rushed down the hallway to the library, where she could get to work.

When her phone rang two hours later, she saw that it was her father and clicked on. "Papà? Where are you?"

"At the airport in Metaponto, waiting for your mother. She's flying in from Taranto."

Thank goodness. Alessandra needed to talk to her. "Has Dea gone back to Rome?"

"After our talk this morning I put her on the plane."

"You sound more calmed down. Is everything okay?"

"There was a misunderstanding that was all my fault, but I've spoken with Signor Montanari and it's been cleared up."

Except that Alessandra still knew next to nothing. She gripped her phone tighter. "I'm relieved for that. How did Dea seem? She was chilly with me."

"That's because I upset her. After I apologized for minding her business, I explained it was my way of being protective to prevent her from being hurt in case Signor Montanari wasn't being sincere. You did absolutely nothing wrong, so don't worry about it. Now the main reason for my call. Do you have plans for the rest of the day?"

"I'm working on my book."

"Would you have time to do me a favor?"

"Of course."

"Signor Montanari is going to be our guest for the next few days."

What? Alessandra almost fell out of her chair. The change in his attitude toward the other man was astounding.

"He needs someone knowledgeable to show him around today. Since I don't know how long I'm going to be gone, you're the only one I trust to drive him and answer his questions. Your work with the institute has given you vital insight into the importance of any changes or disturbances to the environment here in the south. Will you do it?"

His compliment warmed her heart, but it was already getting a workout because it meant she would be spending time with a man whose name was renowned throughout Italy. Her father had yet to explain what he'd found out about Dea's relationship with Signor Montanari.

"Yes." But Alessandra was so attracted to him, she would have to be careful it didn't show. No way would she give her sister a reason to suspect her of coming on to him when she'd met him first.

"Get him back in time, *piccola*. I've asked him to join us for dinner. Liona has put him in the guest apartment on the third floor. He's probably eating lunch right now. Your mother's plane is arriving so I have to get off the phone. *A piu tarde, figlia mia*."

Rini had just finished a second cup of coffee when the beautiful woman he'd seen yesterday on the stairs walked in the dining room. He should have realized right away that she wasn't quite as slender as Dea, but he preferred her curves. "Signor Montanari? I'm sorry if I've kept you waiting. I'm Alessandra." She sounded slightly out of breath and looked flushed.

Earlier in the morning, after the count had asked him about his relationship with Dea, he'd left the castle for the airport. Rini thought it odd to be questioned about her, but he let it go.

At that point the count said that while he was gone, his daughter Alessandra would give him a tour of the property. According to him, she understood the impact of drilling on the environment better than anyone else and he would be in the best of hands. If she was an engineer, Rini had yet to find out.

He got up from the table. "We meet again. I've never met identical twins before."

"Dea's the older sister by three minutes."

"Which accounts for the difference," he teased. "I can see that." He smiled and walked toward her. "Call me Rini."

After a slight hesitation she shook the hand he extended. "*Benvenuto a Posso*, Rini. Papà told me you'd be our guest for a few days and asked me to show you around today."

"That's very kind of you, but I don't want to inconvenience you." He couldn't read her thoughts.

"It's all right. Papà said this was important."

She'd dressed in a simple short-sleeved peach top and jeans. Her tanned olive skin indicated she spent a lot of time in the sun. His gaze traveled from her cognac-brown eyes to her neck-length slightly tousled brown hair rippled through with golden highlights.

As she pulled her hand away, he noticed she didn't wear nail polish. The reason she looked so natural was her lack of makeup. Except that she did wear lipstick, a coral color that blended with the golden tone of her skin and drew his attention to her voluptuous mouth.

He remembered Dea's mouth being sculpted the same way before she'd kissed him. How remarkable that identical twins could look so much alike, yet on closer inspection were so different.

"Your father said you're the one who knows everything."

"Oh, dear. I hope he really didn't say it like that."

Rini got the idea he'd embarrassed her. "He meant it as a compliment."

"I'm his daughter so he has to say it," she commented in a self-deprecating manner. "If you're ready, we can go now."

"Please lead the way."

He followed her ultrafeminine figure out of the castle to a Land Rover parked near the main doors. Rini had done his homework. Her island home was renowned as an Italian treasure. What a coincidence the castle was home to both women!

Before Rini could credit it, she climbed in the driver's seat. "You'll need to move the seat back all the way to accommodate your legs," she said after he opened the passenger door.

One corner of his mouth lifted as hc did her bidding and climbed in. They attached their seat belts and she took off across the causeway to the mainland. She drove with expertise, as if she could do it blindfolded. After leaving the small town of Metaponto, they headed for verdant hills that were covered in ancient olive groves.

"My father explained why you're here. Now that we're on Caracciolo property, tell me why the CEO of Montanari Engineering wants to lease this particular piece of property in order to drill. A lease means taking on a lot of controls." She didn't mince words and was all business.

"Your land may not be for sale, but a lease means compromise that benefits both parties and could be lucrative." Rini looked out over the mountainous, sparsely populated province of Basilicata. "Hidden in the arch of Italy's agricultural boot is the home to Europe's biggest on-shore oil field."

"That's what I've heard."

"Italy produces one hundred and twelve thousand barrels a day, one tenth the North Sea's level. My goal is to double Italian oil production within the next five years. If not on your land, then I'll find others because as you know, the south is underdeveloped."

"Your goals are very ambitious."

"Agreed, but the potential of this particular untapped oil field is huge. We're hoping to drill for the billion-plus barrels of crude oil that lie beneath it. Your father and I are hammering out ideas to preserve the existing environment while drilling for oil to boost the suffering Italian economy."

"You sound like a politician."

"Everyone should be concerned over our country's unemployment problems. I'm particularly anxious for us to bring down the country's twelve-percent jobless rate through new employment. The goal will be to obtain oil, yet maintain sustainable development of agriculture that will offer real career paths for the future."

"I have to admit you make a good case." She kept driving to the top of a ridge that overlooked the huge valley. Onorato Caracciolo was a clever man to send Rini out with his daughter first. Rini had a hunch it would be a smart idea to win her over to his idea since her father appeared to place great trust in her knowledge and intelligence. But after the misunderstanding involving his other daughter, he needed to walk carefully.

"If you wouldn't mind stopping, I'd like to get out and look around."

She pulled off the road and turned off the engine. While he walked a ways, she climbed down and rested one curving hip against the front fender to wait for him. When he returned she said, "I know you see oil beneath the property. But what I see is a fertile field that has been here for centuries. Your plan would create giant, unsightly scabs."

His eyes narrowed on the features of her beautiful oval bone structure. "If you're imagining dozens of derricks, you'd be wrong. My gut instinct is to build several right here in the shadow of the mountain out of sight. The existing road to the south travels straight to the sea, where the oil would be transported to tankers. One would barely be aware of the activity."

"And if you find it, does that mean more derricks?"

"We'll make that decision later."

Her softly rounded chin lifted. "What if you don't discover any?"

"Preliminary reports from this part of Italy indicate vast reserves. We'll find it, but we'll proceed slowly with your father having the final say in how long we are allowed to drill. Let me ask you a question."

"Go ahead."

"If I were to appeal to Queen Joanna herself and explain the benefits, what do you propose she would say? Forget how long ago she ruled. Your father tells me you're a historian writing a biography on her. Your research means you know her better than any other living person today. Was she a risk taker?"

He could hear her mind working.

"She backed Antipope Clement VII against the un-popular Urban VI. For that she was given this papally owned land eventually bequeathed to our family. So yes, I'd say she was a risk taker."

Rini's lips twitched—he was fascinated by the knowledge inside her brain. "You think she would have granted me an audience?"

She stared at him. "I have no idea."

"Humor me and put yourself in Joanna's place."

A smile broke the corners of her mouth he found more and more enticing. "It was a man's world. I wouldn't have trusted any of them. You, particularly, wouldn't have been given a second audience."

"Why single me out?"

"Because you're handsome as the devil, increasing the odds of Joanna being tricked. Give me a little more time to think about your ideas that have persuaded my father to give you a hearing."

"You mean you're not tossing me out on my ear just yet?"

She opened the driver's door. "Of course not. That's for Papà to do." On that note she climbed in and started the engine.

He went around to the other side, glad to hear she wasn't shutting him down yet. "In that case, let's take the road that leads to the sea. En route you can tell me more about the subject of your future best seller."

"I'd rather you gave me more reasons why you think this project of yours outweighs the many negatives. My father will want a report to run by my mother and her sister, Fulvia. The property comes through my father's line, but he always leans heavily on the opinions of his wife and sister-in-law."

"Who makes the ultimate decisions?"

"When it comes to business, the three of them go back and forth until there's a consensus."

"He's a man surrounded by women."

She smiled. "As my Aunt Fulvia says, behind every successful man *is* a more successful woman."

Food for thought. "Do your parents love each other?"

"Very much."

"That's nice. Before my mother died, my parents had the same kind of relationship."

"I'm sorry for your loss. It sounds like you've been lucky to have great parents too," she murmured on a sincere note as they started down into the valley. "What does *your* father think of this latest idea of yours?"

"Though he and I are always in consultation over business, this is one time when he doesn't know where I am, or why." He angled his head toward her lovely profile. "I've taken this time to do reconnaissance work on my own. I told no one where I was going, not even my best friend. That's why I was so surprised when I thought you were Dea. I couldn't figure out how you could have known my destination."

She darted him a questioning glance. "So it really was pure coincidence that you had business with our father?"

"I was introduced to her as Dea Loti. But the misunderstanding has been cleared up. The simple fact is, I thought you were she. But I shouldn't have called out to you before I'd met with your father for an explanation, then none of this would have happened. To be honest, I wasn't ready for you to disappear on me the way you did."

Her pulse sped up. *Did he just say what she thought he said?*

"I was a mess and hoped no one would see me sneak in the castle."

"Not from where I was standing."

She swallowed hard and appeared to grip the wheel tighter. "When Dea and I were younger, we got taken for each other a lot. Not so much now that she's become a top fashion model. She's the true beauty. I've always believed I looked different even though we're identical. But I'm aware other people can't always tell the difference. Under the circumstances I understand why my shorter hair gave you a shock."

Not just her hair. As he was coming to learn, many things about her were different from her sister and other women. She was so genuine and charming, it knocked him sideways. "Your hair is attractive and suits you."

"Thank you."

"I can see why your father wants to protect you." Rini decided not to argue the point further when her physical beauty was self-evident. But Alessandra Caracciolo had been born a twin and he'd heard it could be a blessing and a curse, so he left it alone.

They'd reached a crossroads that would take them back to Metaponto and the causeway, but Rini wasn't ready to go home yet. To his surprise he found he wanted to get to know her better. *Much better.* Besides her intelligence, she spoke her mind and was like a breath of fresh air. "Do you have time to drive us along the coast? I want to inspect the shipping access."

"We could do that, but if you want to get a real feel, you should view everything by boat."

That idea sounded much better. "When we reach Metaponto, let's find a marina where I can charter one for tomorrow."

"You don't need to do that. I'm sure my father will want to take you out on our cruiser so you can talk business."

"Then let me buy you dinner in town in order to repay you for driving me around today."

"Thank you, but that's not necessary. My parents are expecting you to eat with them and I have plans after we get back."

He had no right to be disappointed that she'd just turned him down. She was probably involved in a relationship right now. Why not? She was a stunning woman. He imagined that men flocked to her.

After having shown him around the property for her father, she'd done her duty and had other things to do. Though it was none of his business, for some odd reason the possibility of her being interested in another man didn't sit well with him.

Wednesday morning Alessandra was just getting out of the shower when her phone rang. She reached for her cell and checked the caller ID. "Mamma?"

"*Buongiorno,* darling."

"I'm so glad you're back home. How's Zia Fulvia?"

"I thought she was better. That's why I came home yesterday. But after your father and I finished having dinner with Signor Montanari last evening, we got a call from her. She's having a bad reaction to her new pain medication and it has frightened her. I told her we'd fly to see her this morning. Your father and I are on our way to the airport and will stay with her for another night to watch over her."

"I can't believe you've already gone," Alessandra said in surprise. "I haven't even seen you yet." She needed to talk to her.

"I know. Where did you disappear to last evening? I expected you to join us for dinner."

"I'm behind on my book. After I brought Signor Montanari back to the castle, I went straight to the library to work."

Before Signor Montanari's explanation about Dea, Alessandra had tried hard to hide her attraction to him. But once she knew he and her sister were not involved and never had been, the news had thrilled her so much, she might have given herself away if she'd gone to dinner with him.

"I'm sorry we missed you, darling. I want to hear all about your scuba-diving trip, but it will have to wait another day." Alessandra had already forgotten about that. "Your aunt is really distressed."

"The poor thing. Give her my love and tell her I'll visit her soon."

"She'll love that. By the way, your father wants to know if you would be willing to show Signor Montanari around again? Today he wants to explore the coast by boat. Would you take him out on the cruiser?"

She sucked in her breath. "First let me ask you a question, Mom. What do you think about his idea to lease the property for drilling?"

"To be honest, I don't like the idea at all."

"I didn't think so."

"It seems a travesty to change anything about the land or what lies beneath it. Your father knows how I feel. Though your father believes Signor Montanari's ideas have merit, I'm not persuaded. There's a great deal to discuss before anything is decided."

"It sounds like Papà doesn't feel as strongly as you."

"Let's put it this way. He likes Signor Montanari's vision and is willing to hear more. What's your opinion?"

"He talked a lot about bolstering the economy by providing more jobs. My suspicion is that he's hoping to run for a high-level government position and this could be the feather in his cap."

"He's a brilliant man. That's what brilliant men do." *But not with Caracciolo land.* That's what her mother was really saying. The time Alessandra had spent with him yesterday had persuaded her he was worth listening to, but these were early days. "Alessandra? What's wrong? You don't sound yourself."

"I just wish I hadn't brought Dea into the conversation when I was talking with Papà. He ended up phoning her."

"Your father told me what happened. But when he learned that Signor Montanari had been a guest of Leonides Rossano on his yacht the other night and happened to get introduced to Dea, your father realized he'd made something out of nothing and overreacted. It certainly didn't have anything to do with you."

"But I didn't know the truth until Signor Montanari told me as much while I was driving him around."

"I'm sorry. It's understandable you thought he and your sister were involved."

"I didn't know. When I saw Dea at breakfast yesterday, she didn't explain anything."

"Well he made it clear to your father that meeting Dea was like ships passing in the night."

"But maybe Dea had hopes it could be more." Already Alessandra knew a man like Rinieri Montanari only came along once in a lifetime. She and Dea weren't twins for nothing.

"Why do you say that?"

"If their chance meeting had been so insignificant, how come she flew home last night?"

"Because your father was worried."

"He was," she conceded. "But she didn't even come in my room to talk to me."

"Alessandra—during dinner I got the impression that the CEO of Montanari Engineering is a force to contend with. If he'd been interested in your sister, he would have made future plans to let her know how he felt."

"You're right, but what if she finds out I'm showing him around?"

"What if she does?" After a silence, she asked, "You're attracted to him, aren't you? Otherwise you wouldn't think twice about this. There's nothing wrong with that! I'll admit my heart skipped several beats when I met him at dinner last night."

Her mother's instincts were never wrong.

"He said he truly enjoyed being shown around by you. I could tell he meant it. Don't blow up a simple misunderstanding your father has apologized for into something major."

"You're right. I'm being foolish."

"You are. Go ahead and show Signor Montanari around until we get back from Taranto. I'll call you tonight."

"Okay. Love you. Give Zia Fulvia a hug from me."

Alessandra hung up, realizing she was transparent to her mother, who understood the situation completely. She felt better after their talk. The longing to be with Signor Montanari again was all she could think about.

She pulled on a pair of pleated khaki pants and a blouse with a small tan-on-white geometric print. Once dressed, she went downstairs to the kitchen for coffee and a roll. The cook made her some eggs. While she ate, Liona poked her head in the door. "Alessandra? Did you see Alfredo when you came down the stairs?"

"No."

"He ate his food, but now I can't find him. He usually stays on the main floor while I'm working around. Maybe he's gone off sick somewhere."

"I'll look for him." She ate a last bite, thanked the cook, then began a search, wondering if Signor Montanari was around. "Alfredo—" She called his name several times. When she reached the front foyer, she worried that he'd slipped past some visitor at the entrance.

She opened the door and almost ran into the gorgeous man who'd haunted her dreams. He was just coming in. The sight of him made her heart leap. He held the big marmalade cat in his arms.

"*Buongiorno*, Alessandra," he said with a white smile. "I've been waiting for a limo and found him lying outside the door wanting to get back in."

"Liona will be so relieved. Here. I'll carry him to the kitchen."

"I'll be happy to do it."

"I don't mind."

She could tell he didn't want to give up the cat, who seemed perfectly happy to be held by him. It surprised her because Alfredo didn't like many people. "Then follow me." She opened the door and showed him the way.

Liona was thrilled to see them walk in the kitchen. The housekeeper reached for her cat.

"He found Alfredo outside the castle," Alessandra explained.

"The poor thing is getting confused. I'll take him back to my apartment. *Grazie, signor.*"

"*Prego, signora.*"

Alessandra trailed him out of the kitchen. "That was very nice of you. Her cat is getting old." She followed him to the entrance, but there was no sign of a limo yet, only three tour buses bringing tourists to tour the part of the castle open to the public. "I hope the driver didn't already come and leave."

"I'll call to find out." He reached in his jeans pocket.

Her eyes traveled over his rock-hard body. His blue crewneck shirt had the kind of short sleeves that only looked good on a man with a well-defined physique. In a minute he clicked off. "It'll be a while due to an accident near the causeway."

"What were your plans?"

His veiled gaze slid to hers. "To charter a boat."

"There's no need to do that," she said on impulse. "Since my father isn't here to take you, he suggested I drive you where you want to go in our cruiser."

"But that means interrupting your work."

"It's all right. As Papà reminded me, you're a busy man. Since you're here, you need to make the most of the time. I'll do my own work later." The talk with Alessandra's mother had taken away the guilt she'd been harboring over Dea. There was nothing she wanted more than to spend more time with him.

"Then I'll call off the limo."

"While you do that, I have to run in and get a few things. I'll meet you at the Land Rover in five minutes."

Alessandra hurried inside and up the staircase to her room. Her heart raced abnormally hard to think they were going out on the boat together. She filled her duffel bag with some necessary items, then rushed back down to the kitchen and stashed water and snacks in the top of it. She never knew how long she'd be gone, so she never left without being prepared.

When she walked out to the car beneath a semi-cloudy sky, she found him waiting for her with his own backpack. It had been years since she'd felt this alive around a man. This time when she unlocked the door with the remote, he opened her door and relieved her of her duffel bag so she could get in. He walked on around and put their things in the back before climbing inside.

"Our cruiser is docked on the other side of the island." She started the engine and drove them the short distance.

"It's right in your backyard!"

She smiled. "I know. Can you believe how convenient?"

Once she'd pulled up to the pier, they both got out. He obviously knew his way around a boat. After depositing their bags, he undid the ropes while she got on board and found them both life preservers. She put hers on first.

"Who's the scuba enthusiast?"

"You're looking at her."

His piercing dark brown eyes scrutinized her. "How long have you been a diver?"

"Since I was nineteen. Have you ever done it?"

"I learned at fourteen. It's probably my favorite activity."

His admission excited her no end. To scuba dive with him would be like a dream come true. "Mine, too," she admitted. "Excuse me for a minute."

She disappeared below and pulled out a special oceanography chart of the area for him to look at. When she came up on deck she discovered he'd climbed on board and had put on his preserver. "Here." She put the rolled-up chart on the banquette next to him. "You can look at this as we proceed." Alessandra started the engine at a wakeless speed and drove them toward open water.

"This cruiser is state of the art."

She nodded. "A huge change from our old boat I took everywhere until my father bought this for me so I could go on longer trips."

"For pleasure?"

"It's always a pleasure, but I'm part of a team working for the Institute of Archaeological and Monumental Heritage."

Her response seemed to surprise him. "Where did you go to college?"

"I received my master's degree from the University of Catania. Our job is to identify and retrieve buried structures of archaeological interest."

"Living on an archaeological wonder, you come by your interest naturally."

She nodded. "My area of academics is to study the advanced techniques for nondestructive testing and remote sensing. Hopefully our work will expand our knowledge and help restore the historical buildings above and below the water in this area of Italy."

He sat on the banquette across from her with his hands clasped between his knees. She felt his eyes probing her with new interest. "It's no wonder your father told me I would be in good hands with you. You're an archaeologist. I thought maybe you were an engineer.

"Your father knew that you're exactly the person I need to consult while I'm here. Like you, I'm anxious to identify where the drilling will cause the least amount of destruction to the environment, both on land and water."

"Tell you what. After I give you a tour of the coastline, we'll go to my office at the castle. Since you're an engineer, you can watch a series of videos we've produced that will open your eyes to the many roadblocks you'll have to consider in order to drill and transport oil."

"I'm indebted to you, Alessandra."

"You have no idea what kinds of snags you're up against, so don't get too excited, *signore.*"

"Call me Rini," he urged for a second time in his deep male voice that affected her insides. "I like snags. They make life exciting."

Though she agreed with him, she needed to be careful not to let this man get under her skin. Alessandra had a hunch he wasn't just talking about the search for oil. He had a way of infiltrating her defenses no matter where she turned. She had a feeling that if she got involved with him, he had the power to hurt her in ways that she would never get over.

"Why don't you consult the map I brought up? It will explain a lot as we go."

As they cruised along the coast, she glimpsed a half smile that broke the corner of his compelling mouth before he did her bidding and unraveled it for his perusal. He was such a breathtaking man, she could hardly concentrate.

It was hard to believe he wanted to be with her and not Dea. For some reason Rini Montanari hadn't been interested in her sister. She couldn't comprehend it.

Probably Dea hadn't been able to comprehend it, either. But Alessandra didn't know what went on in her sister's mind and would be a fool to make any more assumptions about anything.

Just be excited that he wants to be with you, Alessandra.

CHAPTER THREE

By five in the afternoon Rini had seen as much as he needed for a preliminary assessment. Alessandra had been a fountain of knowledge. Depending on Onorato's willingness to continue their talks, he wanted to bring out a team from the Naples office to begin an in-depth exploration.

But at this point business wasn't on his mind. During their outing he'd grown hungry. She'd brought along water and snacks, but he wanted a big dinner and intended to surprise her by taking her out for a meal. He'd seen a helipad at the side of the castle and went below deck to call for a helicopter.

With her expertise she guided the boat to the pier and shut off the engine. He discarded the life preserver and jumped to the dock to tie the ropes. In a moment the rotors of the helicopter sounded overhead.

Alessandra looked up. "I guess my parents are back. That's a surprise. Mother told me they could be gone for several days." She removed her preserver.

"I think that's *my* helicopter."

She blinked. "You sent for yours?" Did he see disappointment in her eyes?

"I chartered one to take us to dinner. Last night you turned me down. Tonight I decided not to take any chances on another rejection."

Her eyes slid away from his. "Where are we going?"

Good. She'd decided not to fight him. "That's my surprise. Bring what you need and leave the rest in the boat. We'll retrieve everything later."

"You don't want to change clothes?"

"There's no need."

She nodded. "I'll only be a moment." Before long she came back up on deck having applied a fresh coat of lipstick.

Avoiding his help, she climbed out of the boat and they made their way to the helicopter in the distance. But she couldn't refuse him when he opened the door to assist her into the back. Their arms brushed and he inhaled her light, flowery fragrance, which made him more aware of her.

Within seconds they lifted off and the pilot flew them due east. For the next little while her gaze fastened on the landscape below. When they started their descent to the city of a hundred thousand, she darted Rini an excited glance. "I love Lecce! It's a masterpiece of baroque architecture."

"I haven't been here in several years, but I remember a restaurant near the cathedral and hope it's still as good."

He'd arranged for a limo to drive them into the city nicknamed the Florence of the South. They got out and started walking along the narrow, shop-lined streets to the square for their dinner.

Lots of tourists, plus music from the many eating

places, put him in a holiday spirit, something he hadn't felt in years. Alessandra stopped in front of every shop and boutique, all of which were made from the soft local limestone. The facades were a mass of cherubs. She delighted in their faces as well as the displays. He hadn't felt this carefree in years.

"Oh, Rini. Look at that precious cat! It reminds me of Alfredo." They'd stopped in front of a souvenir shop selling the famous *Cartapesta* items of saints and animals made out of papier-mâché and painted.

"I think you're right. Let's buy it for your housekeeper." Without waiting for a response, he lifted the three-inch orange crouching cat from the shelf and walked inside to pay for it. The clerk put it in a sack. When he exited the shop, Alessandra stared up at him.

"She'll be thrilled."

He handed her the gift. "Will you keep it until we get back to the castle?"

"That was very kind of you," she said in a quiet voice. After sliding it in her purse, they walked out to the square.

"If my memory serves me correctly, our restaurant is on the right, halfway down the colonnade. We'll eat what they bring us. There's no menu." After the call to arrange for the helicopter, he made a reservation at the famous restaurant. When they reached it, the maître d' showed them inside to a table that looked out on the square.

Mugs of *caffé in ghiaccio con latte di mandorla* arrived. She smiled between sips. "I'm already addicted to that wonderful almond flavor."

"Agreed. How about the antipasto?"

She experimented. "These are fabulous. I could make a whole meal on the salmon-and-oyster bruschetta alone."

"I like the little tortillas with olives."

"There's nothing not to like, Rini." Soon they were served angel-hair pasta with sardines. If that wasn't enough, they were brought mouthwatering apple crostinos for dessert.

"I'm so full, I don't think I can move. Thank you for bringing us here. I haven't had a meal like this in years."

He loved it that she enjoyed her food. "It's the least I can do after everything you've done for me. I'm in awe of your knowledge. Not only that, you're a master sea woman." He put some bills on the table, then got up and escorted her out of the restaurant. Night had fallen, adding to the beauty of the square.

"A *sea woman*? Sounds like a new species." Her soft laughter charmed him.

"Until your father gets back, I'm hoping to spend a few more days on the water with you. It's true I'm here on business, but I've decided to take a few days to mix pleasure with it."

He led them through a street to find a taxi so they could head back to the helipad at the airport. Once on board they took off, then he turned to her. "Your scuba equipment has been calling to me. How about we pick up some gear for me tomorrow and you take us where you go diving. I'll charter us a boat."

"That would be ridiculous when we can use my boat."

"I wouldn't want you to think I'm taking advantage of you."

"Can we just not worry about that?"

"That's fine with me. What I'd like to do is camp out. I'll be your buddy. Could I tear you away from your work that long, or would it be asking too much?"

After they reached the island and got in the car, she eyed him speculatively. "After the exquisite meal, it pains me to have to turn you down. I'm afraid I'm behind on my project, but you're welcome to take the cruiser and go exploring on your own."

He didn't believe her excuse. She could be warm and engaging, but if he got too close, she'd retreat. After finally meeting a woman who thrilled him in so many ways, he couldn't take the disappointment that she put other plans first. It was driving him crazy.

"If you don't go with me, I won't have a buddy. You're so smart and know so much, a trip without you wouldn't be fun. What if we go out early after your work is over for the day? Say two o'clock?"

"I'm not sure I can be finished by then." She got out of the car and started walking to the entrance in an attempt to elude him.

He caught up to her. "Then we'll play it by ear."

"You never give up, do you?" But she said it with a smile. "All right."

Those two little words gave him hope, but the minute they went inside the castle, Liona and her cat were there to greet them. "You have a visitor, Alessandra. He insisted on waiting for you. I've put him in the small salon."

Him? Maybe Rini had been right and she was seeing someone.

"Thank you, Liona." She pulled the sack out of her purse. "This is for you. Signor Montanari bought it for you."

The older woman smiled. *"Veramente?"* She opened the sack and pulled out the cat. "This looks like *you*, Alfredo. You must have bought this in Lecce!"

Rini nodded. "It caught our eye."

"Mille grazie, signor. Come on, Alfredo. Let's look at this treasure together." She put the cat in her arms. *"Buona notte,"* she called over her shoulder.

Alessandra's eyes darted to him. "You've made her night."

He cocked his head. "But it appears yours isn't over yet, so I'll leave you to your guest and see you tomorrow. *Dormi bene.*"

After wishing her good-night he headed for the stairs, which he took two at a time to his room on the third floor. Full of adrenaline because she'd finally agreed to be with him tomorrow, he pulled out his phone and returned Guido's call. Though it was late, his friend would probably still be awake. On the third ring he answered.

"Rini? I'd given up and was headed for bed."

"Sorry. I just got back to my room."

"Where are you?"

"In a castle on the island of Posso."

Guido chuckled. "Sure you are. So what's happening? Are we still on for Saturday?"

"I'm not sure."

"Don't tell me it's work again."

"Not this time."

"That sounds serious."

"I am. Have you got a minute?"

"Since when do you have to ask me a question like that? Go ahead. I'm all ears."

For the next little while he unloaded on his friend, leaving nothing out. When he'd finished, Guido whistled in response.

"In my gut I know Alessandra likes me, but she's keeping me at a distance. I asked her to go scuba diving tomorrow and she finally gave in, but she's not easy to understand. She doesn't wear a ring, but tonight a man was waiting for her when we got back from dinner."

"Then the first thing you need to find out is if she's committed."

Rini's brows furrowed. "I don't think she is. The housekeeper referred to the man as a visitor."

"All's fair then. Are you thinking she's being hesitant because you met her sister first? You know, that kind of unwritten law thing."

"Maybe."

"The only way to find out is go after her and learn the truth for yourself."

"I'll do it. Thanks for the advice."

After a long silence, his friend said, "I've been wondering when this day would come."

Guido wasn't the only one...

"I'll call you later in the week to make final plans for Saturday. Ciao."

He rang off, but he was feeling restless and decided to go for a walk before trying to get some sleep.

* * *

Alessandra waited outside the castle entrance while Bruno drove to the dock to get his scuba gear. When he came back, she approached the driver's side of his van. "Did you find everything?"

He nodded. "I'm sorry to have bothered you so late. I have to leave on the diving trip for the institute in the morning. I wish you'd join us. We'll be out there for another three days at least."

"What spot this time?"

"The same one. We haven't begun to explore that area thoroughly."

"I agree."

"Will you come? I know you're busy on your book, but we need your expertise." His gray eyes urged her to say yes. "I'd rather buddy with you than anyone else."

I know. But she didn't feel the same. "Bruno? Please don't take this wrong, but I want to keep our friendship on a professional basis and won't be buddying with you again."

He looked surprised. "Does this mean there's someone else?"

Exasperated, she said, "It means I'd prefer to keep my work separate from my personal life. I hope you understand."

Tight-lipped, he accelerated faster than necessary and took off.

"Someone didn't seem very happy," a deep male voice said behind her.

She whirled around in shock. "Rini, I—I thought you'd gone to bed."

"It's a beautiful night. I was afraid I wouldn't be able to sleep, so I decided to go for a walk around the castle. Did the fact that my kidnapping you to Lecce upset certain plans you had with your visitor?"

"If I'd had plans, I wouldn't have gone with you. That man was Dr. Tozzi from the archaeological institute. He came to get his scuba gear out of the cruiser. Tomorrow he's going on another exploratory dive with the others for a few days."

"You two dive together a lot?"

"There's a whole group of us. Last week we went out on our boats from Metaponto. He happened to be my buddy that trip, so that's why his scuba gear ended up in the cruiser. Tonight I told him he'd have to find another buddy because I would like our relationship to stay completely professional. "

"He doesn't have his own boat?"

"Yes, but he forgot to transfer his equipment after we'd finished. The institute has a state-of-the-art oceanography boat, but he won't bring it out until we've made a positive find."

"I see. Are you supposed to go out with them again?"

"Yes, but I have to divide up my time."

His dark brows lifted. "You're a very important person, besieged on every side, so I have an idea for tomorrow. While you work on your book for part of the day, I'll run in to Metaponto to get me some gear. Then we'll join your group. En route you and I can talk over your father's business. That way you can please everyone, including me. What do you say?"

She let out a sigh. Already he was reducing her to

mush. "I'll get up early and work until lunch, then we'll leave for Metaponto. The dive shop will have the gear you need. From there we can head for the dive site and meet up with the others."

"I'd like to stay out overnight and camp."

"I would, too. It's one of my favorite things to do."

"Good." His eyes blazed. "I shall look forward to it. I'll see you at lunch."

He took off for another run around the tiny island without giving her a chance to say anything else. Alessandra hurried inside the castle, secretly excited to go diving with him. Thoughts of buddying with him left her breathless. The idea that they would protect each other was so appealing she couldn't wait.

At six the next morning she showered and dressed quickly before heading to the library to work on her book. While she was knee-deep in research, Liona entered the library.

"Alessandra? Signor Montanari is eating his lunch in the dining room."

Her head lifted. "It's that time already?"

"*Si*. One o'clock."

"I can't believe I lost track of time. Tell him I'll be right there."

She raced out of the room and up the stairs to freshen up, then hurried back down with her packed duffel bag. When she entered the dining room he stood up to greet her. The man looked amazing in white cargo pants and a dark brown crewneck shirt.

"Sorry I'm late."

His dark eyes traveled up her jean-clad legs to her

white pullover, then found her gaze. "We're in no hurry. Sit down and eat lunch."

"I'd rather not take the time now. While you rent scuba gear, I'll grab us some food and drinks at the nearby deli to hold us over until tomorrow."

"With the announcement of an overnight on the water, you've made my day, *signorina.*"

Everything he said and did made her pulse race. Her feelings for him were spilling all over the place. She didn't know how to stop them. *She didn't want to stop them.*

He followed her out of the room with his backpack and they left for Metaponto in the cruiser. At the dive shop they loaded up with extra tanks. Once they'd bought drinks and groceries, they gassed up the cruiser and headed west. She handed him the special ocean chart he'd looked at before.

"We'll be diving at the midway point between Metaponto and Crotone. Some of the finds date back to the Magna Graecia. We're looking for some columns from the sixth century before Christ reputed to be there.

"If we're really lucky, we'll see the remnants of a temple dedicated to the goddess Hera. This area of the Ionian is a treasure trove, but as you realize, all the artifacts are buried, making them almost impossible to discover."

Rini looked up from the chart to flash her an intriguing smile. "It's the *almost* impossible that fires your blood, *non è vero*?"

She nodded. But artifacts weren't the only thing that fired her blood. The flesh-and-blood male who was a living Adonis had made her come alive without even trying. She'd taken one look at him that first evening in the castle foyer and had fallen so hard, she feared she would never recover.

It was too late to wish he'd gone back to Naples. Already she hated the idea that he would have to leave at all. Her thoughts were crazy. This was the renowned Rinieri Montanari she was talking about, not just any man.

Alessandra imagined that every woman who met him couldn't get enough. Even her mother had been bowled over by him. But the fact that he was still a bachelor meant there was a big reason he didn't have a wife.

Maybe he'd lost a great love and could never bring himself to marry. Or he enjoyed women, but couldn't commit to one for fear of feeling trapped. So no matter how attentive he was being right now, Alessandra would be a fool to think *she* would be the one woman in Italy who could do what no other female had done and win his love.

She glanced at him. "How long has it been since you went diving?"

Rini folded up the chart. "A year, but don't worry. You can count on me." Deep down she knew she could trust him. He engendered a confidence she'd never felt around other men. It didn't bother her that he'd just said he wasn't concerned about the time that had passed since his last dive.

"How have you stayed away from it so long?"

"Too much work."

"But there are lots of marvelous diving sites in the

Naples area. Surely you could have taken some time off."

"True, but even though the office is there, I don't live in Naples and am always anxious to fly home at the end of the day."

That was a surprise. "Where is home?"

"Positano."

"Oh—such a glorious spot with fabulous diving opportunities."

"My friends and siblings did it with me for several years, but for most of the last year my sister Valentina lived with me while she was expecting her baby. That meant no diving for her. As I told you earlier, we'd just lost our mother in a car accident. I divided my time between visiting my father at our family home in Naples and staying around the villa for my sister in order to keep her company."

Alessandra hadn't realized he'd carried such a load. She was touched by the way he cared for his family. "Did she have her baby?"

"*Si.* My nephew, Vito, is thriving. The man Valentina married has adopted him. They live in Ravello with his son, Ric. Both babies were born the same day at the same hospital."

"You're kidding—"

"What's really amazing was that the babies got switched. Valentina brought the wrong baby home while the man she married took home Valentina's son."

"*What?*" She almost lost control of the wheel. "How awful! Where was the mother?"

"They were divorced. At birth she gave up her mother's rights to Giovanni. It was a nightmare after the babies were returned to their birth parents. By then Valentina and Giovanni had bonded with the children. At that point they began to see each other so they could be with both babies and they fell in love."

A smile lit up her face. "That's the greatest love story I ever heard. How hard to love the wrong baby, but how sweet they were able to make everything work out. The person I feel sorry for is the mother who gave her child away. I can't comprehend it. I love my mother so much, I don't want to think what it would have been like if she hadn't been there for me. In fact I can't wait until the day comes when I can have my own baby."

He seemed caught up in his own thoughts before he said, "Fortunately she came to her senses and has now worked out visitation so she can help raise her son."

"That's the way it should be!" But Alessandra couldn't help but wonder about the father of his sister's baby. Still, she didn't want to pry.

"I can read your mind, Alessandra. Vito's father was one of Valentina's engineering professors at the University in Naples, but he didn't want marriage or children. My sister suffered terribly, but today she's so happy, you would never know she'd been through so much trauma."

Alessandra could relate to the trauma. Her hands tightened on the controls. She was living proof you could get through a broken heart and survive the emotional pain, but not everyone could end up as happy as his sister.

"So she's an engineer, too."

"Yes. A brilliant one."

"What does her husband do for a living?"

"He's the CEO of the Laurito Corporation."

Alessandra smiled at him. "That's an amazing combination. Your sister was blessed to have a brother like you to watch over her." She was coming to find out Rini was an extraordinary man. He'd even bought that little gift for Liona.

"Our family is close."

Alessandra could say the same where her parents were concerned. Before long she could pick out the red-and-white scuba flags from two boats ahead. "There they are!" The group had already started diving in an area near the coast. "If anything of significance is found, Dr. Tozzi will bring out the institute's boat. Today we're still exploring."

Alessandra brought her boat to a stop and lowered the anchor. After she raised her flag, she looked back at Rini. He'd already slipped on his wet suit. By the gleam in his eyes she could tell he'd been anticipating this dive.

"I'll be right back." She took her wet suit below to change. Talk about excited. She could hardly keep her fingers from trembling before going back up on deck.

In a moment they'd put on their weight belts and buoyancy-control devices. He reminded her of the film phenomenon James Bond. She finished dressing and put her goggles in place. "We'll be going down eighty feet. Ready?"

"Si, bellissima."

He shouldn't have said that to her. The deep tone of his compliment curled to her insides, disturbing her concentration. She ended up jumping in the water after he did, almost forgetting to keep her goggles and regulator in place.

The air temperature registered eighty degrees, but the water was cooler. Once below the surface she pressed the button to let out some air. The weights carried her down, down. Rini stayed right with her, watching her as their ears adjusted to the pressure. She could tell by the way he moved that he was a pro. It made her feel perfectly safe.

Eight minutes later they reached the sea floor with its clumps of vegetation and only a smattering of tiny fish. He stayed with her as she moved toward the area where she could see the group working. They all waved to her. She motioned for Rini to swim with her beyond the circle and examine a nearby area. The ridge in the distance looked promising, but as she brushed some of the debris away, it turned out to be more debris instead of a column lying on its side.

Rini found some interesting spots and waved her over to him, but every investigation came up short. She got the feeling they were searching in the wrong area. After a half hour he tapped his watch. She'd been about to do the same thing because it was time to go up and it would take a while.

They started the ascent, listening to the rhythm of their breathing through their regulators. She felt like they were the only people alive and loved this dive that had been magical for her. The sheer pleasure of enjoying this experience with him, of depending on him, could never be equaled.

Once they broke the surface, he helped her onto the

transom before levering himself on board. Before she could sit down on a banquette, another boat approached them.

"Alessandra—"

"Ciao, Bruno." She waved to him and the three others from the institute who rode with him.

"I was hoping you'd make it. Who's your friend?"

"Bruno Tozzi, meet Signor Montanari." The two men nodded. She refused to tell him anything about Rini. "It's too bad we haven't turned up anything interesting yet."

"We'll have to keep searching tomorrow."

Another of the divers said, "Why don't you join us in Crotone for dinner?"

"Thank you, but I'm afraid we have other plans. We'll do another dive with you in the morning."

"*Bene.*"

In a minute their boat drove off. Alessandra was glad he'd gone and hurried below deck to get out of her wet suit. When she came up on deck a few minutes, she found Rini already changed into his clothes. He'd organized their gear near the back of the boat and had taken down the flag.

His eyes played over her. "It's growing dark. Do you have a place in mind where we can camp?"

"Yes. A small, secluded cove five minutes from here. I'll raise the anchor." She turned on the boat lights and they headed for the coast. Her heart fluttered in her chest when she thought of spending the night out here with him. Because she knew this area so well, they arrived quickly. She cut the engine and the momentum swept them onto the sandy portion of the isolated beach.

Alessandra turned to him. "Do you want to eat on deck, or in the galley?"

"Since the food is already up here, let's stay put, shall we? I'll do the honors and serve you for a change."

"Well, thank you."

In a minute he had everything laid out on the opposite banquette and they could pick what they wanted—fruit, meat pastries, cheese rolls, drinks, chocolate and almonds.

He sat back in the chair opposite her and feasted. "After that dive, this is heaven," he admitted with satisfaction.

"I can tell you're a seasoned diver, Rini. It was a privilege to be with you today."

"Now you know how I feel to have joined you. I'm excited about tomorrow's dive. Maybe we'll find something, but even if we don't, it doesn't take away from the thrill of being with an expert like you."

His compliments sounded so sincere, she was in danger of believing them. "I loved it."

After a brief silence, he said, "Dr. Tozzi was upset to see you out here with me, so don't deny it."

"I wasn't going to." She reached for some more grapes. "I'm glad you were with me. I've told him I'm not interested in him. Now he's seen it for himself."

Rini's dark brows furrowed. "Is that the reason I was invited along?"

He couldn't really think that, could he? It would mean he felt vulnerable. She couldn't imagine him having a vulnerable bone in his body. She leaned forward. "Of course not!"

He bit into another plum. "Is there an important man in your life?"

Yes. I'm looking at him. "Not in years."

"Why not?"

"I could ask you the same thing," she blurted without thinking. "Why does Rinieri Montanari sail alone?"

"I asked you first," he returned. "A beautiful, fascinating woman like you has to have a history."

Alessandra wasn't used to hearing those adjectives attributed to herself. If he only knew it, she was totally enamored with him. "You don't really want to know."

"I wouldn't have asked otherwise." At this point he'd put the leftover food back in the sacks she would take down to the galley later.

"I fell in love with Francesco at twenty-two. He was a chef from Catania when I was in my last year of undergraduate school. He swore undying love for me and said he'd found his soul mate. I believed him. We talked about getting married.

"One weekend Dea came to visit. I was excited for her to meet him. She stayed in my apartment with me and the three of us spent time together. After she left for Rome, where she was pursuing a modeling career, everything seemed to change. He suddenly told me he had to go on vacation and would call me as soon as he got back. During those two weeks he didn't phone me once.

"I thought I'd lose my mind until I heard from him. I imagined every reason under the sun for his absence except the one he gave me. He didn't have the decency to tell me in person. Instead, he sent me a letter telling me he'd fallen in love with Dea and knew I couldn't forgive him."

Lines darkened Rini's features in the semidarkness.

"At the time it was terrible. Dea didn't come home for two months. When she did, she told me he'd followed her to Rome, but it was over between the two of them almost before it had begun. She thought he was a loser and told me I was better off without him.

"Though inwardly I agreed, my pain had reached its zenith because Dea always had this power to get the boys interested in her. But when it came to Francesco, who I thought was committed to me, something broke inside me. I suffered for a long time. But it happened over six years ago and is buried in the past." She took a drink of water. "Now it's your turn to tell me the secrets of your heart, dark or otherwise."

CHAPTER FOUR

RINI FELT LIKE he'd been stabbed in the chest. Too many emotions rocked him at once. There was someone he needed to talk to before he bared his soul to Alessandra.

"I'm afraid my story would take all night. Let's reserve it for tomorrow evening after another dive. If you don't mind, I'd like to sleep up here tonight."

"Then you'll need the quilt and pillow on the bed in the other cabin in order to be comfortable."

"I'll get them."

"You sound tired after that dive, Rini. I am too, so I'll say good night."

"Buona notte."

He waited an hour before going below to bring up the bedding. Once he'd made himself comfortable on the banquette at the rear of the cruiser, he pulled out his phone and called his sister. Rini knew it was too late to be phoning, but he had to talk to her.

After four rings he heard her voice. "Rini? What's wrong? Has something happened to Father?"

"No, no."

After a short silence she asked, "Are you ill?" He

could hear Giovanni's concerned voice in the back-ground.

"Not physically. But I'm wrestling with a problem that needs your slant. Do you mind?"

"What a question! After all you've done for me, I'd give anything to help you if I can. Tell me what's going on."

He raised up on one elbow. "Let me give you a little background." Without wasting words, he explained his dilemma from beginning to end.

"Ooh" was all she said when he'd finished.

"Forgive me if this touches too close to home, but you're the one person in the world who would under-stand her pain after Francesco went after her sister."

"Rini? I got over Matteo's womanizing and it sounds like she has gotten over her pain, too, so forget her past. You only have one problem. Let this woman know how you feel about her and prove to her that your love for her is everlasting. If Mamma were still alive, she would tell you to follow your heart and not let anything get in the way."

He could hear his mother saying those very words. "Alessandra was really hurt."

"So was I. It passes when the right man comes along. Trust me."

He breathed deeply. "You make it sound so simple."

"Nothing worthwhile is simple, Rini. But look what happened when I followed my heart instead of letting go of Ric, the baby I thought was mine..."

"You mean instead of listening to me tell you not to

get involved with Giovanni," he groaned. "I was a fool to interfere."

"Of course you weren't! I know you were only trying to protect me. But it all worked out and I'm now an ecstatic wife and the mother of two angelic boys."

His eyes closed tightly. "But from the start Giovanni wanted you enough to defy convention, too. That's why it worked."

"Rini, tonight you're alone with her on her family's cruiser. Do you seriously think that would have happened if she weren't absolutely crazy about you?"

"Her father asked her to show me around."

"But to dive? Camp out over night? Have faith, dear brother. A little patience wouldn't hurt until she realizes she can trust you with her life."

A lump had lodged in his throat. "*Ti amo*, Valentina."

"*Ti amo. Buona notte.*"

Rini lay back down, thinking about what she'd said. Even if a miracle happened and her attraction grew into love, she didn't know about his infertility, an insurmountable hurdle in his mind.

The next thing he knew, the sound of gulls brought him fully awake. Clouds blotted out the sun. He sat up to check his watch. Seven thirty. Was Alessandra still asleep? He gathered the bedding and took it below to the other cabin. Her door was still closed.

One thing he could do was fix them his favorite prosciutto ham and eggs to go with their breakfast. As he was putting their plates and mugs on the table, she appeared in the doorway wearing jeans and a T-shirt that molded to her beautiful body.

"You've got color in your cheeks."

"I went for a walk."

He'd had no idea. What a wonderful bodyguard he'd made! "If you'd wakened me, I would have gone with you. Sit down and I'll serve you."

"Umm. Everything smells good."

He poured them coffee and sat opposite her.

She took a sip. "How did you sleep?"

Rini stared at her through shuttered eyes. "There's nothing better than spending the night under the stars. What about you?"

"It's fabulous out here, but I confess diving makes me tired. I fell asleep once my head touched the pillow."

"That's good. How soon do we need to join the others?"

"They'll be out there by nine o'clock."

He swallowed the last of his eggs. "Just for the fun of it, what would you think if we enlarged the search area by traveling a quarter of a mile farther east from them to dive at the same distance from the coast?" He wasn't ready to share her with the others yet. "I consulted the chart. The depth of the sea floor isn't quite as great there. Maybe seventy feet. Who knows? We might make a discovery."

Her lips turned up at the corners. "Your mother must have gone crazy to have a son who went around with such an excited gleam for adventure in his eyes."

Rini liked the idea that she'd noticed. "Is that what I have?"

"Oh, yes. It probably got you into a ton of trouble." He chuckled. "So what do you say?"

"I like your idea. Later on this afternoon we can join the others for another dive."

"Sounds like a plan." Pleased she was willing to go along with him so they could be alone a little longer, he got to his feet to clean up the kitchen. She cleared the dishes and they made quick work of it. He'd never experienced this kind of togetherness with a woman before. Rini couldn't imagine letting her go.

"Thanks for fixing the delicious breakfast. I'll change into my wet suit and meet you on deck."

He bounded up the stairs to put on his own gear. To spend a whole day with her doing something they both loved couldn't have excited him more.

In fifteen minutes they'd arrived at the spot he'd suggested for a dive. They had the whole sea to themselves for the moment. She lowered the anchor and erected the flag. Together they put on all their equipment. "Ready?" he called to her.

Her brandy eyes clung to his, pulling at his heart strings. "Let's go!"

They jumped in the water. He experienced delight as they sank lower past more tiny fish. Once they reached the bottom, they explored around all the vegetation that grew taller and was more plentiful than at the other spot. He saw traces of some deep-sea-fishing tackle caught by the undergrowth. It was like playing hide-and-seek as they swam here and there like little children let out to play.

His eyes followed her as they moved through a new chute. He was so mesmerized by the fun he was having, he almost ran into her because she'd suddenly stopped.

When he looked beyond her, he saw a large round-ish shape like a big boulder covered in debris ahead of them.

The hairs lifted on the back of his neck and knew she was feeling the same electricity. Something was here that didn't belong. He swam to one side of it and waited for her to approach the other side. She was the expert.

Her hands began to brush away the layers of silt. He helped her. After five minutes of hard work, they uncovered part of what looked like a sculpted mouth. Alessandra's eyes stared at him with a glow through her goggles. This was a fantastic find and they both knew it.

While he marveled, she tapped her watch. He'd been too engrossed and forgot the time. They needed to go up to the surface now! It was hard to leave after what they'd just discovered, but they would be back later.

Rini knew the rules by heart. Keep his breathing steady as they rose, but it was hard when his adrenaline was gushing. He could only imagine Alessandra's joy. This was her life!

They broke the top of the water and swam toward the boat. Like déjà vu he helped her on board the cruiser, then climbed in himself.

"Oh, Rini," she cried, having removed the belt and breathing apparatus. "We found something that could have belonged to the Temple of Hera. We've got to find Dr. Tozzi and bring the others here!"

Without conscious thought he grasped her upper arms, bringing her close to his body. "Congratulations!"

Her eyes, the color of dark vintage brandy, searched his. "It was your inspiration that brought us here."

For a moment he was caught up in the wonder of her beauty that went soul deep. "I'll never forget the experience of winding through that undersea garden with you."

"Neither will I," she whispered.

He pulled her closer and closed his mouth close over hers. The unexpectedness of it must have caught her off guard because she began kissing him back with a fervency he could only have dreamed about.

Hungry for her, Rini drove their kiss deeper, marveling over her response to him. Sensation after sensation of desire caused him to kiss her senseless. Only the wake from a passing boat that bounced the cruiser reminded him how far gone he was.

Alessandra seemed to feel it, too. She tore her lips from his and moved out of his arms. "If—if you'll mark this spot on the chart, I'll drive," she stuttered.

He didn't like it that she'd headed for the controls, leaving him bereft. So much for him practicing the patience Valentina had talked about. Rini hadn't been able to keep himself from crushing her in his arms. He'd wanted that divine fusion to go on and on.

While Alessandra raised the anchor and started the engine, he reached in his backpack for a pen. He found the rolled-up chart on the banquette and sat down to fill in the information, but it was difficult. To his surprise the wind had kicked up. He looked overhead and noticed that more clouds had been amassing. Three hours ago it had only been overcast and there hadn't been this breeze.

She drove as fast as the elements would allow. Finally

in the distance he saw the flags of the three boats. They drew closer and waved to several groups of divers in two of the boats. Soon Alessandra drew alongside one of them. "How long has Dr. Tozzi been down?"

"He and Gino should be coming up any minute."

"Did you find anything?"

They shook their heads.

"Well, all is not lost. We have some amazing news." She cut the engine and lowered the anchor while they waited in the rocking crafts for the head of the institute to appear. Rini shared a private glance with her. He could feel her eagerness to impart their finding.

Rini watched until he saw two heads pop out of the water. The divers reached their boat and climbed in. The second the good doctor removed his headgear, his gaze shot to Alessandra.

"You missed this morning's dive."

"We did our own dive farther east and raced here to tell you what we found." In the next breath she told everyone about the head.

"You uncovered a mouth?" The doctor sounded incredulous.

"I wish we could show it to you now, but the weather is acting up. Maybe by early evening we can do another dive. In the meantime, why don't you follow us to the cove where we spent the night on the beach? The site is right off the coast from there and a little east where we can eat before you leave for the port."

Everyone agreed it was a good idea. Alessandra raised the anchor and started the engine. Once again they took off for the cove. While he stayed on the cruiser, Alessandra climbed out to chat with the others. They decided the storm wouldn't hit until evening, but it would be better not to go out diving again today.

"Are you staying here again tonight?"

"I'm not sure what our plans are, Gino, but we'll definitely be here tomorrow at nine to show you the dive site, unless the weather is worse."

Rini had checked ahead. There'd be a storm later. On impulse he picked up the chart and got out of the boat to show it to them. "In case we don't get together, I've marked the coordinates on here if you want to write them down."

Dr. Tozzi glanced at it and made notes on the pad in his pocket before handing it back to Rini. "Thanks."

"You're welcome."

The group prepared to leave. Nothing could have made Rini happier. So happy, in fact, that he handed Alessandra the chart, then helped push the other boats back in the water and waved everyone off.

Alessandra had to suppress a smile. Rini couldn't have been more helpful. How could any man measure up to the famous CEO who could scuba dive and read ocean charts with the best of them?

In a few more days, when he'd finished up business with her father, he'd fly off to Naples and his busy life that sent him all over the country. She had to remember he was only here in the south of Italy for a few more days. To think of him leaving was killing her.

If it turned out her parents agreed to let his company do some drilling, Rini would send out their experts.

From time to time she'd see him coming and going from the castle. But for today and tomorrow, they would be together and it thrilled her heart.

She turned to him. "How would you like to do something fun?"

He cocked his dark head. "What kind of a ridiculous question is that to ask a man alone with a beautiful woman?"

"Just checking," she teased and got back in the boat with her heart thudding in her chest. "If you're game for a bumpy ride, I know a place where the food is divine. By boat it will take us about an hour and a half. When we get there we'll enjoy an early dinner and stay overnight."

"That good, hmm?"

"Yes."

"Only if you'll let me drive us. So far *you've* done all the work."

"I don't mind, but if that's what you want."

"It'll relieve my guilt."

"Over what?"

"I like to feel useful."

"You were amazingly useful when you pushed all the boats off the sand. You reminded me of Hercules."

His deep laughter resounded in the air.

"I'm not kidding. They would have had a terrible time in this wind without your help."

"If I impressed you, then it was worth the pain."

Her eyes scrutinized him from head to toe. "You did it so effortlessly, I doubt there's a sore muscle in your body."

He returned her gaze, sending the color flooding into her cheeks. "I guess it comes from both of us living in and out of the water."

She looked down. "Would you believe I still need to get out of my wet suit?"

"Do you need help?"

She felt the blush break out on her face. "I think I can handle it."

"While you do that I'll push us off and we'll get going."

Her chest fluttered as she hurried below deck to change and freshen up. After ascertaining that her parents had left her aunt's and had gone back to the castle, she joined Rini. He'd changed clothes and was seated in the captain's chair wearing his life preserver. "Tell me where to go."

Alessandra reached in the cubbyhole for her regular map and opened it, but the wind made it difficult to keep steady. "We're here. Keep following the coast past Metaponto, then we'll cut a diagonal and head straight for Taranto."

"That's where your aunt lives?"

"Yes. Our mother's titled family descends from the Duca di Taranto, although the title is now defunct, like my father's."

"Ah. It's all making sense." He put the map back and handed her a life preserver. "Sit across from me so we can talk."

She grinned. "Aye, aye, sir, but I don't think we'll be able to hear each other."

"As long as we're together, I don't care."

The man could read her mind. She sat on the banquette and stared out at a sea full of white caps. The moderate swells slowed them down, but she was having the time of her life. Since he hadn't vacationed in a year, Alessandra suspected he was happy, too, especially after he was the one to have picked the area where they'd made an underwater find. Every time he looked at her, his dark eyes burned with charged energy, melting her to the spot.

Outside Metaponto he stopped long enough to switch gas tanks. "I remember seeing Taranto's naval base and shipyards from the air."

"Then you know it's a big commercial city and port. Our Taranto relatives live in one of the eighteenth-century palazzi in the old town center. I've let my aunt know we're coming to see her. She broke her hip and has a nurse around the clock, but she loves visitors. Be warned she'll insist we eat dinner with her before we leave."

"I don't want to impose."

"She'll love it, Rini. Since you're a seafood lover, get ready to enjoy the most luscious roasted oysters you've ever eaten in your life. The cook prepares them in a special sauce followed by sea-bream-and-mussel soup. It's out of this world. Mother would steal her if she could."

He eyed her speculatively. "What's the other reason you're taking me there?"

You could never fool a man like Rini.

"She's mother's brilliant older sister by nine years and was married to a general who died two years ago. When Mamma was thirty, she almost died giving birth to me and Dea. Fulvia couldn't have children and was there to do everything. She won my father's devotion. As I told you earlier, her opinion goes a long way with both of them. I'd like you to tell her your business ideas for developing the property."

His features sobered. "Are you saying your mother doesn't approve?"

"I'm afraid not. Both of them were raised to be purists and believe that the former papal legacy should remain untouched."

"What about *your* opinion, Alessandra?"

She took a deep breath. "I've listened to my father and think your idea is an important one. If a lot of oil is found, it *will* help the economy. But what's important is what Zia Fulvia has to say."

Those dark eyes searched hers. "Why are you trying to help me?"

A good question. "I believe in you *and* an even playing field."

"I'm humbled by your faith in me." He rubbed his jaw where the shadow of his beard was showing. She thought him irresistible. "Will I find her difficult?"

"Yes."

She loved the bark of laughter that came out of him.

"But you told me you like snags because they make life more exciting."

When he smiled, she felt herself falling toward him. "I did say that, didn't I? Let's go and get this over with. It couldn't be worse than a visit to the dentist."

Alessandra kept chuckling as the cruiser pounded the white water on its way to Taranto. She'd never met anyone with a sense of humor like his. He was getting to her with every minute they spent together.

Due to the wind they made slow progress. It was after five when they passed through the outer and inner sea to pull into the private dock reserved for her aunt's family. Alessandra called for the limo that drove them to the Taranto palazzo in the old town.

"Tarantos have lived here for over four hundred years," she explained as they turned into the court-yard with its fountain supported by Taras, the son of Poseidon from Greek mythology. "You'll think you've entered a fabulous museum. Fulvia and Mamma were raised princesses and Fulvia still lives like one."

"She won't shudder at the sight of us fresh off the boat?"

At seventy-seven Fulvia was still all woman and would probably faint when she saw the gorgeous male Alessandra had brought with her. "No. She's used to my showing up a mess after a day at sea."

Rini helped her out of the limo. "Lippo," she called to the older man who opened the ornate front door at the same time. *"Come stai?"*

"Bene, grazie, Alessandra."

"Please meet Signor Montanari."

"Piacere di conoscerla."

She looked at Rini. "Lippo and Liona are cousins. Our families couldn't live without them."

"Your families are close-knit in many ways," Rini murmured. "Does he have a cat, too?"

Alessandra chuckled. "He would, but my aunt has allergies."

"Signora Fulvia is in the drawing room, but she's tired since your parents left and is still off her food."

"We won't stay long."

"After you've spoken with her, dinner will be served in the small dining room."

"*Grazie*, Lippo."

Alessandra led Rini through hallways of marble floors and walls lined with gilt-framed portraits to her aunt's favorite room. Still a beauty, she sat in a wheel chair surrounded by the mementos of her deceased husband, who'd enjoyed a distinguished military career.

"*Buonasera*, Zia. I've missed you." She hugged her aunt. "I'm so sorry about your hip."

"A hazard of old age. Don't let it happen to you, *cara*." Her brown eyes flicked to Rini, assessing him with uncommon interest. No woman could help it. "Your fame as an engineer precedes you, Signor Montanari. Alessandra, why don't you see if your dinner is ready while I have a chat with him? Then I'll ask the nurse to take me to my room."

Her aunt had to be more miserable than she looked in order to get down to business this fast. "You poor thing. Please don't overdo it. I'll be right back." She shared a private glance with Rini before leaving the room. Though she felt the slightest bit apprehensive, he seemed perfectly at ease.

She didn't think anything could throw him. If he couldn't achieve his goal with her father, Alessandra knew he'd look elsewhere for oil because he was a man on a mission.

* * *

By nine thirty the bad weather had turned ugly. Rini felt the rain as he helped Alessandra into the limo and gave the driver instructions to return them to the private dock. Though she'd told him they could stay the night at the palazzo, the illuminating conversation with her aunt had turned him inside out and he'd wanted to leave.

Her aunt had told him something that had nothing to do with his business meetings with the count. She'd brought up an alarming personal issue that had a direct bearing on Alessandra and her sister. He needed to think long and hard about it for the good of the Caracciolo family before he shared it with Alessandra, *if he ever did*. The only solution was to kill his feelings for her. In order to do that, he needed to leave the castello and search for hydrocarbons elsewhere in the south.

"I'd rather get back to the cruiser. It will do fine while we wait out the storm." He imagined it would last all night.

"Well?" she asked with a smile after they'd gone below deck to the small room she used as an office. The rain pounded down outside. He stretched out in one of the chairs and extended his legs, crossing them at the ankles. Across from him sat the woman he considered the greatest beauty of the Taranto family bar none.

The humidity had curled the tips of her delightful hair. With her pink cheeks, she reminded him of one of the adorable cherub faces from Lecce. Her physical looks were a given. But what he found truly exquisite was her spirit—she had decided to give him a fighting chance to carry through with an idea, although it would never see the light of day now.

"I loved the tour of the palazzo and the meal was superb."

"It always is, but I'm talking about your chat with my aunt. How did it go? She was too tired to talk to me before she went to bed."

None of it was meant for Alessandra's ears. "I thought I was talking to a strong minded woman."

Laughter bubbled out of her. "She's tough all right."

Choosing his words carefully he said, "We talked pro and con. Her knowledge and directness impressed me before she asked to be excused to go to bed."

She eyed him curiously. "That's all you can tell me?"

Tight bands constricted his chest. "There isn't anything else."

"Oh, dear. It doesn't sound like it went well."

"I have no idea. But be assured I enjoyed meeting her and I'm indebted for your help. Since it's getting late, why don't you go on to bed? I've got business calls to make. Sleep well."

After they'd left her aunt's palazzo the night before, Alessandra couldn't believe the change in Rini. He seemed to have turned into a different man, and was aloof, preoccupied. What on earth had they talked about that made him so unapproachable?

She went down to her cabin and cried herself to sleep over the way he'd just shut her out. She'd been waiting for him to kiss her again, but it never happened. What he and her aunt had talked about had changed him in some way.

When Alessandra woke up the next morning, Rini was already at the wheel. The weather had to be better, otherwise the cruiser wouldn't be skimming across the water with such speed.

Why hadn't he knocked on her door to waken her? Anything to let her know he was aware of her.

She couldn't understand it and got out of bed to dress. After making coffee in the galley, she went up on deck with her duffel bag in the hope he would be in a better frame of mind to talk to her.

But the second she saw the set jaw of that handsome face, she knew instinctively that now wasn't the right time. He was in no mood to confide in her. She walked over him. "I thought you might like this."

He eyed her briefly before taking the cup. "Thank you. You're an angel. As you can see, the storm has passed over. We'll have you home soon."

Home?

Her fear that something terrible was wrong had come to fruition. She frowned. "I thought we were going to dive. It's a great morning for it."

"I'd like to, but I'm afraid something came up while I made some business calls last night. I need to discuss them with your father. Please don't let that stop you from joining your group once you drop me off."

Diving was the last thing on her mind. She moved around and straightened the scuba equipment. They were almost to the island. Soon he eased the cruiser to the dock. When it was safe, she jumped out with her duffel bag and tied the ropes, leaving him to shut down the engine.

He joined her at the Land Rover. Their silent drive to the castle only took a minute, proof he was surprised she hadn't stayed in the boat before taking off again. Alessandra had the impression he couldn't wait to get away from her.

Sure enough, as soon as she'd parked the car, he reached for his backpack and got out. Alessandra followed him inside the foyer of the castle. He looked back at her. "I phoned your father earlier. He's waiting for me. Thank you for showing me your world. I loved every second of it."

So did I. Why are you acting like it's over? Rini— what's going on?

But he kept her in the dark. Without lingering, he walked toward her father's office.

With a heart that had fallen to the floor, she went up the staircase to shower and change into clean clothes. Her mother was probably in the day room so she hurried downstairs to talk to her. She would know what was going on with her father and Rini. This was a nightmare.

When she wasn't there, Alessandra went to the dining room and found it empty. "Hey, Alfredo. Are you looking for Liona?" She picked up the cat. On her way to the kitchen she heard the rotors of the helicopter. Someone must be arriving from the mainland. She kept on walking to the kitchen. No one was in there.

She lowered the cat to his food and water dishes, then she took off for her father's office. Maybe her mother was in there and she would find the three of them deep in conversation. After hesitating, she knocked on the door, unwilling to stay away any longer. "*Scusi*, Papà."

"Come in, *piccola*."

She found her father alone. "Where is everyone?"

"Your mother drove Liona to Metaponto for her dentist appointment." That explained why Alfredo looked lost.

"I—I thought Rini Montanari was still with you," she stammered.

He sat back in his leather chair. "He was here earlier to tell me that after thinking everything over, he decided that erecting oil derricks on our property would be a scab on the legacy Queen Joanna left to the family."

Those were the very words Alessandra had used. To hear her father say them brought inexpressible pain.

"He says he's off to search for another area to drill. After thanking both you and me profusely for our time and hospitality, he called for a helicopter and left."

Her legs started to buckle. She grabbed the first chair before she fell. "That's it? No other explanation?"

Her father smiled warmly. "Only to say that you discovered a large head while you were diving yesterday and he presumes it'll make you famous."

Except that Rini was the one with the inspiration to know where to dive.

"Oh—one more thing. He told me you're the most charming, lovely, intelligent woman he ever met and he understood why I wanted you to show him around. I could have told him that about you, but it's nice he discovered it for himself. As for the oil-drilling proposal,

I have to admit I'm glad he withdrew it. Neither your mother or Fulvia were in favor of it."

"I know." A boulder had lodged in her throat.

"Fulvia phoned your mother early this morning. We were surprised to learn you'd taken him to see her. It made her very happy to see you while she's recovering."

But the visit had turned out to be devastating for Alessandra. Once again her world had been destroyed. This time she knew she'd never be able to put it back together.

Alessandra took a quick breath. "Since the weather kept us from making another dive, I decided to pay her a visit. She was tired, but seems to be getting along fine."

"She was very impressed with Rinieri's honesty."

Honesty? What on earth did that mean?

Feeling ill, she got up from the chair. "I've been away from my work too long, so I'd better get busy or my editor will lose his patience. I'll be in the library if you need me." She hurried over to give him a kiss on the cheek before leaving the office.

When she reached her desk, she buried her face in her hands and sobbed. Several messages came in on her phone, all from Gino wanting to know if she would be joining them for the afternoon dive. None were from Rini.

Alessandra texted him that she couldn't make it, then left the castle in the Land Rover and drove to the mainland. After grabbing some food, she drove to the ridge where she'd taken Rini on that first day. The recent downpour had greened up the fields. She walked around, playing back their conversation in her head.

Alessandra was convinced that the excuse he'd given her father not to drill wasn't the real reason he'd backed off.

Deeply troubled, she returned to the castle and got busy on the historical biography she was writing on Queen Joanna. But by Saturday morning she couldn't stand it any longer. Rini had been cruel not to have contacted her, if only to say goodbye. After what they'd shared scuba diving, she wasn't about to let him walk away until he'd listened to a few things she had to say.

If this was how he ended every relationship with a woman, no wonder he was still a bachelor. He'd been clever to abort their growing attraction before it burned out of control. Rini had been every bit as hungry for her as she'd been for him when they'd kissed. So why had he done this?

He'd been the one to pursue her, to want to scuba dive with her. There'd been no stopping him getting his way because she'd wanted to be with him so badly, too, and still did. So what had changed everything? Alessandra needed answers and she wasn't going to let him get away with it.

After telling her parents she'd be home late, she drove the Land Rover to Metaponto and took a commercial flight to Positano. Without her father's knowledge she'd looked up Rini's home address on his computer.

She could have gone to the Montanari office in Naples, but figured he'd be home on the weekend. If she walked in on him entertaining another woman, that was too bad. She needed answers.

Three hours later the limo she'd hired wound around

the lush vegetation of his property. It stopped in front of a magnificent two-storied, ochre-colored villa, probably built at the turn of the century. Good heavens, the hilltop town above the Amalfi Coast was gorgeous beyond belief!

Alessandra marveled to know that Rini lived in this flower-filled paradise. The exterior was drenched in purple and red bougainvillea, robbing her of breath. So did the view of the sea from such a dizzying height.

A warm midafternoon sun shone down on her as she got out of the back. "Stay here, please," she said to the driver. She walked past several cars in the courtyard on her way to the front entrance. Alessandra hoped that meant Rini was home.

After using the bell pull, she waited for someone to answer and heard female voices inside. One said, "I'll get it, Bianca."

The moment the door opened, Alessandra knew she was looking at Rini's sister, who was a real blond beauty. Even though their coloring was different, the extraordinary family resemblance brought Rini to mind with a pang.

"*Buon pomeriggio, signorina.* Can I help you?" She'd answered the door in a bathing suit covered by a short lacy wrap.

Her heart was pounding too hard. "I hope so. I'm here to see Rini."

She studied Alessandra for a moment. "Aren't you the famous Diorucci model?"

CHAPTER FIVE

THIS WAS DÉJÀ VU all over again.

"That's my sister, Dea. I'm Alessandra Caracciolo."

"Well, you're both absolutely stunning."

"Thank you."

"I'm afraid my brother isn't here. I'm Valentina Laurito. Was he expecting you?"

"No." She swallowed hard. "I wanted to surprise him."

A mischievous smile broke the corners of his sister's mouth. "So did I. Bianca informed me he went fishing this morning and hasn't come back yet, but she's expecting him soon so I stayed."

Fishing...

While she took in the disappointing news, an older woman appeared in the foyer carrying a darling blond baby boy, the image of his mother. She made the introductions. "Have you come far?"

"I flew in from Metaponto."

"That's quite a ways. Won't you come in and wait with me while I give my son a bottle? We're out by the swimming pool. Vito loves his Zio Rini and keeps waiting for him to walk out."

Alessandra knew the feeling well. "If you don't mind, I'd love to."

"Tell your driver to come back for you later."

She did the other woman's bidding, then walked through Rini's elegant villa. The patio furniture included tables, chairs and a large swing. Alessandra saw plastic toys in the water. Valentina took the baby from the housekeeper and settled him in his baby swing with a cover to shield his eyes.

"We have extra bathing suits if you'd like to change and take a dip."

"Thank you, but no."

"You might like it after your flight."

"It didn't take that long. Besides I get in plenty of swimming." Valentina was so easy to talk to, Alessandra needed to be careful what she said to her. Rini was a private person who wouldn't appreciate her getting too familiar with his family. Especially not after he'd left the castle permanently.

She found a lounge chair close to the swing to watch the darling baby. In a minute she heard rotors overhead and her pulse leaped. What would Rini think when he found her out here with his family? Maybe she shouldn't have come, but it was too late now because moments later her gaze darted to the tall, dark figure striding toward them from the other end of the pool wearing jeans and a T-shirt.

"There's your *zio*!" Valentina cried.

"Vito—" Rini called to him. The baby turned his head toward his uncle and lifted his arms.

That's when Rini saw her and his eyes narrowed. "Alessandra," he murmured.

Without missing a beat he came close and picked up the baby in his arms, kissing him. "What a surprise. Two visitors in one afternoon."

"Alessandra has flown here from Metaponto, but I can't persuade her to take a swim."

"That's because she scuba dives for the archaeological institute from Catania and probably enjoys a break from swimming."

Valentina's head swung toward her. "Rini's a master diver, too!"

"I know. Your brother was instrumental in helping me make a find the other day. I'm indebted to him."

"Rini," his sister virtually blurted with excitement. "You didn't tell me about that." Her eyes took in the two of them.

With enviable calm he explained, "While I was looking for new oil fields, I tagged along with Alessandra. She lives on an archaeological treasure."

"Zio Salvatore called me when he couldn't find you at the office. You know how upset he gets."

He played with Vito, avoiding Alessandra's eyes. "I'm back from Calabria now and got in touch with him."

"That's a relief. So how was fishing?"

"Good. Guido caught two trout with the lure I gave him. We ate them for lunch."

"Lucky you. I'm glad you came home when you did. Vito and I waited as long as we could, and now we've got to get back to Ravello. Giovanni will be wondering where we are." She turned to Alessandra. "It was so nice to meet you."

"You, too. Your little boy is wonderful."

"Thank you. I think so, too. I have another son, Ric, but he's with his birth mother today." She took the baby from her brother's arms and disappeared into the villa.

Alessandra was left alone with Rini. Her pulse raced at the way his eyes ignited as he studied her for a moment without saying anything. She was glad she'd worn her white dress with the blue-and-green print, a favorite of hers. For once she'd knocked herself out trying to look beautiful for him. She'd even worn some eye makeup and had spent time on her hair.

"I think you know why I'm here," she said, answering the question he hadn't asked. "You didn't say goodbye." Her accusation hung in the air.

His hands went to his hips in a male gesture. "If you'll excuse me for a minute, I'll be right back."

"Promise?" she responded. He'd arrived dressed in outdoor gear with a navy crewneck shirt. With that hint of a dark beard on his jaw, she was almost overcome by his male virility. Alessandra had missed him so terribly, it hurt to look at him.

A nerve throbbed at the corner of his compelling mouth. "I swear it."

He left the patio on a run. She found a chair under the umbrella table and took in the sight of his own private Garden of Eden. So many species of flowers and trees astounded her, as everything looked perfect. All her life she'd lived in a castle surrounded by sand and water.

Alessandra loved the isolation, but being here in Rini's home made her appreciate what she'd been missing.

The fragrance from the roses intoxicated her. She got up and walked around to smell the various varieties. Soon she heard footsteps behind her. When she turned, she discovered that the woman Valentina had introduced her to had come out on the terrace. She pushed a cart of food and drinks to the table. "Rinieri will be right out, *signorina*."

"*Grazie*, Bianca."

From the corner of her eye she saw a baby sandal left on one of the chairs. She started to retrieve it when Rini came out on the patio dressed in tan trousers and a silky black sport shirt. Freshly shaved, he looked and smelled fabulous.

Alessandra held up the sandal. "Your sister left this in her wake. I'm afraid her fast exit was my fault."

"You're wrong." He took the little sandal and put it on the table. "She couldn't wait to join her husband. They're crazy about each other." Rini held out a chair for her. "Sit down and we'll eat. One trout apiece wasn't enough for the appetite I've developed."

"I'm hungry, too. They only served snacks on the plane."

In a minute they filled up on shrimp salad with penne, dried tomatoes and slices of grilled eggplant that melted in her mouth. Rolls and lemonade with mint leaves made their meal a feast, but clearly Rini was a fish man.

Filled to the brim, she sat back in the chair. "I'm waiting for an explanation."

He wiped the corner of his mouth with a napkin before his gaze fell on her. "All along there's been something I should have told you about myself, but I never seemed to find the right time."

"What? That you lead a secret life? That you have a wife hidden somewhere?"

"Nothing like that. After the visit to your aunt's, I decided that I'd wasted enough of your family's time and thought it best to leave so you could get on with your dive."

She shook her head. "You're a man who was raised with good manners, so your excuse doesn't wash. Something happened during your private talk with my aunt that put you off your desire to drill on my family's property. I deserve to know the truth. It's only fair after providing you the opportunity to talk to her."

His eyes glittered. "You're treading on dangerous ground to ask for the truth."

Her hands gripped the sides of her chair. "Now I know I'm right. As you can see, I'm a grown woman and can take whatever you have to tell me."

Lines darkened his striking face. "I'm not so sure."

"Are you afraid I'm too fragile if you tell me a secret about yourself I don't want to hear?"

He eyed her somberly. "I have no desire to bring hurt to you."

Bring? Such a cryptic comment brought a pain to her stomach. "What do you mean? In what way?"

"You need to leave it alone, Alessandra."

Anger sparked her emotions. "I don't accept that."

"I'm afraid you're going to have to." He sounded so remote, her insides froze.

"In other words you really meant it to be goodbye the other day."

Rini leaned forward. "I'd hoped I'd made that clear when I left the island the other morning without letting you know my intentions."

The forbidding CEO of Montanari's had spoken. *Don't you dare break down in front of him.*

She struggled for breath. "Don't worry. You've made me see the light. You and Francesco aren't that different after all. After he disappeared from my life, he sent his goodbye in a letter rather than face me. You flew off and left it to my father to do the honors. What is it about some attractive men? They seem to possess every quality except the one most vital."

A white ring appeared around his lips. She was pleased to see he wasn't completely impervious to her judgment of him. "Don't worry. Keep all your secrets! I'm leaving." She started to get up.

"No, Alessandra—you want the truth of everything, so I'll tell you. I never planned to, but since you've come all this way, I can't handle seeing you in this kind of pain. No one deserves an explanation more than you do."

"Go on."

"Where your aunt is concerned, we only talked business for a moment. The main thrust dealt with you."

"*Ma?*"

Rini nodded slowly. "She loves you."

"I love her, too, but what does that have to do with anything?"

"She wanted clarification and asked to know what happened when I met Dea."

The moment he'd spoken, she stirred in the chair and averted her eyes. "I—I can't believe she brought up something that was none of her business." Her voice faltered. "Mother must have said something." After a long pause she said, "How uncomfortable that had to be for you."

"Not uncomfortable. I found it refreshing. You're a lot like her, you know. If I didn't know better, I'd think she was your mother."

Alessandra's head lifted. She blinked. "You're kidding—"

"Not at all. You and your aunt have a sense of fair play I admire very much. It's clear you both want the best for everyone. I told her nothing happened. Guido's father asked us to dance with the models he'd introduced us to. I had one dance with Dea, then she left. That was it. After my explanation, your aunt wanted to know my intentions toward you."

Alessandra shot out of the chair. "She had no right! I don't see how she could have asked you that when we hardly know each other!"

He stared up at her. "That's not true, Alessandra. Your aunt told me you've never taken a man to meet her before and what we had was something special. Naturally she's aware you've been showing me around for your father."

"So?"

"She realizes we would have learned a great deal about each other already."

"Well yes, but—"

"Her concern for both you and Dea is commendable," he interrupted. "So I had to be brutally honest and tell her that I didn't feel a connection to her. Since you and I met under the most innocent and extraordinary circumstances, she demanded to know if I felt a connection to you."

Alessandra paled.

"Don't you want to know what I said?"

"It's none of my business," she whispered.

"That's not an answer and you know it."

She turned away.

"I told her that my attraction to you was immediate and has been growing out of control." Her groan resounded in the air. "You feel it, too. I know you do. Out of loyalty to both her nieces, your aunt vetted me to make sure I wasn't using *you* to gain access to the legacy."

"That's absurd. I would never have thought that about you."

"But it's a mercenary world. She knew how hurt you were years ago and wanted to protect you."

"So you withdrew the proposal to prove to my family you had no ulterior motive? That's why you walked away from me?" Her voice rang out.

Instead of answering her, he reached for her and drew her over to the swing, pulling her down on his lap "Look at me, Alessandra."

She shook her head. "I'm afraid to."

"Because you know I want to kiss you. The other morning while we were on the sea floor uncovering the mouth on that head, I was reminded of you. When I kissed you on the boat, I was half out of my mind with desire. My motives *are* ulterior, but intensely personal."

"No, Rini. We mustn't. Not out here where Bianca can see us."

"*I* must, *bellissima*."

He curved his hand against the side of her face and turned it toward him. Obeying blind need, he covered her trembling mouth with his own. She tried to elude him, but he drove his kisses deeper and deeper until her little cry allowed him the access he craved. Maybe he was dreaming because she slowly began returning his kisses with a heart-stopping hunger that caused him to forget everything except the heavenly woman in his arms.

His hands roved over her back and shoulders while they gave and took pleasure from each other's mouths. He felt her fingers slide up his neck into his hair. Every touch fed the fire enveloping him.

"Alessandra," he moaned. "I can't get enough of you. Do you have any idea how much I want you?"

"I want you, too," she confessed, covering his face with kisses.

"During the dive I was dying to grasp your hips and pull you into a secret cave where we could make love for months on end."

"Our wet suits would have presented a problem."

"But not now." He eased her down on the swing, where he had the freedom to look at her to his heart's content while he kissed the living daylights out of her.

Rini had never known this kind of all-consuming

desire before. The way she responded to him let him know something earthshaking had happened to her, too. She'd already had one love affair in her life, but it had been a long time ago. He was thankful it hadn't worked out because he was convinced she'd been reserved for him.

But what if she couldn't handle what he needed to tell her? He kissed her nose and eyelids. Before things went any further, she deserved to know the whole truth about him. Though terrified of her reaction, he couldn't stop now.

"You're the most divine creature this man has ever met. Since your aunt wanted to know my intentions toward you, it's only fair I tell you something about me first."

"You don't have to do this, Rini. You don't owe me anything. Please. I never dreamed my aunt would get personal with you like that."

"I'm glad she did. It woke me up to something I've been unwilling to face for years."

Her anxious eyes searched his. "What do you mean?"

"I've remained a bachelor for a reason."

"If you're allergic to marriage, you're not the only man. Until my father met Mother, he decided he'd always be single."

"That hasn't been my problem. In truth I've never gotten to the point in my adult life when I needed to state my intentions. But with you, it has become necessary."

She lifted a hand to caress his jaw. "Why?"

He kissed her succulent lips. "You're not just any

female I happen to have met. I'm not talking about the fact that you were born titled from both sides of your illustrious families. This is something that affects you as a woman. Don't you know you're head and shoulders above any woman I've ever known? Your pure honesty demands the same from me."

"Papà said my aunt was impressed with *your* honesty." She shivered. "What honesty is that? If your intention is to frighten me, you're doing a good job."

"*Frighten* might not be the best word." He sat up and got off the swing. "What I tell you will change the way you view me, but this has to come from me. I'll understand if you say it's been nice knowing you before you go your own way."

"For heaven sakes just tell me!"

Rini had angered her. This was going wrong. "From the time I could remember, I played soccer. By seventeen I was playing on a winning team with my friend Guido. On the day of the championship game, I got injured. At the hospital tests were done and I was told I was infertile. Over the years I've undergone tests, but the diagnosis is always the same…"

Her haunted eyes had fastened on him. She didn't move or cry out, but he saw pain break out on her face.

"Like anyone, I grew up thinking that one day I'd get married and have children. It was something I took for granted. Even after my first diagnosis, I didn't really believe it. I thought that surely in time the problem would go away and I'd be normal like everyone else. But every year I was tested, I was told that nothing had changed."

"I'm so sorry," she whispered, sounding agonized.

"So am I, Alessandra, because the diagnosis has impacted my life."

"So *that's* why you left me without saying goodbye? You thought I wouldn't be able to handle it?"

His lips thinned.

"Of course a woman wants babies with the man she marries. But there are other ways to have children."

"It's not the same. The other day when I was telling you about Valentina, you said you couldn't wait until you could have your own baby. It's a natural urge to want to procreate."

"Yes, but—"

"But nothing. I can't give any woman a baby, so I've been living my life with the reputation of being a dedicated bachelor. No one but my doctor, and now *you*, know I'm infertile."

"It happens to people, Rini. How tragic that you've let it rob you of the joy of life! It kills me that your fear has prevented you from settling down with a woman because you can't give her what you think she wants.

"I know you'd make a marvelous father, Rini. That's why there's adoption. Thousands of couples do it. For you to have lived your life since seventeen with such a dark cloud hanging over your head doesn't bear thinking about."

"You're very sweet, Alessandra, but you're not in my shoes." Her incredible reaction was all he could have hoped for and let him know her support would never be in question. His doctor had told him the right woman would be able to handle it.

But there was still something else to keep them apart.

All of it stemmed from his conversation with her aunt and her implied warning. Even now he held back, thinking it was better that she believe his infertility presented the biggest problem for them.

Alessandra stared at him. "What you're saying is that you're going to let this stand in the way of our having a relationship. If you really mean that, then you need counseling before you deny yourself the greatest joy in life."

"Therapy won't help me," he responded bleakly. He rubbed the back of his neck. "Combined with the conversation I had with your aunt, a relationship with you won't work."

"We're back to my aunt again?"

"She told me some things in confidence I can't share. Don't be upset with her. It's because she loves you."

"Rini—" she cried out, aghast. But she'd felt him withdraw emotionally from her. It had been a huge mistake to fly here after all.

Alessandra pulled out her cell and called for the limo to return to his house. Once off the phone she got up and walked over to the table to drink the rest of her lemonade. "Please tell the cook the food was delicious. Now if you'll excuse me, I'm going outside to wait for my ride."

Rini moved faster than she did and caught up to her outside the front door of the villa. "Alessandra—"

"It's all right, Rini. Though your explanation wasn't the one I expected, I got my answer, so thank you. Please forgive me for barging in here uninvited. I give you my promise it will never happen again."

When the limo turned into the courtyard, she rushed

to get in the backseat on her own. Rini was right there, but she refused to give him the satisfaction of meeting his eyes and closed the door herself. As the limo drove off, Rini's heart plummeted to his feet.

"Where do you wish to go, *signorina*?"

"The airport, *per favore*."

Alessandra didn't look back as they turned away. *No more looking back.*

Just now she'd wanted to comfort him over his infertility, but she sensed he wouldn't have been willing to listen to her. For him to have revealed his agony to her had been huge for him. Now that he'd told her the truth, he'd backed away, certain that she—like any other woman—wouldn't see him as a complete man.

Was that image of being incomplete the reason for his meteoric rise in the business world? Had he worked day and night to compensate for what he saw as an inadequacy? She'd detected the love in his voice when he'd talked about his sister and her babies. Pain pierced her heart to realize that every time Rini eyed his nephew, he was reminded that he could never give a woman a child from his own body.

She'd seen the way he'd kissed and loved Valentina's baby. The man had been there for her throughout her pregnancy. Yet all that time, he'd been gutted by the knowledge that he'd never be able to look forward to having a baby from his own body. Her heart ached for him.

As for his conversation with her aunt, that was something else again. If he'd been sworn to secrecy, then she wouldn't be getting an explanation out of him. Alessandra could go to her aunt and demand to know the truth, but it wasn't her right.

On the flight back to Metaponto, she stared out the window of the plane. Rini Montanari had been an earth-shaking interlude. But interlude was all he'd prepared for their association to be and became the operative word in her romance-less life.

Sunday evening the helicopter dipped lower over Ravello. Rini was late for his brother Carlo's birthday party, which Valentina and Giovanni were hosting.

For the last three weeks Rini had traveled to four areas of Calabria in Southern Italy, exploring the possibility of developing more oil sites. But he'd been in agony since Alessandra had left his villa and couldn't concentrate.

Nothing he'd visited turned out to be as promising as the land owned by the Caracciolo family. But he'd written that off. Unfortunately, blotting Alessandra from his heart was another matter entirely. With love in her eyes, she'd reacted to the news that he was infertile as if it was of no consequence to her. She'd assured him it didn't matter. The way she'd kissed him, as if he was her whole life, he'd believed her.

But her aunt's fear that a relationship with Alessandra might cause a permanent rift between the twins had prompted him to back away. Fulvia had told him how close the girls had been growing up, how much fun they'd had as children. But everything changed when Alessandra fell in love and then was betrayed by her sister and the man she'd thought she would marry.

The girls had finally gotten past it, but now they'd reached another impasse because Dea had met Rini first. Apparently she'd been devastated when he didn't want to date her. Hearing that Alessandra had been showing him around the property had upset her.

Though the situation was totally unfair, Fulvia had looked him in the eye and asked him if he wanted to be responsible for bringing on more pain between the two of them that might last. It was his decision to make.

In the end, Rini couldn't do it, so he'd had to let Alessandra go. All he could do was watch news clips on television about the discovery of the Temple of Hera beneath the waters off Basilicata in the Ionian.

Dr. Bruno Tozzi and his team had been given credit for the find and Alessandra's name had been mentioned. Every few days more information was being fed to the media about more discoveries of a courtyard and temple walls.

Rini was proud of Alessandra and the amazing work she was doing. Thanks to the coverage, he was able to keep track of her without having to make contact with her father. But having said goodbye to her had thrown him into a black void.

Once Rini arrived at the Laurito villa, he was besieged by family. He played with Carlo's daughter, then took turns enjoying the two baby boys. Giovanni chatted with him for a while, but it was Valentina who sequestered him in the sunroom just off the terrace. He couldn't get out of it.

"I thought you'd be bringing Alessandra with you. She's fabulous!"

"That's over."

"Why? I know you're in love with her."

His eyes closed tightly. "It can't work."

"Rini—are you saying she doesn't love you?"

He inhaled sharply. "She's never said the words."

"Have you?"

"It doesn't matter."

"Yes it *does*! Alessandra came to your house unannounced. I saw the look in her eyes when you walked out on the patio. If ever a woman had it bad…"

"There are things you don't know and I can't tell you. Don't make this any harder on me."

"Okay." She patted his arm. "I'll leave it alone. Keep your secrets and come on back out. Papà wants to talk to you and find out what new areas you've found for drilling."

"I wish I had better results to report."

Together they joined the others. Near midnight he flew back to his villa and did some laps in the swimming pool before going to bed. To his chagrin, sleep wouldn't come. He spent most of the night outside on a lounger.

Three weeks… If he didn't see Alessandra again soon, he'd go mad. But he had certain knowledge that bound him to stay away from her. Early Monday morning he put his emotional needs in the deep freeze and left for his office, prepared to announce some new sites for drilling that would please the board. He worked steadily until Thursday, when his secretary put through a call from his sister.

"Valentina?"

"Have you heard the news?" She sounded frantic.

His gut clenched. "What is it?"

"The seismic research facility in Malta registered a six-point-nine quake in the Ionian. The impact was felt all along the coast. It affected the diving site where Alessandra has been working with the institute."

Earthquake? He broke out in a cold sweat. *If anything happened to her, his life wouldn't be worth living.* To hell with what her aunt had told him. He needed to go to her and wouldn't let anything stop him.

"According to the news, apparently two or three divers were injured and transported to chambers at various hospitals on the coast. I found out the institute's oceanography boat docks at Crotone, so I'm sure some of the victims were taken there."

"I'm on my way. Bless you, Valentina."

He alerted his pilot and flew to the Naples airport, where he took the company jet to Crotone. En route he phoned to make certain a rental car was waiting. Following that he made calls to the three hospitals in the town, but no one would give him information about the injured because he wasn't a relative. Other injuries over the southern area had been reported and hospitals all along the coast were filling.

Emergency vehicles and fire trucks filled the parking area of the first hospital. He made it to the ER and learned that one diver had been brought there. No one would give him information, but one of the ambulance crew helped him out by telling him they'd transported a male diver here.

Thanking him, Rini drove to the next hospital. Again it was the wrong one. He made the rounds until he reached the last hospital. When he spotted Bruno Tozzi in the waiting room, he knew Alessandra had to be here. Avoiding conversation with him, Rini walked through the hospital to the director's office. He'd do whatever it took to be granted permission to see her.

"I'm fine," Alessandra assured her parents after she'd spent six hours in the chamber.

"Are you in pain?"

"No, not at all. The doctor told me I have a light case of the bends."

"Dr. Tozzi wants to see you."

"He worries about all the team, but I'm not up for visitors. Tell him I promise to call him tomorrow when I'm feeling better."

"All right. We'll find him out in the reception area and be back in two hours. The doctor said you'll be here overnight. We'll stay with you and drive you home in the morning. Try to rest in the meantime. Love you." They kissed her before slipping from the room.

No sooner had they gone than the door opened again. It was probably the nurse coming in to check her vital signs. When she saw who entered the room, her heart fluttered dangerously fast.

"*Rini*—what are you doing here?" After three weeks of not seeing him, the sight of his tall, well-honed body wearing a navy blue business suit was too much to handle in her weakened state.

"When I heard what happened, I couldn't stay away."

She turned on her side, trying to hide from him. "Did you talk to my parents?"

"They don't know I'm here."

Her breath caught. "You shouldn't have come. We've said all there is to say."

"I had to be sure you were going to recover," he said, his voice throbbing.

Tears stung her eyes, but she refused to let him see them. "I don't see how you found out where I was."

"A simple deduction after Valentina phoned me with the news about the epicenter of the quake."

She sighed. "How did you get past the desk? No one is allowed in here."

"I have my ways. Alessandra, you could have died out there. The doctor said you lost consciousness. It could have been fatal. Do you have any idea what I've been going through thinking I might have lost you?"

"Maybe now you know how I felt when you let me leave Positano and I knew it was over with you." A bitter little cry escaped her lips. "My parents will be taking me home in the morning. The only reason I can imagine you're being here is because of your guilt.

"What a surprise I'm going to survive! Surely it's a relief to you. That way you don't have to tell me what you've been holding back. It would only add to your guilt."

"Alessandra—" His mournful voice reached that vulnerable place inside her before he'd come around the side of the bed. She felt him cup her face with his hand. "*Grazie a dio* you're alive and safe."

She kept her eyes tightly closed. "I admit I'm happy about it, too."

His fingers toyed with her hair, sending fingers of delight through her exhausted body. "I once came down with a case of decompression sickness and know how it feels."

"One of the hazards when you're having fun."

"You don't need to pretend with me. I know you've had a fright and need sleep. Do you mind if I stay here with you for a little while?" He leaned down and kissed her lips. It felt like the touch of fire.

"The doctor won't like it, but that's up to you."

Peering at him through slits, she watched him draw a chair to the side of the bed next to her. He looked like a man with the weight of the world on his powerful shoulders. She needed him to go away and never come back, but she couldn't find the words.

In a minute a nurse came in to bring another bag for her IV. She checked Alessandra's vitals and left without saying a word to him. The man could get away with murder. "What did you do to get permission?"

"I told the administrator that Montanari Engineering would make a generous donation to the hospital if they'd let me in to see you."

There was no one like him, her heart cried out. "Rini Montanari. That was a naughty thing to do."

"It worked. That's all that mattered to me. To find you alive means everything. These last three weeks without you have been a hell I never want to live through again," he admitted, his voice breaking.

His pain was tangible. "Now you'll have to make

good on your offer and work all hours of the day and night to recoup the loss."

"It'll be worth it since the hospital helped save your life. You're the most precious thing in my world. I love you, *bellissima*," he said in the huskiest voice she'd ever heard. "Now go to sleep and don't worry about anything."

When Alessandra woke up in the middle of the night, she decided she'd been dreaming that Rini had come to visit her. Had he really said he loved her? There was no sign of him. The night nurse came in and helped her to the restroom, then walked her back to bed.

CHAPTER SIX

THE NEXT MORNING Alessandra awakened to find her parents in the room. They'd brought her a fresh change of jeans and a soft top, which she slipped into. At 11:00 a.m. the doctor discharged her with the proviso that she rest, stay hydrated and do no diving for at least fourteen days.

It felt good to be wheeled outside to her parents' limo. They made her comfortable before driving her back to the castle. Yet not at any time had they or the medical staff mentioned that Rini Montanari had been a visitor.

She'd really experienced a whopper of a dream to imagine he'd left his office to fly to Crotone in order to find out if she was all right. Alessandra was terrified it would take years, maybe a lifetime, to get over him. But what if she couldn't? The ache in her heart had grown acute.

Instead of going upstairs, she told her mom she wanted to stay in the day room and curled up on the couch under a quilt to watch television. Supplied with water and nuts, she didn't lack for the creature comforts. Alfredo wandered in and jumped up on her lap. He supplied the love she craved.

"Alessandra?" She lifted her head to her mother. "Are you up for company?"

"If it's anyone from the diving group, could you tell them I need a few days?"

"It's Rinieri Montanari."

She reeled in place.

"He said he visited you at the hospital, but the nurse put something in your IV and you fell asleep. He's anxious to know how you are."

Rini *had* been there!

She hadn't dreamed it after all and couldn't believe it. Thrilled, yet tortured by what her mother had told her, she couldn't concentrate on anything else. "I—I look terrible."

"That would be impossible," her mother assured her, "but if you want me to send him away, I will."

"No—but don't tell him to come in yet. Could you hand me my purse? It's over on the credenza."

Her mother did her bidding. Alessandra's hand trembled as she brushed through her hair and applied a coat of lipstick.

"Ready?"

Alessandra nodded. While she waited, she checked her phone to find a dozen texts from friends, one of them from Bruno, who wanted to know how soon she'd be back. Fulvia had sent her love and condolences. She wanted a good talk with her when she was feeling better.

Alessandra's editor was thankful she was all right

and told her not to feel pressured about delivering the book. He hadn't given her a deadline. But there was no message from Dea, the one person Alessandra wanted to talk to. The pit grew in her stomach as she realized her own sister hadn't tried to contact her. Why?

"You don't look like you've been sick," said the deep, familiar male voice she was dying to hear.

She looked up at the sinfully gorgeous man. "You're right. I'm a fraud."

Rini walked over to her. He'd dressed in jeans and a pullover sweater in slate blue. Combined with the soap he used in the shower to assail her, his presence had put her senses on overload. He reached down to scratch behind the cat's ears. "You have the right instincts, Alfredo. I'd trade places with you if I could."

In the next instant he leaned down and pressed a warm kiss to her mouth. "Welcome back to the land of the living. Your doctor told me you lost consciousness down there."

"Only for a moment. My buddy Gino knew exactly what to do. It all happened so fast."

"We can be thankful the divers with the institute are experts." He stood there looking down at her with an intense expression.

She squirmed. "Rini?" Her voice shook. "Why are you here?"

"Though I had my reasons, I treated you badly when I left here the first time without saying goodbye. My behavior was worse when you flew to Positano to see me and I wouldn't explain myself. I thought I was doing the right thing both times, but your accident has changed the way I feel about everything.

"I love you and I've never said that to another woman in my life. Almost losing you has made me realize I could no longer let my reason stand in the way of being with you, so I'm back to find out if you'd be willing to start over again with me."

While she sat there in shock, Liona wheeled in a tea cart laden with a meal for them. "If Alfredo is bothering you, I'll take him out."

"Oh, no. I love him right here. Thanks, Liona."

After she left, Rini got up and served both of them a plate of food and her favorite iced tea. His gaze found hers. While they ate he said, "Life has given both of us a second chance. What I'd like to do is invite you to my villa for a week where we can spend real time together."

Alessandra couldn't believe what she was hearing. She said the first thing that came into her head. "Can you take a vacation?"

"Of course. I want to get to know you without work or interruptions getting in the way. The nice thing about being CEO is that I can arrange it when I want. The doctor told me you shouldn't dive for at least two more weeks. You've shown me your world. Now it's time I showed you mine."

She smiled. "Like fishing?"

"Only if you'd want to."

"Rini, I adore the outdoors. Hiking, camping, all of it."

"The mountains are beautiful this time of year.

Could you talk to your editor and ask for an extension to turn in your book?"

"He already told me to take all the time I need."

If only Rini knew she loved him so much she felt like she could move mountains for him, but she was afraid. "When the week is over, *then* what? Will you consider you've done everything possible to obtain my forgiveness?

"Will we say goodbye like sensible people who've enjoyed their interlude together but knew it had to come to an end? You'll go your way because you can't offer me any more than what you've already done? I'll go mine?"

His jaw hardened. "Why don't we stop worrying about the future and just take things one day at a time? I need help because I've never done anything like this before."

She took a deep breath, surprised to hear the vulnerability in his voice. "Like what?"

"Invite a woman I care about to stay at my house."

"I've never done anything like it, either." Talk about needing help...

"The doctor told me you need rest and that you shouldn't fly until tomorrow. So if I leave you now, will you think about my invitation? I'll call you in the morning. If you decide you want to come, I'll arrange to pick you up in the limo and we'll fly in the company jet to Positano." He stood up.

"Where will you be in the meantime?"

"At the airport in Metaponto. I'm working in my office on the jet and will stay in the bedroom overnight.

I'll give you until ten a.m. to get in touch with me. If I don't hear from you by then, I'll be flying back to Naples."

She knew he meant it. This was it.

"If you'll give me your phone, I'll program my number for you."

Alessandra handed it to him. "Rini, whatever my answer is, I promise to call you."

Lines marred his arresting features. "I can't ask for more than that." He put the phone on the table. "You need rest now. Take care of yourself, *adorata.*"

The second he disappeared from the day room she wanted to call him back and tell him she'd go with him right now. But she needed to keep her wits about her. The decision to spend a week with him would change her life forever.

She kissed the cat's head. "Who am I kidding, Alfredo? My life changed beyond recognition the day he approached me in the foyer."

He said they'd take things a day at a time. She had no choice but to do what he wanted because at this point she knew she couldn't live without him. If it was only for a week, so be it. The man was so complicated it was driving her crazy. Somewhere in the mix, Rini's inability to give a woman a child had stunted his vision of life. She wanted to help him explore the world of adoption so he'd realize he could know total fulfillment.

With her heart ready to burst from the joy his invitation had brought her, she lay down and didn't awaken until hours later, when she heard her parents' muffled voices talking about her sleeping her life away.

Alessandra sat up, disturbing Alfredo, who jumped to the floor. "What time is it?"

"Time for you to be in bed. Let's get you upstairs."

Later when her mother tucked her in bed she told her about Rini's invitation. "I want to accept it, but I'm afraid."

"Don't let what Francesco did keep you from reaching out for your own happiness."

If her mother only knew this had nothing to do with Francesco. But at least she had her parents' blessing.

Liona brought her breakfast at eight, after which Alessandra pressed the button programmed to phone Rini.

"Am I going to hear what I want to hear?" he answered in that deep voice. She thought she heard a trace of nervousness and loved him for it.

"Maybe, unless you've had a change of heart during the night."

"Alessandra—don't keep me in suspense."

Her mouth had gone dry. "I want to come, but I need time to pack."

"How much?"

She chuckled. "Do we have to leave by ten?"

"I don't care when we leave today as long as you're with me."

"Then can we say noon?"

"I'll be at the castle at twelve and we'll eat on the plane during the flight."

"It sounds wonderful. Ciao, Rini."

After ringing off, she hurried around her room to get ready for her trip. She needed to pack everything under the sun. Normally she traveled light, but not this time. Besides sportswear for their outdoor activities, her plan was to bring a few new bikinis and evening dresses that would knock his socks off.

She turned on her radio to some light rock music. The cat wandered in her room and probably thought she was out of her mind as she danced around filling her two suitcases.

"Alfredo? You should see his gorgeous villa."

"Whose villa would that be?" asked a familiar female voice.

Alessandra spun around. "Dea!" After being caught off guard, she hurried over to her sister and hugged her. "I didn't know you were coming." With Rini coming for her, she couldn't believe the bad timing.

"Evidently not. Papà told me about your accident so I came home to see how you are. I thought you'd still be in bed recovering. I never expected to find you flying around your room having a conversation with the cat. What's all the packing for?"

"I—I'm going on a trip," she said, her voice faltering.

"I gathered as much." Dea's eyes looked at the bags on the bed. "I do believe you've emptied your drawers and closets. Are you finally giving Bruno Tozzi a chance? He's been after you for over a year."

"Not Bruno. I've never been interested in him that way. Actually I'm going to be a guest at Rini Montanari's villa." She'd had no choice but to tell her sister the truth.

At the mention of his name, any goodwill Alessandra had hoped could be resurrected between her and Dea on this visit had vanished. Her sister paled. Rini really had hurt her by not asking her out again. "Are you talking about the one in Naples or Positano?"

Of course her sister would know all about Rini. She'd danced with him on his friend's yacht. "I assume Positano."

"Is this because you showed him around the property for Papà?"

"Dea? Please sit down so we can talk." Alessandra closed the lids on her bags. "He'd been scuba diving with me. It's a sport we have in common. When he heard about the earthquake, he flew down. Yesterday he came by the castle to invite me to stay with him for a week."

"You mean he hasn't been here all month?"

"No. He's been gone for weeks on business. I was surprised to see him again." So surprised she'd thought she'd been dreaming when he came to her hospital room.

Dea's eyes followed her around while she packed her cosmetics. "I was shocked to learn he had business with Papà in the first place."

"Let's agree it was a shock all the way around." Alessandra was so uncomfortable she could hardly bear it.

Her sister studied her for a minute. "Be honest with me. Are you going with him because of what happened with Francesco?"

"No, Dea—not at all! How can you even think that?" Alessandra cried. "Whatever happened is long since buried in the past." She sank down on the end of the bed. "What do you want me to say?"

"Have you fallen for him?"

"I care for him very much."

"As much as you did Francesco?"

"You can't compare relationships. Francesco was my first boyfriend. I was young. As you reminded me, he ended up being a loser."

"Don't you know why I told you that?"

Alessandra frowned. "What do you mean?"

"He wasn't interested in me. Within a day of his arriving in Rome, he was chatting up another model."

"Oh, Dea—I didn't know that."

"I thought Mother would have said something. I'm telling you this to warn you about Rinieri Montanari."

Alessandra didn't want to hear it.

"On the yacht, his best friend's father, Leonides Rossano, confided in me that Rinieri was Italy's most eligible bachelor—as if my best friend, Daphne, and I didn't already know it. I read between the lines and deduced he'd been a player for years. Alessandra—he might end up breaking your heart after he gets what he wants from Papà."

"You're wrong about that, Dea. He doesn't want anything from him," she replied, defending Rini. "He withdrew his proposal weeks ago and has been looking elsewhere for oil in the southern part of Italy."

"I didn't know that. Sorry." Dea stood up, but Alessandra could tell the revelation had shaken her. "How soon is he coming for you?"

"At noon."

She looked at her watch. "It's almost that time now. I don't want to be around when he arrives, so I'll join the parents while you get the rest of your packing done. I'm glad you're recovered. Even gladder that I wasn't the one under the water when the quake struck."

A rush of warmth propelled Alessandra toward her sister. She put her arms around her again. "Thank you for coming. You don't know how much it means to me."

Dea hugged her back. "You've always been the brave one." She kissed her cheek before disappearing from the bedroom. Alfredo followed her out the door.

The brave one?

An hour later those words were still chasing around in Alessandra's psyche as Rini helped her out of the limo to board the Montanari jet.

Once they'd attained cruising speed, his steward served them an incredible lunch of lobster pasta with *sfogliatelle* for dessert. The shell shaped pastry had a divine ricotta filling with cinnamon. The wonderful flavor was beyond description.

They sat in the club area by the windows. His dark eyes never left hers. "I'm glad to see a smile. When I picked you up, you seemed preoccupied. For a moment I was afraid you still didn't feel well enough to come. We could have left tomorrow."

"I'm fine, Rini, but I have to admit I'm still a little tired."

"After what you experienced, that's understandable. When we get to the villa, you can rest all you want."

She looked out the window, wishing she felt the same excitement he'd engendered in her when she'd told him she would accept his invitation. But Dea's unannounced arrival had taken her by surprise. Though touched that she'd come to see her after her scuba-diving accident, her sister's questions about Rini had put a damper on this trip.

He was doing everything in his power to make her comfortable and had no idea Dea had been at the castle when he'd picked her up. She didn't want him to know, let alone tell him what her sister had said. Dea hadn't been unkind. Alessandra had been grateful for that, but she couldn't help feeling that her sister was suffering in some way.

Alessandra remembered how she'd felt when she'd first talked to Rini in the castle foyer. The immediate, overpowering attraction she'd felt for him had to be swallowed in the knowledge that he'd already been with Dea. She'd wondered then if she'd ever be able to get over him.

Yet today, her sister had to handle the news that Rini wanted to be with Alessandra enough to invite her to his home. If Dea had felt the same overwhelming attraction to him that night on the yacht, then who knew how long it would take her to get over Rini, especially if he ended up being in Alessandra's future. The thought haunted her.

"I think you really are tired." Rini got out of his seat and adjusted hers so she could lie back. "Our flight won't last long, then we'll put you to bed in the guest bedroom until you're feeling your old self."

"Thank you." But she no longer knew who her old self was. Life had taken on new meaning since she'd met him.

* * *

Something was wrong beyond Alessandra's fatigue. Rini had sensed it the moment she'd met him outside the castle doors with her suitcases. He'd expected to be invited in to speak to her parents, but she'd whisked them away as if she was in a great hurry. Rini hadn't questioned her about it. In time he'd get answers. They had a whole week. Today was only the beginning.

Once the jet touched down, the helicopter flew them to the villa. He carried her luggage while she made her way along the path that led to the back patio. She looked over her shoulder at him. "You truly do live in a garden. At home I smell the sea air. Here, I'm assailed by the most heavenly scents."

"After living in Naples with the occasional scent of sulfur from Vesuvius in the air, I chose this flower-filled mountaintop on purpose. Follow me through the house. Your room faces on the pool. You can walk out the French doors at any time and take a swim. Come on. Let's get you in bed."

He saw her eyes widen in appreciation when they entered the bedroom off the hallway. "It's a lovely room. Those blue hydrangeas on the coffee table take my breath."

"I'm glad you like them. Go ahead and freshen up. I'll be back in a minute." He put her cases down and left to get her a bottle of water from the kitchen. Rini had given Bianca the next three days off so he could be alone with Alessandra and wait on her himself.

When he returned, he found her sitting on the side of the bed still dressed in white culottes with a sharp front crease. She'd layered them with a multicolored blue silk top and looked so sensational, he couldn't take his eyes off her.

"I thought I'd find you under the covers. This is for you." He put the water on the bedside table before opening the shutters to let in the early evening light from the pool area.

She smiled up at him, but it lacked the joie de vivre he'd seen while they'd been out diving. "I'll sleep tonight. Now that I'm in your world again—but only because you invited me this time—I want to talk to you. Please sit down."

He sat in one of the upholstered chairs by the coffee table.

"Where's Bianca?"

"On a short holiday."

"So it's just you and me?" He heard a slight tremor in her voice.

He frowned. "Are you worried about being here alone with me?"

"Of course not." She got up from the bed and walked over to smell the flowers. "Can we have a frank talk? You said you wanted to start over again. I want that, too, but I need to understand you better."

Rini sat forward with his hands clasped between his legs. "Would I have brought you here if I didn't want the same thing? We've got all the time in the world. Go ahead. Ask me anything."

She darted him a curious glance. "You say that, but I wonder if you really mean it."

"Where's this doubt coming from?"

"I don't know exactly. Tell me about what happened when you first met Dea. Being twins, she and I have shared a unique past. Sometimes it has been eerie."

"In what way?"

"It's hard to explain, but there are times when even though we're two people, we think as one."

Rini got to his feet. "I've heard that happens to twins. But what does that have to do with me?"

"I'm not sure and am only feeling my way," she cried softly before turning away from him.

He put his hands on her shoulders and pulled her against him. "You sound frightened," he whispered into her fragrant hair.

"I am."

"Of what? Of me? Tell me." He shook her gently.

"I've been going over the conversation that my aunt had with you about me and Dea. You told her that you felt no connection with Dea, but it was different with me." Alessandra turned around in his arms. "But it doesn't provide all the answers."

"What more do you want?"

Her eyes searched his. "Will you bear with me a little longer and tell me your feelings when you realized I wasn't Dea?"

His hands slid to her face. "After I left your father's office and went back to my hotel in Metaponto that first night, I couldn't get you off my mind. Make no mistake. It was *you* I was thinking about. From a distance you had Dea's superficial features, the same features that had drawn me on the yacht. But the second you said you weren't Dea, I realized my mistake.

"You looked so adorable standing there in your shorter hair and man's shirt that didn't cover up your bikini. Tanned, no makeup, bare-legged, full of energy, duffel bag in hand. I thought, I've got to get to know this exciting woman! I told your aunt I felt a connection so powerful with you, I couldn't wait to get back to the castle the next morning to see you again."

He felt Alessandra's anxiety before she eased out of his arms. "Thank you for being so honest with me." She was shivering.

"Now that I have, do you want to tell me what's going on in your mind?"

"After I entered the castle, I heard a voice call out *signorina.* You'll think I'm out of my mind, but when I saw you walk toward me, it was like seeing the prince who'd haunted my dreams come to life before my very eyes. I felt your imprint on me before you said a word.

"But the second you started talking, I realized you thought I was Dea and my dream was crushed to grist. She'd had a history with you. She'd been there first. I'd never experienced such envy in my life. I've heard of love at first sight, but I never imagined it would happen to me. My pain that she'd met you first was too excruciating to bear."

Her eyes glistened with unshed tears. "Until I learned the truth of your relationship with Dea during our drive, I'd been forced to keep my feelings bottled up and pretend nothing was wrong in front of my father."

Her words shook Rini. *"Adorata."* He reached for her, but she took another step back. "I haven't finished. There's something else you need to hear."

Rini couldn't take much more and attempted to get his emotions under control. "What is it?"

"When Dea and I were little girls, we had many of the same likes and dislikes that in some cases baffled everyone. One of the things we had in common was to talk about the princes we would marry one day. We played our own form of house with a miniature castle and all the characters Papà had made for us.

"Our mother and aunt gave us beautiful clothes to dress our dolls. Dea always had the most glamorous and stupendous outfits because they knew how much she loved fashion. I was given a fabulous boat that would sail me and my prince around the castle and the world."

The lump was growing in Rini's throat.

"We played for hours about living in the castle all our lives and being happy forever with our princely husbands and children. In our case it wasn't pure fiction considering the lives of our titled parents and heritage."

"Alessandra—"

"Let me finish," she interrupted. "You were there when she first laid eyes on you. You saw what I can't see. Rini, I'm convinced that when Dea met you on the yacht, she had the same experience I did. She saw you sitting there and knew you were the prince of her dreams. It was one of those times we were both the same person. By the expression on your face, I can tell I'm right."

He closed his eyes tightly for a minute. *Incredibile!* This talk with Alessandra answered the questions that had lingered in his mind about Dea. In view of what he'd just learned, the way she'd linked her arms behind his head and the ardent kiss she'd given him when they'd stopped dancing as if she'd been claiming him for her own made a strange kind of sense. Her actions had borne out Alessandra's theory.

Guido had acted nonchalant about it, but Rini had seen the glint of envy in his friend's eyes. That was the only time he'd ever known him to show a side of emotion that surprised him. But Rini couldn't be that cruel to Dea or Alessandra by telling her what Dea had done that night to show her attraction to him. It had to be a secret he would take to the grave.

His head reared. "What you're saying is, Dea is now the one devastated."

"Maybe."

"Then we're back to where we were before. If your guilt is going to keep you from enjoying this vacation with me, then I'll fly you back home in the morning."

"No, Rini—that isn't what I want. I just needed to have this conversation with you."

"But it doesn't solve anything, does it?"

"I guess I want you to tell me what we should do."

"If you mean that, then I suggest we table our concerns and enjoy our vacation. We'll just have to hope that time and work will help Dea get over whatever disappointment she's feeling." But that wasn't going to be easy since he still hadn't forgotten the conversation with her aunt. He'd been burdened by it. "As for you and me, I'd hoped to take us on an overnight hike tomorrow."

"You know I'd love that."

"Then we'll pick you up a lightweight backpack and

sleeping bag in the morning." She nodded with a smile. "How are you feeling now?"

"Much better. I'm getting hungry and know you are. Why don't we go out to dinner someplace in Positano."

"I've been anxious to show it to you. If you're ready, we can go now."

CHAPTER SEVEN

As Rini helped Alessandra into the black BMW parked in front, he squeezed her waist and kissed the side of her neck. When he reached for her hand and held on, her heart pounded with anticipation of the night to come. He started the car and they wound through the lush greenery toward the town center. She could see the twinkle of lights from the fabulous villas half hidden behind cypress trees and palms.

The interior of the car smelled of the soap he used in the shower. She was so in love with him it was impossible to hide it from him. If she didn't put Dea out of her mind, she could ruin this incredible time for them.

"Whoa. We're right on the edge of the cliff."

Rini flashed her a smile and parked the car along the side of the narrow road. "We've arrived at my favorite place. You'll love the view from here." She could hear soft rock music as he helped her out. They walked up the rock steps lined with flowers growing out of the vegetation to the little restaurant perched high up. The view from the terrace, where a band was playing, opened to the sea below between two mountain sides.

She gasped and clung to him. "That's a steep drop."

"Kind of like dropping eighty feet with you in our own private world." Trust him to remind her. "Come on, *bellissima*."

He put his arm around her shoulders and guided her to an empty, candlelit table. The romantic ambience made her feel feverish. Rini seated her and asked for wine from the waiter who recognized him. "Will you trust me to order for you?"

"If you'll trust my cooking when we eat along the trail tomorrow evening."

"I can hardly wait." After the waiter walked away, Rini reached for her hand and pulled her onto the small dance floor, where another couple was dancing.

"There's no room for anyone else."

"That's the whole idea," he whispered before biting her earlobe gently. They danced in place, sending her body temperature skyrocketing. "If you knew the dreams I've had about holding you like this. Tonight there's no wet suit to separate us."

She chuckled. "I noticed."

"I never want to be separated from you," he admitted in a husky voice and crushed her to him. Alessandra closed her eyes and rocked in place with him. Never sounded like forever. Was it really possible? But that question led to the troubling question about Dea still hanging over her head, shooting more pain to her heart. So it was better not to think, just relish this night under the stars with Rini.

"I could stay this way indefinitely," she murmured, "but I can see our food has arrived. Let's get you fed."

"How lucky am I to be with a woman who understands me." He walked her back to their table and they plunged into an exquisite meal of octopus on creamed potatoes and prawns, followed by vegetables and *carpaccio* of swordfish with a dessert of *salame de chocolat*.

"If we keep eating like this, I'll have to buy me a larger wet suit," she quipped.

His dark eyes glinted with amusement. "We'll hike it off tomorrow. For now you need to get home to bed. It's been a long day for you."

"I have to admit bed will feel good tonight."

"I knew it." He paid the bill and ushered her out of the restaurant. "Careful as we go down the stairs. Hold on to me."

She didn't need his urging as she clung to him. He walked her to the car, keeping her hugged against his side. Before he opened the door, he lowered his head to kiss her. She'd been dying for it. The passion he aroused in her was so powerful, she almost fainted. Someone in a car driving by let out a wolf whistle, causing her to blush in embarrassment. Rini only chuckled and opened the door so she could hide inside.

"Sorry about that," he murmured as they drove back to his villa.

"No, you're not."

"Would you believe me if I told you I couldn't help myself?"

Yes, if his desire for her was half as great as hers for him. She rested her head against the back of the seat. "This has been a wonderful night. I rarely drink wine and am afraid I drank too much."

His hand reached out to give her thigh a squeeze, sending rivulets of desire through her body. "One glass?"

"Already you're a corrupting influence on me."

Male laughter rang inside the confines of the car. "Didn't you know you've become my addiction? You'd better lock your door tonight."

She rolled her head in his direction. "I trust you, Rini."

"Maybe you shouldn't."

"If I didn't, I wouldn't be going camping with you. Where are you going to take me?"

"Along the footpath of the gods."

"Did you just make that up?"

"No. It's the name of a trail formed by man years ago along the Amalfi Coast. In my opinion it's one of the most striking panoramas of this world. You'll know what I mean when we get going. We'll follow it part of the way through gorges and precipices, then veer inland into the mountains."

"You've given me goose bumps."

"When you uncovered the mouth on that head, it raised the hairs on the back of my neck."

She eyed him with longing. "I can't believe how you just happened to know where to dive."

"Pure selfishness. I wanted you to myself." He pulled into the courtyard and escorted her inside the villa to her bedroom. Putting his hands on her shoulders he said, "Tonight was the perfect way to start our vacation. I'll see you in the morning and we'll get going whenever you're ready. Sleep well."

He gave her a brief kiss before exiting the room. It was a good thing. If he'd lingered, she wouldn't have let him leave.

Before she went to bed, she hung up a few things in the closet, then checked her phone. Her mother had texted her to find out how she was feeling since her hospital stay. There was no mention of Dea, who was probably still there. Alessandra texted her back, telling her she felt fine and that they were going hiking tomorrow. She sent her love to her parents. But when she climbed under the covers, her heart ached for Dea, whom she knew was in deep pain.

The ringing of the house phone at the side of the bed awakened Alessandra the next morning. She checked her watch. Seven thirty a.m. He was a morning man who loved fish. Little by little she was learning those precious things about him. With a smile she reached for the phone. "*Buongiorno*, Rini."

"Hot coffee is waiting for you in the kitchen when you're ready, but there's no hurry."

The excitement in his voice was contagious. She swung her legs over the side of the bed. "If I told you I couldn't make it until noon, you know you'd have a heart attack."

"Please don't tell me that."

"You'll have to be patient with me," she teased. "Ciao."

She hung up the receiver and raced around the room getting ready, once she'd taken a shower. After diving into her suitcases, she pulled on jeans, a T-shirt and hiking boots. She packed a cloth bag she'd brought in her suitcase. Quickly she filled it with extra clothes, socks, a hoodie, a flashlight, matches, cosmetics and a brush—all the little things needed for their hike. She'd attach it to the backpack they were going to buy her.

When she hurried through his elegant home to the kitchen, she discovered she'd only taken eight minutes to get ready. Not bad considering the gorgeous male drinking coffee had assumed she would keep him waiting for hours.

The look of surprise on his handsome face was so comical, she thought he would drop his mug. Alessandra grinned. "Got ya."

His eyes blazed with intensity. In the next breath he wrapped her in his arms and whirled her around. "I figured five more minutes and I was charging in to get you."

"Now I wish I'd waited."

A bark of laughter escaped his throat before he kissed her fiercely. He didn't let her go until she struggled for breath. "I've made breakfast. Go ahead and eat while I take your bag out to the car with the food I've packed."

"You made food for our hike? I could have helped."

"Bianca always has my favorite meat and cheese pies on hand. We'll pack some to take with us."

"I'm salivating already."

She reached for a ham roll and grapes. After swallowing coffee, she hurried out to the car. Rini locked up the house and they left for the town to pick her up a backpacking frame. He knew exactly what he wanted for her and soon they were on their way to the outskirts of Positano, where he parked the car in an area reserved for hikers.

Rini was a master at assembling all the gear, which included a tent, fishing gear plus all the other things they'd brought. "How does that feel?" he asked after helping her adjust the straps. "Is it lopsided?"

"It's perfect and the day is absolutely glorious."

Through her sunglasses she stared at the striking male specimen standing before her wearing his own pack. He carried the bulk of their equipment as if it was nothing and smiled back at her through his sunglasses. "Get ready to be astounded by the sights."

"After you, Captain."

They were off. She followed him along a well-worn path for about a mile. Before she knew it they'd come to a section with a thousand-foot dropoff and no railing. "Rini," she squealed in awe.

"We're at the top of the cliff. You'll notice that people live up here and use this path coming and going."

"It's a miracle. Unbelievable." They continued walking and ran into farms and terraces that grew fruits and vegetables.

"Some people come here for a hike and decide to live here in one of the little houses on these mountains."

"I can see why. It's so peaceful up here, unconnected to anything else."

"You should be here during a storm. The clouds drift in from the sea and literally collide with the cliffs."

"The view from this spot is breathtaking. That water is so blue, I have to take a picture." She pulled the phone out of her pocket and insisted he get in it. They took turns so he could capture her, then they trudged on.

Alessandra really did feel she was walking on the footpath of the gods. One of them was right in front of her. He took such wonderful care of her every step of the way, she felt cherished.

They stopped at noon to eat lunch under a tree, then made a turn into the interior. Rini was an encyclopedia on the flora and fauna, let alone the history of the region governed by Byzantine rule from the third century when Amalfi was a trading post.

He took her past gorges and caves until they came to a mountain stream. "How are you at fly fishing?"

"I've only trolled for fish in the sea. You'll have to teach me."

"You're going to love it. Let's have a snack, then I'll set up our fishing poles and I'll show you how to cast."

It felt good to sit down and relax for a little while. He told her to look in his tackle box and see what kind of fly she'd like to use.

"Do they all work here?"

"Most of them. Look for a gray spider fly."

Alessandra rummaged around until she found one of that color. "This?" She held it up.

"That's it. I'll attach it and we'll walk down to the edge of the water to catch our dinner."

She watched him put her fly on the line before he chose a spot. "Show me how to cast."

He demonstrated five or six times so she could get the hang of it. "Okay. I think I'm ready to try." But it wasn't as easy as he made a look. She hit too low, too high and was too jerky. On her last cast she put the fly rod too far back and her line was snagged by a shrub. "Oh, no!"

Rini didn't laugh outright, but she knew he had to be chuckling as she scrambled up the side of the ravine to retrieve the fly. She made several attempts to no avail. "Help! I can't get it out!" He joined her and carefully extricated it from the prickly bush. "You're so good at this I bet you've never done that."

"You have no idea the mistakes I've made," he confessed after pressing a hungry kiss to her mouth. "Come on. Let's try it again."

"I'm embarrassed and want to watch you fish for a while."

He reached for his pole and aimed for a spot near a rock where the water pooled in the stream. On his third attempt to catch something at the same place, she saw a little fish grab his fly and he reeled it in.

"That was poetry in motion, Rini. I'll never be able to do that."

"Keep at it and you'll become an expert like you are at everything else." He got out his fish knife and removed the hook before throwing the fish back in the stream.

"Why did you do that?"

His eyes lit on her. "It was too small. Maybe he has a big brother or sister swimming around. Now it's your turn to try again."

She reached for her pole. "I'll aim for the same place you did." This time she threw it so hard, her pole landed in the water. *"Diavolo!"* she cried and jumped into the fast moving stream to catch it. But her boot tripped on a rock and she felt flat on her face. Her pole was carried farther downstream and got stuck around a bunch of rocks.

Like lightning Rini was there to help her up. By now they were knee-deep in the water. She lifted her head, not knowing whether to laugh or cry. His body was shaking with laughter, but being polite, he held it back. She loved him so much, she couldn't stay angry and started to laugh.

"Apologies for the slip."

His smile enveloped her. "Which one?"

"Both!" She broke free of his arms and made her way carefully downstream to recover her pole. "Ooh—a big trout just swam past me. I wish I could have grabbed it!"

Rini's deep male laughter poured out of him in waves. He moved toward her.

"No, no. I can make it back to shore myself. You're probably thinking, is this the scuba diver?" To her horror, the moment she said the words she slipped on a moss-covered rock and fell on her face, making another big splash.

When she stood up sputtering, there was Rini taking a picture of her. "That's not fair." Alessandra made a face. "This is ridiculous." She raised her rod and stomped out of the water, flinging herself down on a grassy spot. "Don't you dare laugh again."

Rini raised his hands. "I wouldn't dream of it. I was hoping we could hike farther to a small lake, but under the circumstances we'll camp here. I'll set up the tent so you can change out of your wet clothes."

"I'm all right. Let's keep going. Maybe I'll have better luck at the lake. I'll just troll for a fish by walking through the water and trailing my line."

One dark brow lifted above eyes that were dancing in amusement. "You're sure?"

"Let's go." She put on her backpack, deciding to carry her pole as is.

Rini started out first. All along the way she heard him chuckling, but he never turned around. A half hour later they dropped into a dark green gorge. With night falling fast, she was reminded of a primeval forest. The water from the stream emptied into a silvery narrow lake maybe a soccer field long. "It's shaped like a fat eel!"

"Spoken like a scuba diver. My father always thought it looked like a cigar."

"What about your brother?"

"A long blimp."

She laughed. "And you?"

"The Veil Nebula."

Alessandra blinked. "You love astronomy?" He nodded. "Did you ever consider becoming an astronomer?"

"No. The universe is too far away. With engineering I can get my hands on something once I design it."

"You like the tactile."

He nodded. "We'll set up camp here."

"I love this spot."

"Tomorrow we'll explore the other end of the lake. The water trickles down to become a waterfall and cas cades to the sea."

"I wish we didn't have to wait."

His gaze trapped hers. "You know the old saying. All good things come to those who wait."

"But I don't want to. Aren't I awful?"

"Later tonight I'll tell you what I think."

His words filled with promise almost caused her legs to buckle. In seconds he'd found them a grassy area and pulled out the blue-and-white two-man tent. She helped him erect it. They worked along in harmony. Finally she was able to go inside and change into warm gray sweats and tennis shoes. All her clothes needed to be dried outside, including her boots.

While he built a small campfire, she laid their sleeping bags side by side. The whole time Alessandra worked, she feared he could hear her heart thudding through the walls of the tent. Tonight they'd be sleeping together. This was the kind of heaven she never imagined could happen to her.

The light from the flames flickered, revealing his tantalizing male features. He'd thrown on a tan crewneck sweater over his jeans. His beautiful olive skin and dark coloring had been bequeathed by his Neapolitan ancestry. She could feast her eyes on him all night.

He watched her approach. "Come and sit down. I've made coffee to go with our pies."

"You're wonderful." She kissed his jaw before making a place next to him. "I'm sorry I couldn't contribute anything for our dinner. I'll do better another time."

"I'm counting on it," he murmured.

Her pulse raced as she sipped her coffee from the plastic mug. "Did your mother camp with you when you came out here?"

"Many times. Valentina, too. It's dark in this part of the mountains. She would bring her hand telescope and pass it around. I remember the hours she taught us about the constellations. Then she and Papà would slip into their tent and leave the three of us to enjoy the wonders of the universe. When I grew old enough, I understood they sneaked away to enjoy the wonder of each other."

"Oh, I know all about that." Alessandra chuckled. "Our family went on expeditions to Sicily. One time at the Valley of the Temples, we'd set up our camp. I thought we'd explore that first night while there was still light. But our parents told us to run along and enjoy ourselves.

"My sister and I eyed each other. We could always amuse each other. But it was another one of those times when we were both thinking exactly the same thing. You could say that night contributed to our enlightenment. I never looked at my parents the same way again."

Rini ate another pie. "I can relate." He let the fire burn down.

She sat cross-legged in front of it. "You've never told me where you went to school."

"University of Naples, then MIT in Cambridge, Massachusetts."

"You didn't meet a special woman during those years?"

He swallowed the rest of his coffee. "Yes, but I had a goal to finish my education and didn't let anything get in the way."

"Still, you know what I mean."

"She didn't matter enough to distract me from my agenda since I knew I couldn't give her a baby."

"I'm glad it didn't work out. Otherwise I wouldn't be with you now."

Rini stirred and got to his feet. "I want to continue this conversation, but would rather do it in the tent. Give me a minute to put out the fire." While he went over to the stream half a dozen times for water to douse the flames, Alessandra put the food away, then found her flashlight and took a trip behind a fat bush.

She kept the light on for Rini. Once she'd removed her tennis shoes, she entered the tent and lay down inside one of bags. Before long he joined her having exchanged his sweater and jeans for a dark blue sweatshirt and pants. His dashing smile took her breath. "I'm having the most fun I've ever had in my life."

"So am I."

He zipped up the tent flaps and opened the little screened window for air. Then he stretched out on top of his sleeping bag and turned toward her. "Do you mind if we keep the light on for a little while? I want to look at you while we talk."

She rolled on her side to face him. "I love looking at you, but you already know that."

"Alessandra?" He reached for her hand and kissed the palm. "Though I want to make love to you and never stop, I can't wait any longer to tell you what's on my mind first."

"What is it?"

"I'm helplessly in love with you, *adorata*, and want to marry you."

A cry escaped her throat. "Rini—"

"That couldn't be news to you." He sat up to face her. "I fell in love with you that first day. You weren't the only one who had a surreal experience."

Joy permeated her body. "I hoped you felt that way, but I hardly dared to dream I would ever hear those words."

"I've been afraid to say them because of the burden it puts on you."

She raised up on one elbow. "What burden? If you're talking about the fact that you can't give me babies, we've already had this conversation. It doesn't matter."

He shook his head. "Of course it does. But putting the reality of adoption aside, I'm talking about something else that I should have discussed with you weeks ago."

Weeks?

With that word Alessandra got a sinking feeling in the pit of her stomach and sat up. "This has to do with my aunt, doesn't it?"

Lines marred his features, letting her know she was right, and her frustration grew. "Instead of going diving that morning, you drove us back to the castle because you said you had business with Papà."

"I did," he muttered.

"That's interesting. When I came down to the office later to find you, he told me you'd gone. I heard the helicopter. According to him you were no longer interested in drilling for oil on our property. As a footnote he said you thanked both of us profusely for our time."

Her voice quivered, but she couldn't stop it. "I thought I was in the middle of a nightmare."

Rini was quiet so long, she couldn't stand it. "What went on with my aunt behind closed doors that caused you to leave without even having the decency to say goodbye to me in person? If what happened was so terrible, why didn't you tell me immediately?"

"I held back because I didn't want to betray a confidence that could bring pain."

"You've said that before. To whom?" she demanded.

He stared her down. "Everyone involved."

"I don't understand." Her tears had started. He brushed them away with his thumbs.

"My feelings for you ran so deep, I was afraid to spend another moment with you. The only thing to do was get away and never see you again."

She shuddered. "Don't you know how cruel that was to me? I'd fallen hopelessly in love with you and you knew it."

"Listen to me." He grasped both her hands. "I slipped away because I thought it was the best thing to do considering that I never intended to see you again."

Alessandra couldn't take much more. "Then why did you come back?"

"You know the answer to that. When I heard about the earthquake and knew your diving team had been affected, I came close to having a coronary. Nothing could have kept me away, not even my reason for leaving you the way I did in the first place."

"The accident didn't turn out to be that serious."

"It could have been deadly," he argued. "Don't you

know *you* were the most important person in my life? To think of losing you was so terrifying, I flew out of my office and left for Crotone. I had to search for you at two other hospitals before I found you. The moment I saw you again and your doctor told me you would recover, I realized I couldn't walk away from you a second time."

"Even if what you're about to tell me will hurt everyone?" Her question rang inside the tent.

"Yes. I have to risk it because I've just asked you to be my wife. But I was premature and don't want your answer until you've heard the whole truth from me."

A groan came out of her. "How long are you going to make me wait? Please just tell me what it is and let it be the end of all the secrets."

The sick look on her face devastated Rini, but she needed to hear everything. He drank part of his bottle of water first, then screwed the top back on. "Did you know that Dea flew to Taranto to see your aunt the morning after being on the yacht?"

A delicate frown marred her features. "That's news to me. I thought she told you she had some fashion shows that kept her in Naples."

Rini nodded. "That's what she told me. Does your sister have a special bond with your aunt?"

"Yes. Many times over the years she's gone to stay with her. My aunt took care of her after she was born so Mamma could have a break from two children at once. I usually spent time with our mother. I adore my aunt, but I'm pretty sure Dea developed a deep attachment to Zia Fulvia that has lasted. Our aunt is very glamorous and exciting. Naturally it meant the world to her since she couldn't have children.

"I've always appreciated that Dea and I were raised to be individuals. Neither Mamma or Fulvia played up our twin status. We were never dressed alike or put in the same classes at school. They wanted us to be able to express ourselves in our own way and have our own friends. Dea gravitated to Fulvia."

"Yet interestingly enough, in some ways you're more like your aunt than she is."

"You told me that before." She took a ragged breath. "You still haven't told me why Dea went to see her."

After listening to the explanation of Alessandra's background, Rini was beginning to understand a great deal. "Your sister wanted to talk to her about me."

A haunted look crept into her lovely face. "I'm surprised my aunt would reveal something that private to you."

"So was I, until she explained herself. I'm convinced that what she told me was motivated out of pure love for both you and Dea."

Alessandra lowered her head. "What did she do? Ask you to stop seeing me?"

"No. That's exactly what she didn't do. For the first few minutes she told me a story about a wonderful, brilliant girl who fell in love with a chef from Catania named Francesco and got her heart broken. Fulvia feared this girl would never get over it and never be able to forgive her sister, whom she'd always felt was more beautiful and loveable than herself. To Fulvia's great surprise and joy, this girl *did* get over her heartache. She seized life to the fullest without blaming her sister for anything."

"What?" Alessandra's head flew back in shock.

"That's right," Rini murmured. "Then she told me a story about another exciting, bright girl who fell for an engineer named Rinieri Montanari. He represented her prince incarnate, but she discovered he didn't feel the same way about her and she wanted to die."

Alessandra's chin trembled. "Oh, Rini..."

"*Oh, Rini* is right. Your aunt asked me to think carefully before I took another step. She feared Dea might not be as strong and courageous in battling her heartache as was the scholarly twin she'd always envied."

"Dea envied me?"

The shock on her face was priceless and told him this was a woman without guile. "She left me with a question and a warning before she went up to bed. Her exact words were, 'Is the recent love you feel for Alessandra greater than the lifetime love between twin sisters? Whatever you decide, you'll have to live with the consequences forever.'"

Rini didn't know how she'd respond after telling her the truth, but he hadn't expected her to turn away from him and sob into her pillow. *"Cara—"* He lay down next to her with his arm around her shoulders. She convulsed so much, all he could do was hold her and kiss her cheeks and hair until the tears eventually subsided. "Talk to me, *bellissima*."

After a long time she turned over, her face blotchy from crying. "The warning she gave you felt like someone just walked over my grave."

"Why do you say that?"

"Because when I found out you'd met Dea first, I determined to put you out of my mind. Nothing was worth coming between my twin and me since we'll be sisters forever. I was taken by surprise when Papà asked me to drive you around the property. Much as I wanted to be with you, I knew it would be taking a great risk. Fulvia's words have just confirmed my worst fears."

Gutted by her response, Rini shut off the flashlight and lay down on his back. "I'm sure your aunt didn't want me to reveal our conversation to you, but my world changed after your accident and I had to tell you."

"I'm thankful you did. I know she spoke to you out of love for Dea and me." He heard Alessandra's heavy sigh. "It took a lot of courage on your part to tell me and I admire you for keeping quiet about it for as long as you have in order to protect Dea."

"What worries me now is where you want to go from here."

"I don't know, Rini. In the morning I'll have an answer. Thank you for the greatest day I've ever known. *Buonanotte.*"

He heard the rustle of her sleeping bag. She'd turned away from him physically and emotionally. Unable to lie this close to her without reaching for her, he stood up and went outside to walk around. A three-quarter moon lit up the night sky. He didn't need a flashlight or a fire to see the forested landscape. The lake shone a mystic silver.

She's not going to marry you, Montanari. I can feel it in my bones.

Rini felt like he was burning up with fever. The cool night air brought some relief. He eventually planted himself beneath the trunk of a pine tree close to the tent so he could keep an eye on her. Several times he nodded off, but was wide awake at six craving coffee.

After making it, he heated it on the ultralight stove. Once he'd downed a cup, he walked over to the stream. Though he cast his line half a dozen times, nothing was biting yet. Maybe it was an omen to prepare him for what was to come.

He could have kept the secret he'd shared with her aunt, but wouldn't have been able to live with it long. Alessandra's tearful breakdown proved to him he'd done the right thing telling her. But it was possible he'd written the death sentence on a future life together with her.

Near eight o'clock she stepped outside the tent with a false smile, dressed in another pair of jeans and a white pullover. One by one she produced their sleeping bags, all rolled up and snug in their cases. He didn't have to hear a word from her to know their vacation had come to an end.

Her eyes darted to his. "*Buongiorno*, Rini. I detected coffee. It smells so much better out in the forest, don't you think?"

Without saying anything he poured her a cup and handed it to her.

"*Grazie.*" She eyed his pole. "I heard your line snaking in the air. Evidently you didn't have any luck fishing this morning or you'd be cooking our breakfast."

Rini had all the chitchat he could take. "Why don't you just tell me what I already know," he groaned.

This morning she was dry-eyed. "Papà once said that Zia Fulvia was the wisest woman he'd ever known. After what we talked about last night, I'm convinced of it. I'm honored by your marriage proposal, Rini. No thrill will ever equal it. But even if I'll love you to my dying breath, I don't want to see you again. I'm ready to hike back to the car whenever you say."

CHAPTER EIGHT

A WEEK AFTER returning to the castle, Alessandra realized she couldn't go on in this state of limbo. Even if she could dive again, she didn't want to. The thought of working on her book was out of the question. She unpacked all the gorgeous clothes she hadn't worn and put them away. Rini was on her mind night and day.

Though her parents didn't question her when she returned home having cut her vacation short, she knew they wanted to. But her father didn't probe and she was thankful for that. Her aunt came to stay for a few days to enjoy a change of scene. Soon she'd be able to get around without the wheelchair.

Fulvia was as warm and loving as always, giving nothing away about her private conversation with Rini. They did some puzzles as a family and Alessandra learned that Dea was back in Rome after another sensational show in Florence attended by some VIPs in the television industry.

But talking about Dea had been like pressing on a thorn until she was bleeding all over the place. The day after her aunt flew back to Taranto, Alessandra told her parents she was taking the Land Rover to visit friends in Metaponto and wouldn't be back until evening.

She gave Alfredo a kiss on the head before leaving the castle. "I don't like lying, but this is one time no one can know where I'm really going."

Once she reached the airport, she boarded a flight for Rome. The plane landed at noon. After hailing a taxi, she asked the driver to take her to the elegant apartment complex in the heart of the city where Dea had been living for the last year. The five-hundred-year-old street where it was located was a warren of fabulous shops near the Pantheon and the Piazza Navona.

When Alessandra approached the desk manager, he called her Signorina Loti. "You've mistaken me for her. Would you please ring her room? I'm her twin sister and have flown a long way to see her."

The middle-aged man did a double take. "*Scusi, signorina.* It's astonishing how much you two look alike. Except for the hair… I suppose in this case it will be all right to let you in."

"Thank you, *signor.* You're very kind."

Dea had a fabulous apartment on the third floor. Fulvia had come to Rome to help her furnish it in a lavish style. After she'd been let in and freshened up, she went out again and left a note for the manager to give Dea when she came in from work.

Four hours later she returned to the apartment building having eaten and done a little book shopping while she thought about what she was going to say to her sister.

"*Signorina?* Your sister came in ten minutes ago."

"Grazie."

Her heart pounding with anxiety, Alessandra took the lift and knocked on her apartment door. Dea opened it looking gorgeous in harem pants and a filmy short-sleeved top of aqua. "This is a surprise."

"For me, too."

"Come in."

They hugged before she walked into the living room. She put down her sacks and turned to her sister. "Forgive me for not letting you know I was coming. I didn't decide until this morning."

"No problem. I thought you were still on vacation in Positano."

She shook her head. "I returned early."

Dea eyed her critically. "What happened to change things?"

"That's what I want to talk to you about. Do you have time, or do you have other plans?"

"Not tonight. If you want juice or fruit, it's in the fridge."

"Thanks, but I've already eaten.

Her sister sank down on the sofa. "Go ahead. What's on your mind that has brought you all the way here?"

"The last time we saw each other, you asked me if I was seeing Rini because of what happened with Francesco."

"And you told me no. Why are we talking about this?"

She sucked in her breath. "Because I'm tired of ignoring the elephant in the room and I have a feeling you're sick of it, too."

Dea averted her eyes. It told Alessandra her sister knew exactly what she was driving at.

Tears sprang into Alessandra's eyes. "I'm going to tell you something I've never admitted to you before. From the time we were little, I looked up to you as my big sister."

"Three minutes hardly qualifies me for that title."

"It did for me because you came out first and no one let me forget it. You were beautiful and made friends easily. Everything you did was elegant and perfect. As I grew older, I felt more gawky and insecure around you. By our teens guys flocked around you. I'm ashamed to admit I was so jealous of you."

She had to be getting through to her sister because Dea lifted her head and stared at her in disbelief. "You... were jealous of me?"

"Oh, yes. When Francesco followed you to Rome, I didn't want to believe it, but deep down I wasn't surprised. I'd seen the way he'd looked at you. He never looked at me like that."

"I'm sorry, Alessandra," she cried.

"No, no. Don't be. You didn't do anything to attract him. You don't have to. It always happens because you're you. For a long time after that I lived in denial about it. Finally I realized I needed to grow up and face the fact that I could never be like you. It meant I had to work on myself."

"But you're perfect just the way you are!"

It was Alessandra's turn to stare at her sister in wonder.

"It's true. All my life I've been the one jealous of

you. You're beautiful without even trying and you're smart. You write books and do all these amazing things with the underwater archaeological society. I've envied your love of adventure and hated it that I have so many stupid fears."

Alessandra shook her head. "I had no idea."

"We're a mess," Dea muttered. "Since it's truth time, want to tell me why you're not still with Rinieri? He's the most gorgeous hunk of manliness I ever saw."

"I agree," she said quietly. "But I wish I hadn't met him."

"That's the biggest whopper of a lie you've ever told."

"Dea—"

"It's true. You're mad about him. So what are you doing here with me?"

"Y-you know why," she stuttered.

"Because I had a giant-sized crush on him first? That's true, but he wasn't enamored of me no matter how hard I tried to entice him. It killed me that he didn't want to see me again. I even told Zia Fulvia."

Alessandra swallowed hard to hear the admission she already knew about.

"She laughed and said, 'Dea Caracciolo—do you want to conquer every man you meet? What would you do with all of them? It's not natural!'"

Alessandra's laughter joined Dea's.

"She gave me a simple piece of advice that made sense. 'When the true prince of your dreams comes along, it'll work. Until then, dry your tears and do your thing you do better than anyone other woman in the country.'"

"Fulvia's wonderful."

"She is. So are you, and Rini Montanari is absolutely smitten with you. Otherwise he wouldn't have invited you to his villa for a whole week. The famous bachelor has fallen to his knees. If you don't snap him up, then you're a fool."

"You mean it?"

"Oh, come here." Dea reached out and hugged her hard. "I have something else to tell you that should make you happy."

"What?"

"I made a play for him. He didn't bite."

"What kind?"

"On the yacht, I kissed *him* good-night right on the mouth."

"Good grief!"

"Don't worry. He didn't kiss me back and turned me down when I asked him to go out to dinner with me the next night. Only an honorable man would do that. You're a very lucky woman and I'll welcome him into our family with open arms."

"I love you, Dea, and want only the best for you."

"I know that, and I love you, too."

"Let's never let anything come between us again."

"Never."

"We're sisters forever."

Forever.

"Now let's go on a shopping spree and find you an outfit that will deliver the coup de grâce the moment Rini sees you. Why not show up at his office and dazzle everyone in sight?"

"I only want to dazzle *him*."

"Then let's do it!"

The Montanari office complex dominated a portion of a city block in the downtown business center of Naples. At four in the afternoon, Alessandra was met by whistles and stares as she stepped out of the limo in her Jimmy Choo heels. She was wearing the designer dress Dea had picked out for her. It cost a fortune but she didn't care because she felt transformed in it.

The solid off-white pullover dress with long sleeves had a row of trendy buttons up the side from the tulip-styled hem to the neck. Around her shoulders she wore a flowing ivory-and-tan print scarf that matched the tan-and-ivory lace of her shoes.

Her hair glinted with streaks of gold among the brunette. She wore new lipstick in a deep pink with a soft blush on her high cheek-bones and a touch of eye shadow Dea said brought out her eyes. She'd never been so decked out. Her sister said she'd never looked more beautiful. Alessandra felt like she was moving in a fantastic dream.

His office building was like a small city, forcing her to pass through security before she could approach the bank of elevators. Her pride in his accomplishments made her throat swell with emotion as she rode one of them to the thirty-sixth floor, where his headquarters was located. She approached the secretary in the main reception area.

"I'm here to see Signor Montanari."

The attractive, thirtyish-looking woman looked up, then blinked. "You're Dea!"

Alessandra smiled, not minding it at all. "No, but you're close. I'm her sister."

"Do you model, too?"

"No. I scuba dive."

"Oh." Her blue eyes rounded. "Which Montanari did you wish to see?"

"Rinieri."

"I'm sorry, but the CEO is in a board meeting and can't be disturbed. If you'd like, I'll make an appointment for you."

At least he was here and not out of town. "Thank you, but no. I'll wait until he comes out."

"It might be several hours."

"I don't mind." *I'd wait forever for him.*

She sat down on one of the love seats with her ivory clutch bag in hand. Twenty minutes later she saw an attractive, dark-haired man who bore a superficial resemblance to Rini walk into the reception area and hand something to the secretary. His brother? A cousin?

The secretary must have said something to him because he turned in Alessandra's direction. Their eyes met before he walked over to her. "I understand you're here to see Rinieri?"

"Yes, but he didn't know I was coming. I wanted to surprise him."

The flattering male admiration in his eyes made her efforts to look beautiful worth it. "He's going to be surprised all right. I'm going back in to the meeting. I'll let him know someone is out here waiting for him, but I won't give you away."

Her heart fluttered in her chest. *"Grazie."*

"Prego."

Twelve men sat at the oblong conference table. Rini's Zio Salvatore scowled at him from a few seats down on the right. "I think we're moving too fast. Look what's happened in Greece!"

"If we don't strike now, someone else will." Rini was tired of the deadlock. Tonight he'd reached the end of his rope. He was ready to take off for places unknown to forget his pain. Guido had tried to talk to him, but Rini was in such a dark place, he wasn't fit company for anyone. Something had to change or his life wasn't worth living.

"My son's right," Rini's father said. "With this uncertain economy, we have to take advantage of these opportunities while we can."

While everyone offered an opinion, Carlo came back in the room. His brother's brows lifted, a signal that he wanted to talk to him about something. It would have to wait until they'd resolved the issue before the board.

"Let's take a vote," his cousin Piero said.

"We're not ready yet!" This from Rini's great uncle Niccolo.

The arguing went on another fifteen minutes. Rini received a text on his phone. Just so you know, Octavia said you have one more appointment before you leave tonight. The person is waiting in reception.

Since when? Rini didn't have the time or inclination

to do any more business once he left this room, but he nodded in acknowledgement to Carlo, who sat at the other end of the table. When five more minutes hadn't yielded a consensus, Rini brought the meeting to a close.

"It's late. We'll reconvene on Monday and take a vote then." Salvatore couldn't have been more pleased that no action had been taken yet. He came from the old school, unable to abide the kind of progress Rini felt the company should be making.

After slipping out a side door into his private office, Rini rang Octavia. "Send in the person who's been waiting. Since they're infringing on my weekend, tell them I can only give them one minute. My helicopter is waiting."

"Yes, sir."

While he leaned over his desk long enough to sign a pile of letters ready to be mailed, he heard a knock on the door.

"Come in."

"Signor Montanari? Please forgive me for barging in without an appointment, but this is a matter of life and death."

He knew that voice and spun around, convinced he was dreaming.

"Cat got your tongue?"

The vision before him left him breathless. He *had* to be dreaming!

"The last time we were together, you asked me an important question. I couldn't give you an answer then, but I'm prepared to give you one now. But maybe too much time has passed and you'd like to unask it."

He could hardly breathe. "Remind me of the question."

"You asked me to be your wife." The tremor in her voice made its way to his heart.

"I remember. But you had an irreconcilable conflict that prevented you from answering."

Her eyes filled with tears. "Since then I've *un*-conflicted it."

His breath caught in his lungs. "How was that possible?"

"Two days ago I flew to Rome and had the conversation with Dea we've needed to have since she visited me in Catania. It was the heart-to-heart kind that immersed two sisters in tears. It was a time of love and forgiveness for all past hurts and misunderstandings. In the end she told me something I needed desperately to hear. So do you.

"She said, 'I wanted Rini Montanari to want me, so I made a play for him and kissed him good-night right on the mouth. He didn't bite.'"

Rini's head reared. "She admitted that to you?"

"Oh, yes. There's more. She said she invited you to dinner but you turned her down flat."

He shook his head. "I don't believe what I'm hearing."

"I do. That's because you're an honorable man, my darling. Not only for turning her down because you didn't have those kinds of feelings for her, but for keeping that secret to yourself in order not to hurt her or me. She thinks I'm the luckiest woman alive. I am! She said to tell you that she welcomes you to the Caracciolo family with open arms. That's a good thing because I plan to be your wife. I can't live without you!"

She ran into his arms, almost knocking him over while she covered his face and mouth with kisses. "*Ti amo*, Rini. *Ti amo*."

"Hey, bro?"

Rini's eyes swerved to the door. Carlo had just walked in on them, but he came to an abrupt standstill and a huge smile broke out on his face. "Well, look what my *fratello* snagged on his last fishing trip! I wouldn't have missed this for the world. Looks like Guido's the only living bachelor left in Naples. I'll make sure you're not disturbed."

He closed the door. By now Rini had sat down in his chair with Alessandra in his lap. They kissed long and hard until he started to believe this was really happening. She looked and smelled divine.

"How soon can we get married, *bellissima*?"

"Whenever you want. I think the chapel in the castle would be the perfect place. Dea and I had a chapel in our play castle. We always planned elaborate weddings with our dolls. We even had a doll priest. Did you know Queen Joanna married one of her husbands there?"

Rini hugged her hard. "I can't think of a place more fitting for you."

"And you, because you're my prince. We'll invite all our friends and family. We have room for everyone. The cook will plan a wedding feast with all the fish you can eat." He started chuckling. "Dea will help me find the perfect wedding dress and Fulvia will help Mamma do everything else. We'll ask your sister to bring her babies and we'll dress them up like little princes. Alfredo will walk around excited because there's going to be food. And Papà will play the host with a twinkle in his eye."

By now his chuckling had turned to deep laughter. "There's one thing *I* want to do. Plan the honeymoon," he whispered against the side of her neck.

"I was hoping you'd say that. Can we leave now and go somewhere private where I can kiss you as long and wickedly as I want?"

"What a ridiculous question to ask the man who's headlong in love with the most gorgeous woman alive."

"I hope you'll always feel that way."

It took them a while to stop kissing long enough to make it to the roof. Rini told his pilot to fly them to Positano. "We're getting married, Lucca."

He grinned. "Tonight?"

"Don't I wish. It'll be soon."

With a background of Vesuvius, the helicopter rose into the evening sky. Rini was so full of emotion, he couldn't talk. While they were in the air, he pulled a ring out of his breast pocket. He'd bought it a month ago and had been carrying it around, keeping it close to him like a talisman.

"Give me your left hand, *adorata*."

Her whole countenance beamed as she did his bidding. He slid the ring on her finger. "It's fabulous, Rini!" She held it up close to inspect it. "The diamond and setting—this is like the one on Queen Joanna's hand in the foyer of the castle!"

"The foyer was the place I fell in love with you. She's

the reason you and I met. In a way I owe her my life. I'm glad you noticed."

Her beautiful eyes rounded. "You silly man. How could I not notice? Just wait till you see the ring I have planned for you."

Joy was a new emotion for him. So new, he clung to her hand, unable to find words.

CHAPTER NINE

ALESSANDRA STOOD OUTSIDE the closed chapel doors with her father, where they could hear the organ playing. After waiting a month for her wedding day, she was so anxious to be Rini's wife, she'd started to feel feverish in anticipation.

"Papà? Why are we waiting?" Everyone was inside including her husband-to-be, whom she knew was equally impatient to be married at this point.

Her distinguished-looking father, outfitted in wedding finery and a blue sash befitting the Count of Caracciolo, turned to her with a gleam in his eyes. "Your aunt has worked her magic."

"What do you mean?"

"As you are a princess of the Houses of Taranto and Caraciolla, the Archbishop of Taranto is going to preside. We're giving him time to enter the nave through the side entrance."

A quiet gasp escaped her. "Rini's not going to believe it."

"He's going to have to get used to a lot of surprises being married to my darling *piccola*."

She smiled at him. "You're loving this, aren't you?"

He leaned over and kissed her forehead. "Almost as much as you. After all the weddings performed in your playhouse castle, you're going to be the star in your very own. You look like an angel in all that white fluff and lace."

"Dea found it for me."

"Of course. That explains the long train."

"It's spectacular."

"So are you. I see your mother gave you her tiara to wear."

"Something old and borrowed. Papà? Do you like Rini? I mean really like him?"

"I think he's an exceptional man who has met his match in you."

While they stood there, Dea came around the corner toward them. She looked a vision in pale lavender carrying two bouquets. She handed the one made of white roses to Alessandra. "I outdid myself when I picked out this wedding dress for you."

"I love it. I love you."

"Do you know where you're going on your honeymoon yet?"

"Rini's lips are sealed."

"Lucky you." Dea kissed her. "It's time."

The doors suddenly opened and Dea took her place behind Alessandra and her father. Together they entered the ornate chapel with its stained glass windows, where a lot of history had been made. Every single person she loved was assembled. The archbishop added a solemnity to the occasion in his ceremonial robes. But she only had eyes for the tall, dark-haired man turned out in dove-gray wedding clothes standing near the altar.

The dazzling white of his dress shirt set off his olive skin coloring to perfection. He was her prince in every sense of the word. She prayed her heart wouldn't give out before she reached his side. His dark eyes seemed to leap to hers as she reached his side. While the archbishop addressed the congregation, Rini didn't remove his gaze from her.

"Surely heaven is shining down on these two people this day while they are joined together in the most holy ordinance of the church," the archbishop began.

Rini's hand held hers. He rubbed his thumb over her palm and wrist. She was trying to concentrate on the sacredness of the occasion, but his touch sent fire through her entire body. By the time they came to exchanging vows, he'd reduced her to a weakened state. Thank heaven the words were finally pronounced.

"I now pronounce you, Rinieri di Brazzano Montanari, and you, Alessandra Taranto Caracciolo, man and wife in front of God and this congregation. What God has joined together, let no man put asunder."

Her clear conscience over Dea had freed her from bondage. They both kissed with restrained passion, forcing themselves to hold back. But she was bursting inside with love for him. When she turned to face her family, her joy was so great she could hardly contain it.

"It won't be long now," Rini whispered in an aside. He squeezed her hand as he led them down the aisle and out the doors to the great dining hall that had once seen the courtiers of kings and queens. He reached around her waist and pressed her against his hip while they greeted their parents and guests. She saw her father hand something to Rini before they took their places at the head table.

Guido and his parents sat together before he took over the emcee job. "One good thing about this marriage. Alessandra has taken him off the market. Now *I'm* the most famous bachelor of Naples." He ended with a wonderful trail of anecdotes about Rini that had people bursting with laughter.

Dea took her turn. "Alessandra and I were joined at the hip in the womb. It feels strange to be on my own at last, but I couldn't be happier for her." She shared more nuggets of personal moments with Alessandra to delight their audience. Alessandra turned beet-red.

One by one, the members of both families paid tribute. Valentina brought tears to everyone's eyes in her tribute to Rini, who'd been so wonderful to her after their mother had died. Carlo reminisced over his own touching memories of Rini when their mother was alive.

There were more speeches, but she could tell Rini was restless. In a move that appeared to surprise him, she rose to her feet with some difficulty considering the length of her train. "Rini and I want to thank everyone for making our wedding day unforgettable. Zia Fulvia? What would we do without you? In fact, what would we do without our marvelous staff, my darling Liona and her cat Alfredo and the families we cherish."

Rini got to his feet. "I couldn't have said it better, but I hope you'll understand that we need to leave."

"Sure you do," Guido quipped loud enough for everyone to hear. Dea laughed at his remark. Alessandra hid her head against Rini's shoulder as they left the hall on a run. He led her through the hallway to the foyer. They raced out the doors to the Land Rover. He stuffed her inside and ran around to drive them to the helipad.

Their pilot was all smiles as he helped her on board. Once they were strapped in, they took off with Rini seated in the copilot's seat. "*Complimenti*, Signora Montanari."

"*Grazie*, Lucca. My husband won't tell me where we're going."

"We'll be there soon, *bellissima*."

"It was a beautiful wedding, don't you think?"

"Yes, but I thought it would never be over."

"Mamma said the wedding is for the bride. She was right."

The pilot flew east to the Adriatic, then dropped to a luxury yacht making its way through the water. Her eyes darted to Rini's in question.

"Guido's parents insisted on providing their yacht for our honeymoon. We can stop anywhere we want and scuba dive in Croatian waters. There are caves you'll love to explore."

"It sounds wonderful, but as you once told me, I don't care where we go as long as we're together."

Lucca set them down on the yacht's helipad with remarkable expertise. Rini jumped out and reached for her, carrying her across the deck to a stairway with the master bedroom on the next level down. She could see everything had been prepared for them ahead of time.

Flowers overflowed the living area of the suite, creating a heavenly perfume.

"At last." The way he was looking at her caused her limbs to quiver. He wrapped his arms around her and undid the buttons of her wedding dress, while he gave her a husband's kiss that never ended.

Somehow they gravitated to the bedroom, leaving a trail of wedding clothes and a tiara. The covers had been turned down. He followed her on to the mattress, burying his face in her throat. "Alessandra, I can't believe you're my wife. I've been lonely for you for years."

"You don't know the half of it. I love you so terribly. Make love to me, darling, and never ever stop," she murmured feverishly until they were devouring each other and conversation ceased.

For the rest of the night they communicated with their bodies, trying to show each other how they felt in ways that words couldn't. Rini took her to another world, where she felt transformed. When morning came she couldn't bear for the night to be over. Even though he'd finally fallen asleep, she started kissing him again to wake him up. His eyes opened.

"You've married a wanton. Forgive me."

In a surprise move he rolled her over so he was looking down at her. "I wouldn't have you any other way. You're perfect." Another long, deep kiss ensued.

"But was it…good for you?"

He moaned. "What a question to ask me? Can't you tell what you've done? I'll never want to go to work again."

"I don't know if I'll be able to let you go."

"Then our problem is solved. *Buongiorno, moglie mia.* Welcome to my world."

She pressed another avid kiss to his compelling mouth. "We're not dreaming this, are we? This is real. You really are my husband."

"You'd better believe it, but in case you're in any doubt, let me prove it."

To her joy he proved it over and over. Except for taking the time to eat, she drowned in her husband's love. They didn't surface for three days.

At the end of that time they planned to go up on deck. But before they left their room, Alessandra rushed around in her robe to pick up their wedding attire still all over the room. It would be too embarrassing for any of the ship's staff to see the hurry they'd been in after arriving in the helicopter after the ceremony.

"Darling? I found this in the pocket of your suit." He'd just come out of the bathroom with a towel hitched around his hips. She handed him an envelope.

"Your father slipped this to me at the castle."

"I wondered what it was."

Rini opened it and pulled out a letter.

"What does it say?

"'Alessandra's mother and I wanted to give you a wedding present, but it's for selfish reasons on our part. If you want to drill on our land, you have our permission. That way we know we'll see you part of the time when you have to be at the castle to supervise everything.'"

He looked shocked. Alessandra slid her arms up his chest and around his neck. "Now you know how much they love and trust you."

"I never expected this."

"That's one of the reasons why they did it. But my guess is, Fulvia helped Mother see that your vision can help our country."

"Is that what you think, too? Your opinion is the one that matters to me."

"You know I do. Otherwise I would never have taken you to see my aunt."

"We can thank providence you did. She proved to be the catalyst that helped you and your sister put away your demons."

She nodded. "One problem solved and one to go."

He kissed her with almost primitive desire. "We don't have another one."

"You're almost thirty-three and not getting any younger. Neither am I. If we're going to adopt children, we need to do something about it soon. These things can take time."

His brow dipped. "Are you desperate for a child already? Or tired of me already?"

"Rini... I'm not going to dignify either of those questions with a response. I'm simply looking ahead to our future. When I saw you playing with Ric and Vito a couple of days ago, I could picture you playing with our own children.

"I'm not saying we're ready now. Maybe the day will come when you'll want to consult one of the attorneys who work for you and we'll make an application to begin the process. But if it upsets you, I promise I'll never bring it up again."

He let out a ragged sigh and crushed her in his arms.

"I'm sorry I got so defensive. It's different when you know you can't have your own baby. I don't know if I could be a good father."

"No one knows if they're going to be able to handle it. I bet if you ask Carlo, he'll tell you he was nervous before their daughter was born."

"But he knew it was his."

"But he didn't see the baby until she was born. If we adopt, we won't see the baby until it's born. What difference will it make?"

He smiled. "You're right. It won't."

"Come on. Let's go on deck and soak up a little sun."

"I have a better idea. How would you like to fly to Montenegro for dinner? We've been away from the ship for three days. Wear that gorgeous outfit you showed up in at my office."

"You liked that one? I'll start getting ready right now."

"I like you in anything when you have to wear clothes, but if I had my way…"

"That works for me where you're concerned too." She giggled and ran into the bathroom, but he caught up to her before she could lock the door.

EPILOGUE

Eight months later

RINI WAS AT the drilling site when his cell rang. Hopefully it was Alessandra telling him she was back at the castle after her visit to her editor in Rome. Her book on Queen Joanna would be coming out shortly and the publisher wanted to set up some book signings.

But when he checked the caller ID, he saw that it was Maso Vanni, the attorney who'd helped him and Alessandra make application for adoption. The unmarried mother from Naples who'd been the right match for them was expecting her baby in a month. Rini hoped everything was all right. The last thing he wanted was to give his wife bad news.

He clicked on. "Maso? What's going on?"

"Lauretta Conti is in labor."

"What?"

"The doctor is trying to slow things down, but my advice is for you and your wife to get to the hospital as soon as you can."

"We'll be there!" He rang off and phoned Alessandra, but her voice mail was on. He left her the message that he was on his way to the hospital in Naples because Lauretta Conti might be having her baby in the next little while.

After leaving instructions with the crew, he drove to Metaponto for his helicopter flight to the hospital in Naples. There was no time to shower or change out of his khaki work clothes. En route he tried several times to reach Alessandra. "Please answer as soon as you can, *cara*."

Once at the hospital he was shown to Lauretta's private room. The doctor said they couldn't stop the baby from coming. "My patient needs a Caesarean. You're about to become a father."

Rini had never felt so helpless in his life.

"The nurse will show you where to scrub."

The situation was surreal as he washed and put on a gown. He was given a mask and gloves. Before long he returned to the room and stood by the head of the bed. He and Alessandra had met with Lauretta several times in preparation for the baby's arrival. Where was his wife?

Suddenly things began to happen. The anesthesiologist administered a spinal and a team came in while the doctor performed surgery. Everyone seemed so calm. When he heard a gurgling sound, a thrill shot through him. A second later the newborn cry of the baby filled the room.

The pediatrician took over and Rini was told to follow him to the room next door. "I understand you're going to be the father of this baby."

"Yes." But fear held him in its grip.

"Where's your wife?"

"She's on her way." She would be when she got the message.

"He's strong for a preemie. Six pounds, twenty-one inches long. Seems to be breathing on his own. As soon as we clean him up, you can hold him."

The baby had a dusting of dark hair. Rini watched in fascination as the doctor checked him out. One of the nurses came in and put the baby in a little shirt and diaper, then wrapped him in a receiving blanket.

"Sit down, *signore*, so you can hold your son."

Nothing had seemed real until she placed the baby in Rini's arms and he was able to look at him. The sight of the beautiful boy caused his heart to melt. He didn't make a peep. Rini couldn't tell the color of his eyes yet. His little mouth made an *O*.

"You've got a cute *bambino* there," the nurse said. "Don't be afraid of him. He won't break. I'll get a bottle ready for him."

Taking her advice, he put the baby on his shoulder and patted his back. The warmth of his tiny body was a revelation. Emotion swamped him as he realized this baby would look to him forever as his father. Rini removed the mask and kissed his little head, wanting to be all things to him. A longing to protect him and give him everything possible filled his soul.

"Here you go." The nurse handed him the bottle. "He'll be hungry soon. Tease his mouth with the nipple and he'll start to suck."

He followed her advice. Like magic the baby responded and started to drink with gusto. "Hey, you like this, don't you? I like food, too. I'm a big eater. Always have been."

"Like father, like son." His wife's voice.

He turned his head. "Alessandra... How long have you been standing there?"

"Long enough to watch you bond with him. I knew it would happen."

Tears filled his eyes. "It did. I was terrified when I got here, but when the nurse put him in my arms..."

She smiled down at both of them. "Fatherhood took over."

"You need to hold him."

"I will in a minute. It's enough to watch the two of you. What did the pediatrician say?"

"He seems fine and his lungs are functioning even though he came early."

"We're so blessed." Her eyes glistened with moisture. "Can you believe we're parents now? I'm a new mom and didn't even have to go through labor."

"You're the most gorgeous mother in the world."

"And you're already a natural father. I can tell he's so happy to be there with you. He has almost finished his bottle."

She put her arms around his shoulders and stared down at the baby with her cheek against Rini's. "We're going to learn how to do this minute by minute. I love you for being willing to adopt. I know it wasn't an easy decision to make."

Rini was close to being overcome by his deepest feelings. "I never dreamed I would see this day."

"I know. It's a surprise since you're a true man of vision."

He cleared his throat. "I don't think you have any idea how much I love you for marrying me when you knew I couldn't give you a baby."

"But you *have* given me one, darling. He's in your arms and you're both in mine. What more could a woman ask for in this life?"

* * * * *

HOW TO BE A
BLISSFUL BRIDE

STACY CONNELLY

To Cindy—

So glad our love of romance (and especially of Special Edition) has brought us together as friends and fellow writers!

Chapter One

Chance McClaren took a deep breath of cool, ocean-scented air and willed his body to relax. Closing his eyes, he let the sound of the waves rushing against the rocky shoreline wash over him. Faint sunlight barely broke through the November haze, but he focused on the warmth against his skin. Gradually, his muscles started to relax. Neck, shoulders, arms. Not his right leg, but that tightness was due to more than tension.

He could do this. He could smile, he could play along. He could pretend...for as long as it took for his body to heal. For as long as it took to get the hell out of Clearville.

Opening his eyes, he hazarded a glance over his shoulder and scowled. The old lady was still there. Hovering over him. Staring down at him. Watching him.

Turning at the waist until the joints in his back popped, Chance muttered, "You're losin' it, man."

He rubbed at the back of his neck, the skin there feeling bare without the weight of the familiar camera strap. As a photojournalist, Chance had the gift of capturing a moment for everyone to see. Of making still images come alive for people half a world away.

But bringing life to a photo was one thing. Imagining that his family's Victorian hotel, the old lady behind him, was living, breathing, watching him... That was something else.

"Please come, Chance," his younger sister, Rory, had pleaded. "You haven't been to Hillcrest House in years. Being here will be good for you."

His sister had always loved the old gal. Chance's lips twitched in a smile. The hotel *and* their Aunt Evelyn, who ran the place and would slay him with a killer glare for even thinking of her as old.

Rory and their cousin, Evie, had moved to Clearville months earlier to take over while their aunt went through cancer treatments. Aunt Evelyn was splitting time between staying with his parents and staying with Evie's parents as she recovered from surgeries and chemotherapy.

Even if they hadn't had their hands full, Chance couldn't have stayed at his parents' house for another minute. He loved them, he did. But the worry and the lingering sorrow in their gazes, even now that they knew he was safe—knew he was *alive*—weighed down on him. Suffocated him.

They'd never understood his desire to see the world, to live his life with his backpack and camera gear the only baggage allowed. He was free to come and go as he pleased, to live his life the way he wanted, and his work made a difference! He had contacts around the globe. He could go into places other journalists couldn't go and tell the stories that might otherwise remain unheard.

His parents had always had a straighter, safer path in mind for him. One that included following in his father's footsteps and taking over the small photography studio

Matthew McClaren owned, buying a house and settling down with a wife and kids.

Chance had jumped the curb and taken his life off-road when he left home at eighteen and had never come close to veering anywhere near that white-picket-fence neighborhood again. He wasn't the settling kind, and while his parents might not understand that, Chance always believed they respected what he'd accomplished, respected the heights he'd achieved in his career...

Or at least he had until that whispered conversation he'd overheard, the one that made it clear he couldn't stay under his parents' roof any longer than necessary.

We're your family, Chance. We love you.

His mother's words, the confusion on her face when he walked out—first as a hotheaded kid and then again, just a few weeks ago—cut deep. But he'd known if he didn't leave, he would only end up saying something he would regret.

His parents hadn't wanted him to be alone while he was recovering, and he'd thought staying with Rory and Evie might be enough to ease their concern while still giving him space to breathe.

Now he wasn't so sure.

"Oh, Chance, this will be so perfect!" his sister had gushed the moment he set foot inside the family hotel. "Our current photographer is moving away soon."

He'd forgotten about the whole all-inclusive wedding destination business that had been his aunt's brainchild about a year ago. He didn't know how considering, as the hotel's wedding coordinator, the ceremonies were all Rory talked about. Especially now that she'd found a groom-to-be of her own.

"You can fill in while you're here!"

Wedding photographer? Yeah, that was right up there

with fashion photographer as a worst nightmare. "Not exactly my thing, Rory."

He felt like he'd kicked a puppy as he watched the excitement in his little sister's eyes dim. Jamison Porter, Rory's fiancé, had studied him carefully during that first meeting and suggested, "Why don't you let your brother get settled before offering him a job, sweetheart?"

At that, Rory had recovered quickly, wrapping her arms around him in a far more cautious version of her usual exuberant hug. "Of course! What was I thinking? We have the cottage house set up for you."

The caretaker's cottage was a small wood and stone structure on the grounds, but well away from the hotel itself. Chance welcomed the privacy even if staying there felt like living in a very girlie dollhouse thanks to Rory's decorating skills.

But he'd take the dollhouse over his childhood bedroom. And it was only for a month—maybe two. His leg was getting stronger every day, and Chance refused to think he wouldn't make it back to 100 percent.

And after a few days of consideration, he'd even agreed to fill in as wedding photographer—which he still couldn't quite believe. But he needed something to keep his mind active, to keep moving.

He'd traveled to some of the most desperate, poverty-stricken, war-torn areas in the world and yet nothing—nothing—was quite as scary as walking into a room filled with marriage-minded women riding high on romance.

Shuddering, he shifted his weight to his right side, testing his leg without the help of the crutches he'd only recently left behind. Sharp shards of pain sliced through muscle and bone. He'd pushed himself too hard, the packed sand more of a challenge than he'd expected. He had a long walk back to the hotel in front of him.

He pulled in a breath before taking that first step, beads of sweat popping up along his hairline and instantly cooling in the ocean breeze. The stormy blue-gray water was nearly the same color as the stormy blue-gray sky. Nearly the same color as a pair of stormy blue-gray eyes that had haunted him for months.

Alexa Mayhew had been draped in gold the night they met. Beneath a sparkling crystal chandelier, she'd glittered with the grace and elegance of a goddess. She was tall and slender, with a poise and prestige that allowed her to move in elite circles where most mortals wouldn't be welcomed. And yet he'd sensed a restlessness inside her the moment their gazes met across the ballroom, a need to throw aside the fake smiles and polite facade and grab hold of something real...

Or so he'd thought until she made herself clear. She'd been slumming their weekend together. Different worlds, different lives...different bank accounts.

Reaching into the pocket of his baggy khakis, he fingered the small jeweled hairpin he'd been carrying with him since that weekend. In his line of work, he'd learned to travel light. No extra baggage allowed. And yet, he hadn't been able to leave the small reminder behind any more than he could convince himself to return it to the woman it belonged to. Such a small thing, he hadn't thought carrying it with him could hurt.

He'd certainly never imagined it would save his life.

He wasn't superstitious and he wasn't sentimental. He certainly didn't believe in love at first sight, so why was he having such a hard time letting Alexa go?

"Welcome to Hillcrest. And I understand congratulations are in order?"

Standing in the elegant lobby of the Victorian hotel,

Alexa Mayhew hoped she managed a smile to fool the bright-eyed wedding coordinator.

"It's not official yet," she murmured, trying to somewhat inconspicuously hide her left hand in the folds of her wide-legged gray trousers. Her naked left hand, unlike the woman in front of her who sported a sparkling rock on her own third finger.

"But we'd still like a tour of the grounds while we're staying here if that's possible." Griffin James wrapped an arm around Alexa's shoulders and pulled her tight to his side. "Isn't that right, sweetie?"

Alexa stumbled slightly at the sudden move before regaining her balance. She and Griffin had checked in earlier that day after a long drive from Los Angeles. Worn out from hours in the car and feeling more than a little nauseous from the twists and turns on the mountain roads leading into the small Northern California town, she had lain down for a short rest while Griffin had—

Alexa tried to withhold a sigh. Who knows what Griffin had done? Announced their impending engagement from the top turret of the towering Victorian mansion, for all she knew.

She shot her could-be fiancé a glare he returned with a wink and a grin, knowing she could never stay mad at him. He'd been her best friend since childhood, the one person she could turn to when times got tough. The one person who could always make her laugh—which was pretty much what she'd done when he proposed.

"Griffin," she started to protest.

"Come on. It'll be fun. A good chance to take a look around." His eyebrows rose pointedly, reminding her why he had chosen this particular hotel.

Alexa hadn't really cared where they stayed, too eager to accept his offer of a break away from the demands of her grandmother's charity foundation. And from the demands of her grandmother.

From the time she'd gone to live with Virginia Mayhew, the wealthy philanthropist had instilled in Alexa a sense of responsibility. In the past decade or so, she had become the face of the foundation. She spent countless hours fund-raising, overseeing charity events, speaking with the media, all in an effort to give back.

But for the first time in her life, Alexa had something she wanted to hold on to...just for herself. She needed to get away, and though she was aware of the faint and almost constant vibrations coming from the cell phone tucked in her purse, she refused to check the barrage of emails and text messages.

Understanding Griffin's unspoken professional interest in looking around the hotel, she said, "We'd love a tour."

"I have some time free now if you're not too tired from traveling," the woman offered. "And I'm Rory, by the way. Rory Mc—"

A high-pitched whistle sounded, and she glanced at the phone in her own hand. A dreamy smile lit her already beautiful face at the text flashing across the screen. The moment lasted only a split second before she appeared to snap back to reality. A slight blush rose to her cheeks as she slipped the phone into a hidden pocket in the folds of her full skirt. "Sorry about that. That was *my* fiancé and... Well—" she shot a woman-to-woman look at Alexa "—you know how it is, right?"

"Of course." Even as happy as the other woman looked, Alexa would bet Rory hadn't laughed out loud when her fiancé proposed.

"Let's start inside, and then I can show you around the grounds. We remodeled the gazebo over the summer, and it's always a popular spot—depending on the time of year for the ceremony. Have the two of you picked a date yet?" Rory asked.

Griffin shot Alexa a questioning look, calling her out on dragging her feet—literally across the richly patterned carpet and in giving a definitive answer to the question he'd asked.

Fall decorations highlighted the elegant lobby—a cornucopia on the concierge desk; red, yellow and orange leaf garland wrapped the deep walnut carved columns, and a huge grapevine wreath dotted with tiny pumpkins and squash hung above the river-stone fireplace in the sitting area. Scents of cinnamon and cloves filled the air.

All signs of how quickly time was flying by. Hard to believe Thanksgiving was only three weeks away. Especially when every time Alexa closed her eyes, her thoughts drifted back to the end of summer.

"Sometime before April, I'm thinking," Griffin answered wryly when Alexa stayed silent.

"Hmm, that's not much time," the wedding coordinator warned before holding up a hand. "Not that we couldn't pull it off."

"Yeah, well, it's kind of a…predetermined time frame."

As Rory started talking about the history of the hotel, Alexa jabbed an elbow into Griffin's side. "Would you stop?" she muttered from behind her smile, voice low enough for only Griffin to hear.

"What? It's true. By April, you'll be—"

"I know. I know. But don't you feel at least a little bit guilty going through with this tour when it's doubtful we'd get married here anyway?"

"Naw, it's kinda fun." Griffin tipped his golden blond head toward the wedding coordinator. "It's like getting a tour from Snow White…"

"Behave," she warned him, though past experience told

her it would do little good. Besides, he was right. Their guide did resemble the Disney princess, but beyond that... Alexa frowned, a memory tugging at her mind like an elusive song lyric she could almost but not quite capture.

"As much as I love this place's history," Rory was saying, "it's the air of romance that brought me back here." Leaning closer, she confided, "My cousin, Evie, wouldn't like hearing me say this, but I have to tell you that Hillcrest is, well, special. People have a way of finding their own happily-ever-after here."

Griffin made a sound Alexa hoped the wedding coordinator would believe to be an indulgent laugh. "Hear that, sweetheart, our own happily-ever-after."

Alexa didn't want to think about romance in the air or happily-ever-after. For almost as long as she could remember, she had been one to play it safe. Her jet-setting parents had loved action and adventure—skiing in St. Moritz one day and sunbathing in the Bahamas the next. They'd let life take them wherever the wind had blown, sweeping in and out of her childhood like a hurricane.

After they died, her grandmother had provided Alexa with the stability she craved. No more wondering. No more worrying. No more whirlwind.

Not until that night almost four months ago when she'd hosted a fund-raiser for one of the many charities her grandmother supported. When she'd met the striking blue-eyed gaze of the most handsome man she'd ever seen. Her heart had stopped, her breath had caught and she'd been swept up in something beyond her control.

Even in that first electric connection, she'd known. There would be consequences. She couldn't cast aside years of living each day with a carefully laid out plan and then expect to pick up where she left off like nothing had happened. Not when Chance McClaren had happened.

In those first few weeks following the charity auction, he'd played constantly on her mind. Laughing and teasing her thoughts as if he'd stood right beside her, whispering in her ear. After all, he had promised he'd be in touch, and Alexa had jumped at every call, scrambled for her cell phone at every text, scoured her email every few minutes over calls and texts and emails that *weren't* from Chance.

By the time he did call, some five weeks later, she'd already come to a decision. What they'd had was a fling. Nothing more, and it was over. She'd sensed his surprise. No doubt there were dozens of women who would be thrilled to hear from him no matter how long it had been since he'd called. But in the end he'd agreed and abided by her wishes.

She hadn't heard from him again and did her best not to think of him.

Alexa told herself the mental roadblock would eventually work…right up until the moment she realized she'd missed her period. She was pregnant, the father of her child a man she barely knew. A whirlwind who'd stormed in—and out—of her life with a recklessness that left her head and heart spinning.

How was she supposed to tell a man who lived out of a backpack that he was going to be a father? Alexa had rehearsed what she would say dozens of times as she made dozens of calls, trying to reach him.

And then fate seemed to take the decision out of her hands as she woke one morning to see the headline scrolling across a national news channel.

Photojournalist Chance McClaren killed in bomb attack in Kabul.

"How long have you worked here, Rory?" Griffin asked their guide as she led them back to the lobby after showing them the elegant ballroom. The hotel's old-fashioned feel filled the room from the dark, carved check-in desk, to the wall of small cubbyholes for guest messages, to an actual phone booth and its replica of an early 1900s phone.

But like any modern hotel, the lobby was a busy spot with families coming and going, bellhops pushing packed luggage carts, and employees offering advice for things to see and do in the nearby Victorian town of Clearville.

Rory stopped to allow a chatting couple to wheel by with a stroller. And as she had for the past few months, Alexa locked in on the baby strapped inside. Her breath caught at the sight. An infant with her eyes closed, her chubby cheeks pink with sleep, her head slouched to one side. So sweet, so small...

She wrapped her arms around her waist. Before she'd gotten pregnant, she hadn't understood that she wouldn't need to wait for her baby to be born to feel such a deep connection with the new life inside her. She was amazed by how much she already loved the child growing in her womb. How she loved the idea of a little boy or little girl with dark hair and startling blue eyes like—

No, she wouldn't think about the baby's father. She wouldn't.

She watched with a combination of anxiety and anticipation as the mother stopped for a moment to adjust the lacy pink sock barely clinging to the toes of the tiniest foot she'd ever seen.

"Well, I've worked here as a wedding coordinator for the past six months or so," Rory was saying, "but my family has owned the hotel for decades. My Aunt Evelyn runs the place now, but the McClarens have—"

"What—" Alexa stopped so suddenly, Griffin almost knocked her over. "What did you say your last name was?"

"McClaren." Rory's blue gaze—her familiar blue

gaze—swung back and forth between Alexa and Griffin. "Didn't I say that earlier?"

"Alexa?" Griffin's arm tightened around her shoulders as she swayed against him. "What's wrong?"

"Nothing."

Everything...

It wasn't easy to spot the resemblance between masculine, rugged features and this delicately feminine woman, but Alexa must have subconsciously noticed the similarities. The rich, almost black hair, the high, sculpted cheekbones, those blue eyes...

The thick, patterned carpet swirled beneath her feet as the room spun. "I'm not feeling very well. I think I need to lie down..."

"Of course. I'll walk you back to the suite."

To the suite. Alexa fought a hysterical laugh. That wasn't nearly far away enough to escape the dizzying thoughts whipping through her mind.

The McClaren family hotel... *Chance's* family's hotel?

And before she could make her escape, the hotel's carved entry doors opened and in walked the father of her child.

Chapter Two

At first he thought he was imagining things.

It had happened before, after the explosion. The blast that shattered his leg had also left him with a serious concussion—one that had him drifting in and out of consciousness for days. In that confused state, he'd seen Alexa at his side. Heard her voice. Smelled the honey-lilac scent of her skin.

He hadn't stopped to think that her presence made no sense. The wealthy granddaughter of one of California's biggest and most generous philanthropists might raise money for victims of war-torn countries, but she didn't travel to war-torn countries.

She certainly wouldn't have belonged in a crowded field hospital where understaffed doctors and nurses did their best to care for those injured in the series of bombings.

But he'd been so sure of her presence that he'd nearly gotten in a fight with one of the doctors once he reached semiconsciousness, unable to understand why the man refused to let him see Alexa. Why he was keeping her away when she'd been *right there*?

Later, as the uncertainty clouding his mind started to clear, he realized it had all been some kind of delusion. He'd been embarrassed to have been so fooled by his own mind. Unsettled that a woman he barely knew—a woman he'd spent no more than a weekend with and one who wanted nothing more to do with him—had been the person he'd reached for, clung to, even in such a confused state.

And so even though he'd thought of calling since he'd returned to the States, he'd purposely not picked up the phone.

Now, as the color drained from her face, he wished he had.

She looked as beautiful and ethereal now as the night they'd met. That night, she'd been wrapped in gold, her blond hair intricately woven on top of her head, her smooth bangs held in place by the jeweled butterfly hairpin. Today, she was draped in silver, her shoulder-length hair caught more sedately in a ponytail at her nape. As he watched, she hugged her arms around her waist, her blue-gray eyes huge in her gorgeous face.

"Chance—" his sister's expression brightened as she caught sight of him "—come meet two of our guests. Alexa Mayhew, Griffin James, this is my brother, Chance McClaren."

He didn't remember moving, but he suddenly stood in front of Alexa, inches away from the woman who'd been on his mind and under his skin for months. "Alexa…"

"Chance."

She reached out, her hand hovering in the air between them as if she wasn't quite sure that he was truly there, and his heart clenched. The uncertainty in her expression hit hard as he grasped her hand in his. The soft skin, the sweet scent, all of it real this time.

"Alexa," he said again, a whisper of sound beneath his breath.

"Chance. I— It's…" Her throat worked as she swallowed. "So good to meet you."

Meet him? Meet him! She'd done a damn sight more than *met* him in a hotel room in Santa Barbara almost four months ago.

Shock held him motionless, Alexa's hand still in his, until the man at her side spoke. "If you'll excuse us. Alexa isn't feeling well."

The man—Chance couldn't even recall what his sister said the guy's name was—had a protective arm wrapped around Alexa's shoulders. Chance had barely spared him a glance earlier, but summed him up now with a quick look. Wealthy, sophisticated, handsome. Someone very much a part of Alexa's world.

The swift slice cut deep, but Chance had endured worse pain. That was one lesson he could thank Lisette for. Finding his fiancée in bed with another man had cured him of any belief in love, marriage, or even whatever the hell it was he thought he and Alexa had found in a five-star hotel penthouse suite.

But cured or not, he couldn't help taking a few shots of his own. "You look so…familiar. Are you sure we haven't met somewhere before?"

"I, uh, don't think so."

"No? So we didn't meet—I don't know, parasailing along the Waterfront? Or maybe bungee jumping off the Bridge to Nowhere?" Chance wouldn't have thought it possible, but Alexa turned even paler, and he really started to feel like an ass. He stopped himself before he mentioned her last whispered wish.

Making love under the stars.

"Alexa is hardly the type to go bungee jumping," the golden boy at her side said drily.

"Maybe someday she'll have the opportunity to take that chance."

Her turbulent blue-gray eyes met his. Their gazes lingered, clung, like they had that night in Santa Barbara.

Come on, Lexi, he'd whispered, *take a chance.*

And she had. For a weekend. And no, they hadn't had time to fulfill her wild and thoroughly facetious bucket list wishes of parasailing or bungee jumping. But he'd flown high enough and fallen hard enough that for a moment he thought he could have died happily in her arms…

But it was just a moment. One weekend, and Chance had never met a woman that he couldn't forget once he moved on. Maybe that was the problem. Ever since the explosion, he hadn't been moving. Not on to a new job, not on to a new assignment, not on to a new country across the world. He was stuck. And like some kind of shark, if he didn't keep in constant motion, he couldn't breathe.

That was the only reason why his chest hurt as he gazed at Alexa.

The man by her side glanced between them before murmuring, "Something tells me that's not happening anytime soon."

Chance opened his mouth to argue like the fool he was when his cousin, Evie McClaren, spotted the group from across the lobby. "Chance, there you are. I've been looking for you."

"If you'll excuse us," Alexa murmured to Rory.

"Oh, of course. We can finish the tour later."

"Thank you for taking your time with us this afternoon."

Always so polite, always so damn proper, Chance thought with a twist of a smile that had Alexa's elegant head lifting to an even higher angle when she caught sight of it. "Mr. McClaren."

"Ms. Mayhew… It's been a pleasure."

He drew out the word long enough for a riot of color to storm her cheeks before she turned away. Her golden boy kept his arm around her shoulders as he turned her toward the hallway leading to… Her room? His room? Theirs?

Chance shoved his hands in his pockets, fists clenched tight enough that the hairpin gouged into his palm. He didn't care about women—any one woman—enough to be jealous. Not anymore.

"Chance? Hello, Chance?"

His cousin waved a hand in front of his face to capture his attention. "Your doctor's office called about moving your therapy appointment." She gave him a stern look. "They said they tried your cell, but you weren't answering."

"Oh, Chance." Rory frowned at him, her blue eyes so similar to his own darkening in concern. "You really should have your phone with you especially when you go out by yourself."

Chance sighed. "Yes, Mom."

His cousin's arch expression wasn't nearly as concerned as his sister's. "Not your mom. Also not your secretary. Answer your own darn phone calls."

"Yes, Evie."

At the moment, the very thought of therapy exhausted him. Dammit! He used to run for miles, and now just a twenty-minute walk on the beach left him weak, winded… and in a hell of a lot of pain.

Something that must have been more obvious than he wanted to consider as Rory said, "Speaking of Mom… She says she hasn't heard from you lately and is talking about making a trip down to check on you."

Chance's jaw tightened. "You can tell her I'm fine, Ror."

"You can tell her yourself," his sister chided. "And are you so sure about that? You look…" She hesitated, biting her lower lip, her soft heart clearly worried about hurting his feelings.

"Scary," Evie interjected.

"Evie!"

"What?" His sharp-witted, sharp-tongued cousin flicked a slender hand in his direction. "He's frightening the guests. I thought that poor woman was going to faint at the sight of him."

"Oh, I don't think that was about Chance," Rory argued. "It's a big decision, you know. Choosing where to get married."

When he first woke after the explosion, a dull roar had filled his head, the pain making it almost impossible to think. With that bomb his sister dropped, a second wave hit like an aftershock.

Alexa. Married. *At Hillcrest.*

"Chance…are you sure you're okay?"

He ran a hand down his face, several day's growth of stubble scraping against his palm. "When?" he asked, his voice sounding just as rough.

"What?"

"When's the wedding?"

"Oh… Well, they haven't picked a date yet either. Why?"

"I was just wondering if I'd still be here when it happens." Hell, he needed something to make him forget about the woman. Maybe seeing Alexa marry another man would do the trick. So far nothing else had worked.

"Don't they make the cutest couple?" Rory sighed.

"Adorable." And watching them exchange vows, promising to love each other until death did them part and sealing the words with a kiss… Chance's jaw locked tight. He'd just as soon stick that hairpin into his eye.

"Seriously, Chance," Evie interjected, tucking a strand of straight, chin-length hair behind one ear, "we both know I'm nowhere near as love-stupid as this one—"

"Hey!" Rory protested as their cousin waved a hand her way.

"—but if you're going to photograph the weddings around here, you need to get on board with this whole happily-ever-after crap."

"Oh, lovely," his sister muttered. "We'll be sure to put *that* in one of our brochures."

"I'm on board, Evie."

Her pointed gaze raked him from the tip of his too-long hair, to his faded to gray T-shirt, to his rumpled khakis. "Frightening the guests," she repeated.

"I'll get a haircut. And shave," he added when her look didn't change. He all but groaned, "And go shopping."

"Before this weekend?" Rory asked, catching her lower lip between her teeth once more.

"This—" He choked back a curse. This weekend was his first official Hillcrest House event.

Chance McClaren—wedding photographer.

"All right. All right. Before this weekend. You know, the two of you really should be nicer to me," he said without thinking. "After all, I almost—"

He cut himself off before he could finish the old joke, one going back to a serious injury when he was a kid. A skateboarding accident had left him in a coma followed by months of physical and occupational therapy.

Rehab had been hell, not so different from what faced him now, and he'd pushed himself as hard as he could, determined to get back to the reckless, daredevil kid he'd been before the accident. Not that he hadn't pulled out the sympathy card every chance he got.

Work his tail off to get back on a skateboard? *Sure thing*.

Pick up his dirty socks? *Come on! Didn't everyone know he was, like, seriously injured?*

But unlike in the past when Rory would meet his melodramatic statement with a give-me-a-break eye roll, this time her blue eyes filled with emotion as she said the word he hadn't. "Died, Chance." Her voice broke on his name. "You almost died."

A wave of guilt crashed over him when he thought of what his sister, his parents, his family had been through. *Not my fault*, he reminded himself, but the words didn't erase the lingering shadows from his sister's eyes whenever she looked at him.

"I'm fine, Rory. I'll be back to my old self in no time."

Reaching out, his sister squeezed his arm and gave him a sad smile. "That's what I'm afraid of."

"Rory…" His voice trailed off as she walked away, and Chance knew better than to go after her. She needed time by herself, and he wasn't sure he could catch her if he tried.

"You really are a jerk sometimes." Disdain, not sorrow, filled his cousin's icy gaze, and it was almost a relief to have Evie glaring at him. Anger he could handle, and he wondered if she was, in her own prickly way, trying to make things easier on him.

"You do realize that I had no idea what some overeager journalist was reporting. I was stuck in the hospital—"

"You were unconscious in a makeshift first-aid station half a world away."

And that is your fault, Chance. Evie didn't say the words, but he read the accusation.

"It's my job, Evie." A job he loved despite the dangers. "And you know your sister and your parents. As far as they are concerned, their job is to love you. You shouldn't make it so hard."

And then she, too, walked away, leaving him standing in the middle of the lobby with chatting guests and employees passing him on all sides. A harried businessman barked orders into his phone, jarring Chance's leg with his brief-case as he hurried by. White-hot pain seared through him, and he clenched his jaw to keep from crying out. Sweat broke out on his upper lip, and he sucked in a deep breath.

Despite what his family thought, he was not typically foolish or reckless. His job required calculated risks, but he always weighed his options before making a decision— even if he had only a split second to do so.

The smart thing to do would be to walk away. There was no payoff to be had here. No final shot to wrap up the story. No reason to slowly, painfully make his way over to the reception desk—except for one foolish, reckless urge.

He wanted to remind Alexa Mayhew that they had, in-deed, met before.

"You're sure you're all right?"

Griffin had asked the same question half a dozen times since they left—escaped—the lobby for their hotel suite. He'd led her through the tiny living area with its small shades-of-blue love seat and coffee table straight to the whitewashed dining room, where he fixed her a cup of herbal tea.

She hadn't taken a sip until she was sure she could lift the mug without her hands shaking and then had to swal-low a burst of hysterical laughter along with the brew. Chamomile. Did Griffin really think the soothing benefits would help in *this* situation?

Chance. Here. At Hillcrest.

The last fifteen minutes were such a blur, the moments

so surreal, she could almost believe she'd had some kind of out-of-body experience. The second she saw him, her brain had shut down even as her limbs kept going, her mouth kept moving.

Nice to meet you?

What had she been thinking? She'd been stunned, yes, but to look him in the eye and pretend they'd never met? Alexa didn't know Chance McClaren well—other than in the biblical sense—but even she had to realize a man so *macho* would take that kind of flat-out dismissal like a challenge. She didn't remember? Well, then, he would just have to remind her, wouldn't he?

Take a chance.

The play on words had been the phrase he'd used to get her out onto the dance floor, into his arms and, by the end of the evening, into his bed.

Take a chance.

Easy for him to say. He wasn't the one who'd ended up pregnant!

"Alexa?"

Jarred from her thoughts, she cupped her hands around the warm white ceramic mug and met Griffin's worried gaze. "I'm fine now. Really. I think I was just—overwhelmed for a minute back there."

He seemed to think she was referring to the tour and the wedding coordinator's ideas for their perfect wedding. He had no reason to think anything else since Alexa had never told him the name of the man she'd had that weekend fling with.

"I meant what I said, you know. Maybe it wasn't the most romantic proposal—"

"Griff—"

"But the two of us—the *three* of us—we make sense, Allie."

His offer and the sincerity in his golden gaze wrapped around her like one of his exuberant hugs. They'd met when she was eight years old—the day of her parents' funeral. Her grandmother's estate had been filled with people— inside and out. Mourners draped in black inside and paparazzi with long-lens cameras outside. She had spent most of her childhood feeling lost and alone, but she'd never felt as invisible as she had in that crowd. Neither her parents' jet-setting friends nor her grandmother's old guard seemed to have any idea what to say to a young orphan. Though she had overheard plenty of what they had to say about her...

Poor thing. What on earth do you think Virginia will do *with her?*

I'm sure she'll be sent to boarding school. I'm surprised Stefan and Bree hadn't enrolled her already.

To say she had slipped away unnoticed would have been a huge understatement. No one had paid attention to her when she was there; why would anyone notice when she was gone?

Alexa hadn't given much thought to where she was going. Slipping out the back entrance, she ran. For miles it had seemed, traveling that much distance before ever leaving her grandmother's property and stumbling onto the neighbor's vast estate next door.

Though the grounds were as sculpted as her grandmother's with high hedges, flower gardens and fountains, this yard had a swing set, and that was where Griffin found her.

And as if he'd come across a homeless kitten, he'd taken her back to his house, fixed her a glass of milk and a bowl of cereal. And when his mother found the two of them sometime later, Griffin had announced, "This is Alexa. Her mom and dad died, so she's gonna live with us."

She felt the same way now as she had then. Like Griffin was the one person she could count on. And she loved him. She really did. She just wished—

Alexa shook her head. Maybe that was her problem. Always wanting more than she had. The oh-so-typical poor little rich girl.

"You're my best friend, Griffin." Setting aside the mug, Alexa rounded the table to take his hands. "You have been since we were kids, and if I ever lost that, if I ever lost your friendship—"

"Not gonna happen. I promise you that. Scout's honor."

"You were so never a Boy Scout." After giving his hands a final squeeze, Alexa pushed him toward the door of their suite. "Go! You know you don't want to be stuck in this room with me."

Recently, Griffin's father had expressed an interest in Hillcrest House. Evidently, he had heard that a competing national chain had made an offer on the Victorian hotel, and he'd asked Griffin to go see whether the property was worthy enough to make a counteroffer.

Alexa was more than a little surprised Griffin had agreed. He had his own dreams that had nothing to do with becoming a hotel magnate. Dreams that could come true—if he found a way to prove himself responsible to his father.

"Just so you know, I'd never think of myself as being stuck with you." He paused with a hand on the doorknob. "Only lucky that you were by my side."

"Go! Before you make a ridiculously hormonal woman start to cry!"

He left with a wink and a wave, and the reality of the past few minutes hit like a hurricane, practically knocking Alexa off her feet. She sank into the blue love seat, the strength all but sapped from her muscles, and pulled a matching pillow against her chest.

Chance McClaren…

Seeing him had been like—seeing a ghost.

A living, breathing ghost.

Because despite that initial news report, Chance Mc-Claren had not died in the bomb attack.

Two days later, every news channel in the country was scrambling to revise their headlines. Chance was injured but alive in a hospital in some foreign city Alexa had never heard of.

But for those two days between, shock had left Alexa blessedly numb after the roller-coaster ride of emotions she'd experienced since the night they met.

She'd spent her childhood waiting for her parents to call, watching out windows for them to show up out of the blue. Waiting, wondering, hoping, only to have that hope dashed time and time again when one nanny or another would tell her that her parents weren't coming.

Until the day when her grandmother arrived and put an end to all of it. To the waiting, to the wondering, to the hoping. Her parents weren't coming. Not ever again.

She'd relived every twist and turn, every jolt and jerk, every stomach-in-her-throat loop-the-loop after Chance left, and when she read that first news report, a small, desperate part of her had been—relieved.

This child—a child she already loved, a child who would love and need her—would be all hers, and she wouldn't have to share. She wouldn't have to tell Chance he was going to be a father. Wouldn't have to worry that he would wreak havoc crashing in and out of their lives. She wouldn't have to face the pain of knowing she'd cursed her baby with a childhood destined to be so similar to her own.

She wouldn't.

Because Chance was dead.

Only then he wasn't. But it was almost easier to pretend he was.

Alexa barely had a chance to take a breath, forget to take the time she needed to recover from seeing him again, when a knock sounded at the door. She gave a small laugh as she pushed off the love seat cushions. Typical Griffin. "Forget your key?" she asked as she pulled open the door.

Only it wasn't Griffin standing on the other side. A living, breathing Chance McClaren arched a dark brow and said, "I don't recall you giving me a key…yet."

Chapter Three

Heat licked a path from her chest all the way to her cheeks, and she was tempted—seriously tempted—to slam the door in his face. But she'd been Virginia Mayhew's granddaughter too long to react in such a way. Though, really, what etiquette book had a chapter on something like this?

How to greet a weekend fling father of your unborn child. Or better yet, *What to say to a man who figuratively, if not literally, had come back from the dead.*

"Come on, Lexi, aren't you going to invite me in?"

One hand gripped the edge of the doorframe in a casual pose, but she wasn't fooled. His blue eyes were shadowed, his unshaven jaw clenched, the muscles in his arm standing out in stark relief. He looked like he'd fall over if he let go. And the heart she'd tried so hard to harden ached for him.

"Please don't call me that," she murmured even as she stepped back and allowed him into the suite and, she feared, back into her life.

She kept her back turned as she led the way toward the suite's living area. The space had felt cozy when Griffin had been there with her. Now, with Chance, she felt the walls closing in.

"What should I call you? After all, that is how you introduced yourself that night, isn't it?"

Alexa nearly groaned at the reminder. She'd been calling herself a fool ever since. What had she been thinking? One look into Chance's startling blue eyes back in the lobby, and she'd remembered. Even now a rush of energy, awareness, attraction arced between them, and Alexa knew she hadn't been thinking much at all.

For one weekend, with this one man, she'd let herself feel. She'd known there would be a price to pay for abandoning the tight control that had shaped her life for the past twenty-plus years. She just hadn't realized until she found out she was pregnant that her child would be the one to pay it. But only if she told Chance the truth...

"What do you want, Chance?" She picked up the pillow that had fallen from the love seat and carefully tucked it back against the armrest, smoothing a ruffled corner as if nothing mattered more.

"Oh, I don't know." His eyes glowed like superheated flame as she straightened to meet his gaze. "I hear congratulations are in order."

So she was right, Alexa thought. She had wounded some sense of macho pride when she pretended not to know him. Throw in an almost-engagement, and the man she'd last spoken to months ago was suddenly at her door.

She took a step backward, needing some space from the heat coming off his body in waves, only to bump up against the white wicker coffee table. He countered her move, trapping her there unless she wanted to start scrambling over furniture to try to get away. "Chance—"

"For someone who claims not to take risks, you sure move fast when you want to."

Alexa wasn't sure her skin could get much hotter without setting her hair on fire. He knew just how fast she had moved, falling into bed with him the very night they met. Looking back, the entire weekend seemed like some kind of dream, a magical moment out of time. One that, even with the pregnancy, she hadn't been able to bring herself to regret—until now. Until Chance made her feel ashamed. "I—"

"Four months, and now you're suddenly engaged?"

"Engaged? You mean Griffin?"

He raised an eyebrow. "Do you have another fiancé I don't know about?"

"No, of course not." She didn't even have the one he did know about. Not really.

"Unless..." His gaze narrowed dangerously. "Were you engaged when we met?"

"What? No! I certainly wouldn't have slept with you," she hissed beneath her breath as if the entire hotel might have been listening in, "if I'd been engaged to another man at the time."

He searched her expression, his stance easing ever so slightly at what he saw there. She caught a hint of the ocean mixed with his own masculine scent, and her focus drifted toward his lips even as she wondered if she would taste the salt on his skin...

He's here. I can't believe he's really here.

Sucking in a quick breath, Alexa snapped herself out of the dangerous direction her thoughts had taken. Chance might have just come from a walk on the beach, but she was the one who needed to throw herself into the frigid waves!

What had he been saying? Oh, right. He'd just accused

her of cheating on her fiancé. "Griffin James and I have known each other since we were children, but he only recently asked me to marry him."

"Just like that?"

"What?"

"You've known each other for years and then what? You woke up one day and decided to get married?"

"We're well suited." Alexa cringed, hearing her grandmother's words coming out of her mouth. Her grandmother would be thrilled if she accepted Griffin's proposal. Virginia had been pushing the two of them together since high school.

"Right. Whereas you and I were only well suited in bed."

Alexa stared at him. "What are you doing here, Chance?"

He opened his mouth but no sound escaped. He ran a hand through his disheveled hair, looking at a loss, out of sorts and so completely different from the man she'd met four months ago. "Hell if I know," he finally sighed.

Alexa fought it, she really did, but her heart cried out at the unexpected vulnerability in his expression. He looked...awful. At the charity auction, he'd fit in with the sophisticated crowd—breathtaking in a tuxedo that outlined his six-foot-something frame with a perfection that would bring any red-blooded woman to her knees. His dark hair had been brushed back from his wide forehead, revealing his classic bone structure, gorgeous blue eyes and a pair of dimples to die for.

Today his hair fell across that forehead in disarray. His face looked gaunt. The spark was missing from those sapphire blues, the dimples nowhere to be seen beneath the rough stubble.

Four months wasn't much time, but so much had happened. She had a new life growing inside her, and

Chance—Chance had almost died. "I heard the news reports."

Cringing, he asked, "Which one?"

"The one that said you'd been killed in a suicide bomb attack."

"Bad reporting."

"It doesn't look that far off." She hadn't noticed earlier, but he stood off-center, resting the majority of his weight on his left side. How close had he come to dying?

"I'm fine. I'll be back in the field in no time."

Right, Alexa thought bitterly, because who would let nearly getting blown up make them rethink their life choices?

A few years before her parents were killed in an avalanche while skiing in the Italian Alps, they had survived a plane crash. The small jet had experienced engine failure, and the pilot had made a miracle landing on a middle of nowhere country road. But instead of making her parents rethink their high-flying, jet-setting lifestyle, surviving the near-death incident had only made them feel that much more invincible.

Alexa could only imagine Chance would react the same—taking more risks, accepting more challenges until his luck ran out way too soon.

At the moment, though, it was hard to think about him being thousands of miles away, putting his life in danger, when he was right there, close enough to touch. And it was all Alexa could do not to erase the mere inches between them, to throw her arms around him, to see, smell, touch, *taste* that he was really and truly alive and well—

Hormones, she thought desperately. She'd read how pregnancy could lead to a skyrocketing of emotions, but the rationale failed to erase the dizzying rush of desire flooding her veins. *Nothing more than a momentary lapse.*

Unfortunately, her lapses were all too common at least

where Chance McClaren was concerned. But just because she'd made a mistake didn't mean she would keep making them. From now on, she would make no more impulsive decisions; she would do her thinking with her head, not her heart.

And certainly not with her hormones.

Taking a sanity-saving step back from the hold Chance had over her, she whispered, "You should go before…"

His lips twisted in a mockery of a smile as he came to his own conclusion as to what she was afraid might happen. "Right. Wouldn't want your fiancé catching you alone in a hotel room with a guy you slept with."

Alexa opened her mouth to argue only to stop. What would be the point? Maybe it was better for Chance to think she and Griffin were engaged.

"But don't worry. We'll have plenty of time to see each other around."

She shivered slightly at the promise—*warning*—in his expression. "Why is that?"

"Didn't my sister tell you? I'm your wedding photographer."

Alexa smiled at the waitress who topped off her glass of water before looking across the small table to find Griffin staring at her. "What?"

"You're not eating."

After the confrontation with Chance, Alexa had wanted nothing more than to escape the hotel. When Griffin returned to their suite and suggested a trip into town, she'd instantly agreed. They'd spent the afternoon browsing through the charming stores along Main Street. She would normally have loved taking in the Victorian architecture— the turrets, the wraparound porches, the elegantly detailed trim work and bright colors of the painted ladies—but she couldn't concentrate.

She sighed as she picked through her salad. Couldn't eat.

After surviving bouts of morning sickness her first trimester, her appetite had come back with a vengeance. So much so that when she'd reminded Griffin she was eating for two, he'd asked, "Are they both linebackers in the NFL?"

But now, with her nerves so frazzled from the confrontation with Chance, she could barely swallow a bite. "If you want, we can go somewhere else," Griffin offered.

He'd spotted the old-fashioned diner with its black-and-white floors, stainless-steel eat-in counter and red-vinyl-covered booths. Despite—or perhaps because of—the five-star restaurants boasted by many of his family's hotels, he'd always enjoyed a basic burger and fries.

They were seated toward the back of the diner, and Alexa had a view of the entire place. The booths and barstools were crowded with a mix of tourists and locals. Pink-uniformed waitresses called out orders to a cook behind the counter, and fifties music bounced through the speakers. The smell of grilled meat and fried food would have been mouthwatering if she'd had any kind of appetite.

"No, this is fine." She stabbed at a piece of chicken in her Cobb salad.

Dunking a fry in a pool of ketchup on the corner of his plate, Griffin casually asked, "That was him, wasn't it?"

Alexa froze, midchew, convinced he couldn't be asking what she thought he was asking. But his gaze was so certain, reminding her that she'd never been able to pull anything over on him. Still, she swallowed and reached for her glass.

"I'm sorry..." After taking a sip of slightly tart apple juice, she asked, "Who's 'him'?" Childish of her to play dumb when Griffin knew her so well. She might as well close her eyes and pretend the world—pretend *Chance McClaren*—couldn't see her.

"You know." He nodded to the spot hidden beneath the opposite end of the table. "Your baby daddy."

Alexa set her glass back on the white-fleck Formica table with a thunk. "Have I told you how much I loathe that term?"

"Do you have a better expression in mind?"

Weekend fling...

Sperm donor...

Father of her child...

None of them did anything to settle the nerves spiraling through her stomach.

"Besides, it doesn't matter what I call him. I'm still right, aren't I? He's the one."

The one. Somehow that sounded even worse than all the others. Yes, Chance McClaren was the one man who'd made her forget herself for a long weekend. The one man who'd gotten her to take a chance, to risk stepping outside her comfort zone. The one man who'd made her feel free.

A flutter of movement in her belly seemed to mock that thinking. *Not so free now.*

But Chance was not the one when it came to the man Alexa might have picked to father her child. Not the one when it came to a man she would choose for a stable, long-term relationship.

She knew that in her head, in her heart. So why didn't her stupid body get with the program and settle down? Why were chills still racing down her spine and gooseflesh rising along her skin after seeing him again?

"How did you figure it out?" Alexa had told Griffin she was pregnant, keeping most of the details, including Chance's name, to herself. She wasn't sure why, other than saying his name would have brought back even more memories. And she'd been trying so hard to forget.

"Other than the sparks you two were striking off each other?" Griffin downed a fourth of his cheeseburger with one bite before adding, "After seeing the way you reacted, I did some quick online research on the guy. Turns out he was at that benefit in Santa Barbara, the same one where you met your mystery man."

Alexa sighed, knowing Griffin had her cornered. "I still can't believe he's here. A part of me thought I'd never see him again."

"Because you thought he'd been killed?" A hint of chiding filled Griffin's voice that she hadn't told him the whole story.

"You read the reports?"

"It was hard not to. Plug McClaren's name into a search engine, and every headline touts how the guy came back from the dead."

Alexa pushed the chopped tomatoes in her salad into a small pile. "I know. And I would have told you, but you were in the middle of those meetings with your father." Meetings over Griffin's trust and the stipulations that, so far, had kept him from obtaining the money. "And by the time you were home..."

"Chance was alive."

"Yes."

"Safe to say the two of you aren't as finished as you made it seem."

Alexa shook her head. "You're wrong. It's over." She gave a half laugh. "It never really started. It was a weekend fling. Nothing more."

"You don't have weekend flings, Alexa."

"I know!" She longed to cover her face with her hands at what had been such an out-of-character thing for her to do. She feared it wasn't so out of character for Chance, yet another reason why things could never work out between them.

"So don't you think that means something?"

"That I've become a desperate, lonely woman?"

"Okay, first, that's not true. And second, there had to be something about Chance McClaren for you to sleep with him that first night." His expression was wry as he pointed out, "I've seen you take longer before deciding on a pair of shoes."

She refused to meet his gaze as she added a dash of pepper before spearing a quarter slice of hard-boiled egg. "Shoes are important."

"Allie. Come on."

Alexa swallowed. "It wouldn't work between the two of us. We're too different. We want such polar opposite things out of life. I told him that when he called. And that was before I even knew I was pregnant!"

"Wait." Griffin pointed a thick-cut fry in accusation. "You didn't tell me that."

"What?"

"That he called...or that you were the one to call things off."

"I didn't. Not really." Leaning forward, she stressed, "I hadn't heard from him in five weeks, Griffin."

"And what was Chance doing during those five weeks?"

"He—" Alexa cut herself off, realizing she hadn't asked where Chance had been or what he'd been doing. "He was probably off in some desert or jungle or swamp, God knows where."

"Which probably made it hard to make contact," Griffin chimed in with a logic that had Alexa feeling very illogical.

"Whose side are you on, anyway?"

"Yours. Always." He leaned back in the booth before saying, "I found something else when I was looking around online. Something I should have remembered. It was the twenty-year anniversary of your parents' deaths, wasn't it? Not long after you and Chance met?"

The exact anniversary had been the very day he'd called. "I don't see what that has to do with anything."

"Oh, come on, Allie. You can't tell me you don't see the similarities. But whatever your parents' faults were, they were their own. Don't hold Chance responsible for them."

"What are you saying, Griffin?"

"What you already know. He has a right to know that he's going to be a father."

The last thing Chance wanted to do that evening was head into Clearville for dinner. The Victorian town held a certain appeal for visitors and for locals who made their money off those tourists, but the place had always struck Chance as too cute. And now, as smiling pumpkins and pilgrims battled with Santa and Rudolph for prime window display real estate, it was worse than he remembered.

Rory, of course, loved it.

"I can't wait to start decorating Hillcrest for Christmas!" Wearing a thigh-length red coat, his sister already looked in the holiday spirit. She waved a hand at the glowing storefronts along Main Street. "I wanted to start putting up a few small touches here and there—just a wreath or two—but Evie insisted we wait until after Thanksgiving."

"For once, Evie and I agree," he said wryly.

"I'm so glad you'll be here for the holidays. I don't remember the last time we were all together at Christmas."

Home for the holidays? Oh, hell, no. Christmas was several weeks away, which might as well be an eternity. He wouldn't still be in Clearville then. He *couldn't* be. But even as he opened his mouth to argue, he swallowed a curse as the toe of his shoe caught on an uneven spot on the sidewalk, and his full weight landed on his right leg.

Six months, his doctors and therapists had warned him, before he could expect full range of motion. Before he could walk without limping, without pain.

"Chance—"

"I'm fine." He cut Rory off before she could ask the question he was already so sick of hearing.

"Are you sure you should be off your crutches so soon?" she pressed.

Pushing yourself won't make your body heal any faster, his doctor had warned. *You aren't building up muscle. You're regrowing bone, and that takes time.*

Chance didn't have time. He'd been riding a wave of success with recent recognition from the World Press along with nominations for international photography awards. While on the sidelines, several key assignments had been given to other photographers. He had to keep his name and his pictures out there. Whatever it took.

As they stepped inside Rolly's diner, Chance came face-to-face with another reason why he needed to get out of there. Anywhere but Clearville.

"Oh, look, there's Alexa and Griffin!" Rory announced as she sent the couple a quick wave.

Seated at a booth toward the back of the restaurant, Alexa lifted a weak hand in response while her golden boy fiancé was all smiles. As Chance's gaze caught Alexa's, as the distance between them—the crowded tables, the chattering waitresses, as the whole damn diner—disappeared in that powerful moment of memory, of connection, he could almost feel sorry for the poor SOB.

If Griffin James hadn't been the one seated across from Alexa. If he hadn't been the one holding her hand, hearing her voice, smelling the honey-lilac scent of her skin.

Sharing her hotel room...

Yeah, who was the poor SOB now?

"I didn't expect to see them here," Rory was saying as she slid into an empty booth.

Chance had had plenty of time to curse the limitations of his injury but rarely more so than in that moment. Unable to fully bend his knee, he had to take the seat on his left, to keep his right leg stretched out. A seat that faced the back of the restaurant and gave him a perfect view of Alexa and her fiancé.

"Yeah, this is hardly Alexa's kind of place."

Rory frowned as she lifted the laminated menu that probably hadn't changed since the last time Chance had eaten there. "How would you know?"

"I know...women like her," he finished. "Wealthy, spoiled, too good for everyone around her."

Not that Alexa had seemed like any of those things the night they met.

Setting the menu aside, his sister took a deep breath. "You know how much I hate admitting Evie's right, but you really do need to get on board if you're going to be our photographer."

If? *If?* She'd all but begged him to fill in! "I told you I'd get a haircut and all that."

"I'm not talking about how you look. I'm talking about your attitude about love and marriage...and women."

"Excuse me?"

"I know Lisette did a number on you—"

Now it was his turn to toss the menu aside. "This has nothing to do with Lisette," he stated flatly.

"Then what?"

"It's—"

We come from different worlds, Chance.

He watched as Griffin James, a man very much a part of Alexa's world, reached over and cupped her cheek in his palm.

"Nothing," he told Rory finally. "It's nothing."

Chapter Four

"**D**on't worry. Everything's under control." Even as Alexa spoke the words into her cell phone, she fought a burst of hysterical laughter that would certainly be enough to send her grandmother's panicked assistant over the edge. Not to mention the state it would leave Alexa in.

Under control? As she listened to Raquel rattle off the dozens of details her grandmother had needed handled in the three days since Alexa left, she couldn't imagine anything being further from the truth.

Chance was alive.

Chance was here.

She needed to tell Chance he was the father of her baby.

The phrases had circled endlessly through her mind, robbing her of any hope of a good night's sleep. She'd always been an early riser, part of the strict schedule her grandmother had established and one Alexa couldn't seem to break no matter how hard she tried. Or no matter how many hours she'd spent tossing and turning the night before.

Her doctor had encouraged exercise and warned her about too much stress, so Alexa had set out on a early morning walk. As she'd breathed in the cool morning fog, a bit of pressure eased from her chest. The breeze rustled through the pines, carrying a hint of salt air, and she was glad she'd thought to grab a thigh-length beige sweater to wear over her tunic-style cream blouse and tan leggings.

But any sense of relaxation had come to an abrupt end as she remembered that Chance wasn't the only one Alexa needed to tell about her pregnancy. And while she had no idea how Chance was going to react, she had a good idea what her proper, old-fashioned grandmother would have to say.

Tuning back into the conversation and Raquel's laundry list of concerns, she reassured the younger woman, "You'll do fine."

"But the Giving Thanks benefit—"

"Everything is going as scheduled. I confirmed with the vendors this morning." Alexa could hear Raquel relaying the information back to her grandmother and Virginia's protests in the background. "Tell my grandmother—"

"You can tell me yourself, Alexa." Virginia Mayhew's crisp voice cut across the line.

"Like I was saying to Raquel, everything is under control. I contacted—"

"*You* should be here working on the benefit. How does it look for you to be off on vacation at the most critical time of the fund-raising season?"

Considering she typically dealt with vendors by phone or email, Alexa knew things didn't "look" any different. She also knew that wasn't her grandmother's point. Alexa was the face of the foundation, and that face was always supposed to be in the public eye.

But Alexa was tired of constantly living behind a public persona. She wanted to live her own life. A life where she could go outside without the perfect clothes, perfect hair, perfect makeup. A life where *she* could be something less than perfect. "It's only for a few days, Grandmother."

"This isn't a good time. I told you that before you left."

"Yes, you did," Alexa acknowledged, but it was never a good time. Which was why she hadn't taken a vacation in...she couldn't even remember how long. "I'll be home soon."

Alexa hung up feeling the familiar weight of expectation pressing on her chest. She had started volunteering for the Mayhew Foundation when she was still in her teens and had dedicated her adult life to helping raise money for those in need.

Taking a deep breath, Alexa pressed the button on the side of her phone. For the first time, she was going to think of *her* needs. She'd longed for a break from the nonstop schedule for the past year or so, but doubted she would have made the stand if not for her pregnancy.

Growing up in her grandmother's house, Alexa's world had been filled with directives as to what a Mayhew did not do. A Mayhew did not slouch, did not sulk, did not argue, did not cry...

Only with Griffin had Alexa ever felt she could let down the walls her grandmother's rules had built around her and truly be herself. Only with Griffin...and with Chance.

Not that her feelings for the two men were at all the same. With Griffin, she felt safe. With him, she could say and do whatever she wanted.

With Chance, she felt *dangerous*. With him, she had said and done things she'd never imagined, and now...

Alexa was certain getting pregnant following a weekend fling would fall within the "did not" constraints.

But telling her grandmother would have to wait. First, she needed to tell Chance.

Some wistful part of her hoped that he would be stunned, yet overjoyed by the news. Sweeping her up into his arms the same way he'd swept her off her feet in Santa Barbara.

After confessing she'd never done something so out of character, so impetuous as to sleep with a man she'd just met, they'd teasingly come up with the list of crazy, adrenaline-fueled exploits for her to try next—all with Chance right by her side.

How about rushing headlong into the adventures of parenthood, Chance? How do you feel about holding my hand on that wild ride?

But after seeing him again, it was almost impossible to imagine a happily-ever-after ending. The charmingly seductive man she'd met the night of the charity ball seemed so...different now. Had the injury somehow changed him? Or had she allowed herself to start to fall for a man who didn't even exist?

Maybe he would even deny the baby was his. She supposed that would serve her right after foolishly pretending not to know him, and after she'd told him not to contact her in the first place, but the idea of Chance turning his back on their child made her heart ache.

I want this baby. A child to care for, to nurture, to love. The baby might have been unexpected, but not unwanted. Never unwanted. At least not by her.

Alexa slid the phone into the pocket of her sweater and glanced back toward the hotel. She'd walked farther than she'd realized, the Victorian turrets silhouetted by the gray autumn sky. She thought she'd taken the path that would lead to the gazebo Rory mentioned during their tour, but instead she caught a glimpse of a small cottage between the trees. She couldn't help smiling as she recalled Griffin's comment. If Rory was Snow White, then Alexa could certainly imagine seven dwarves living in the cute stone and wood structure.

She was tempted to take a closer look but stopped short when the front door opened. Her breath caught in her throat as Chance stepped outside, erasing any thoughts of fantasy dwarves and replacing them instead with the reality of six feet of living, breathing male.

Standing on the small porch, he stretched his neck from one side to the other. As his gaze swung in her direction, Alexa automatically ducked. She cringed, imagining what her grandmother would say if she could see her now, crouching behind a row of hedges before he could spot her.

A Mayhew does not skulk in the bushes, Alexa.

As she watched from her leafy vantage point, he ran both hands through his tousled dark hair and arched his back. Her mouth went dry as his faded T-shirt rode up above the loose waistband of his sweatpants, revealing a slice of muscled abs and tanned skin. Heat licked at her cheeks, and she wasn't sure which flame burned brighter—her arousal or her embarrassment.

Hiding was one thing. Spying was something else entirely!

Really, she needed to stop. And she would...in a minute.

Because beyond arousal and embarrassment, Alexa couldn't help noticing that his sweatpants weren't just loose. The elastic band threatened to slip past his hip bones.

Her stomach clutched. How much weight had he lost? As he took a few steps, his limp was more noticeable than the day before. Was his leg worse...or with no one around and no reason to pretend everything was all right, was he allowing himself to give in to the pain?

He would hate for her to witness even a momentary weakness, and she carefully ducked deeper into her hiding spot. She'd wait a moment or two for Chance to go inside before making her way back to the hotel.

She hazarded another glance toward the cottage and breathed a sigh of relief when she saw the porch was empty. She needed to tell Chance about the baby, but not yet. Not until she could be calm and in control, and until she was sure she could do that... Well, she'd be hiding in the bushes.

Pushing to her feet, she swore beneath her breath as the branches caught in the loose knit of her sweater. She nearly jumped out of her skin when a deep voice behind her asked, "You lose something?"

She spun around, slipping on the damp ground and stumbling against the solid, masculine wall of his chest. Chance instinctively caught her, his hands warm and roughly seductive against her upper arms. Each individual fingertip struck a pinpoint of sensation, and the back of his thumbs pressed against her overly sensitive breasts.

She jumped back quickly, but the damage had already been done. Her body still tingled from the sudden contact, the air around them still crackled with undeniable intensity, and she knew she'd made a big mistake not leaving when she'd had the chance.

"You scared me half to death!"

He gave her a sardonic grin. "Sorry, didn't mean to sneak up on you while you were...?"

His words drifted away, a dark brow winged upward in query, and Alexa wrapped her sweater around her waist. "I was out for a walk," she sniffed, trying to maintain an air of dignity.

His smirk marked her as a liar. "Next time maybe you'll try the beach. That's my favorite spot."

Alexa had a view of the rugged coastline from her suite along with the uneven, rocky pathway that led to the beach. It was not what she'd consider a leisurely stroll. As he turned, Alexa realized he hadn't been stretching on the porch; he'd been warming up.

Without stopping to think, she reached out and caught his arm. His skin was warm, undeniably masculine muscle beneath a dusting of dark hair, and for a moment, she forgot what it was she wanted to say.

Forgot everything but the memory of sliding her hand down that same arm as she'd slipped the white tuxedo shirt from his broad shoulders.

Chance froze beneath her touch, and Alexa swallowed. "Are—are you sure that's a good idea?"

His heated gaze dropped to where her hand still rested on his forearm. "Are you sure *that's* a good idea?"

Snatching her hand back, she said, "I meant pushing yourself so hard."

"Hard was being stuck in traction. You don't have to worry about me, Alexa. I heal fast."

She couldn't imagine what that had been like for him. For a man who was always on the move to not just be stuck in a hospital bed, but to be held in place, immobilized by ropes and pulleys.

She was dying to ask him what had happened, what he'd gone through, beyond the news reports she could barely bring herself to read. After that first devastating headline, she hadn't known what to believe. Was he truly recovering or was that information wrong, as well?

But she knew better than to expect an honest answer. Especially not after he pinned her with a look and added, "Before long, I'll move on like nothing ever happened."

The way he thought she'd moved on to Griffin? Alexa swallowed but asked, "What about your job here?"

"You mean…wedding photographer? That *isn't* my job, Alexa. That's a favor to my sister. One I never should have agreed to," he added beneath his breath.

"Why? Photographing weddings will be a piece of cake compared to what you're used to."

"What I'm used to—" he muttered. "What I'm used to is photographing some of the worst of humanity. I'm not sure I trust myself to still recognize the good."

His vulnerability grabbed hold of the secret she kept, tugging the words straight from her heart. She longed to reassure him of the good in the world, of the something *great* the two of them had created together. But would he see their baby that way? When he was so dead set on pushing himself to get better so that he could *move on*?

So instead, she pointed out, "Your sister clearly trusts you."

"My sister tends to trust everyone. It's one of her biggest failings." Chance glanced around the towering trees and the Victorian hotel in the distance. "Rory's always thought this place was magic."

With her arms still crossed at her waist, Alexa could feel the slight swell of her belly. She and Chance had made a baby. It might not have been magic, but as far as Alexa was concerned, it was a tiny miracle.

A miracle she needed to share. Swallowing against the lump in her throat, she whispered, "Chance…"

He straightened abruptly. "You should go. I'm sure your fiancé is wondering where you are."

"Chance, we need to talk—"

"I think you said everything you needed to say during our last phone call."

Goodbye was pretty much all they'd said during that phone call, and so much had happened since then. Finding out that she was pregnant, the bombing, the reports of his death. "But…"

He started to turn away, then stopped. Alexa's heart jumped to her throat as he reached up a hand and brushed his fingers through her hair. A muscle in his jaw clenched, and she could only stare helplessly into the firestorm of emotions in his sapphire eyes.

For a split second, she thought he was going to pull her closer, to kiss her the way he had that first night underneath the sparkling stars. To kiss her the way he had every night since in her dreams.

His voice gravel rough, he said, "I think you must have dropped this."

Only after he moved away from her did she lift a hand to the spot above her ear. Her fingers brushed against a thin piece of metal. She pulled the hairpin from her hair and stared at the bejeweled butterfly clip she hadn't seen in four months.

Not since she wore it the night of the charity event in Santa Barbara.

"Doesn't the gazebo look amazing?" Rory asked Chance, her smile almost blinding in an otherwise overcast day.

He lifted a shoulder in a shrug as he adjusted the camera to account for the hazy morning. His sister was wearing a bright red sweater over a black-and-white polka-dot dress—an outfit that was sure to pop against the white lattice of the gazebo.

He cringed at the thought, left over from his days of fashion photography where he'd worked behind a camera to capture fantasy rather than reality. He would have thought after seeing behind the curtain, knowing all the hours of hair and makeup and wardrobe that went into creating a picture-perfect shot, that he would have been able to tell the difference.

And yet for months, Lisette had had him completely fooled.

He had to give her credit for one thing, though. The first time they met she'd told him she would do anything to make it as a fashion model. She'd been up-front about that. He just hadn't realized "anything" included lying, manipulating and finally cheating on him.

When he confronted her, she'd pleaded, she'd cried, she'd begged him not to throw away everything they had over a "mistake." But in that moment, he finally realized he'd witnessed that full range of emotions from behind the camera and that it was all a performance. When he refused to budge, Lisette had dropped the act.

We're not so different, Chance, so don't pretend you're better than me. We both know our careers are more important than anything...or anyone.

Chance wasn't so sure that was true ten years ago, but it was now.

His hands tightened on his camera as he thought of the call from his editor the other day. "I'm sorry, Chance," the man had added after telling him he was giving the prime assignment to another photojournalist. "You know we can't sit on breaking stories. If there was any way to know when you'll be back..."

Chance had swallowed the promises he longed to make. As much as he wanted to grab his gear and go, he couldn't. The harder he pushed his body, the harder his body was pushing back.

Are you sure that's a good idea?

He'd barely been able to get out of bed after the grueling pace he'd set that day on the beach. He couldn't even pretend work had been the only thing on his mind as he'd pounded across the hard-packed sand until his lungs were burning and his leg was on fire.

Because hadn't he wanted to believe he'd seen something in Alexa's eyes when he'd run into her outside the cottage? Something that said what they'd shared had been more than a final fling before marrying her "well-suited" fiancé?

Chance swore. Maybe that old expression was true—once a fool, always a fool.

"Sorry, Chance, what was that?" Rory asked, breaking into his thoughts and returning his focus to where it should have been all along.

"I was just thinking…" He waved a hand at the gazebo with its lattice trim and elegant scrollwork. "Looks the same as it always did."

"Right, the same as it did ten or fifteen years ago when you last saw it. You weren't here a few months ago when it was practically falling down." Her smile turned almost secretive as she ran a hand over the railing leading to the circular platform. "Jamison did an amazing job remodeling it in time for his best friend's wedding. This place is…special to us."

Special? Combine that with the satisfied look on his sister's face and—Chance groaned. "Okay, stop. Now! Before I have to scrub my brain out with soap."

"Oh, grow up! We're both adults here."

"Uh, no. I'm an adult and you're my baby sister, and if you tell me much more than you already have, I'll have to punch your lawyer-boy fiancé in the face. Where is he, anyway?"

His sister had asked him to take some pictures for updating the hotel's website and for new brochures touting the place as *the* wedding spot. Rory and Jamison were going to pose as a happy couple with the gazebo as a romantic backdrop, but his sister's fiancé had yet to show. "Didn't you say you had a deadline to get these shots to the printer?"

Rory sighed. "I do, but Jamison decided to stay in San Francisco for another day or two. His former in-laws are having a hard time with Hannah moving away."

Chance didn't feel much sympathy for the older couple, knowing the problems they'd caused when Rory and Jamison first got together. "So they call, and he automatically runs home?"

"Like I said, they're having a hard time. Jamison is doing all he can to make the transition easier." Rory lifted her chin to a stubborn—and familiar—angle.

Chance knew she wouldn't say anything against her fiancé, but he had to wonder. "Are you sure Jamison isn't simply making it easier for his in-laws to manipulate him? And letting them use his daughter to do it?"

"They've lost their daughter, and Hannah is their only grandchild. This isn't *easy* on anyone. And besides, they're her family."

"Family," he echoed. "You say that as if it makes everything and anything okay. Even if—"

We just want what's best for you, Chance.

Even if they didn't know him at all.

"Chance..."

His sister was no fool. But whatever Rory suspected, he wasn't going there. Not now. Probably not ever when for all he knew, Rory felt the same way.

Maybe—maybe it would be better if his leg never healed...

"So if Jamison's a no-show, what are we doing here? You want some shots just of the gazebo?"

Lingering worry and hurt swirled in his sister's gaze. "No, I—" Her expression cleared, and she glanced over his shoulder. "Oh, perfect. Here they are now! When Jamison had to leave town, I asked another couple to step in."

Chance knew without looking back exactly who was standing behind him. The hair on the back of his neck rose as a familiar awareness surged through him. He didn't need to turn around, but like some kind of polarized magnet, he couldn't stop the sudden pull.

As Alexa's startled gaze locked on his, Chance's hands tightened around the camera. He was sure heiress and philanthropist Alexa Mayhew had never given modeling a second's thought, but she could have made a fortune at it. Wearing a soft pink sweater draped over a loose floral print dress, she looked as fashionable as ever. Her blond hair fell to her shoulders in soft waves, tucked back behind one ear.

It was all Chance could do to keep from lifting his camera and snapping the moment.

In the months since that weekend in Santa Barbara, especially those first agonizing weeks in the hospital, he'd regretted not taking Alexa's picture when he'd had the chance.

Oh, with her family's wealth and Alexa's status as the face of her grandmother's foundation, he could have found dozens of images online. But none that he had taken. He wanted to photograph the Alexa only he could see, the sensual side she'd revealed to him during their weekend together. He wanted to capture that part of her for himself—

And didn't that sound downright creepy?

"I asked Griffin and Alexa to help out, and they agreed," Rory was saying behind him.

Because yes, Alexa's fiancé was there, too, but Chance couldn't drag his gaze away from Alexa.

Ever since the morning outside the cottage two days

ago, Chance had done his damnedest to keep his distance, but the hotel simply wasn't big enough for both of them. There were still those unavoidable moments. A brief second when they passed each other in the lobby. When they'd seen each other across the hotel restaurant. And he'd felt it every damn time.

The rush, the attraction, the awareness arcing between them. As powerful and elemental as a bolt of lightning, raising the hair on his arms on end and making him feel... alive.

And as she drew closer, a flash of gold and diamond in her hair sparkled despite the cloudy skies. Her chin lifted, almost as if she were challenging him to notice, to remember...

Chance swore beneath his breath. Like he needed the reminder. Hell, he'd given the damn thing back to her as a way to cut ties. To convince his stupid heart of what he hadn't been able to bring himself to believe—it was over.

She'd been more than clear in that last phone call, so why would she choose to wear the hairpin now?

During his months together with Lisette, he hadn't figured her out until it was too late and the damage to his career had already been done. And in hindsight, without head-over-heels lust blinding him, the attention-grabbing, spoiled beauty wasn't that hard to pin down.

But did he really think he'd have a clue what was going through the mind of a far more complicated woman like Alexa after their single weekend together?

Color rising in her cheeks, she finally broke the lingering glance and turned to her fiancé. "What did we agree to?" she asked quietly.

"You didn't tell her?" Rory asked.

Griffin was all smiles as he shot Alexa a wink that had

Chance's hands tightening on his camera. "I thought it would be a surprise. Surprise!"

Rory laughed and explained, "We need some pictures taken for our website and for some brochures for the hotel. We're in a bit of a time crunch and… Anyway, I need a couple to pose with the gazebo as the romantic backdrop, and when my fiancé got called away, I thought you and Griffin would be perfect! If you don't mind, Alexa?"

Griffin was already guiding her toward the gazebo's steps, his arm wrapped possessively around her slender waist. "You're always willing to help out when someone needs a hand."

Chance could see she was practically dragging her feet across the damp ground. "Of course, I'd like to help but—"

"It will only be a few shots. And Chance is a marvelous photographer."

Alexa drew in a deep breath and offered Rory a smile. "Just a few shots," she agreed.

"Perfect!" His sister clapped her hands in excitement. "Chance, are you ready?"

Ready to see Alexa in the arms of another man? Because walking in on Lisette hadn't been bad enough?

Clearly the universe felt he hadn't learned his lesson when it came to falling for the wrong woman.

Chapter Five

As the face of her grandmother's charity, Alexa had learned long ago to hide behind a smile. Band canceled at the last minute? No problem. Famous couple who were presenting the charity with a check were now at war? Piece of cake. Countless minor emergencies filling her days, her nights, her weekends, her life? That's what she was there for.

But this...

"If you could see your boyfriend's face right about now..." Griffin said in a low voice as they posed on the gazebo with Chance as the photographer and Rory as artistic director. "He looks like he wants to kill me."

"*I* want to kill you right now!" Pins and needles pricked every inch of her flesh, heightening her awareness to the point when every breath seemed an effort and she could count every single beat of her heart. Suffocating beneath Chance's impassive stare, she wanted to sink through the gazebo floor. "And he's not my boyfriend."

Self-consciously, she lifted her hand to tuck her hair behind her ear only to remember her hair was already back. Held in place by the butterfly hairpin Chance had returned to her two days ago.

She hadn't known exactly when she'd lost the hairpin the night of the charity event. Down in the marble and gold lobby as she mingled with the other arriving guests? In the ballroom during the five-course meal? On the dance floor where Chance first held her in his arms? Or later when he'd held her in her hotel room?

The impact of Chance returning the hairpin hadn't immediately struck her. She'd left it behind; he'd found it and returned it. Except he couldn't have possibly known he would see her. Not at Hillcrest House. Possibly never again, considering the way they'd left things with that last phone call.

So why, when fate…or *whatever* brought them back together again all these months later, had he still been carrying her hairpin with him?

You don't have weekend flings, Alexa, Griffin had pointed out. *Don't you think that means something?*

She was still coming to grips with what that weekend meant to her. It was easier to believe Chance had walked away without looking back. But what if some part of him wanted to hold on to what they'd found that weekend—like he'd held on to that hairpin? What if he'd wanted to *stay*?

"You'll forgive me. You always do." Griffin's expression turned serious as he added, "It's been three days, Allie. You said you were going to tell him."

"No, you said I *should.*"

"And deep down you agree whether you're willing to admit it or not. You just need a little push."

And Griffin was good at pushing her. Into the deep end of the pool when she'd been nine and too scared to jump despite months of private swimming lessons. Out from behind a curtain and onto center stage at one of the first fund-raising events she'd organized.

And now he was pushing her to talk to Chance.

"Griffin—"

"Just a second." Stepping back, he reached into his pocket and pulled out his phone. After a quick look at the screen, he shot her a sympathetic glance. "Sorry, I've got to take this. I'll just be a minute."

Reaching out, Alexa desperately grabbed his arm. "Griffin!"

Leaning close, he pressed a kiss against her temple. "Talk to him," he murmured before he backed down the stairs and walked away.

Standing alone in the gazebo, Alexa felt ridiculously abandoned. "I'm sure he'll be back in just a minute," she told Chance and Rory, certain of no such thing.

Five minutes later and even that small amount of certainty started to wane. But when Chance lifted the camera strapped over his head, she pleaded, "Can't we wait just a few minutes longer?" She'd promised—or at least Griffin had promised—to help Rory, and Alexa didn't want to let the other woman down. "Griffin—"

"I'm not waiting for Griffin," Chance stated flatly. "Here."

Rory's eyes widened as she fumbled with the camera her brother handed to her. "Chance, what are you doing?"

"Point and shoot, Rory. It's not that hard."

"Not that hard? Easy for you to say! If I end up breaking this thing—"

"You won't."

But instead of turning and walking away like Alexa thought he was going to, Chance stalked toward her. Reaching out, she grabbed hold of the gazebo's railing as she felt herself swaying closer as he stomped up the steps.

His gaze captured hers, and her thoughts flashed to that night four months ago.

Chance backing her into the bedroom, his low laughter striking sparks along every inch of her exposed skin when she'd suggested turning off the lights.

Do you always kiss with your eyes closed, Lexi?

Maybe, she had confessed while thinking, *Among other things.*

Then prepare to see all you've been missing, he vowed, and to say she'd had her eyes opened was a serious understatement...

"Your fiancé's an idiot."

"Excuse me?" Alexa blinked, the muttered words not the ones she'd thought she'd hear.

"He's an idiot to walk away from you."

Conscious of his sister only a few yards away, fiddling uncertainly with the camera in her hands, Alexa murmured, "Well, at least I can be sure Griffin's coming back."

"You made it pretty damn clear you didn't want me back, princess."

In the days that followed that magical weekend, doubts had quickly crept in. That instant connection...it couldn't have been as strong as she remembered. The feeling of belonging she'd found in his arms...that was all part of the fantasy. None of it was real because she didn't believe in love at first sight, did she...

Did she?

She couldn't. Not with a man like Chance McClaren. A man who lived life in a lane so fast it didn't have a speed limit, a man who would leave her time and time again before leaving her for the last time.

So she convinced herself the connection wasn't strong, and she had told him she didn't want to see him again.

"Um, are you sure about this, Chance?" Rory called

out, the camera that had looked so much a part of Chance held awkwardly in her much smaller hands.

"You wanted a couple to smile for the camera, right?" he called over his shoulder. "So come on, Lexi," he said beneath his breath. "Smile."

Nerves carved a hole in her stomach as she inhaled the scent of his aftershave. He'd gotten a haircut since she'd seen him last and had scraped away the thick stubble coating his rugged jaw. But for all his instructions, his unsmiling features appeared carved from granite.

"No one is going to believe we're a couple. Not even in a photograph."

Bending his head low to hers in what Alexa inanely realized would make a poignant picture, Chance murmured, "Just fake it... You know, like you did in Santa Barbara."

"Well—" Rory cleared her throat as she handed the camera back to Chance "—I think we got some...interesting shots."

Though her smile remained in place, he couldn't possibly miss the "what the heck was that?" arch to her eyebrows. He couldn't begin to explain to his sister what had just happened. Hell, he couldn't explain it to himself.

One minute he'd been photographing Alexa and Griffin, clinging to every ounce of control he possessed to keep from storming up the gazebo stairs and knocking the other man into next week, and then in the next—the guy was gone, walking off and leaving Alexa alone.

Embarrassed color kissed her cheeks in the fading light. She'd lifted a hand to her hair, and he couldn't help noticing once more that Griffin James had yet to put a ring on Alexa's slender finger. In fact, the only diamonds she wore were the ones Chance had given to her. Or at least had given back to her.

And before he could take a moment to talk himself out of it, he had climbed those steps, but the only blows had been the ones Alexa landed.

No one is going to believe we're a couple.

How many times did she need to tell him? he asked himself as he shoved his camera and lenses into his bag. He didn't belong in her world, and she'd already chosen a man who did. End of story.

So he'd shot back that jackass comment about faking it, determined to hold on to his self-righteous anger only to lose it the moment he wrapped his arms around her. Desire thrummed through his veins and it had taken all his self-control not to pull her body tight to his until he could feel every inch of her against every inch of him.

It was goodbye, he'd told himself, and this time when he walked away, there'd be no looking back. Just moving forward, the way he had always done. Onto the next job, onto the next shoot. His life was his work. In the field, he was known for his single-minded concentration. His ability to focus on the shot and block out all other distractions around him.

But Alexa was a distraction unlike any he'd ever known. With her slender arms around his neck and her honey-lilac scent haunting his senses, Chance didn't know how he was supposed to let her go.

He'd never been one for holding on, had always been the one to leave—like he had left Alexa after their weekend together. But she'd followed him. In his thoughts, in his dreams, in the darkest moments after the explosion when her presence—imagined though it was—had pulled him through.

"Chance."

"Don't," he'd protested gruffly, sure she was going to remind him once again of the differences in their lives.

He might have made a name for himself as a photo-journalist, but that didn't mean he fit in Alexa's wealthy, privileged world. So why had hearing her say the words hurt so much more than he'd expected?

"Don't say anything. Just…"

"Feel?" she'd whispered back, her voice breaking on the word and on the memory.

But that was the problem. He felt too much for a woman promised to another man. How many times had he told himself over the past months that those nights in Santa Barbara weren't as incredible as he remembered? That the long, lonely nights spent in some godforsaken war-torn country had somehow magnified his last pleasurable experience into so much more than it was?

Like putting the object of a crush on some untouchable pedestal, his memory elevated his experience with Alexa to a height real life could never equal.

But after touching her again, holding her in his arms, Chance knew it was all a lie. The reality of Alexa was more than memory, more than imagination could ever offer.

His movements were rough, impatient as he jerked the zipper on his camera bag closed. He needed to get the hell out of Clearville. He'd known coming here was a mistake, as much of one as going home had been.

He had a studio apartment in LA he saw half a dozen times a year at most. He could stay there. The three flights of stairs would be hell on his leg but a picnic compared to what staying in Clearville was doing to the rest of him.

Strains of music drifted out over the grounds, and Rory glanced back toward the hotel. "We have an anniversary party set for this evening. Sounds like the DJ is getting set up. Alexa, why don't you come with me? I'm sure you'd enjoy seeing the way we've decorated for the event."

"I'll wait here for Griffin, and we'll join you in a minute."

"Oh, okay. Um, Chance, you'll need to email the final shots over to the printer."

"I'll go through and do some touch-up work and send them over. Unless you want to have final say?"

"No, of course not. After all, you are the *professional*."

He didn't miss the slight emphasis on the last word. A reminder that Alexa was a guest and a potential Hillcrest bride...

"I can't imagine what your sister is thinking," Alexa muttered as Rory walked away.

"You're worried what my sister is thinking? I figured you'd be more concerned about your fiancé."

Her gaze cut to his, her expression a little wounded, a little guilty. "Chance, there's something I need to tell you... About Griffin...and about our time together in Santa Barbara."

"You've said enough already, and it's not like I haven't heard it all before."

"What—what does that mean?"

"Do you think you're the first rich girl to go slumming?"

Her jaw dropped. "You think— That is *not* what I was doing. If anyone is a fake, Chance McClaren, it's you! You played me in Santa Barbara. You fooled me into thinking you were charming and—and sensitive—and kind."

"I'm still plenty charming when I want to be."

He advanced on her, but she held her ground. Reminding him once again that his golden goddess had a spine of steel.

"Oh, you'd like to think so, wouldn't you? But I've got news for you. You're like the chicken pox. Now that I've had you, I'm immune."

Her head was raised to a haughty height, but that only made the pulse pounding in her long, elegant neck more noticeable. He cupped his hand around her nape, her silken hair teasing his skin as his thumb laid claim to that tell-tale throbbing. "You sure about that, princess? 'Cause I'm more than ready to put it to the test."

Alexa gasped his name when he pulled her body flush with his, but that wasn't what held Chance in place. Instead, it was the soft strains of a familiar melody—the song they had danced to in Santa Barbara.

They both froze, caught in the moment…in the memory.

Anger, desire, longing—all of it charged the air around them until the hair on the back of his neck rose. Alexa's lips parted, the slight intake of breath enough to draw him even closer, to pull him into the promise of her kiss and the memory of making love.

Until the music cut off abruptly, putting a sudden end to something that had never truly started. The empty silence was jarring, too…loud for him to ignore all he couldn't say to a woman engaged to another man.

Chance ignored the sharp pain in his leg as he jerked away. "Go back to your world, Alexa, and stay out of mine."

The past few minutes should have sent her scurrying back to her fiancé. Hell, she was right after all. He wasn't the man she'd met in Santa Barbara. He couldn't blame her for not recognizing him. At the moment, he barely recognized himself.

But instead she stood her ground, her eyes glittering with unshed tears as she raised her arms from her sides. "I can't."

"Why not?"

"Because I'm pregnant!"

Chapter Six

Blinking back furious tears, Alexa couldn't imagine a worse way to tell Chance about the baby. Shouting out the words in a fit of anger and hurt and...desire. That was as far from the calm, logical conversation she'd planned as she could get. But maybe she shouldn't even have been surprised. From the moment she met Chance McClaren, her plans had all landed in one huge handbasket.

"Pregnant?"

He echoed the word blankly, a mix of consonants and vowels that held no possible meaning in his world. "How—"

"You have to ask?"

"How do you know it's mine?"

Alexa told herself she'd expected the question, that it was her own fault Chance had to ask. But it didn't stop the hurt slicing through her. "It's yours." Still seeing the suspicion in his eyes, she said, "Griffin's a friend. Just a friend."

"A friend you were going to marry."

"He asked me to marry him. I didn't say yes."

"You sure as hell didn't say no or the two of you wouldn't be here, looking at a wedding venue." His gaze narrowed to a thin slice of blue. "He knows, doesn't he?"

"About the baby? Yes."

"You told him, but you didn't tell me." His voice had a hollow sound to it as if she'd cut the heart out of him and left him empty inside.

She forced herself to face the truth. She'd started to fall for him that weekend in Santa Barbara. She wasn't sure she believed in love at first sight, but she'd felt something. Something magical. She never would have slept with him if she hadn't. That was why she'd been so hurt when she hadn't heard from him. When the days of loving someone who would leave her without a backward glance had returned with a vengeance.

And when she found out she was pregnant…

She hadn't wanted her child to feel that same longing, that same pain.

"I needed someone to talk to, and Griffin's always been there for me…as a friend. He's always been the person I turn to, the person I count on—"

"The person you were counting on to raise my child?"

"Chance—"

"How the hell did you expect me to be there when you'd already given me the 'hit the road' speech? I wasn't there? I wasn't someone you could trust? How am I supposed to trust *you* when you were the one keeping the fact that you're pregnant a secret? You should have told me, Alexa. Me! As soon as you found out."

"You're right, Chance. This is all my fault. I really should have tried harder to get ahold of you. I should have— What? Dug out my Ouija board to let my dead baby daddy know he was going to be a father?"

Shock washed over his features, wiping away some of her anger. "I *tried* to get ahold of you, and I couldn't. The cell number you'd given me went straight to voice mail, so I reached out to the last magazine you'd published with. They wouldn't tell me anything other than that you were on assignment and then—"

Her voice broke as the memories, the pain she'd buried, denied, rose to the surface. As fresh as if she were just hearing the news. As real as if Chance was lying broken and bleeding a half a world away rather than living, breathing in front of her.

"Alexa..."

Ignoring him, she pointed a shaking finger into his chest. "So don't tell me about what I should have done."

"The reports were wrong. You know that. You must have heard that later. I'm here. I'm fine."

"This time. But next time when you aren't so lucky? When the reports are right? I know what it's like to lose my parents. I don't want to— I don't want that for our child."

"Alexa—"

Brushing the tears from her cheeks, Alexa rushed past Chance, not stopping when he called after her. Not surprised when he didn't come after her.

But at least this time she was the one to walk away.

Chance didn't know how most men reacted to finding out they were going to be a father, but as soon as the initial shock wore off, his first instinct was to run. As far and as fast as he could—which took him only a mile down the beach. The pathetically short distance and the amount of time it took him to get that far only added to the trapped, suffocating feeling.

You can't outrun this one.

The mocking sound of his conscience pounded in his

head, louder than the cool ocean air rasping in and out of his lungs, louder than the waves breaking against the shoreline. A million miles wouldn't be far enough to distance himself from the panic that had set in the moment Alexa broke the news.

A father.

Bending at the waist, he braced his hands on his knees and wondered for a moment if he was going to be sick.

He was going to be a father.

He should have been excited. He should have been overjoyed. Instead, all he felt was…guilt. And fear.

Despite the risks he'd taken in life, Chance had never given much thought to dying. Not even with his list of close calls as a kid to the more recent bomb attack. Dying was inevitable regardless of how he lived his life. He could take calculated risks or he could live life in a bubble, but one way or the other, the end result was the same.

Worrying about it didn't change a thing.

But the idea that he could have died without knowing he was going to be a father, that his child could have grown up without ever knowing him, hit hard. As hard as the blow Alexa had delivered in telling him she was pregnant in the first place.

Expect the unexpected.

It was a familiar motto in the field where things rarely went as smoothly as planned on paper. He'd learned to think fast and move faster. But as he stood on the beach watching the waves rush toward the shore, the sand beneath his feet might as well have been quicksand.

He couldn't move, couldn't think.

Alexa was right. For most of his adult life, he'd avoided commitment, ties, responsibilities beyond those that came with his job. Hell, even when it came to his career, he'd made the decision to work freelance, where he was able to choose which assignment to accept and which to turn down.

He had the freedom to pack up and hit the road—just like he had that morning in Santa Barbara when he'd left Alexa behind. Sure, he'd called a few weeks later after the assignment ended and he was back in town. Thinking they could pick up where they left off. But was she really supposed to be thrilled when he called with nothing more to offer than another weekend of sex and five-star room service?

Of course she wanted more. She deserved more, and now with a baby on the way... The only question was did Chance have it within him to give more? Or was he going to leave that to Alexa's *good friend* Griffin James?

Chance wasn't sure how long he stood on the beach, but the lights in the hotel were glowing by the time he started back. Music drifted through the night air, and a flurry of activity surrounded the large tent set up on the south lawn. The white canvas gleamed thanks to the moonlit night and the hundreds of twinkle lights shining like stars in the nearby trees. Staff members were scrambling around, calling out instructions to each other as they put on the final touches for the anniversary party. Place settings, water glasses and a red rose on every table.

Rory did an amazing job, but his sister was the last person he wanted to run into. Sucking in a deep breath, he turned away. The loose gravel path crunched beneath his uneven gait, but he pushed forward. If he could just keep moving, he'd figure this out. One foot in front of the other, and before long, he'd be—

Standing a hundred yards outside the hotel.

He had to talk to Alexa.

Too many important decisions, life-altering decisions,

had to be made to let the silence fester and grow to the point where neither would be able to hear the other no matter how much was said.

As his foot hit the first step, a voice called out from one side of the wraparound porch. "Hey, Chance, photo shoot over?"

Chance's hand tightened on the railing as Griffin James stepped out from the shadowy alcove. Despite Alexa's vow that she and the other man were nothing but friends, her words did little to ease the jealousy that had been eating him up inside since Griffin and Alexa had arrived. Not when Griffin was the man she could count on, the man she could trust, the man she'd turned to with the news that she was pregnant with *Chance's* baby.

"Not just the photo shoot," he warned grimly.

"Not just... Ah." The puzzlement cleared from the other man's expression as did his friendly smile. "She told you about the baby, didn't she?"

"My baby," he stated, though just saying the words was enough to make his head spin.

"You might be the baby's father, but there's more to parenthood than biology. Alexa knows that better than anyone."

"What's that supposed to mean?"

"Her own parents barely remembered they had a daughter. They left her behind for one adventure after another until they finally got themselves killed when she was eight."

A child... Her parents had died when she was just a child. She'd spent so much of her childhood without them, growing up alone. And the fear he'd failed to leave behind on the beach clawed at him once more.

I almost died...

Chance clenched his jaw until his back teeth ached. So not funny anymore.

"They cared more about freedom and fun than family," Griffin was saying, accusation slicing through every word. "Sound familiar?"

"I left because of my job." Even to his own ears, the words sounded hollow. "I had an assignment."

"Do you think that mattered to Alexa when she found out she was pregnant and you were gone? Do you think it mattered when she thought you'd been killed?"

The questions were no different from the ones circling through his own mind. He couldn't stop them. Couldn't shut them up. Griffin, though... Chance's hands tightened into fists. He had a pretty good idea how to shut *him* up. "I didn't know she was pregnant. If I had—"

"If you had, then what?" Griffin challenged.

Chance opened his mouth, but when the words wouldn't come, Griffin came to his own conclusion.

"Alexa needs a man who'll be there for her...and for her baby. If that's not going to be you, well, don't be surprised if it ends up being me."

"Like hell!"

"What is wrong with you?" Rory demanded, her eyes narrowed with an anger he hadn't seen since he'd accidently decapitated one of her dolls when they were kids. "What were you thinking?"

Holding an ice bag against his jaw, Chance tried to meet his sister's furious gaze. Not easy to do when his left eye was already swelling shut. Though Griffin James was tougher than he looked, Chance had gotten his blows in. If not for his injured knee, he would have taken the other man down in no time. As it was, Chance didn't know how long they'd grappled together...before they'd both ended up toppling over the railing and falling from the porch.

Bloodied and bruised, the fall knocked the wind out of

them, giving two of the hotel porters the opportunity to break up the fight. Chance didn't know how Rory and Evie heard about it, but as soon as his sister arrived, she had pushed him into Evie's office, out of sight of the guests.

Last he'd seen of Griffin James, Evie had been helping the man to his feet, offering to call a doctor and to comp his stay.

"Griffin James is a guest! What on earth would make you hit him?"

Chance locked his jaw and ducked out of the way as she raised a napkin toward his face. Even when furious, she was still trying to mother him. "We'll be lucky if he doesn't sue! Not to mention the damage this could do the hotel's reputation. Did you even think about that?"

"He deserved it. You have to trust me, Ror." He just wasn't ready to explain all the reasons why.

His sister stared at him. "So in other words, no. You didn't think. You just…acted. To hell with the consequences or with anyone else who might get hurt in the fallout."

Tears glittered in her eyes, and Chance knew this tirade had nothing to do with the fight with Griffin. And the frustration that Chance hadn't come close to burning off rose up.

It's not my fault! he wanted to yell. He hated the hell those reports had put his family through, but he couldn't change what had happened. "Rory—"

"No, don't. Whatever you're going to say, I'm sure I've heard it all before. This is your life, Chance. Go ahead and live like no one else in it matters."

A part of Alexa wanted nothing more than to throw her clothes into her suitcases and book the first flight back to LA. She'd spent far too much of her childhood trying to carve out some tiny piece where she fit in, where she was wanted, where she belonged to force her way into Chance's life.

He wanted her to go back to her world? Fine. Her grandmother had a team of lawyers on retainer. She could hide behind a wall of suits and never have to deal face-to-face with Chance again.

Only she didn't want that. Not for herself or for her child. She didn't want to outsource her emotions or hire other people to fight her battles. She needed to work this out with Chance, to come to some kind of understanding.

She'd dropped a bombshell on him and should have expected to be hit with some of the fallout. Her world wasn't the only one that had been upended since that night in Santa Barbara. At least she'd had some time to come to grips with the news that she was pregnant. She'd given Chance all of five minutes before running off.

Hearing the door to the suite open, Alexa pressed the cool damp washcloth beneath her eyes a final time before hanging it on the towel rack and leaving the bathroom. The last thing she wanted was for Griffin to see that she'd been—

"Griff!" She gasped as she caught sight of him. His dress shirt was untucked, a grass stain marred one shoulder and the front... Bright red blood splattered across the pale blue silk. "My God! What happened? Were you mugged?"

It hardly seemed possible that such a crime would take place in the quaint small town, but she couldn't come up with a better explanation. Rushing to his side, she took his arm. "Did you call the police?"

Griffin waved aside her concern. "No, of course not," he protested, his voice sounding thick and nasally.

Alexa stared down at him as he dropped onto the sofa, his head tilted back against the cushions, a cloth napkin held to his nose as he tried to stop the bleeding. "Why on earth not?"

"Because I didn't think you'd want me to get your boy-friend's ass thrown in jail."

"*Chance* did this? Why?"

Hand still pressed to his nose, he shot her a knowing look. "Why do you think?"

Sinking onto the couch next to him, Alexa could practically hear her grandmother's arch, aristocratic voice echo-ing in her head.

A Mayhew does not cause a scene.

"I told Chance about the baby, but are you saying he just *jumped* you?"

"Not exactly," Griffin said, only it came out sounding more like *nob exally.*

"Griffin…"

"I might have pushed him into it."

"Why?" Lifting her hands helplessly at her side, she protested, "You were the one who wanted me to tell him about the baby!"

"That doesn't mean I didn't want to punch him in the face for getting you pregnant in the first place."

"Are you okay?"

"I'm fine. Evie McClaren was very solicitous in tak-ing care of me," he said with a rakish wink he couldn't quite pull off thanks to the bright pink bandage across his eyebrow. "I'm pretty sure she's afraid I'm going to sue."

"And…is Chance okay?"

"No worse off than I am. Unfortunately. Although his sister did look like she wanted to kill him, so there's al-ways that."

Alexa dropped her head into her hands with a groan. Great. Now, thanks to her, there was a rift between Chance and his family. "I don't understand why you had to do this."

Sitting up straight, Griffin reached over and pulled her hands down. "Because you deserve a man who's willing to fight for you. And I'm not talking about me."

Alexa's throat tightened with unshed tears, making words impossible...had she even known what to say.

"And now I think it would be best if I head home in the morning."

"You're leaving?" Somehow the squeak of panic escaped the lump in her throat. "But what about the research you were doing for your father?"

"I'm tired of playing by his rules, hoping that what I do will be enough for him to finally hand over my trust fund. Besides, I don't get feeling from either Rory or Evie that they have any interest in selling the hotel. From what I understand, their aunt is the one who makes final decisions, and she's off on some mysterious sabbatical that no one's talking about."

"I don't want you to go," Alexa protested.

"I know. But you need to do this on your own, Allie. I've been holding you back too long."

"Holding me back from what?"

"From taking chances. From spreading your wings."

"I don't know what you're talking about."

"If your grandmother asks you to host an event, who's the first person you call?"

"The caterer."

Griffin's lips twitched. "The second person."

"You," Alexa admitted a little grumpily.

"Right. Because you hate hosting or going to those kinds of events alone."

"And because you're my best friend. You've always been there for me."

"I think I've been there too much. I've become your safety net. You're going through life with me as your plus-one, knowing there's no chance you'll fall in love with me or end up getting hurt."

As much as she wanted to argue, Griffin was right. If he hadn't been overseeing the expansion of one of his family's overseas hotels the weekend of the charity event in Santa Barbara, if he'd instead been at her side as he usually was, she very well might have refused when Chance asked her to dance and certainly wouldn't have taken him back to her room.

"Isn't not getting hurt a good thing?"

"It is, but not if playing it safe keeps you from finding real happiness."

And as much of a mess as her life was currently in, Alexa couldn't bring herself to regret the baby growing inside her... Or the weekend she'd spent in Chance's arms.

"Do you really think I'm going to find that kind of happiness with Chance McClaren?" The words that were supposed to come out in an unbelievable scoff sounded far more wistful.

"I think you found something with him in Santa Barbara."

Alexa shook her head. "I've told you that I wasn't myself that weekend."

"Maybe. Or maybe with Chance, that's exactly who you were always meant to be. He fought for you. Clearly he cares about you. More than he's probably willing to admit. And if you feel the same way, then it's your turn. You need to show you're willing to fight for him."

Alexa had never been one to fight for herself, but to fight for Chance? For their child? That was one battle she had to find the courage to take on.

Chapter Seven

That's exactly who you were always meant to be.

As much as Alexa wanted to pretend she didn't know what Griffin was talking about, she couldn't. For some time she'd wanted to break free of the carefully crafted walls she'd built around her world. She'd lived the past ten years as the face of the Mayhew Foundation, but she wanted to be so much more than that. To be more than a pretty face smiling for the media. To show that she had a mind, a heart, a body. To the public, to her grandmother, to herself…

Somehow Chance had seen that.

Take a chance.

That weekend in Santa Barbara, she'd taken a huge risk. She hadn't wanted to admit it at the time, but she'd opened her heart to Chance only to slam it shut again when he'd left with hardly a moment's notice. And then after the news reports of his death, well, she'd pretty much thrown away the key.

The anniversary party was still going strong—light, laughter and music drifting over to the path that led to the small cottage. She hugged her arms over her chest, wishing she'd thought to wear a sweater. The nighttime temperature would be considered balmy by most people, but Alexa was used to the warmth of Southern California.

The tiny cottage looked even more magical in the faint moonlight, and was the last place she could picture Chance living. But this was only temporary. A place for him to recover before he moved on. She didn't even know if he *had* a permanent residence.

Pushing the troubling thought aside, Alexa hurried up the front steps and knocked on the door. She listened for movement inside but couldn't hear anything over the pounding going on inside her own chest.

Maybe he hadn't come back to the cottage, but if he was in the same shape as Griffin after the fight, she couldn't imagine where else he would want to go.

"Chance?" she called out when he didn't answer after knocking a second time.

Alexa was ready to turn back when she heard a crash from inside. "Chance!"

Heart pounding in her throat, she grabbed the door handle, surprised when the cool metal turned in her hand. She gasped when the door was suddenly pulled open from the inside, jerking her forward and straight into Chance's chest.

His naked, damp chest...

The cottage was dark with only a faint glow coming from the front porch. Swallowing hard, her other senses were overwhelmed by his nearness, the feeling of warm skin over masculine muscles and the scent of soap and shampoo. And despite the desire thrumming through her veins, she couldn't help giving a small laugh.

"What?"

She heard the scowl in his voice as his arms dropped away and he stepped back.

"Lavender."

"What?"

"You smell like lavender."

Chance swore. "I ran out of the soap I brought with me and grabbed whatever my sister had."

The unexpected moment eased some of the tension tightening her chest, and Alexa took her first deep breath since…she found out she was pregnant, it seemed.

"Are you okay? I thought I heard something fall?"

"This place is like a damn china shop. I can't turn around in here without breaking something."

Her heart stuttered as Chance lifted an arm, but instead of reaching for her, he flicked on the wall switch over her shoulder. Griffin's bruises should have prepared her, but she still cringed at the first sight of Chance. The black eye. The swollen jaw.

But try as she might, she couldn't keep her eyes focused on his face. Her gaze lowered to the broad shoulders, muscled arms, the dusting of dark hair over his well-honed chest and abs. The weight Chance had lost since the accident only served to further define every masculine ridge. As if the accident had somehow pared down the man she'd met into this hardened, stark version in front of her.

She took in the drawstring gray cotton shorts, somewhat relieved to realize he hadn't answered the door totally in the buff, and then gasped again when she saw his leg.

"The scars aren't exactly pretty, I know," he said as he turned away from her.

"No, it's not that. It's—" Alexa truthfully was horrified by the violent reminders of what he'd gone through. What he'd *lived* through… But that wasn't what had her grasping his arm. "You need to sit down. Your knee's totally swollen. You should probably see a doctor to make sure—"

"No, no doctors." Despite the implacable tone of his voice, Chance still allowed Alexa to lead him to the feminine floral print couch. "I've seen enough doctors to last me a lifetime."

"Well, maybe you'll think about that before you get in another ill-advised fistfight. For someone so determined to *move on*, you certainly aren't making things easy on yourself."

Chance muttered something that almost sounded like *I'm not the only one*, but Alexa couldn't be sure she'd heard him right.

She reached for a lacy pillow, intending to use it to prop up his leg on the steamer trunk coffee table in front of him, but he caught her wrist. "I was coming to see you." Rolling his eyes, he added, "Both times."

"What?"

"I was coming to see you when Griffin and I got in the fight and just now. I was getting cleaned up so I could come see you without looking like a—"

"A bloody, beat-up mess?"

"Hey, your *good friend* looks as bad as I do."

Alexa shook her head at what was an almost exact repetition of what Griffin had said. "Because that's what's important here."

"You're what's important here," Chance vowed, sending a small thrill through her and his thumb stroked the inside of her wrist. "You and the baby."

Of course. Wasn't that what she had told herself earlier? So she had no reason to feel somehow disappointed that Chance's priorities were exactly where they should be. "Right. The baby." Pulling away from his gentle grasp, she waved her hand toward the doorway leading to the dining room. "I'll go get you an ice pack. The kitchen's..."

Chance nodded. "It's that way."

When he started to push up from the couch, Alexa demanded, "What are you doing?"

"I'm getting dressed. We need to talk."

As if they'd end up doing something else otherwise. Which, considering the difficulty Alexa was having keeping her eyes from straying, might be more of a possibility than she dared to admit... "Good—good idea. I'll, um, be back with the ice pack."

She didn't find an ice pack in the tiny kitchen, but she did spend a good five minutes with her head in the freezer anyway. She pressed a bag of frozen corn to her forehead, foolishly hoping that might cool her heated thoughts as she glanced around.

The kitchen was decorated with the same shabby chic touch as the living room, with white cabinets, an old-fashioned cobalt blue tile countertop and delicate tea saucers decorating the soffit.

Spotting an amber bottle of pills near the sink, Alexa lowered the bag of corn. The prescription was for pain meds as she'd hoped, but judging by the full bottle, Chance hadn't taken any of them. As hard as he was pushing himself with runs on the beach, appointments with physical therapy—oh, and not to mention, ridiculous fights—she couldn't believe he hadn't needed the pills.

Walking back into the tiny living room, Alexa breathed a small sigh of relief to see Chance sprawled against the corner of the couch fully dressed. If only seeing him so relaxed didn't pose a different temptation. His blue-and-gray flannel pajama bottoms and faded T-shirt looked so soft, she wanted nothing more than to cuddle up next to him. To have his arms around her as she rested her head against his chest as they talked about their hopes and dreams for their baby's future.

So simple, and yet so complicated...

She placed the frozen-vegetable bag on his knee before holding out a bottle of water and two of the pills. But Chance was already shaking his head. "I can't take them. They make me...loopy."

"Loopy?"

"Yeah, like a teenager with his first beer buzz. I never know what I'll do or say or... So just forget the pain meds."

"Oh, wow, who would have thought? Chance McClaren, Mr. Live For The Moment, is a control freak."

"That's not true."

"Then take the meds. As long as you take them as prescribed, you'll be okay."

She held his glare for at least a minute, and she could only imagine how much pain he had to be in to grudgingly accept the pills she held out to him. He downed the water, and she tried not to notice how the muscles in his neck worked as he swallowed. Tried not to remember how she'd kissed that very spot as he lowered her to the hotel-room bed for the first time.

"Are you feeling okay?"

Alexa blinked. She was feeling more than a little overheated, but could Chance actually see those thoughts written on her face?

"You know, morning sickness or whatever?"

"Oh, that. No, not anymore." Perching on the edge of the sofa cushions, she added, "I get tired easily, and I'm starving half the time, but I feel fine."

"And the baby's healthy?"

A hint of vulnerability in his blue eyes had Alexa's heart softening. "The baby's fine."

"I wish you would have told me sooner."

"Chance..."

"I—I'm trying to understand why you didn't, but seeing you here with Griffin... I've acted like a total ass."

"I told you Griffin's just a friend."

"A friend you were thinking of marrying."

"Yes."

"Are you still?" The plastic bottle crackled as Chance's fingers flexed.

"Still what?"

"Still thinking?"

"No, Griffin's leaving in the morning."

"Can't say I'll be sorry to see the guy go."

Alexa opened her mouth to argue only to stop. How would she have felt if she'd arrived in Clearville to find Chance almost engaged? Even to a woman he considered just a friend? Simply imagining a beautiful woman on Chance's arm had jealousy digging deep.

"I am sorry. I should have been up-front about Griffin and the baby from the start. It's just that seeing you here was such a shock especially after—"

"Those damn news reports." Chance sighed as he dropped his head back against the cushion. Leading Alexa to stare at that spot on his throat once more...

Jerking her gaze away, she clasped her hands between her knees. "I honestly did try to get ahold of you once I found out I was pregnant."

"Before the bombing."

"Yes."

"But not after."

"No," she admitted. "After that first report, I didn't know what to think, how to feel. I was just starting to get used to the idea of being pregnant, and then I had to face the thought of raising a child on my own."

"And after?" he pressed.

"And after...after I'd read that you were alive, that your condition was improving, I didn't know what to believe. What if those reports were wrong, too?"

Pushing back against the couch cushions, he sat forward as he met her gaze. "I'm not going to lie. My job comes with risks, but *life* comes with risks. It's not as dangerous as you might think."

"The scars on your knee tell a different story." She spoke again when he would have protested. "And it's more than a job. You're willing to go where not every journalist will go and tell the stories that not every journalist will tell."

Truthfully, Alexa had been drawn to his work before she'd been drawn to the man himself. The night of the charity event, she'd been so impressed that she'd spoken to an acquaintance of her grandmother's, Roslynn St. Clare, about a possible showing for the talented Chance McClaren.

Knowing Chance as she did now, Alexa realized that a gallery showing filled with wealthy patrons and patronizing critics was hardly his style. He preferred to stay on the front line and let his work speak for itself.

"You have a true calling, and I admire that."

"You admire me, and yet you think I'm the type of man who wouldn't want to know he had a child, who wouldn't take responsibility."

Alexa squeezed her hands tighter together. Maybe that was what she was afraid of. Not that Chance would walk away from their child, but that he would stay. Grimly determined and duty bound to do the right thing. She didn't know which was worse—a father who was never around or one who was there but wanted to be somewhere else.

"A child should be more than a responsibility. A child needs to know he or she is wanted, loved... What?" she demanded when she noticed him studying her with a sympathetic expression on his face.

"Just thinking of something Griffin said," he murmured.

Alexa raised an eyebrow. "You mean the two of you actually talked and didn't just start pummeling each other?"

"We did a little of both."

And he clearly wasn't going to tell her what Griffin had said. Which, knowing her friend, could have been just about anything.

Chance leaned his head back again, and Alexa could see some of the tension draining from his body as exhaustion and the pain pills started to take over. "I should go. You need to rest."

She settled her hands against the cushions, ready to push to her feet, but without opening his eyes, Chance reached out and caught her wrist. "Stay," he encouraged.

Her heart suddenly pounding in her throat, Alexa swallowed. Heat radiated from the simple touch of his skin against hers, tiny flames of memory licking to life in its wake.

"I don't think that's a good idea. You should rest."

Chance's eyes opened as he leaned toward her, his movements languid and purposeful at the same time. "I haven't had a good night's sleep since the last time you were in my bed. I can't close my eyes without imagining you there."

Alexa stared at him, dumbfounded. He'd thought about her while he was away? Imagined her by his side, even while they were apart? Those same thoughts, memories, *desires* haunted her dreams, but to think Chance had felt the same way, felt that same longing…

"Chance." His name was a breathless gasp of air as he rose above her and pulled her to her feet. Her legs trembled, and Alexa knew she should leave before it was too late.

But it had been too late from the first time she'd spotted him from across the ballroom. When he'd caught her very much in the act of doing something a Mayhew did not do—interfering with one of her grandmother's biggest donors by diverting the inebriated man's unwanted attention from a young female server.

And Chance McClaren had been watching her all along. But instead of seeing disappointment or disapproval in his gaze, his blue eyes had glowed with amusement and admiration.

But that was then. This was now. So much had changed and yet one thing hadn't changed at all. She wanted him to kiss her now as desperately as she had then.

"Alexa. *Lexi.*" The nickname sent shivers down her spine. To the rest of the world, she was Alexa Mayhew. Only Chance called her Lexi. Only Chance...

Her name was still on his lips when he claimed hers in a kiss, and she buried her fingers in his hair as he pulled her body tight to his.

They were a perfect fit, the muscled strength of one of his thighs between the softness of hers, the curves of her breasts against the wide plane of his chest, the subtle roundness of her belly cradled by his concave stomach.

Their *baby* cradled between them.

Startled by the thought, Alexa jerked back. Her chest heaving as she gasped for much-needed breath, she stuttered, "That's not— We can't—" Swallowing against the arousal she saw reflected in Chance's taut expression, she said, "This is a bad idea."

He stared at her for a long moment before shocking her with a laugh. His white teeth flashed in the first genuine smile she'd seen since she arrived. "That's what you said in Santa Barbara, too."

"Yes, well, this time I mean it."

Her pulse quickened as he stepped forward and erased the hard-fought distance she'd placed between them. "Bad ideas. Ask anyone, I'm full of 'em."

For a brief moment a shadow crossed his features before his expression cleared. Reaching up, he touched the butterfly hairpin in her hair. "My good-luck charm," he murmured.

Alexa swallowed. Though a still-smoldering desire lingered in his eyes, his gaze was slightly unfocused, as well. "You really weren't kidding about the effect pain meds have on you, were you?"

His half smile was teasing, sexy and, yes, the slightest bit loopy. "Told ya."

Ignoring the disappointment coursing through her, she said, "Which is why you need to go to bed. Alone," she stressed, reminding herself as much as Chance. The chemistry, the attraction, the desire to feel his body pressed against hers once more had her resolve trembling right along with her suddenly rubbery legs.

"Not like I can get you more pregnant."

No, no danger there. But the risk that she'd fall even further for him? That was a very real—and very frightening—possibility. "Yes, well, as romantic a proposition as that is, I'm still not sleeping with you."

He gave a sigh heavy enough to stir the hair at her temple, but allowed her to guide him down the hall. With an arm draped over her shoulders, he leaned on her enough for Alexa to wonder if he really had done further damage to his leg. But when he pulled her tighter to his side and pressed a kiss against the top of her head, she wasn't sure if she was holding him up or if he was simply holding her.

With the faint glow from the living room, Alexa had the impression of a very girlie bedroom, complete with canopied lace-trimmed bed. Chance was so not the typical Sleeping Beauty and yet…"Get some sleep."

But before Alexa realized what he planned, he fell back on the mattress…taking her right with him.

"Chance!" Her protest was cut short as she landed on top of him with an inelegant grunt. "What are you doing?"

Rolling with her on the bed, he pinned her to the mattress with a firm arm wrapped around her waist and warm, heavy thigh between her legs. Alexa sank into soft, wildflower-scented sheets, a feminine contrast to Chance's hard, masculine body above hers.

"I told you. I can't sleep without you."

"And I think I told you, I'm not sleeping with you. Chance?" Alexa pushed at his shoulders, her hands sliding uselessly against soft material of his T-shirt and the smooth muscles beneath. "Chance!"

She may well have questioned the truth of his words, especially given what he'd told her about his aversion to pain pills, but actions spoke louder as he settled deeper into the pillows with a contented sigh and promptly fell asleep…with her.

Chance knew he was dreaming again.

The dream was so realistic—like the ones in the hospital during the first days after his surgery. He could feel the silken brush of Alexa's hair across his arm, the teasing warmth of her breath against his neck. He pulled her closer, but instead of bare skin against his, he encountered the softness of some fuzzy material.

Why was she wearing clothes? His dreams always started with her naked in his arms and ended with her slipping away…

"Chance! Chance, wake up!"

He ignored the voice, the one that sounded like Alexa's

but was only a trick. He tightened his grip, determined not to let her get away and equally determined not to wake up. When he opened his eyes, she would be gone.

"Seriously, Chance. I can't breathe here."

"Dreams don't need to breathe," he protested, rolling until he half pinned Alexa's dream self beneath his body.

She laughed at that—maybe a little breathlessly—before saying his name.

With his eyes still closed, his lips found the sensitive spot where her shoulder met her neck. She smelled just like he remembered—something sweetly floral but with that hidden hint of spice. She whispered his name again, even more breathlessly this time, and heat flooded through his veins.

In the real world, too much stood between them for Chance to give into desire. The secret she had kept, the uncertainty of the future, the responsibility of their child. But this was a dream where nothing could come between them.

Nothing but that stupid fuzzy sweater.

"Why are you wearing clothes in my dream?" he complained.

Alexa groaned, sounding as frustrated by the unnecessary clothing as he was. But when she spoke this time, a note of panic entered her voice. "Chance, you need to wake up now." She pushed at his shoulders, but he wouldn't budge. "No, really, you need to wake up. I think someone's here!"

He faintly heard a car door slam, something else completely out of place in his dream and enough to make him wonder... The sound, combined with a sharp pain in his leg as Alexa scrambled out from beneath him, jerked him from the remnants of slumber.

Blinking, he stared at Alexa as she scurried off the side of the bed. With a wide-eyed glance at the window, she straightened the cashmere sweater from his dream and smoothed her hair. Not that it helped. Her clothes were wrinkled, her normally perfect hair tousled, her face free of makeup and still softened from sleep.

His heart did some kind of a slow roll inside his chest. He'd never seen her look more beautiful, and he asked himself again how the hell he'd managed to walk out of that hotel room four months ago.

Was it any wonder he'd pictured her there a hundred times since, and yet for the life of him, he couldn't figure out…

"What were you doing in my bed?"

"What was I— You—" Color bloomed in her cheeks and she shook her head in exasperation. "Do not start with me this morning. And get up! Someone is here!"

What the hell happened last night? He remembered the fight, Alexa showing up at the cottage, taking those damn pain pills… After that, things got a little blurry, but considering she was fully dressed and he—Chance tossed back the covers to confirm—yep, he was wearing a T-shirt and a pair of flannel pajama bottoms, he was pretty sure nothing had happened while she was there.

His reflexes slowed by his still groggy state of mind, he barely blinked as a pair of jeans hit him in the chest and then fell to the floor in a heap. "What—"

"Get dressed," Alexa hissed as she turned toward the open closet door.

He swallowed a groan as he awkwardly bent to snatch the jeans from the floor. "Who's here?"

"I have no idea, but someone—" The knock on the front door interrupted the flurry of activity as she clutched one of his shirts to her chest, her eyes wide with panic.

After a split second of silence, the knock sounded again. "Chance, sweetie!"

Alexa still didn't move, but Chance saw her eyes narrow at the sound of the feminine voice. "Sweetie?"

This time he didn't even try to swallow his groan. He almost wished he had some past girlfriend standing on his front porch as Alexa clearly suspected. "That's my mom," he sighed. Limping over, he grabbed the shirt from her frozen hands. "Prepare to meet the parents."

Chapter Eight

"Your parents?" Alexa's voice rose an octave as the knocking on the front door suddenly seemed to reverberate inside her chest. "I can't meet your parents now!"

She had no experience with anything like this. Not even as a teenager had she been caught in a compromising situation.

A Mayhew does not sneak boys into her bedroom or make out in the back seat of a car.

His gaze washed over her from head to toe. "You could meet the queen of England like this. You look as beautiful as ever."

Heat rose in her cheeks at the compliment as well as at the intimacy of the moment. Even though they'd spent a weekend together, even though they'd made love, an even more powerful connection stretched between them. An unspoken acknowledgment that said they were in this together.

The truth was, she could have left his bed at any time last night. Though he had initially held her tight, the pain pills weren't enough to keep him from a restless sleep. Before long, he'd rolled to his side and then tossed onto his back. She'd even pushed back the covers, ready to slip away, when he called out her name.

At first she thought he was awake, only to quickly realize he was still asleep and reaching out for her in his dreams. "Don't go. Don't leave...again."

And in that moment, she'd known she wasn't going anywhere.

He'd needed her last night, and as impossible as the idea sounded in her own mind, Alexa couldn't shake the thought that Chance needed her now.

His dark hair was mussed, and a pillow crease lined one lean cheek. His morning beard combined with the black-and-blue bruises on his jaw and eye gave him a dangerous air. But there was something almost defensive in his posture even as he joked, "There's always the window if we want to try to make a break for it."

"We? They're your parents," she reminded him.

Chance sighed. "Exactly."

After tossing the clothes onto the bed, he reached for the hem of his T-shirt. Alexa's jaw dropped as he stripped off the shirt and tossed it aside. "What—what are you doing?"

"Hey, you wanted me to get dressed. And it's not like it's anything you haven't seen before."

Seen, felt, tasted... Her face heated even as she protested, "Not with your parents right outside the door!"

His deep chuckle sent another round of nerves dancing in her stomach. "Better than right inside the door... which is where my mother will be in about two seconds if I don't get out there."

"They're going to think we're sleeping together."

"They're gonna *know* once they find out about the baby."

He laughed again when Alexa spun around the second his hands dropped to the drawstring waistband of his flannel pajamas. But memory supplied such mouthwatering detail she almost wondered why she'd denied herself.

The rustle of denim was loud in the otherwise silent room, the rasp of the zipper seeming to run straight down her spine. The hair on her neck stood on end as Chance stepped close enough to murmur in her ear, "I'll try to buy you a few minutes."

"To duck out the window?"

"Or join us in the living room. Up to you."

Alexa used the extra few minutes in the bathroom to wash her face and brush her hair before stepping into the living room, where Chance made the briefest of introductions.

Dozens of unspoken questions were written in his parents' eyes, and it would have been impossible to miss the look the older McClarens exchanged in the split second before Alexa held out her hand.

Chance's mother, Mary, ignored it, enveloping Alexa in a quick hug. Familiar brilliant blue eyes beamed as she said, "It's so good to meet you. I'd like to say Chance has told us so much about you, but he's always been notoriously silent when it comes to his love life."

"Mom…"

Mary met her son's pained protest with an exasperated look. "Well, it's true. We haven't met one of your girlfriends since—"

"So what are you two doing here?" Chance interrupted, silencing his mother but certainly not Alexa's curiosity about the last woman he'd brought home.

"We're heading down to Santa Rosa for a retirement

party for an old friend of your father's," Mary explained as she started tidying the small room, straightening a ruffled pillow, picking up the empty water bottle, pausing only slightly at the now-defrosted bag of corn. "We thought we'd stop by since it's on the way."

"Not exactly on the way," her husband muttered, jingling a set of keys in the pocket of his khakis.

Matthew McClaren had salt-and-pepper hair and the same wide forehead and strong jaw as his son, but classic bone structure wasn't the only similarity between the two men. Alexa hadn't missed the stubborn set to those matching jaws.

Mary, however, smoothed over the moment with a laugh. "It is if you take the scenic route."

"Still," Chance pointed out, "you have a long drive ahead of you—"

"Which is why we left before the crack of dawn. We certainly have time for a late breakfast with the two of you while we're here."

"There was an anniversary party at the hotel last night. The restaurant's bound to be packed right now."

His mother waved aside the warning. "No offense to Hillcrest's restaurant, but you know we've never been big on eating out. Rory told me she made sure to stock the kitchen before you came?"

"Packed to the rafters," Chance answered wryly.

"Perfect! Alexa, you'll lend me a hand, won't you? We'll let the men talk," Mary said with a pointed look at the two males in question.

"I, um, sure," Alexa said weakly with a final glance at Chance before following Mary into the kitchen. She knew perfectly well why she was nervous about a one-on-one chat with Chance's mother. What she couldn't figure out was why Chance seemed just as uncomfortable talking man-to-man with his own father.

Despite her initial concerns, Alexa felt instantly at ease with Mary McClaren. Partly, she imagined, because the older woman kept a constant stream of conversation flowing. Her mouth moved almost as fast as her hands as she bustled around the tiny kitchen, slowing only when she had to search another cupboard or two for an ingredient.

"I am sorry we just showed up out of the blue like this. If Chance had told us— But, well, Chance doesn't say much of anything when it comes to his personal life."

Alexa paused, the plate in her hand hovering an inch above the pale oak table as she waited for Mary to say something more about the woman in Chance's past. But when nothing more was forthcoming, she admitted, "My own arrival was somewhat of a surprise, as well. I've only been in town for a few days."

"But you and Chance…"

"Met a few months ago in Santa Barbara. We, um, planned to keep in touch after he left for another assignment but then—".

Alexa cut herself off as Mary's movements slowed to a stop. She bowed her head for a moment as they both silently acknowledged what happened—what almost happened— *then*…

"You do like pancakes, don't you?" Mary asked Alexa over her shoulder, her smile forcefully bright. "So many people nowadays have food allergies."

"No, no allergies." She couldn't recall the last time she had pancakes, though, more likely to have something as simple as tea and toast in the morning. And during her bout with morning sickness, even that had often been too much.

But now… Finished setting the table, Alexa walked

over to the counter. Her stomach let out a very unladylike growl as Mary dropped a handful of blueberries into the batter and gave a quick stir with a wooden spoon.

"I don't think I've ever seen someone make pancakes without a recipe before. Other than a professional chef."

"Professional?" Mary gave a laugh. "You mean like those cooks on television? Oh, trust me. I'm not in their league. I guess I've just been doing it for so many years I can make them automatically."

Alexa hadn't been talking about television. She'd been referring to the full-time chef on her grandmother's staff. Her face heated slightly at her near faux pas. If Mary didn't think of herself in league with a TV personality who could smile for the camera and beat an egg at the same time, she certainly would have felt outclassed compared to the cordon bleu–trained chef her grandmother employed.

"So if you don't consider yourself a professional, how did you learn all this?"

"I guess I consider myself a professional mom. Not always the most glamorous of jobs and not one that will win you an award, but rewarding enough for me." With her reddish-brown hair streaked with gray and faint lines fanning out from her hazel eyes, Mary McClaren exuded a warmth and comfort that drew Alexa in.

A professional mom. She liked the sound of that. For the past few months, she'd been so caught up in the idea of being pregnant, of having a baby, somehow the thought of being a mother had gotten lost. "So you learned all this after Chance and Rory were born?"

"Oh, no! My own mother taught me to cook when I was still a little girl. It was always such a treat to be with her in the kitchen."

"Oh. Right." Of course. These were skills Alexa was

already supposed to have. All things her mother was supposed to have taught her.

"By the time I had two kids, I barely had time to breathe. Thank goodness this was all second nature by then. Although with a newborn, then the trick came in learning how to do it all one-handed."

"One-handed?"

"It's amazing how quickly you figure out how to hold an infant in one arm and still crack eggs with your free hand."

Alexa swallowed a disbelieving laugh. Holding a baby while cracking eggs. Sure, she'd give that a try. Right after—oh, who knows? Sword swallowing? Fire juggling?

"But then once the kids were older, I was able to pass down all I'd learned. Rory was such a good little student, standing on a stool by my side, so eager to help. I think for Chance, it was more about the bonus of licking batter from the beaters and having first dibs on dessert." Mary's eyes sparkled at the memory. "So what kind of things did your mother teach you?"

Her mother taught her how to smile even when she was crying inside.

You be a good girl for nanny and Mommy will be back soon!

Bree didn't like when Alexa cried when she left or begged her not to go. So Alexa learned to be a good girl, always waiting hopefully for her mother to return.

That hiding behind a smile came in handy as she said, "Oh, my mother taught me so much, it's hard to know where to begin."

But as she watched Mary in the kitchen, Alexa couldn't help thinking that the most important lesson Bree had taught her was how *not* to be a mother.

A lesson Alexa had just over five months to totally unlearn.

* * *

"So how did the two of you meet?"

Chance didn't even try to hold back his groan. "Five seconds, Mom. That must be some kind of record."

His mother had whipped up a feast of blueberry pancakes, maple syrup, scrambled eggs and bacon. The tiny table could barely hold all the serving dishes and plates, and despite the sweet smells filling the kitchen, he didn't have much of an appetite.

Not when he was going to end up getting grilled as the main course.

She gave him a reproachful look as she passed the butter to his father. "It's just a question."

And hardly one that was out of line. Especially not when coming from parents who had just walked in on their son scrambling out of bed with a young woman.

Even if nothing had happened the night before. Which was both a relief and an embarrassment. He'd learned way back as a kid that he and pain pills didn't mix. He'd had plenty of cause to take them during the daring exploits of his youth, and the side effects were never pretty. Walking in his sleep. Talking in his sleep.

Hell, he could only imagine what Alexa had to put up with. Snippets of memory floated through his mind, but it was too similar to what had occurred after the accident, when most of what he recalled had been nothing but imagination.

Alexa's warm, feminine curves beneath his body... Her golden hair spread out across the pillow... Her slender arms around his neck...

I'm here, Chance. I'm right here. I won't leave you.

One thing he knew wasn't imagination or some kind of delusion.

Alexa was pregnant. With his baby. He was still coming to grips with the sudden turn his life had taken.

"We met at a charity event," Alexa was saying to his all-ears mother, her movements graceful and precise as she used a knife and fork to cut her single pancake into tiny bite-size pieces. "Chance was there to sign some of his photographs as part of a silent auction."

Chance's grip tightened on his fork. Alexa couldn't possibly know the minefield she'd just walked into. His job was a decade-old point of contention between him and his parents. His father, especially, and Chance didn't miss the scowl on the elder McClaren's face.

Let the McClaren men talk.

As if his mother didn't know perfectly well that he and his father got along so much better when they weren't talking.

Chance shoved another big forkful of fluffy, melt-on-your-tongue, buttery pancake into his mouth. If he could keep his mouth shut—or full—for a few minutes more, they might all get through this visit unscathed.

He'd done his best to hide his sigh of relief when his mother offered the destination for their trip. His father would be eager to get back on the road, every turn and stop carefully plotted along the way, despite what Mary had said about taking the scenic route.

He swallowed a snort of laughter at that. His dad never took the scenic route. Matthew McClaren was direct to a fault, always on the straight and narrow, never one for taking the road less traveled.

Chance had known from the time he was a kid that getting lost was the best way to find himself. To find out what he was capable of, to find out what he truly needed and wanted out of life.

Discovering that what he wanted was the exact opposite of what his parents wanted for him? Well, that was a hurdle the three of them had yet to successfully cross.

"Chance's work drew some of the highest bids that evening. I can't tell you how many people would pay a small fortune for a McClaren original."

Matthew gave a grunt, the dismissive sound that much more abrasive compared to the pride in Alexa's voice.

Pride? She'd made it clear how she felt about his job and its dangers, and yet...

Sitting by his side at the tiny table, Alexa offered him a small smile. "I would have bid on one of them myself if winning wouldn't have seemed unfair."

"Unfair? Why would it?" Mary asked.

"I had organized the event, so it was best that I not win any of the items. You know, for appearance's sake."

For appearance's sake... She'd told him that night how much she hated living her life with that kind of scrutiny. How she longed to be free. She hadn't told him she'd thought about bidding on his photographs.

He wondered what she and his mother had talked about in the kitchen. His mother wanted nothing more than to see him settled down and married. Hell, she'd been the only one in the family to approve of Lisette. Even Rory, who almost always looked for the best in people, called her his crazy ex-girlfriend.

But for Mary, all she cared about was that while he and Lisette had been together, he'd spent more of his time focusing on *his girlfriend's* career rather than on his own dangerous one.

"Well, I hope you were able to take some kind of memento home from the event."

His gaze met Alexa's, this time her smile more than a little wry. "Oh, yes, I definitely brought something home with me."

A baby. *His* baby.

And while a part of him still wanted to reject a reality he wasn't ready to face, another, bigger part of him wanted to reach over and pull Alexa into his arms. It was the same feeling he'd had that morning while she was throwing clothes at him in the bedroom.

A feeling of connection…

For a man who'd lived his adult life without ties to hold him down, the emotion should have scared the crap out of him. And yet he wasn't willing to break the fragile contact, letting the moment lengthen and strengthen between them.

Until his father interrupted when he demanded, "So what's with the black eye?"

"You know me, Dad, always the one picking a fight."

His father didn't miss the subtle dig judging by the way his grip tightened on his fork.

"Chance, you—"

"It was my fault," Alexa jumped in suddenly. "The fight—everything—was my fault."

His father raised an eyebrow as he glanced over in surprise, almost as if noticing Alexa for the first time. Not that Chance bought into that for a second. Even wearing yesterday's clothes and without a speck of makeup, she looked stunning. With her head held high as she took on his father, defending Chance, she was even more beautiful than the first time he saw her.

Too beautiful for words, and certainly too beautiful to be so easily dismissed as his father waved off her claim. "Unless you're a lot stronger than you look, something tells me there's more to the story."

Before Chance could shove back from the table, Alexa placed a hand on his flexed arm and gave a reassuring squeeze. "There is," she agreed as she glanced from his father to his mother and back again. "It was mostly just

a big misunderstanding, but when it comes down to it...
Chance was looking out for me."

Jealousy still carved a hole in his gut when he thought
of Alexa and Griffin together. Friends, just friends, she
had said, but it was still a blow knowing Griffin was the
man she had turned to. The man she could trust, the man
she could count on. Griffin. And not Chance.

Griffin had been willing to marry her, to prove he was
responsible—when Chance was responsible. For Alexa.
For the baby they had created together.

"So, does this mean the two of you are...serious?" His
father speared him with a knowing look, expecting the
typical answer.

*I'm not ready to settle down. My career comes first. A
family isn't part of my future.*

Alexa had held her own with his father, but now her
hand slid away from his arm and her attention fell to her
mostly empty plate. Immediately missing the contact,
Chance reached over and laced her slender fingers through
his own. As he met her startled gaze, he couldn't help but
think, *Ready or not.*

"I wouldn't call it a 'thing' between us. More like a
baby. And if you'll excuse us, I have a wedding...to photograph."

Chapter Nine

"I now pronounce you husband and wife. You may kiss your bride."

Chance took a deep breath, leaned forward...and lifted his camera for the perfect shot.

The guests gathered in front of the gazebo burst into applause as the newly married couple exchanged their first kiss, and he gave a silent exclamation of his own as he captured the moment with a click of a button.

He'd done it. His first wedding. He hadn't expected it to be so nerve-racking. He didn't know how his sister put up with this week after week.

From his own admittedly ignorant and totally biased view from behind the camera, Chance thought Rory had done an amazing job on the simple afternoon wedding. Red-and-white-flowered garland draped the gazebo's pillars and railing. Matching velvet bows decorated the tie-backs of the chairs on either side of the white lace runner that led to the platform steps.

Even the weather—frequently rainy and overcast in November—had cooperated. The sun had peeked out from behind the clouds during the ceremony, shining down on the tuxedoed groom and his vision-in-white bride. The party would move into Hillcrest's ballroom for the reception, but for now...

He focused on the couple as they made their way down the aisle amid a shower of red rose petals. He didn't doubt the pictures would be perfect, but he still couldn't shake the dizzying feeling of vertigo every time he looked through the lens.

He was totally out of his element, and he knew it. But it was more than that. It was looking through the lens and trying his damnedest not to imagine Alexa in a white gown and flowing veil. Alexa walking down the aisle, bouquet in hand. Alexa repeating the vows, tears filling her beautiful eyes as she promised to love, honor and cherish.

Only just yesterday, she'd been thinking about saying those very words to her good friend Griffin. And even though she'd reassured him she was not accepting the other man's proposal, Chance still couldn't make the leap of seeing himself as the groom. What did he know about being a husband?

What did he know about being a father?

That was the question his father had demanded after Chance dropped his bombshell about the baby. His mother had been over the moon, instantly ready to share what sounded to him like horror stories about pregnancy woes and labor pains and sleepless nights filled with round-the-clock feedings.

But it was his father's words that stuck with Chance.

How do you plan to parent a child from half a world away? Fatherhood isn't something you can phone in like your latest story.

Chance didn't have any answers. He wasn't ready to walk away from his career, but after having Alexa back in his life for only the past few days, he damn sure wasn't ready to walk away from her or their baby.

They had time to work out the details. It was what he'd told his parents before ushering them out of the cottage even as his mother instructed him to keep them up to date on things like the baby shower, the baby's due date, and oh, yeah, by the way, the date of their *wedding*.

Judging by the way Alexa's eyes had widened at his mother's words, Chance figured she was looking for the nearest window to jump out of.

Sucking in a deep breath, he lifted the camera, taking comfort in the familiar weight in his hands. Wondering as he often did how the most important thing he and his father had in common, the one thing they both loved, was also the one thing that had driven such a wedge between them.

He worked for another half hour, taking shots of the bridal party posed on the gazebo platform and lining the steps. But every damn time he had to blink away the image of Alexa standing there— Good God, was that really just the day before? How was it that his life had completely changed in a mere twenty-four hours?

The muscles in his leg burned in protest as he bent to a knee for an angled shot of the bride and groom, reminding him that life didn't need hours. It could change in a split second. Still, it was a relief when the bride announced they were ready to join the guests for the reception.

"Did you get the shot?"

"Did I get the shot?" Forcing a confident smile he was far from feeling, Chance turned and snapped a quick photo of his sister, who glared in return. "Don't you know who you're talking to?"

"Yeah, my obnoxious older brother."

"Hey, I'm here, aren't I? I even got that haircut you wanted."

"Right, and the black eye's a wonderful addition."

Despite the words, Rory's tone was more exasperated than angry. They hadn't had much time to talk since he'd arrived. Rory, busy with the finishing touches before the ceremony started, and Chance with photographing the bride in the moments leading up to the wedding.

"I take it you talked to Mom and Dad."

"Are you kidding? I was *grilled* by Mom and Dad, who seem to think I should have known everything that was going on when clearly I didn't have a clue!" Taking him by the arm, she led him away from the gazebo and toward a curve in the tree-lined path leading back to the hotel, she asked, "Alexa's pregnant?" At his nod, she added, "And the baby's yours?"

"Was that a question?"

"I think it's a somewhat legitimate one." She shook her head at his scowl. "No pun intended. But, Chance, she was engaged to another man."

"He's just a friend."

"And you believe that?"

Chance's shoulders tightened though he couldn't blame Rory for her doubts. His track record with women was far from stellar. Lisette had manipulated him more thoroughly and professionally than the physical therapist who worked on his leg. He supposed he should be grateful she'd been so determined to claw her way to the top of the fashion world. No way would she have risked her figure or her future by getting pregnant—not even as a way to keep a hold on her favorite photographer.

"Why would Alexa lie, Rory?" He pulled up short as he confronted her suspicions. "If she was going to trick someone, Alexa would be better off fooling Griffin James into believing he's the father. The guy's family has almost as much money as Alexa's does."

Chance made a decent living. He'd invested well, and his nomadic lifestyle limited his spending when it came to worldly possessions. But his bank account was pocket change compared to the Mayhew and James fortunes.

"Look, I did some research online about Alexa."

"Oh, good, because you know you can always believe anything you read on the internet."

Ignoring him, Rory said, "She lives with her grand-mother who's something of a recluse. I saw pictures of their home. It's this walled fortress of a place, Chance. It wouldn't surprise me if they have armed guards at the gate."

"What's your point, Rory?"

"I'm just saying, it will be a lot easier for you two to work things out here than back home on her turf."

"Her turf? You make it sound like some kind of battle." He thought of Alexa's wealth, of the dozens of lawyers she could easily employ, the miles of red tape she could use to keep him away from their child. Away from her... It was a battle he couldn't afford to win.

Chance swallowed. It was a battle he couldn't afford to lose.

A high-pitched whistle sounded, and Rory pulled her phone from a pocket in the pale yellow skirt she wore. Her dark brows pulled tight as she read the message on the screen.

"What is it?" Chance asked. "Some kind of wedding crisis?"

His sister shook her head. "I guess that would depend on you."

"What are you talking about?"

"Evie just sent a text." Rory held up her cell. "Alexa's checked out of the hotel."

* * *

Alexa had spent her entire adult life trying to live up to her grandmother's standards, but she was seconds away from throwing a tantrum that would make any reality-star diva proud.

"Griffin James checked out earlier today," she stressed to the wide-eyed maid who stood in the middle of the hotel suite, cleaning cart at hand. "I am still here."

Though why she was still there was rather fuzzy at the moment. Or maybe that was just due to the tears she refused to let fall.

If she had any question about how Chance felt about their baby, he'd made his answer loud and clear.

Alexa would be better off fooling Griffin James into believing he's the father.

Her head had been spinning since meeting Chance's parents that morning, and with Chance busy with the wedding, Alexa had gone back to the suite to say goodbye to Griffin. She'd given him a brief recap of all that had happened, tempted to smack him when he wouldn't stop laughing during her explanation of how the McClarens had all but walked in on her and Chance.

"We still have a lot to discuss—including the fact that his parents are clearly expecting us to get married—but I'm glad I told him about the baby," she'd told Griffin, believing in her heart that things were going to work out somehow.

Now she didn't know what to believe.

"I'm sorry, ma'am," the maid was saying, "but I was told to ready this room for a new guest who will be checking in this evening. Maybe the front desk can help?"

Alexa didn't want to go back down to the lobby. She wanted nothing more than to bury her head in a pillow and cry. But the recently fluffed and perfectly arranged pillows were no longer for her use. She was no longer a guest and had no reason to stay in Clearville. No reason not to return home.

"My luggage... My clothes... Where?"

"I'm sure the front desk..."

"Right." Swallowing her tears, Alexa straightened her shoulders and left the suite only to bump into a solid masculine form in the hallway. "Oh, I'm sorry. I'm—"

"Crying." Chance caught her by the shoulders and ducked his head to get a good look at her face. "Why are you crying?"

Concern furrowed his forehead, the expression on his face sending her already confused emotions into another tailspin. "I'm not— I don't—"

"Come on, let's go back to the room."

"It's not my room. You have a new guest arriving tonight."

The arm he'd wrapped around her waist tensed. "You've checked out?"

"Evidently."

Guiding her back into the suite, he made eye contact with the startled maid. "Out." The one word had the poor girl dropping her dust rag and scurrying out of the suite with her cart in tow.

Dropping onto the blue-and-white-patterned love seat, Alexa stared at the empty doorway. "Do you know what people would say about me if I treated the staff like that?"

"I don't care what people say."

"No, of course not." Alexa cared. Maybe that was part of the problem. Maybe she cared too much. About things people said. About things she overheard...

"Look, Alexa." Chance ran a hand through his dark hair to grip the back of his neck. "Don't go, okay?"

She blinked up at him, the words not the ones she expected to hear. "You want me to stay?"

Dropping onto the cushion beside her, he reached for her hand. "Of course I want you to stay. When I heard you were checking out…"

She shook her head. "I'm not. There was a mix-up with the room."

"We'll figure it out. We'll figure all of this out."

The words were so similar to the ones she'd used earlier, and she wanted to cling to that promise and yet… "Do you really wish I'd tried to fool Griffin into thinking this baby was his?"

"What? No, Alexa!" His hands tightened around hers. "You were there? You heard…that?"

"I went to find you." Remembering why she'd gone to look for Chance, Alexa slipped her hands from his to wrap her arms around her waist. The wild swing of emotions rushed back—from exhilarated to devastated—in the blink of an eye. "I thought I felt the baby move. It's still so early, I can't even be sure, and it's not like you could feel it anyway—"

Her words cut off with a gasp as he reached over, his large palm laying claim to the slight swell of her belly. And Alexa suddenly hoped he *couldn't* feel what was going on inside her body as yearning grew from everywhere his hand touched to everywhere it *didn't*.

"I'm glad this baby is mine, Alexa." Possessiveness and a familiar heat burned in his blue eyes. "What you heard me say to Rory… I guess I'm worried you might still think Griffin would be a better bet as a father."

"As soon as I felt—or at least thought I felt—the baby move, I wanted to share that with you, Chance." Covering his hand with her own, she pressed his palm tighter against her belly, strengthening the already miraculous bond between them. "With *you*, not with Griffin."

"So you'll stay?"

"The room—"

"We'll talk to Evie and figure something out." After reaching into his pocket, he held out his closed fist. "Besides, Cinderella, you don't want to leave this behind, do you?"

She gave a small laugh when she saw the butterfly pin resting in his palm. "Again?"

"You seem to be making a habit of leaving this in my bed."

Feeling the heat rising to her cheeks, she reached out, but Chance's hand closed around hers. "And you seem to be making a habit of finding me and giving it back."

"Lucky thing."

"Last night at the cottage, you said the pin was your good-luck charm."

Chance groaned and immediately let her go. "I told you I'm an idiot on pain meds. Who knows what I was talking about?"

Alexa had the feeling he knew exactly but that he didn't want to explain. As she fingered the fragile butterfly, she tried not to think about a time when Chance's luck might run out.

"When my brother invited you to come down to the reception, I don't think cleanup duty was what he had in mind."

Alexa paused, drink tray in hand, to glance over her shoulder. Rory McClaren held two dessert plates loaded down with wedges of chocolate and raspberry cream cake. "I don't mind lending a hand."

Her plan to simply watch the festivities from the sidelines hadn't lasted long. Sitting toward the back of the ballroom, she'd admired the rose and gerbera daisy centerpieces on each white-clothed table. Matching red velvet bows decorated the back of every chair, the bright color a complement to the ballroom's dark walnut wainscot. She'd been content to watch and laugh at the sight of couples young and old strutting their stuff to the "Chicken Dance" on the parquet inlaid dance floor.

But when the music changed to a romantic ballad and the bride's seventysomething grandfather asked her to dance, Alexa hadn't had the heart to refuse the sweet man. That dance was followed by one with the groom's preteen and adorably serious nephew. No one minded that she wasn't an invited guest, and each time she looked Chance's way, he met her glance with a quick wink of his camera flash.

She couldn't help but watch him throughout the reception as he smiled and laughed with the guests and bridal party, helping even the most reluctant subject relax in front of his lens.

That was the Chance Alexa remembered from Santa Barbara. Charming, funny, with a confidence she found undeniably sexy.

But she'd seen another side of him, too, during the unrehearsed shots when the bride and groom or wedding guests didn't realize he had them in his sights. A serious, determined side. The camera seemed like a part of him in those moments as his focus narrowed and the world around him disappeared.

That must be what he was like in the field. When he would shut off his emotions with the single-minded purpose of getting his shot. When bombs could go off around him and he wouldn't even notice.

"I've never coordinated a wedding, but I know what it's like to plan for large events. There's always something that needs to be done."

Now the reception was starting to wind down. The band

still played to a handful of couples on the dance floor, but most of the guests had left. The Hillcrest House staff had started to discreetly move around the ballroom, sweeping away empty plates and glasses from the white-clothed tables. Not one to sit around when there was work to be done, Alexa had grabbed a tray to help out.

"When it comes to weddings, there's always too much work, but if you're lucky, sometimes there's too much cake. Like a piece?"

At Alexa's nod, Rory set the plates on a nearby table before sinking into a chair with a groan. "My feet are killing me. One of these days, I'm going to start wearing tennis shoes to these things."

Chance's sister looked professional yet eminently approachable in a yellow shirtwaist dress with cap sleeves. Her kitten-heeled slingbacks matched perfectly, and Alexa couldn't imagine her sacrificing style for comfort, no matter how much her feet hurt.

Alexa took a small bite of cake, and rolled her eyes as the rich chocolate and tart fruit flavor melted in her mouth. "This is to die for."

"All our cakes are made by a local baker who owns a café on Main Street called Sugar & Spice. You should check it out while you're in town. I mean, if you're staying?"

Rory's prying was somewhat more subtle than Mary's, but Alexa could certainly see a mother-daughter resemblance. "I'm staying for now, but I have a fund-raising benefit at the end of the month. I'll need to be back in LA by then."

"Chance mentioned the work you do. I can't imagine all the preparation that must go into coordinating those star-studded events." She waved her fork at the ballroom. "I'm somewhat new at all of this. A part of me is still surprised when everything goes off without a hitch."

"I've organized more benefit dinners and charity events than I can count. The only way those events succeed is to rely heavily on volunteers, which means being shorthanded more often than not. I've set tables, arranged flowers, help prep in the kitchen. I've even—"

She laughed at a long-ago memory, the sound drawing a curious look from Rory. "Even what?"

"Back when I was still a teenager, my grandmother hosted a party at the house. The singer she'd hired canceled at the last minute." Alexa shook her head. "And my grandmother, in her infinite wisdom, decided I should fill in as the night's entertainment."

Rory's dark eyebrows rose. "You can sing?"

"After all the countless hours with a private music instructor, you—like my grandmother—would think so," she said wryly. "One good thing to come out of that disaster was that it did put an end to those lessons."

The brunette fought a smile as she dug in for another forkful of the moist, decadent cake, and Alexa strangely felt like she'd passed some kind of test.

"You know, it's been years since I've met one of Chance's girlfriends."

Bonding over bridezillas and celebrity nightmares wasn't enough for Alexa to feel comfortable confessing she wasn't Chance's girlfriend. More like a weekend stand— if such a thing existed.

So instead, she murmured, "Your mother might have mentioned something along those lines this morning."

Rory grinned. "That must have been fun."

"I'd likely use another word for it."

"His last girlfriend did a real number on him. Jerked him around enough in their six months together to give him a permanent case of relationship whiplash." Her tone was easy, but Alexa didn't miss the weight behind it.

"I'm not here to jerk Chance around." Remembering what the wedding coordinator said during their first meeting—about magic and romance—Alexa said, "I'm sorry for not being more up-front about my...history with Chance. I'm sure the next couple who comes through will find their Hillcrest House happily-ever-after."

"Final dance, folks!" the lead singer called out from the small stage in the corner of the room. "Make it last."

An older couple joined the younger kids on the dance floor, including the groom's nephew who had found a dance partner closer to his own age.

"Don't give up on your own happily-ever-after so soon, Alexa," Rory advised with a speculative smile. "Something tells me your story isn't over yet."

Alexa turned in the chair, following the other woman's gaze, and felt her heart skip a beat. Walking up behind her, Chance held out his hand. "Can I have this dance?"

Chapter Ten

Chance's pulse pounded in his veins as Alexa placed her slender hand in his. He'd been dying to hold her in his arms again since... Since she'd joined him at the reception? Since she'd arrived in Clearville? Since he'd left her hotel room four months ago?

He knew the answer was all of the above. And after watching her tonight, he wanted her even more.

She'd been as charming and gracious at this small-town wedding for a couple she didn't even know as she'd been at the celebrity gala in Santa Barbara. He'd watched her make an old man feel young again and make a young boy feel like a man as she'd moved so gracefully in their arms.

Both of her partners had beamed with pleasure and pride as she'd easily smoothed over any of their missteps. Though Chance had every confidence in his own abilities, he didn't doubt the same smile was tugging at his lips.

She was amazing, and the most incredible part was that she didn't even seem to know it.

"You're staring," she accused as she ducked her head slightly and kept her gaze focused on the top button of his shirt.

"I know. It's hard not to when you're the most beautiful woman here."

Anyone could see that, but Chance suddenly realized how often that was all anyone saw. *The face of the foundation...* That was how Alexa had referred to herself, as if beauty was all she had to offer.

"Do you know the first thing that attracted me to you that night in Santa Barbara?"

Alexa blinked up at him, and Chance could tell she didn't know how to answer the question. She had beauty, wealth, sophistication, but so too had many of the women there that night.

As the hostess for the charity event, she'd greeted every wealthy donor by name, welcoming them with a flawless grace. But as he'd watched, he quickly recognized the strength behind the beauty.

"It was seeing how you handled that drunk jerk."

A small smile tugged her lips. "That drunk jerk is one of my grandmother's biggest donors, and a high-tech billionaire."

"Doesn't change the fact that he was drunk jerk. I saw him proposition that server, and I was ready to toss him out on his fat wallet."

"That would have been something to see."

"Yeah, but it might have gotten me thrown out of the event and taken the focus away from all the hard work you'd done for the charity. But you—you were a pro. You handled him so perfectly that the guy didn't even know he was being handled. He handed over a donation and was back in his limo before he knew what hit him."

"It's all part of the job."

"You know it was more than that. You could have notified security, but that might have caused a scene and even more embarrassment for the poor girl." He brushed a strand of hair back from her cheek, mesmerized by the softness of her skin, by the silkiness of her hair. By her...

"That night, I thought you looked like an angel, but the truth is you're human, just like the rest of us, but with a heart of gold. You care about people. And that's—that's what I saw that night. That's what you've shown me again here today."

She shook her head, and that same wayward strand of hair fell forward to tempt him again. "I haven't done anything special today."

"You made your dance partners' days just by saying yes. You've made my day—" his week, his month, his year "—just by saying yes to this dance."

"Thank you, but still... As a wedding photographer, you should know that no one is more beautiful than the bride on her wedding day," she chided gently, and just like when he'd lifted his camera earlier, the images in his brain jumbled together.

Alexa... The bride... Alexa, the most beautiful bride...

"Oh, Chance." Seated with him at a table in the now empty ballroom, Alexa looked up from the wedding pictures he'd uploaded to his tablet. She stopped at an image of the bride adjusting her veil in front of a full-length mirror. Sunlight shone through a side window, casting an aura around the blond-haired woman. "She looks like an angel. This picture is perfect."

"I still need to do some editing," he said, deflecting her praise, but she wouldn't hear of it.

"It's perfect," she repeated.

She'd seen some of his award-winning photos, including the ones he'd donated the night of the charity auction. Those images were raw, stark, brutally honest. So she could understand his concerns that his professional eye might not translate to capturing the hope and romance of a young couple's wedding day.

He needn't have worried.

He shifted at her side, uncomfortable with her praise as she swiped through the next photos. Her breath caught at a picture of a toddler flower girl in a ruffled red dress, her white wicker basket held upside down over her head. Flipping through the pictures quickly, Alexa could view a near live-action video of the little girl's adorably unsteady march down the aisle—her blond corkscrew curls bouncing, her blue eyes bright with laughter, her chubby cheeks almost matching the color of her dress.

In the last photo, the little girl was grinning straight at the camera. Seeing that little girl through Chance's camera lens, through *his* eyes, had her own blurring with tears.

"Weddings are supposed to make you cry. Not looking at wedding pictures. Especially not pictures of people you don't even know." His voice was as gruff as if he, too, was fighting some overwhelming emotion.

"I don't know these people, but— These pictures, seeing them, makes me feel like I'm seeing the real you."

"Funny." Chance gave a soft laugh. "Every time I lifted my camera, I felt like I was seeing you."

"Seeing me?" Puzzled, Alexa set the tablet aside. A different kind of longing gripped her as she met his gaze. She felt like they were back on the dance floor. Despite the slow song, her head had spun dizzily, a feeling that stayed with her even after the music stopped. He overwhelmed her every sense—from the low rumble of his voice, to the scent of his woodsy aftershave, to the brush of his muscular thighs against hers... With his lips mere inches above hers, she'd wanted nothing more than to kiss him again.

She hadn't abandoned the list of "a Mayhew does nots" to the point where she'd be comfortable making out on a dance floor—even an almost empty dance floor.

But the longing and the head-spinning, pulse-pounding desire was still there, reflected back in Chance's handsome face as he brushed a lock of hair back behind her ear. A shiver ran down her spine as he said, "I kept seeing you dressed in white, walking down that aisle, wearing a veil."

Her breath seized in her chest. Her heart beat so loudly against her breastbone she wondered that he couldn't hear it. Surely he couldn't be saying what she thought he was saying? "Chance..."

His smile was wry as he reached up to touch her hairpin. "It wasn't just this butterfly I carried with me all those months. It was you...Lexi."

"We barely know each other!"

"The baby you're carrying goes to show we know each other pretty well."

"Not well enough to—" Alexa couldn't bring herself to say the words.

"Get married?"

Oh, good Lord, he was saying what she thought he was saying!

"Look, I know your parents clearly expect us to get married but—"

"This isn't about what my parents want. It's about me wanting our child to have two parents. For the three of us to be a family."

"Our child does have two parents. Getting married doesn't make you a father."

A muscle in his jaw thrummed. "Getting you pregnant doesn't make me a father either. It takes more than that."

"You're right. It takes caring and commitment—"

"Which is why I want to marry you. To prove to you that I am committed—to you and to our baby. We have a responsibility to do what's best for our child."

Alexa couldn't deny the sincerity or seriousness of his vow. If only he didn't sound like he was trying to convince himself as much as he was trying to convince her.

And it had to be some kind of record, right? To be proposed to by two different men within a two-month period with neither one of them mentioning the *L* word.

She hadn't expected it from Griffin, and it was foolish to think she'd hear it from Chance, and yet somehow she still had...

"So we get married and then what? Do you realize I don't even know where you live?"

"I have an apartment in LA, but we can live wherever you want. That doesn't matter."

"Doesn't matter?" she echoed faintly. She supposed it didn't, not when so much of his life was on the road and everything he owned fit in a beat-up backpack. Something that clearly wouldn't change even if it meant leaving a child—or wife—behind.

"What matters most is that I want to be part of our child's life."

"And how would that work when you're halfway around the world?" Putting himself in God knew how much danger...

"That's not fair, Alexa. That's my job. A job I love."

Ah, and there was the *L* word missing from his proposal, given instead as a reason why he would always be walking away.

"You're an amazing photographer, but the assignments you take—the risks. I was serious about the money people would be willing to pay for your photographs, Chance. I spoke with Roslynn St. Clare. She's a friend of my grand-mother's, and she owns one of the most prestigious art galleries in Beverly Hills. And she was *interested* in your work."

But he was already shaking his head. "That's not me, Alexa. That's not who I am, and even if I wanted to do a show with Roslynn St. Clare, I couldn't."

Even though she hadn't expected him to agree, the sting of disappointment burned the back of her eyes. "Why not?"

"Because I would never know if she was asking for me or if she was asking for you..." At her confused frown, he added, "A friend of your grandmother's, remember? I imagine that friendship pulls a lot of weight."

"If you think I used my family's influence to persuade Roslynn, I swear to you, Chance, I didn't!"

He sighed. "You may not have intended to, but I'd never know for sure, would I?" He shook his head. "I don't know how we went from talking about getting married to talking about my job, but we need to focus on the future. Our future."

And Alexa didn't know how he could talk about *his* career and *their* future as if they were two completely separate things. "I made a mistake in not telling you I was pregnant right away, but I'm not going to keep you from our child. You can be in his or her life as much—" or she feared as little "—as you want. We don't need to get married for that to happen."

"When Griffin asked you to marry him, you said you'd think about it." He cut her protest off with a pointed look. "At least do me the same favor."

"All right," she said finally, not that her agreement was much of a concession. As lacking as his proposal was, she doubted she'd be able to push it from her mind. "I'll think about it."

"And you'll stay in Clearville until the end of the month?" he pressed.

Alexa nodded. "I'll stay."

"She can't stay." Evie stared at him from across the marble reception desk. "When the room opened up, we offered it to another guest. And with the anniversary party last night and the wedding today..." She shrugged a shoulder. "We're booked."

Chance narrowed his gaze as he took in his cousin's enigmatic expression. His short time in Clearville had either already dulled his edge or she was one hell of a poker player. He prided himself on his ability to correctly read a source, knowing at times his life depended on it. And yet he had no idea if Evie was telling the truth.

He didn't even know if she was trying to get rid of Alexa or hoping to push her into his arms.

If the latter was part of Evie's plan, she—hell, *they*—had their work cut out for them.

Chance had never imagined proposing to a woman, which might have something to do with why he'd screwed it up so royally. All that talk about responsibility and commitment... He probably couldn't blame Alexa for refusing to marry him. Not when even to his own ears, it sounded like his *dad* was the one proposing.

He was still sticking with his plan to marry Alexa, to give their child two parents. He just needed her to get on board, and to do that he needed to keep her in town for the next three weeks like she'd promised.

Rubbing his aching forehead, he tried to hold on to his temper. "Evie, I swear if this is some kind of a con—"

" The rooms are full. If you want to go around banging on every door in the place, you can, but I wouldn't recommend it." Tucking a strand of her blunt-cut dark hair behind an ear, she added, "Besides, I don't know what you're all bent out of shape about. She can always stay at the cottage. From what Rory tells me, that's where Alexa spent *last* night."

Family... Sometimes he didn't know if he wanted to throttle them or... Oh, yeah, throttle them.

"I really don't think this is a good idea," Alexa protested, and not for the first time as Chance maneuvered up the steps to the cottage, her designer luggage in each hand and under both of his arms. He'd insisted on carrying her bags, and she felt ridiculously embarrassed for having overpacked.

Honestly, why had she thought she needed to bring so much with her?

So, in spite of his protest, she hurried across the porch to open the front door before Chance tried to somehow do that himself, too.

"You shared a suite with your good friend Griffin," he pointed out as he dumped her bags in the middle of the living room and turned on one of the Tiffany lamps.

"That's different."

"Not sure I see how."

"Probably because Griffin's never seen me naked!" As soon as the words burst from her lips, a flush rose in her cheeks. "I cannot believe I just said that."

Amused, Chance said, "Well, I'm glad to hear it. And it's not like we aren't even. You've already seen me naked, too. Plus, you're the one who said we barely know each other. I can't think of a better way to become more intimately acquainted than to live together."

Alexa didn't think she'd imagined the way he stressed *intimately*, and the spike in her heart rate was exactly why staying with Chance was entirely different from rooming with Griffin.

"Besides, it's late. Do you really want to start calling hotels to see if they have a room available?"

"If you had told me earlier, I would have had more time."

But after Chance came back from talking to Evie, he hadn't said anything about the hotel being full. Just like he hadn't said anything more about getting married, confirming Alexa's belief that he regretted his impulsive proposal.

Instead, he'd taken her to dinner at Hillcrest's elegant dining room, where he'd asked about the kind of food her obstetrician recommended and if she'd had any cravings. She told him about her sudden hunger for big, juicy hamburgers and her love of mint chip ice cream, and he laughed when she confessed that particular craving might have predated her pregnancy.

And it hit her in that moment that by keeping the pregnancy a secret, Chance wasn't the only one who had missed out. She'd also robbed herself of someone with whom to share all the tiny details.

So when he carefully repeated, "If I had told you earlier…" Alexa immediately felt the heavy weight of guilt press on her shoulders.

Catching sight of her stricken expression, Chance swore beneath his breath. "I shouldn't have said that. What's done is done, and what we need to do now is to focus on the baby and how to move on from here. Look, it's been a long day. Let's get some sleep, and if you want to find someplace else to stay, we can talk about it in the morning."

Alexa had to admit she was exhausted. She was also very much aware that the tiny cottage had only one bedroom… and one bed. "I'll, um, sleep on the sofa. You'll be more comfortable in the bed."

Chance shook his head. "Forget it. I rarely sleep through the night anyway."

"You did last night," she reminded him.

His eyes glowed at the memory. "That's because you were there with me."

Chapter Eleven

Chance didn't argue with Alexa's insistence on sleeping on the sofa. Instead, he simply waited. After the long and emotional day, she fell asleep with her head on his shoulder as they watched television. He made the most of the opportunity, lifting her into his arms and carrying her to his bedroom.

He fully expected her to wake up, but the pregnancy must have taken more out of her than she wanted to admit. Other than a soft sigh that had goose bumps rising over every inch of his body, she didn't stir. She snuggled deep into the covers when he placed her in the center of the mattress, and Chance gritted his teeth as he resisted the urge to join her there.

Next time they ended up in bed, he wanted them both awake and aware of the undeniable desire drawing them together.

She'd still been sleeping when he'd left for a physical therapy appointment that morning. His therapist had shaken his head at the sight of his bruises but reassured Chance that his rehab was progressing. He'd been on his way back when he received a text from Rory, asking him to stop by the hotel.

But when he showed up, Rory was busy with the arrival of her fiancé, Jamison Porter, and his daughter, Hannah. Settling into one of the overstuffed lobby chairs to wait, Chance froze when the little girl climbed right into his lap despite the multiple empty seats around him.

"Um, hey, Hannah."

The blond-haired girl giggled. "Hay is for horses, Uncle Chance. I don't have a horse. I have a dolly. See?"

Her body a warm, bubblegum-scented weight, she settled against his chest and right into his heart. "Um, that's nice?"

"Miss Rory gots her for me after I was a flower girl in Miss Lindsay's wedding. I had a basket and I threw flowers and I wore a crown in my hair. Now I get to be a flower girl for my daddy's wedding to Miss Rory! An' after the wedding, Miss Rory will be my next mom!"

His head spinning from the rapid-fire conversation, Chance glanced up as Rory walked over. "Next mom?"

His sister smiled indulgently at her soon-to-be step-daughter. "Four-year-old logic for what it means to get a stepmother," she explained. "Which if you think about it, actually makes more sense as a description."

As far as Chance was concerned, none of the babbled conversation made sense. He fought back a groan as Hannah handed him the doll to play with.

"You should be thanking me," Rory told him. "This will be good practice for you."

The longer Hannah babbled on, the less he understood. Something about dolls or maybe dogs or— He didn't know what. By the time she scrambled off his lap, narrowly missing the family jewels with a deadly knee, he was exhausted.

Something that evidently showed, based on Rory's gleeful laughter. "Oh, my gosh! The look on your face. I don't think I've ever seen my big brother so scared! And of a little girl and her doll, of all things!"

"I have no idea what she was talking about," he admitted.

"She's four, Chance. It's not rocket science," Rory said as she sat beside him. "She was telling you about her dolls and how Jamison built her a miniature gazebo like the one here on the grounds where her dolls can play."

"And she thought I'd want to know about that…why?"

"Because she's *four*," Rory repeated. "Her dolls are important to her, and she wants them to be important to you because you are also important to her."

"She doesn't even know me."

"You're her Uncle Chance. She adores you. Evie, too, although I'm not always sure why since Evie's never been kid friendly."

"And I am?"

"In your own way, yeah. You love adventure, excitement, exploration, and that's what being a kid is all about."

Chance smiled. Rory was right. He'd loved being a kid. There were some parts he'd never outgrown.

"And besides, you're having a baby. By the time your child is Hannah's age, you'll have tons of experience at being a dad." After a slight hesitation, she added, "I talked to Alexa a little at the reception last night. She says she's only staying through the end of the month."

"That's right."

Pointing out what he already knew, she said, "That's

not much time. So what are you going to do? You can't just let her leave."

"I can't exactly force her to stay."

"I'm not talking about forcing. I'm talking about *persuading*."

"That didn't exactly work either," he muttered.

"You asked her to stay?"

"I asked her to marry me."

Rory's jaw dropped in utter shock. "Seriously? You proposed? When? How?"

"Last night, and what do you mean how?" Chance shifted uncomfortably, rubbing at the back of his neck where his collar—hell, his own damn skin—felt too tight.

"Were there flowers? Music? A ring?"

Only if he counted the ones for another couple's wedding.

Throwing her hands up in exasperation, Rory said, "Honestly, Chance, you can't ask a woman to marry you in some kind of knee-jerk reaction and expect her to say yes. Didn't you see Alexa at the reception, willing to dance with perfect strangers just to make them smile? This is a woman who's looking for romance and longing for a man to sweep her off her feet."

The last time Chance opened his heart to romance, Lisette had stomped all over it. What kind of fool would he be if he left himself open for that kind of heartbreak again?

"Morning."

A shiver ran down Alexa's spine at the sound of Chance's voice. She glanced over her shoulder to find him lounging in the kitchen doorway. How was it he could look so good after rolling out of bed to go straight to a physical therapy appointment? Dressed in a faded T-shirt and navy sweatpants, his dark hair mussed from the workout session, stubble shadowing his jaw along with a rainbow of bruises, and her mouth still went dry at the sight of him.

She wrapped her hands around a fragrant mug of peppermint tea, holding on to the warm ceramic to keep from reaching out as he stepped into her personal space and made it his own. "How was your appointment?"

"Good. My therapist says I'm ahead of schedule." He frowned, and she could only imagine his frustration that even ahead of schedule wasn't healing fast enough. "How'd you sleep last night?"

"Better than expected, considering I went to sleep on the couch and somehow woke up in your bed." A hint of annoyance filled her voice, left over from the frustration of his scent, his warmth, his presence invading her subconscious with dreams that left her restless, achy and, as it turned out, alone.

But instead of owning up to what he'd done, Chance had the nerve to grin. "Do you have a habit of sleepwalking?"

"Hardly. I told you, you should take the bed."

"And I told you...I'm not sleeping there without you."

Heat flooded her cheeks, and Alexa only wished she could blame it on the steam rising from her mug. Even though she told herself that giving in to sexual chemistry wasn't a solution, she wasn't sure how much longer it would be before she would be asking him to join her there.

Breaking the sensual spell, Chance glanced over her shoulder at the kitchen counter. "What's all this?" he asked, gesturing to her tablet propped up against the toaster.

The video tutorial she'd been watching while brewing her tea had run its course, the television chef now paused and waiting to be played back. Alexa had hoped to have breakfast made by the time he returned from his therapy appointment. But unlike his mother, she needed a recipe.

She'd been astounded by the overwhelming number of results for something as simple as blueberry pancakes.

Which, as it turned out, might not be so simple after all...

"Do you realize if you type 'blueberry pancake recipes' into a search engine, you get more than two and half million hits?" Two and a half *million*, and she'd never made a single one.

Not seeming nearly as amazed by this revelation, Chance chuckled. "Blueberry pancakes again? Is this some kind of pregnancy craving?"

"I thought you liked pancakes."

"I do, although maybe not for breakfast every day."

"When your mother was here, she talked about cooking for you and Rory when you were kids. About how the two of you would stand on step stools on either side of her and argue over who got to lick the batter from the spatula."

"Yeah, my mom loves to cook, and she always wanted to share that love with us. I hadn't thought about that in a long time." His voice faded off into forgotten memories as he murmured, "Too long..."

Alexa didn't have those kinds of memories of her mother, had precious few memories of her parents at all. "This is the part where I should probably tell you I don't actually know how to make pancakes." Embarrassed by that admission, she added, "We always had a chef on staff," which only made it sound that much worse.

Because her family hadn't stopped at hiring chefs, and it wasn't only her lack of skill as a cook that had Alexa doubting her ability to be the kind of mother their child deserved...

"Hey." Reaching out, Chance took the tea mug from her hands and set it aside to pull her into his arms. With his forehead against hers, he said, "As an annoying and occasionally wise woman reminded me just this morning, we're not having a full-grown kid. We're having a baby. It will be months before that baby is old enough to be eating pancakes, and years before the baby'll be old enough to stand on a step stool by your side to lick the batter from a spatula. We have time to figure this out, to figure *all* of this out."

With her hands fisted in the soft cotton of Chance's T-shirt, Alexa couldn't decide if it was wonderful or scary how easily he read her thoughts. Settling on *wonderfully scary*, she asked, "So what do we do now?"

"Now, we make pancakes. The old-fashioned way." After powering down her tablet, he reached into a cupboard over the stove and pulled out a small blue-and-white-striped tin box.

"What is that?"

"Copies of my mother's recipes." His smile was more than a little wry as he said, "If we're going to learn how to do this, we might as well learn from one of the best."

"Alexa, you're right on time!"

Rory greeted her with a smile as she crossed the lobby. The pretty brunette was dressed for the season in a brown V-neck sweater and plaid burnt-orange skirt. But the warm colors, like the fall decorations, only served as a reminder that Thanksgiving and the end of the month were drawing near.

We have time to figure this out.

Alexa couldn't help the small smile that came to her lips. After some trial and error, and quite a bit of laughter, they had figured out pancakes. She'd waited breathlessly as he took the first taste before proclaiming, "Best pancakes ever."

And when he held out his fork for her to try the buttery, maple-soaked goodness, a different kind of anticipation caught inside her chest as a different kind of hunger sharpened his expression. Alexa wasn't sure how she managed to swallow a single bite, let alone to finish an entire pancake. Recalling the expression about not being able to take the heat, she had quickly gotten out of the kitchen.

She'd spent the morning on the phone with Raquel after informing Virginia that she was extending her stay until the end of the month.

"A Mayhew does not abandon her duties, Alexa."

"I know, and I'm not. I'll check in every day, and I'll be back before the benefit," she'd promised.

Her grandmother had been far from pleased, and Alexa feared she would be even less so once she told her about her pregnancy.

But Alexa wasn't ready for that conversation, and she'd been surprised and relieved when Rory had called her later in the day to invite her to lunch with some friends. Alexa didn't think she could start another cooking lesson with Chance in the kitchen that didn't end in the bedroom.

Wanting to make a good impression, Alexa had debated over what to wear, trying to find a balance between too dressy and, well, way too dressy. Despite the ridiculous amount of luggage she'd brought with her, her expanding waistline was starting to limit her options.

Finally, after the third outfit change, Chance had caught her by the shoulders on the way back to the bedroom.

"What are you doing?" he'd asked.

She waved a hand at the wide-legged burgundy slacks she wore with an ivory scoop-necked sweater and multicolor, knitted scarf. "I need to change."

"Why? You're perfect just the way you are. Relax, Lexi. You don't have to be the face of the foundation. Just be *you*," he had encouraged her.

Keeping that in mind, Alexa took a deep breath and smiled at his sister. "Thank you for inviting me."

"We're heading into town for lunch at Sugar & Spice," Rory told her.

Recalling that the café was owned by the baker who supplied Hillcrest House's wedding cakes, Alexa said, "I'll be sure to save room for dessert."

"It's better to play things safe," a slender honey-blond woman said as she joined them. "I've been known to order dessert first."

"Alexa, this is Lindsay Kincaid, and Sophia Cameron will be here as soon as she's done chasing down Kyle."

"Chasing—" Alexa started at the unexpected feel of something tugging at her burgundy slacks. No, not something. Someone, she realized as she glanced down into a chubby-cheeked face and big dark eyes.

"Looks like you found Kyle." Rory bent at the waist to offer a four-fingered wave at the baby. "Or he found you."

"This is Kyle?" The little boy who'd pulled himself unsteadily to his feet wore a long-sleeved red T-shirt beneath the most adorable pair of denim overalls. A bit of demand entered his babbling as he slapped a dimpled hand against her leg.

"He's not walking on his own yet, but he's the fastest thing on all fours," Lindsay laughed.

A particularly exuberant pat had the boy losing his grip. He teetered for a moment before toppling over and landing on the patterned carpet. Looking a bit stunned, the baby stared up at Alexa for a moment before those big eyes stared to fill.

"Oh, sweetie. It's okay. Don't cry!" Without stopping to think, Alexa bent and scooped up the little boy. He was heavier and studier than she expected as he settled into her arms.

Despite the tears dampening his long lashes, the little boy rewarded her with a drooly smile, showing off two shiny white bottom teeth. The baby patted her shoulder this time, and as ridiculous as it was, Alexa couldn't help but feel like she'd received a stamp of approval.

Five months. In five months, I'll be holding my baby. Our baby.

"Honestly, I don't know how I am going to keep up with him once he starts walking!" A petite dark-haired woman with a huge diaper bag strapped to one shoulder crossed the lobby to join them. Her dark eyes and pixie haircut immediately identified her as the boy's mother. "He only recently learned to crawl, and now every time I turn around, he's broken some speed record in getting away from me."

Handing the little boy to his mother, Alexa said, "He is so cute."

"Thank you. I'm Sophia Cameron, and you've already met Kyle." She bounced the baby in her arms, eliciting a gurgling laugh that had them all smiling.

"I've asked Alexa to join us for lunch."

"The more the merrier," Sophia said, smiling her welcome. "So long as you don't mind this guy coming along. My babysitter canceled at the last minute."

"Of course not. He is so cute…" Noticing the other women exchanging smiles, Alexa felt her face heat. "I already said that, didn't I?"

"You did. Do you have children?" Sophia asked innocently.

Alexa froze, aware of Rory's gaze on her. She wasn't sure how much Chance had told his sister but figured she wasn't revealing any secrets when she said, "Actually, I'm pregnant."

"Oh, how exciting!" Sophia exclaimed.

"Congratulations, Alexa," Lindsay offered.

"It gets even better," Rory added with a grin. "Not only is Alexa going to be a mother, but I'm going to be her baby's aunt."

The two women squealed again, hugging not just Rory but also Alexa. Their exuberance caught her off guard as did the sudden rush of emotion. Sophia was the first to notice. "Oh, my goodness. Are you okay?"

"I'm fine." Alexa wiped at the tears on her cheeks, feeling extremely foolish for breaking down. "It's just—"

The first time anyone had been truly happy to hear about the baby.

Her shock at discovering she was pregnant had barely worn off when the news reports had announced Chance's "death." And then she'd made such a mess of telling him he was going to be a father. She couldn't go back and do things differently, but going forward...

"I'm happy," she told the other women. "I'm crying because I'm happy if that makes any sense at all."

"Are you kidding?" Sophia asked with an understanding smile. "Welcome to my world. When Kyle got his first tooth, I went from overjoyed at how big he's getting to devastated that he's growing up too fast in an instant."

"Alexa."

The deep voice rang out across the lobby, and she glanced up to see Chance striding toward them, an intense look on his handsome face. Reaching her side, he all but glared at the three women around her. "What's wrong?"

She blinked at him, dislodging a lingering tear, and said, "I was about to ask you the same thing."

"Me?" His brows pulled together over the brilliant blue of his eyes. "I'm not the one who's crying."

Butterflies fluttered in Alexa's stomach as he reached out to brush a thumb beneath her eye. Catching his hand in hers, she promised, "I'm fine, Chance. It was just, well, hormones."

His gaze searched hers as if searching for the truth to her words. Seeming satisfied with what he saw there, he stunned her a little by pressing a kiss to her forehead. "If you're sure you're okay."

"She's coming with us to lunch, big brother, where we promise the only tears will be ones of ecstasy over to-die-for desserts. That's assuming you'll let her come out and play."

He didn't appear the least bit embarrassed by his sister's teasing, and as he feathered his fingers through Alexa's hair, the sights and sounds of the elegant lobby faded away until only the two of them existed...

When Chance had entered the walnut-paneled lobby and saw that Alexa had been crying, his overriding instinct had been to rush to her side. Only once he realized she was fine did his focus expand, taking in the smug smile on Rory's face, the two wide-eyed women beside her and the grinning, dark-haired baby one of them held.

"Da-da!" the little boy shouted, his chubby arms reaching out toward Chance.

"Whoa! Hang on there, kid." Catching the boy as he practically dive-bombed from his mother's arms, he murmured, "I'm not a daddy yet."

Although that wasn't entirely true. He was already a father to the unborn child Alexa carried, but it still didn't feel entirely real. The baby was just an idea, a concept he had yet to wrap his mind around. Nothing as substantial as this little guy currently wrapped around his neck.

But when he saw the watery, tender smile on Alexa's face as she reached out to touch the baby's soft cheek before brushing her fingers across his own bristled jaw, the emotional blow was real enough to leave him weak at the knees.

His sister's laughter broke the moment, and she said, "Sophia, Lindsay, this is my brother, Chance. The baby magnet."

Not too long ago, Chance would likely have been annoyed at his sister's teasing. But now... The wonder of it all had him smiling even as the little boy's responding grin had drool running from his dimpled chin and soaking into Chance's T-shirt.

A bit of baby slobber couldn't hurt, and the kid really was cute...

"Da-da!"

"Looks like little Kyle here knows how to spot 'em," Rory said as she patted Chance's soggy shoulder.

"From the moment he was born, Kyle's been a daddy's boy. But Jake's been traveling a lot lately. You miss your daddy, don't you?"

"Da-da!"

His mother laughed at what sounded like a firm agreement. "It is his favorite word, and one that can pretty much mean anything, including a name for big, masculine men."

"No need to apologize. Really," he said, handing the boy back with a surprising amount of reluctance.

As Alexa asked Sophia a question about Kyle, Chance could already see how Rory's friends had accepted her. She smiled and laughed with the other women, and seemed as fascinated by little Kyle as he was, reaching over more than once to grasp the baby's hand or to adjust the strap of his tiny overalls.

"Thanks for inviting Alexa," he told his sister quietly. "I appreciate you making the effort."

"I like her. And I have to admit, I wasn't sure I would, considering your past taste in women."

"Alexa is nothing like Lisette," he argued. And yet hadn't he had doubts of his own, questioning if she'd used her wealth and status to try to get him that gallery showing for his work?

Lisette had been a master at manipulation, going behind his back and working behind the scenes to make sure he was offered jobs at star-studded events and along red-carpet runways, but always for her own benefit.

He couldn't deny that Alexa's motives were pure and unselfish, but her efforts still made him wonder if she could ever accept him for the man he was.

His editor had called again to let Chance know he'd been given the green light on a follow-up to an article he'd written on a refugee camp in Serbia—if he was ready to get back to the job.

"Three weeks," he'd heard himself say to the other man.

Alexa had given him three weeks before she planned to go back to LA, the same amount of time he had to convince her that he could be a husband, a father and a photojournalist.

He watched as Sophia pulled a toy from the large diaper bag hooked to her shoulder. With the boy focused on the stuffed dinosaur, she swooped in to wipe his glistening chin with a small cloth, her movements easy and efficient.

When Kyle reached out again, this time to Alexa, a beatific smile curved her lips as she caught his pudgy hand and pressed a kiss to his palm. He babbled happily as she entertained him with a game of peekaboo using her scarf. Making the little boy belly laugh and making Chance... He didn't know how to describe the sucker-punch feeling inside.

"She's so good with him," he murmured. "She's going to be an amazing mother."

"You didn't think she would be?" Rory asked.

"No, *I* knew… Alexa was the one who doubted it. It will be good for her to spend some time with Kyle."

"Good for Alexa?" she echoed. "Because she's worried about motherhood?"

"Well, yeah."

Too late, Chance turned his attention back to Rory. He didn't know what he'd done to make his sister's eyes narrow like that, but nothing good could possibly come of it.

"Hey, girls, my big brother just had a brilliant idea," she announced as she reached for the baby's bag. "He's volunteered to watch Kyle while we go out to lunch."

"Wait! What?" Pure reflex had Chance catching the diaper bag that hit him straight in the chest—right along with a huge dose of panic. "No!"

Chapter Twelve

"Are you sure Kyle's going to be okay?" Alexa asked as the four of them sat down at one of the white wrought-iron tables inside the Sugar & Spice café. The small space was sunny and cheerful, with buttery yellow walls, white wainscot and primary-colored accents in the ceramic pots of fresh herbs displayed on floating shelves.

The scent of vanilla and cinnamon filled the air and gorgeously crafted desserts glistened behind a gleaming glass display, but Alexa was too distracted by thoughts of the man—and baby—they'd left behind.

"My three brothers have all taken turns watching Kyle, and only one of them has experience with babies, and that was over a decade ago. If Kyle can survive the Pirelli brothers, he can survive Chance."

"Personally, I'm more worried about my big brother than I am about Kyle. Did you see the look on his face when I *suggested* he babysit?"

Pretending to fan herself with a laminated menu, Sophia said, "I'd rather talk about the look on Chance's face when he first came charging over. He looked like he was ready to rescue Alexa from fire-breathing dragons."

"Hey, I think I resent that," Rory interjected.

Wishing she could fan her own suddenly heated face without drawing too much attention to herself, Alexa shook her head. "I'm sure Chance was just worried about the baby."

"I've seen a worried-about-the-baby look," Sophia pointed out. "That was not it. That was definitely a man-worried-about-his-woman look."

Nerves danced in Alexa's stomach, and she fisted her hands in her lap, frightened by how badly she wanted to believe the other woman might be right. That the caring and concern Chance had shown over the past few days was more than a sense of responsibility for the child she carried.

Had he given her just a hint that his feelings for her were because of something more than overwhelming attraction or the *result* of that attraction when he proposed, Alexa was afraid she very well might have said yes.

"Stop, Sophia," Lindsay chided gently. "At least allow Alexa some chocolate reinforcement before you start investigating."

"Oh, all right," the brunette agreed. "But you are having dessert first, aren't you?"

Alexa couldn't help but laugh, though she was relieved when the dark-eyed woman's attention shifted to the server who stopped by to take their order. And, no, Alexa did not order dessert first, settling instead for a grilled turkey panini with a garden salad for a side.

As the server walked away, Lindsay leaned forward,

her eyes bright with excitement as she said, "I'm so glad everything for the shower is coming together."

At Alexa's questioning glance, Rory explained. "Lindsay's sister-in-law, Nina, is due right before Christmas, and we're having the shower at Hillcrest."

"And we can't thank you enough for offering to let us use the parlor room, not to mention asking Chance to take pictures."

Rory waved aside the thanks. "Hey, as long as he's here, I'm planning to put him to work."

As long as he was there.

Alexa's appetite faded as worry about the future grabbed hold. She had promised Chance she would stay through the end of the month before heading back to LA. But she had no idea where Chance's next assignment might take him.

"Nina's going to be so surprised. It's her third baby," Lindsay was saying, "so she said she didn't want a shower."

"But we couldn't let that happen."

"Absolutely not. A baby is always something to celebrate." Seeming to have read into all Alexa hadn't said earlier, Rory repeated, "Always."

As the server arrived with their food, Alexa forced herself to focus on the positive. "Thank you again for inviting me. This looks wonderful, and it's nice to get out." Alexa cut herself off before she could add "with friends." That would be assuming too much, and while neither Sophia nor Lindsay questioned her tagging along, Alexa hadn't missed the whispered conversation between brother and sister. She was certain Chance had had something to do with his sister's sudden invitation.

"Of course. And, Lindsay, you and Alexa have something in common," Rory told the blond-haired woman as she added a splash of vinaigrette to her salad. "She's in charge of fund-raising for the Mayhew Foundation, her grandmother's charity organization."

Turning to Alexa, Rory added, "Lindsay works for the chamber of commerce, and she just organized a rodeo benefit for a local horse rescue a few months ago."

Lindsay shook her head. "Jarrett Deeks and his wife, Theresa—who also happens to be Sophia's cousin—did the majority of the legwork. I mostly helped with the advertising and reaching out for donations. Still, I was happy that the rodeo was such a success. And the best part is that they've already been able to make some upgrades to the stalls and take on more horses with the money raised."

"How wonderful that you can see the good your work has done firsthand."

"Well," Lindsay said, her cheeks brightening at the praise, "it's nothing on scale to all you've accomplished."

The foundation had raised millions of dollars over the years, but rarely did Alexa see that money put into use. She talked to people who knew people, and made sure the events went off without a hitch. And then at the end of the night, she would present the head of the charity with a big check—literally—as she smiled and posed for pictures.

But then she would move on. To the next charity in need and to the next celebrity golf tournament, star-studded concert or golden gala. The foundation received pictures of improved schools or health clinics or housing for those in need. But that wasn't the same as seeing the benefits firsthand.

"I've actually been considering taking on a different role at the foundation," Alexa said, speaking her thoughts out loud for the first time to an audience who didn't know her well enough to judge. Who wouldn't limit her possibilities with all a Mayhew did not do. "I'd like to be more hands-on and work with the charities to come up with financial plans for how to best use the funds raised. Finding a way to maintain donor interest in those projects might help the public realize charities don't just need money during fund-raising drives or at the holidays."

Embarrassed by her own unexpected outpouring, Alexa cut herself off and reached for her glass of water. "Sorry, I'm probably getting a little far ahead of myself."

But Lindsay only shook her head. "That sounds like a really good idea. In fact, I'd love to do some brainstorming with you while you're here. That is if you don't mind."

"And I can set up something with Jarrett and Theresa if you want to take a look around their rescue and see what they've accomplished so far," Sophia offered.

"I wouldn't mind at all," Alexa said, surprised and pleased by how readily the other women had embraced her ideas. Starting out small would be a great way to get her feet wet as well as an opportunity to give back to the small town she was coming to love.

The sound of a muffled ringtone had Sophia pushing back from the table. "Oh, excuse me for a second," she said as she dropped her napkin on the chair and answered her cell.

The three women talked a bit more about Lindsay's position at the chamber of commerce as well as the town's areas of need before Sophia returned to the table. "Sorry about that. Jake, my husband, has been out of town. I thought he'd be back tonight, but he's been delayed."

"Is everything okay?" Lindsay asked.

"He has assured me 'not to worry.' Which means that's all I'll be doing until I hear from him again."

"What does your husband do?" Alexa asked, recalling what the other woman had said earlier about her husband's frequent travels.

"He's a private investigator."

The unexpected answer had Alexa setting her sandwich aside. "Wow. That sounds interesting."

"Jake swears it's not, and that ninety percent of the time, it's totally boring. It's that ten percent that keeps me up at night."

"I don't imagine it's much like they show on television."

"Don't even get him started on those comparisons! Although my brothers love to tease him. For his last birthday, they all bought him Hawaiian shirts in tribute to *Magnum, P.I.* You know, that popular detective show from the eighties? Believe me when I tell you Jake is not a Hawaiian shirt kind of guy."

"Still, it must be hard when he's gone." Alexa tried to imagine her son or daughter calling a man other than Chance "da-da" and didn't think she'd handle it nearly as well as Sophia had.

"It is." The brunette's smile trembled a bit, revealing that it wasn't as easy as she made it seem. "But I have friends and family to help out, and I know he misses me as much as I miss him. But this is more than a job to Jake. It's so much a part of him that I can't imagine him doing anything else." Her dark eyes brimmed with emotion as she added, "His love for me has always been completely and irrevocably unconditional. How can I possibly deserve that unless my love for him is the same?"

Though Chance was sure Rory thought otherwise, he did occasionally listen to his sister. And when he did, more often than not, he was forced to admit she was right. Which probably accounted for why he didn't listen more often.

He hated admitting she was right. He especially hadn't liked it when she'd pointed out how lacking his proposal to Alexa had been.

Were there flowers? Music? A ring? Didn't you see

Alexa at the reception, willing to dance with perfect strangers just to make them smile? This is a woman who's looking for romance and longing for a man to sweep her off her feet.

Alexa deserved all of that and more, but other than that first weekend together, he'd shown her very little of it. Something he was trying to make up for as he led Alexa down the gravel path from the cottage.

"Are you sure your eyes are closed?"

"I'm sure, although why they are closed, I don't know," Alexa said, her hands to her face. "Is this some kind of payback for leaving you to babysit Kyle?"

"You do know what they say about revenge being sweet," he teased. He did still owe Rory for that whole bait and switch she'd pulled the other day. "I cannot tell you how much energy that kid has."

After two hours, he'd been exhausted and overwhelmed—but so excited to meet his own kid, he didn't know how he was going to wait another five months.

Of course, he couldn't blame Alexa if she wasn't quite so eager. He'd seen the look on her face when she'd walked into the cottage. Every toy, every piece of clothing, every diaper had been tossed out of the oversize diaper bag. Kyle had had a field day playing with all of it—but none of it for more than fifteen seconds at a time.

From there, he'd moved on to a stuffed bear left over from Rory's childhood. A perfectly suitable plaything, Chance had thought, until the little boy pulled off one of the bear's button eyes and popped it into his mouth. Panicked, Chance had scooped up the baby, holding him upside down until he spit out the button much to the little boy's dismay.

Figuring if the kid was hungry enough to eat inedible objects, lunch ought to be a piece of cake. After a scene involving pureed peas that would have done the special effects artist from *The Exorcist* proud, the cottage was soon littered with the majority of Chance's wardrobe as he'd had to change his shirt. Three times. By the end of the meal, both he and Kyle were half-naked. The little boy keeping on his long-sleeved T-shirt, diaper and one sock while Chance settled on wearing just his jeans.

Finally, after having been sufficiently worn out, Kyle had settled down in Chance's arms for a nap. Which was where Alexa had found them an hour or so later.

Alexa, he had to admit, had been a trooper. She'd helped him redress Kyle, pack up his numerous belongings and return him to his mother—more or less in the same shape as when she'd left him.

"Poor baby," she commiserated now.

"Me or the kid?"

"Oh, you. Definitely you."

"I just hope Kyle didn't end up eating his other shoe. I'm telling you, I have no idea where that thing went."

"I have a feeling it will turn up somewhere."

"Okay, we're here." Positioning Alexa for the best vantage point for his surprise, he said, "You can open your eyes."

Dropping her hands, she let out a gasp as she caught her first glimpse of the gazebo. A table draped in white sat in the middle of the platform. Covered dishes gleamed in the twinkle lights draped overhead, and colorful pots of burgundy, orange and yellow mums lined the steps along with garland draped on either side of the stair railings. "Oh, Chance. How beautiful!"

"I thought after the busy day we've both had, that a nice quiet dinner would be just what we needed."

A nice *romantic* dinner, he could almost hear Rory whispering in his ear.

He'd bungled his proposal to Alexa. Badly. While he might not be ready to put his heart on the line, Alexa was a woman who deserved candlelight dinners, wine—or for now sparkling cider—and flowers.

"We've kind of gone about this all backward," he admitted as he guided her up the steps. "To say we rushed things in Santa Barbara might be a bit of an understatement."

"You think?" she teased, the candlelight reflected in her eyes as she sank into the chair he pulled out for her.

"And I certainly rushed that proposal the other night, so I was thinking that maybe we could not start over, but just a few steps back and take things a bit slower this time."

Her lashes lowered as she ducked her head almost shyly. "I think I'd like that." And then dispelling any sense of shyness as well as most of the thoughts from his head, she added, "Although I was looking forward to another cooking lesson for dinner."

"Well, there's always breakfast in the morning." Which left so many possibilities open for tonight.

All of which would once again fall into the "rushing things" category.

"Are you warm enough?" Chance asked sometime after they had finished the mouthwatering meal from the hotel restaurant. He had to hand it to Evie, who'd somehow convinced the up-and-coming chef to leave San Francisco to come work at Hillcrest. The man had outdone himself with roasted Cornish game hens, sautéed asparagus and brown sugar sweet potatoes.

Alexa had wanted a better view of the stars while they ate their dessert, so Chance had switched off the lights and carried the plate over to where she'd taken a seat on the stairs. She had her arms wrapped around her knees, and although he had warned her to dress warmly and brought two propane heaters out for the occasion, he wanted to make sure she was comfortable.

"I'm fine," she reassured him as he sat down beside her.

He wrapped an arm around her shoulders—just to be safe—and felt something sweet and powerful settle into his chest as she rested her head against his shoulder.

"Mm, pumpkin cheesecake," Alexa almost groaned as he offered her the dessert, the sound sending a burst of heat straight to his gut. And when she closed her lips around the fork, it was all he could do to form a coherent sentence.

"Evie's all about offering guests a seasonal menu."

"Everything was wonderful."

"Not bad for a first date?"

She laughed a little at that. "Not bad at all."

They sat in a comfortable silence as she dug into the crumbly graham cracker crust. She had just set the plate aside when she pointed to a streak across the night sky. "Oh, look! A shooting star…" She sucked in a breath, and though the movement was slight, Chance felt her pull away. Her shoulders slumped as she drew her legs up onto the next step, curling into herself as if trying to shield her heart.

He tightened his arm around her, an instinctive urge to protect her from anything, everything, rising inside him. "Alexa? What's wrong?"

"That's what my grandmother sometimes called my parents. Shooting stars."

"Do you want to tell me about them?"

"They were like Christmas and New Year's and the Fourth of July—fun and exciting."

And only came around a few times a year. Alexa didn't say the words, but he heard them in the wistfulness in her voice. His heart broke a little as the moonlight touched on the sad smile on her beautiful face. Reaching over with his free hand, he threaded his fingers through hers and squeezed. "I'm sorry, sweetheart."

"It was a long time ago. Twenty years ago." Her shoulders straightened slightly as she turned to face him. "The day you called was—that was the anniversary of my parents' death, Chance."

"Oh, Lexi..."

"I spent the first half of my childhood waiting for them to call, to come home. I saw myself falling into that same pattern with you, and I didn't want to be that little girl again."

"And so you told me it was over."

"Yes." That abrupt conversation still stung, but Chance felt he understood better now. "I'm sorry..."

"I don't want to hear that you're sorry. I want to hear that it's not true." Chance heard the touch of desperation in his own voice and forced his grip on her slender hand to relax. "That maybe that weekend meant more than a meaningless fling..."

"It meant...enough to scare me. To leave me feeling vulnerable."

"Just like that phone call left me feeling. All that talk about different lives. I saw you that night at the hotel, surrounded by some of the wealthiest people in California, and there I was—a high school dropout who's spent most of his adult life living out of a beat-up backpack, thinking to myself, 'What the hell am I doing here?'"

"But that—that's not what I meant!" It was her turn to tighten her grip, the skin-to-skin communication mattering as much as the words. "Not at all! Chance, you're talented, successful, famous! That's why you were invited to that benefit. That's why half the people were in attendance, to meet you!"

He gave a rough chuckle. "I'd say half is a definite exaggeration. But the point is, you belonged there, and I didn't."

"You're so confident, so at ease in your own skin, I honestly can't imagine a place where you wouldn't belong."

It had suited him well over the years, his ability to adapt, to fit in. But Chance wasn't sure he'd ever felt as truly comfortable, as completely in the present as he had with Alexa by his side. He wasn't working an angle, wasn't digging deeper to uncover some hidden truth. He'd allowed himself to simply enjoy the moment, to accept the chemistry and connection for what it was.

"The only time I felt like I belonged that night was when I held you in my arms." Alexa glowed in the soft moonlight, but Chance still saw the shadows from a childhood where she'd been so easily left behind. "I wanted to carry that feeling, to carry a piece of you with me, Alexa. That's why I didn't give the butterfly hairpin back."

"So you had it with you...the whole time?"

"The whole time," he echoed. It had become his touchstone, a good memory to combat all the bad.

"And you still think it's lucky?"

"I know it is," he said, thinking back to the day when the small memento had saved his life.

He'd been moments away from stepping inside a building to interview an outspoken political dissident. After paying off the guide who had led him to the meeting place, Chance had stuck his hand back into his pocket. His fingers had brushed against the butterfly, and in an instant he'd been taken back to that weekend. Back to Alexa.

His head hadn't been anywhere near where it should have been—preparing for the interview—something that in another place or time might have gotten him killed. But in that moment, with Alexa filling his thoughts, he'd taken an extra moment to refocus. He'd waited outside a minute. Maybe two. But long enough that when the building some twenty feet from him exploded, he was far enough away to survive.

He had Alexa to thank for that, but the story wasn't one he planned to share with her. Not now. Not ever.

But almost as if reading his thoughts, she asked, "Can—can I ask you about your work? If you don't want to talk about it—"

"No, it's okay. What do you want to know?" But even as he asked the question, he braced himself. His job had always been a sore spot. First with his parents and later with Lisette.

"When did you first realize you wanted to be a photographer?"

The easy question caught him off guard, and he felt himself relax. "When I was still a teenager, not too long after my dad gave me one of his old 35 millimeter cameras."

"Your dad?"

"He's a photographer, too."

Alexa was silent for a moment before she said, "I noticed some tension between the two of you. At first I thought it was about the baby, but it was there even before you made your announcement."

"It isn't you, Alexa, or the baby. It's me. It's always been me. I'm—I'm not who my parents want me to be."

"What does that mean?"

"They love me, I know that, and I love them. And if I was a different person—maybe a better person—then maybe I could change. Maybe I could put aside my own dreams and do what they want me to do. But ask anyone. I'm selfish. Always thinking of myself first and my family second. Or to hear my father tell it, not thinking of them at all."

Not thinking of Alexa or the baby at all. That was what his father had said after pulling him aside in the final moments before they drove off. And that accusation hurt more than Chance wanted to admit. Because his father thought so little of him? Or because deep down, he couldn't help wondering if the words were true.

"What do they want you to be?"

"When I was a kid, I was always the wild child. The one who thought the word *no* simply meant I should do what I want without getting caught." He gave a short laugh. "Only I almost always got caught—doing stupid stuff, mostly. There wasn't a dare I could back down from or a chance I wouldn't take even as a little kid."

"So you were...you. Even then."

"Yeah, I guess that's one way of looking at it. I thought I was invincible until I was twelve or so and found I wasn't as hardheaded as everyone thought."

"What happened?"

"I was messing around on a skateboard. Trying a trick on a half-pipe that I was nowhere near skilled enough to complete. I landed wrong, hit my head and...ended up in a coma."

"Oh, my God!"

Chance heard the shock, the concern in Alexa's voice. Just a fraction of the emotion that his parents must have felt, but as for Chance, he didn't remember the accident or the weeks and months that followed. He hadn't understood how he could wake up one day only to discover everything had changed.

"I fully recovered, but in a way, I'm not sure my parents ever did. Not completely. After the accident, they couldn't protect me enough. For the longest time, they didn't even want me out of their sight."

"And you hated that."

"Hated it, rebelled against it. Fought even harder to do whatever I wanted, whenever I wanted. And then when I was fourteen or so, I started to get interested in photography. At first they were all for it. I think they hoped if I channeled all my energy into photography, I'd be happy taking pictures of, I don't know, kittens and puppies. But I was still me. I still wanted to be out hiking and climbing and biking—only with a camera in hand.

"After high school, my parents wanted me to go to college and work part-time at my dad's studio. Taking family photos, graduation shots, baby pictures." Even after all that time, just thinking about being trapped in that small studio—both physically and creatively *stuck*—was enough to make Chance want to take off at a dead run. "Instead I took off for LA, and I never looked back."

"And you have an incredible career. You can't tell me your parents aren't proud of the man—the photojournalist—you've become."

"I always thought so until this happened," he said, stretching out his right leg and still feeling the reminders of the damage done by the explosion in the strain in the joint and muscles. "Until I woke up in the hospital after my last surgery and overheard my parents talking about how it might be better if I never fully regained use of my leg again."

"Oh, Chance…"

Just saying the words out loud, he was taken back to that moment. To the sterile white walls, the beeping of the machines, the sharp, antiseptic smell of the recovery room. His parents hadn't realized he was awake, and in truth, he hadn't been. Drifting in and out of consciousness, but aware of enough to know he hadn't misunderstood any of what he heard.

"This is my life, the career I've always wanted. The one

I dreamed about since I was a kid and that they would actually be *glad* if I were injured badly enough to have to give it up…" His throat burned, searing all the way down as he swallowed the words he couldn't bring himself to say.

"Chance, they're your parents." Her gentle blue-gray gaze pleaded with him as she said, "They love you—"

"Love," he bit out roughly. "If that's love, I don't want any part of it."

Chapter Thirteen

If that's love, I don't want any part of it.

At the bitterness slicing through Chance's voice and straight to her heart, Alexa could have cried. Not for herself, but for him. Beneath the anger, the rejection, she heard the pain. How often as a child had she wondered what more she could have done? If only she'd been smarter, funnier, more interesting, then maybe her parents would have stayed. Maybe they would have lived.

The situation wasn't exactly the same. Her parents hadn't loved her enough to stay. Chance's parents loved him too much to let him go. But too much or not enough, that love wasn't *unconditional.*

She couldn't deny that she understood the fear and the longing in his parents' desire to keep their son safe. As much as she admired his talent, his courage, his convictions, she hated the thought of him putting his life in danger.

She'd already felt a fraction of what it would be like to

lose him when she heard the news reports. But that was before she'd truly gotten to know him beyond the sexy, confident man she'd had such an entirely out-of-character fling with. She'd seen his moments of doubt and vulnerability, how the horrors of what he'd witnessed through his lens haunted him. She'd seen him completely in over his head with little Kyle and loving every minute of it.

She'd seen the kind of man—the kind of husband, the kind of father—he could be, and she didn't know how to protect herself from that Chance McClaren.

But then she thought of their weekend together. How being with Chance had made her feel reckless, wild and unafraid. If making love had made her brave enough to take a chance for a weekend, was it possible that loving him with her whole heart might make her strong enough to take a chance on the love of a lifetime?

He pushed away from the steps, his long strides carrying him a few yards before he stopped short. His tall, broad-shouldered form was little more than a shadowed silhouette, but tension radiated from his unnatural stillness. Alexa sensed the slightest movement might send him running. She had an idea of what might make him stay if she had the courage to be the woman she was always meant to be.

"It's getting cold," he said abruptly. "I'll walk you back to the cottage."

Slowly lowering her feet to the ground, she stood and walked over to his side. She ran a hand down his arm, waiting until his muscles relaxed to link her fingers with his. They were silent on the walk back, but the slow pace did little to ease the raw energy building inside him.

Though she had given in to his insistence that she sleep in the bedroom, the cottage was small. The thin wall between them did little to block out the sound of his restless nights, and he was always gone in the morning when she woke. More than once she'd slipped from the bed in the middle of the night to stand by the door, afraid to turn the knob. Knowing if she did, she wouldn't have been inviting Chance into the bedroom, but into her heart.

He stopped on the porch when she tried to draw him inside. "I'm going to go clean up the gazebo. I'll be back later."

Her heart pounding, Alexa swallowed. "Chance?"

He half turned back to her as if caught in a moment of indecision. Stay...or go?

"You asked me my first morning here how I slept the night before. I lied. The truth is, I haven't had a good night's sleep since the last time you were in my bed." Holding his gaze as she repeated him word for word, she added, "I can't close my eyes without imagining you there."

His eyes widened, and this time when he ran, it was back to her. His long strides ate up the distance, his limp almost imperceptible, and her heart trembled a little at what that would mean in the near future. But she didn't want to think about that now. And then Chance kissed her, and she didn't want to think about anything. Not the past or the future. Nothing but the swirling, impatient passion of the present.

She wrapped her arms around his shoulders and held him tight as he backed her toward the cottage. The solid muscle contrasted with the soft cotton shirt, and she couldn't get enough, would never get enough.

He fumbled with the doorknob as if not wanting to let her go for more than a second, and she wasn't sure how they made it to the bedroom. By the time they crossed the threshold, she had already stripped off his shirt, laying claim to the smooth skin of his shoulders and his hair-roughened chest.

He helped pull her sweater over her head, the skirt down her hips, and then he froze. A split second of uncertainty washed over Alexa, leaving her feeling, well, exposed in nothing but her black lace bra and panties. But then she realized what had captured his attention as his gaze locked on the swell of her belly, the low-cut lace flaunting the roundness.

A brief hesitation held them both spellbound. And then Chance stroked his fingers over her stomach. Her muscles trembled at the light touch, but it was the look of amazement that shook her to her soul. "Chance..." Her voice broke, and Alexa knew her heart might soon follow, but she had no choice. She was falling in love with him.

He swallowed hard and then lifted his gaze to hers. "Alexa, I have a confession to make..." Despite the weighted moment and the seriousness of his words, a teasing light entered his eyes. "You're not gonna get a good night sleep with me in your bed tonight."

"Something tells me you'll make it up to me. And besides," she said with a tempting, tender smile as she pressed his palm to her belly and their baby, "it's not like you can get me more pregnant."

His eyes glowed as he lowered his head and brushed his mouth across hers. Alexa reveled in a hint of the dessert that tasted a hundred times richer on his lips than it had on the fork.

But unlike a sweet tooth, which could be sated, every kiss made Alexa's hunger grow. She was dizzy and aching by the time Chance brushed aside the bit of lace undergarments, then stepped away to strip off the rest of his clothes. Eager to be back in his embrace, she threw her arms around his broad shoulders as he lowered her to the bed.

Bracing his weight above her, he asked, "Is this...okay?"

His caring and concern touched her heart as thoroughly and powerfully as his caresses touched her body. "More than okay," she reassured him with a breathless gasp. "It's perfect."

When he lowered himself between her thighs, thrusting inside, she felt whole. And when he took her in his arms, it was like coming home. Chance rocked against her, each shallow thrust striking sparks of desire inside and out. Pleasure spiraled out of control, cresting and breaking. Alexa clung to him, wrapping her limbs around him as he shuddered and rode his own wave of release.

Gradually the rhythm rippling their bodies slowed, then stopped, but still Alexa refused to let go, wanting the moment to last. Wanting to hold on tight...and to never have to let go.

Years ago, Chance had brought Lisette home to Medford to meet his family. She'd acted as though his hometown and the entire state of Oregon, for that matter, was some kind of untamed wilderness. He could only imagine how she would have dismissed the tiny, quaint town of Clearville in a single glance.

Only a few weeks ago, he would have thought Alexa might do the same, but the more time they spent together, the more he realized how different she was from his ex. In a short amount of time, she'd already become a part of his sister's inner circle of friends. Sharing ideas with Rory on decorating the hotel for the upcoming holidays. Meeting with Lindsay to discuss events planned by the chamber of commerce. Planning to talk with Theresa and Jarrett Deeks about fund-raising ideas for the couple's horse rescue.

Hell, she fit in better than he did.

From the orchard where visitors could pick their own apples, to the horse-drawn carriage rides through town, to the dozens of tiny shops along Main Street, she lived it all with a wide-eyed enjoyment that grabbed hold of his heart and wouldn't let go.

Showing her around the town brought back memories of how much he loved coming to Clearville as a kid. The hours he'd spent exploring everything from the rugged coastline to the towering redwoods to the acres of farmland. And now, seeing it all again as an adult with a photographer's eye…

"I told you," Alexa had said at one point as they walked along the beach, her blue-gray eyes laughing at him as she lifted a hand to keep her blond hair from blowing in the ocean breeze. She wore a cream-colored sweater over a pale-blue-and-white-striped dress, the soft material molding to the curves of her breasts and the curve of their baby.

"What?"

"That you should have brought your camera with you. You're dying to capture all of this. Your index finger has been twitching all afternoon," she teased.

"It has not," he argued, even though she was right. Though he'd never given serious thought to nature photography, with such vast and varied landscapes all around him, it was almost impossible not to try to line up the perfect shot in his mind's eye.

But he'd refused to bring his camera.

Something was happening to him here. Something about his time in Clearville was softening his focus, changing the angle of his lens.

What had Alexa said when looking through the wedding pictures he'd taken?

Seeing these pictures makes me feel like I'm seeing the real you.

For so long he'd narrowed his gaze on the turbulent moments of life and human nature. Capturing a darkness t many people wanted to turn a blind eye to. His work was important, yet after such a short time around his family, around Alexa, he could feel himself losing his edge. He was relaxing, breathing easier, slowing down.

All fine and good for recovering from his injuries. But that kind of lax attitude could get him killed in the field. He couldn't just expect to pick up his guard along with his camera before heading out to the next job.

Over the past half decade, he'd traveled an average of nine months out of the year. The grueling schedule was starting to pay off. His articles were gaining recognition; he was being offered more and more choice assignments. Could he really walk away from his career just as he was nearing the pinnacle he'd strived to reach for so long?

He didn't have an answer to that question, and he was running out of time. His leg was getting stronger every day. His editor was expecting him to be on a plane by the end of the month to take an assignment he hadn't told Alexa about yet. And Alexa was expecting—

Alexa was expecting his child and, he feared, more than he knew how to give.

Stepping closer, he watched her eyes widen with sensual awareness as he bent his head toward hers. "There's something else I want to capture, and I'd rather not have a camera in my hands while I do this…"

He pulled her into his arms and kissed her then, the salt from the ocean air and pure seduction of her lips beneath her own wiping away any thoughts of leaving. "Or this…"

Alexa's startled laugh turned into a playful scream as he scooped her up into his arms and charged toward the frigid surf.

"Thank you again for inviting me out to the ranch," Alexa told Theresa Deeks as the two of them stood outside a corral, watching as Jarrett worked with one of the Rockin' R's horses.

Along with running the horse rescue, the Deekses offered rental cabins for tourists and visitors who wanted to stay outside of town. From what she could see, they had picked a prime location. Towering redwoods lined the surrounding acres, climbing toward the clouds overhead and extending to the mountains in the distance. A sense of peace filled the property, with the rustle of the wind in the trees and the whinny of a horse the only sounds.

Alexa wished she could grab hold of some of that peace for herself. The past few days with Chance had been some of the happiest of her life. She loved walking down Main Street with him, strolling through the Victorian shops the town was known for; holding his hand while they explored the grounds around Hillcrest; soaking up the sounds of the ocean as they combed the beach for seashells.

And the nights…she had no doubt about how much he wanted her when they made love or even in the quiet moments after when he would reach for her in his sleep.

On the outside, everything was…perfect. But beneath the surface, she sensed something was wrong. Little ripples of unease that she worried hid turbulent water below. Like that morning when she'd asked him to come to the ranch with her. Confidence had filled his sexy smile as he kissed her. "You've got this, Alexa. You don't need me."

Maybe she didn't *need* him, but she wanted him to be with her…and she was very much afraid he already wanted to be somewhere else.

"I should be thanking you," Theresa was saying. "The rodeo benefit was a first for us, and we're thrilled with the results. The donations and the percentage of the take from the ticket sales were more than what we hoped for, but then trying to come up with the best way to use that money…"

She shook her head, her dark ponytail swinging back and forth. "You wouldn't think that would be a problem, but deciding how to spend the money was almost as daunting as not having the money to spend."

Refocusing on her reason for going out to the ranch, Alexa said, "It's always hard especially for a smaller rescue operation like the one you and Jarrett run here. Trying to figure out where your greatest need is, well, it's like triage," Alexa said. As a nurse, Theresa would be very familiar with the concept.

"That's exactly what it is," Theresa said, her eyes lighting in realization as the two of them walked back to the stables. "I can't believe I never thought of it that way, but with the financial plan you came up with, I feel like I have a better handle on where to go from here. And I love the idea of an open house."

In the past few months since the benefit, Jarrett and Theresa had already put some of the money raised to good use, making improvements to the stables, stocking up on feed and taking in more horses. "You've made some amazing changes already," Alexa said. "From the way you described it, most of Clearville turned out for the rodeo. I'm sure people would love to see how you've put their donations to use, and it's important to keep the rescue in the public eye. I know you're hoping to make the rodeo an annual event, but you can't rely on one fund-raiser to support the rescue for an entire year."

As Theresa led the way into the stables, the two of them discussed contacting local businesses to see who might be willing to volunteer or donate food, entertainment and advertising for the event. Alexa figured the ranch and the horses themselves would be a huge draw. The sights and sounds of the stables were as unfamiliar as the rich, earthy scents of hay and horses, but she was fascinated by the beautiful animals eyeing her curiously from their stalls.

"I don't believe my eyes!"

Startled by the sound of a feminine voice, Alexa turned to see a blonde smiling her delight as she walked down the concrete aisle between the stalls. "I swear that is the first designer outfit I have seen in the six months since I moved here!"

Not completely unprepared for the trip out to the Rockin' R, Alexa had worn boots. But the black suede pair she'd matched with her black, wide-legged trousers and emerald green ribbed turtleneck sweater were nothing like Theresa's or this woman's sturdy, well-worn footwear.

She couldn't help but smile, though, at the other woman's enthusiasm. "Well, you seemed to have survived despite the lack of high-end fashion."

"Never let it be said I can't rock a pair of Wranglers," she said with a full turn that would have done a model on a catwalk proud. Sighing as she ran her palms down the untucked red-and-black flannel shirt. "But I do miss the opportunity to dress up more often."

"You have to excuse my sister-in-law. She's still adjusting to life in a small town where you buy clothes at the same place where you pick up your groceries," Theresa said with a smile at the younger woman.

Alexa hoped she managed to hide her surprise. She'd been charmed by Jarrett Deeks's soft-spoken Midwestern drawl, as well as with his obvious devotion to his dark-haired wife. She wouldn't have imagined that this petite blonde with corkscrew curls and outspoken sass would be related to him.

"Summer, this is Alexa Mayhew. She's a friend of Rory McClaren's."

Summer's cornflower blue eyes widened. "Oh, my

gosh! Do you know Chance McClaren? I am one of his biggest fans. I keep hoping I'll run into him in town, but so far, no luck."

Alexa didn't want to feel jealous that this beautiful, wide-eyed woman wanted the chance to meet her idol. Didn't want to think of the adoring fans he had around the world.

As Summer went on about the color and composition of his photos, Alexa realized the other woman hadn't exaggerated about being a true fan—and not simply of Chance as a handsome, successful photojournalist, but of his photographs.

Jarrett called his sister's name from the doorway to the stables, and the bubbly blonde headed out to give a riding lesson, but not before asking if Alexa would introduce her to Chance.

"Sorry about that," Theresa said as she led the way into the small office in the corner of the stables. "Summer can be a bit exuberant at times, but that's why we love her. And while I'll admit I'm a little biased, she truly is a talented photographer. She's taken all of the pictures for the rescue's website and for our Home, Sweet Home wall."

Theresa waved a hand to the space behind the desk and the collage of horses posing with their adoptive families. But it was another picture that caught Alexa's eye. One of a denim-and-flannel-dressed cowboy hovering midair above a ferocious black bull. "Is that Jarrett?"

"That it is," Theresa confirmed. "Back in his bull riding days."

After watching the cowboy in the corral for only a few moments, Alexa had seen his quiet confidence and skill with the horses, but this—this was something else. "Isn't that...dangerous?"

"That it is," the brunette repeated. "Fortunately, that

was back in the days before we met. Before a pretty serious injury put an end to his rodeo career."

"What would you do," Alexa asked, her pulse suddenly pounding in her ears, "if that injury healed to the point where Jarrett wanted to ride again?"

Theresa exhaled a breath. "Boy, I've never really thought about that before." Leaning back against the edge of the desk, she said, "I didn't know Jarrett when he was competing, but I have an idea of how important it was to him, how much he loved it. Giving it up was hard on him, and if he hadn't turned his attention to rescuing horses, I hate to think of the darker paths he might have chosen. So, even though I know how dangerous bull riding can be, even though a part of me would always, well, hate it, to be perfectly honest, I'd have to do all I could to support him.

"Maybe my own career as a trauma nurse gives me a different perspective. I know how quickly life can change. From illness, to injuries, to accidents, you never know what might happen, no matter how careful you are. For me, it was a car accident."

"Were you seriously injured?"

"Seriously enough," Theresa admitted. "When I first came here, I was still hurting. I honestly didn't know if I would recover to the point where I could go back to the job I loved, and Jarrett was there for me. He had a faith in me that I didn't have in myself."

"But that's not the same thing, is it? Nursing doesn't come with the dangers of being a photo...I mean, bull rider," Alexa amended at the last second.

Theresa's knowing smile acknowledged the slip, but she merely said, "True. But at the time, going back to work meant going back to St. Louis. His life was here and mine, I thought, was there. So, as clichéd as it might sound, Jarrett loved me enough to let me go, which in the end is what gave me the strength to stay."

Letting go of someone she loved... Alexa felt she'd lived her whole life letting go. Could she find a way to hold on to the hope that she might be reason enough for Chance to stay?

Chapter Fourteen

"Are you ready for this?" Chance asked as he pulled into a parking space and cut the engine.

Sucking in a deep breath, Alexa gazed at the three-story building in front of them. "I didn't expect to be so nervous," she admitted, her hands tightening on the seat belt without releasing the latch.

After the tour of the Rockin' R ranch, Theresa had invited Alexa to stay for lunch. Over sandwiches piled high with shaved roast beef, lettuce and tomato, the other woman had asked about Alexa's pregnancy. Before she knew it, Alexa was sharing more personal details than she ever would have expected to with a perfect stranger. But Theresa's compassion and calm demeanor made her easy to talk to.

Maybe it was all part of the pretty nurse's bedside manner even though they'd both been sitting at the kitchen table at the time.

And when Alexa admitted she'd had to cancel her ultrasound appointment back home after her stay in Clearville had lasted longer than planned, Theresa had recommended an obstetrician at the medical clinic in nearby Redfield.

"Will they be able to tell if it's a boy or a girl?" Chance asked.

"Possibly, if the baby cooperates and is in the right position. Do you want to know what we're having?"

"I'm not sure. I think…I'd rather be surprised. To find out in that moment when we first meet our child whether we have a son or a daughter."

In that moment…

After pulling the key from the ignition, Chance climbed from the SUV, but Alexa couldn't bring herself to move as he rounded the hood to open her door.

His eyebrows rose when he realized she was still buckled into her seat. Concern filled his expression as he crouched by her side. "Hey, everything okay? You're not that worried about the scan, are you?"

"No, I'm fine." Alexa shook her head, and she unbuckled her seat belt and grabbed her purse. Her hands trembled as she held tight to the leather strap. Not with fear, but with the faint stirrings of hope. She'd been steeling herself from the beginning to face going through labor alone.

But now, with Chance making it sound as though he wanted to be in the delivery room with her, she pressed a hand to her trembling stomach. She wanted him there. She *desperately* wanted him to be there, but if she started to count on that, to count on him, and if he let her down…

Whenever his cell phone rang and he stepped out of the room to take the call, her heart practically leaped from her chest. Each time, she waited for him to tell her he was taking another assignment, biting her lip to keep from begging him not to go. So far her fears had been unfounded as Chance would slip the phone back into his pocket without saying a word. But Alexa knew the day would come, and she wondered if he had any idea that when he left he'd be taking her heart with him.

Chance was silent as they headed toward the clinic's glass doors. When Alexa turned toward a large directory near the elevators, he guided her down a hall to the left.

"The obstetrician's office is this way."

Her eyebrows rose. "And you know that...how?"

"Because," he explained, "my physical therapist is a few doors down."

Which was true, but Chance had probably paid more attention to the comings and goings from the baby doctor's office than any healthy, single man should. He'd been attending therapy down the hall long enough to have seen a few hugely pregnant women arrive for an appointment one week only to return soon afterward with a newborn infant in their arms.

More than once, he'd lent a hand to a woman struggling to hold an infant in one arm while maneuvering an awkward baby carrier or enormous stroller with her free hand. And he'd wondered where their husbands, the fathers of their children were. Why were so many of the women trying to handle all this alone?

The way Alexa will be alone when you go on assignment.

Guilt tightened around his chest, making it almost impossible to breathe. The trapped, suffocating feeling was the same one he used to get on his visits home. When his mother's not-so-subtle hints about settling down and his father's more pointed comments about wanting Chance to take over the family business had sent him running.

And he'd never stopped.

For years, he'd been racing toward his goals—tracking down an elusive source, following the story wherever led, grabbing hold of the acclaim, the awards, the highest achievements in his field.

But when he thought of leaving Alexa, of leaving their baby, he didn't feel like he was running toward his future. But more like he was running away from his past.

Heading toward the reception area, Alexa smiled at the young woman behind the desk. "I'm here for an appointment with Dr. Fitzgerald. My doctor in LA was supposed to email my records."

"Yes, Ms. Mayhew. We have them here. In looking over them, the doctor noticed some…gaps in the father's medical history?" The receptionist glanced at Chance but clearly didn't want to make any assumptions.

His jaw tightened, not as concerned about the gaps in his history as he was about the gaps in his child's future.

Embarrassment colored Alexa's cheeks as she reached for the clipboard, but Chance beat her to it. "Let's fill in some of those blanks."

The receptionist offered him a relieved smile before he and Alexa took two seats in the corner of the waiting room. Sitting ramrod straight in the chair beside him, her hands were locked around her purse strap in a death grip. "I'm sorry," she said quietly.

"Don't, Alexa. I told you before, what's done is done."

But as he filled out the forms, spelling out the details of his recent surgeries word for word, he couldn't help wondering what might have happened if Alexa had gotten ahold of him in the days before the bombing.

If he had dropped everything to go to be with her then, he might not have been injured. He would have known about her pregnancy from the start, but then what? Had he been perfectly healthy over the past three months, did he really think he would have turned down another assignment? He certainly wouldn't have come to Clearville. He wouldn't be sitting at Alexa's side now.

Without the months of recovery, time he'd spent with memories of Alexa filling his waking and sleeping hours, he might never had slowed down enough to consider a life beyond the one he'd always known.

He'd never been a big believer in fate, but… Reaching over, he grabbed Alexa's slender hand. "Some things are meant to be."

She returned his reassuring squeeze, and Chance didn't want to let go. Not even when a nurse called her name a few minutes later. The woman explained that the doctor would perform an exam first, and they would bring Chance back to the room for the ultrasound.

Finished with the forms, Chance had nothing to do but wait—and pace—while Alexa was with the doctor. He stopped abruptly when a turn by the reception desk had him nearly bumping into a very pregnant woman who had just signed in. "Sorry, I'm—"

"A first-time dad?" she guessed with a sympathetic smile.

Running a hand through his hair, he sighed. "That obvious?"

"It's been a while since we had our first, but I still recognize the signs."

Two months ago had anyone told him he would be talking babies and pregnancy with a total stranger, he would have laughed his head off. But as he helped lower the mom-to-be into one of the waiting-room chairs, he asked, "What number is this for you?"

"Our third. Another boy." She rolled her eyes. "Heaven help me." But her dreamy smile as she rested her hands on her large belly told another story.

"You look familiar." Cocking her head to one side, she said, "I know! You're Rory McClaren's brother, aren't y—

I work at a florist shop in Clearville, and we've done the flowers for some of Hillcrest's weddings."

"Oh, right." Great, now he was talking babies, flowers and weddings with a perfect stranger. He may as well forfeit his man card for all eternity. "Chance McClaren."

"I'm Nina Kincaid. It's nice to meet you."

The name rang a bell. Nina… Oh, yeah, this was Lindsay's sister-in-law and the guest of honor for the surprise baby shower at the hotel next weekend.

Did Alexa have friends in LA who would throw such a party for her? Friends who would look after her? Between her absentee and neglectful parents and a grandmother more interested in grooming a successor than raising a granddaughter, Chance could understand why Alexa didn't want to raise their child the same way. He even agreed with her, but he hated the thought of her going back to LA to live alone.

At least in Clearville Rory and Evie were around. His Aunt Evelyn had recently finished her cancer treatments and hoped to be back at work by the beginning of the New Year. Heck, even his parents were only a few hours away, too close for his comfort, but he had no doubt his mother especially was dying for a grandchild to love and—

"Whoa, there, Dad!" Nina advised, though her voice sounded far away thanks to the crazy whirlwind of thoughts circling inside his brain. "You look like you're about to pass out."

Fighting the dizzying sensation, Chance sank back against the waiting-room chair. He wasn't actually hoping Alexa might stay in Clearville… Was he?

Chance didn't know how many photographs he'd taken ver the years, how many pictures he'd studied. But noth-, nothing, compared to seeing the ultrasound of his baby. He—or she—was perfect. The sex didn't matter any more than it mattered that the baby's features were little more than an indistinct blur.

This was his child.

Seeing the pictures, hearing the baby's heartbeat made it all...real in a way it hadn't been before then. He could take a thousand photos, ten thousand photos, and none of them could compare to the one he held in his hand.

"What do you think about Kylee?"

"Hmm?"

Seated together on the couch, Chance held Alexa's feet in his lap. He idly pressed his thumb into her arch. After the past few days, he'd discovered the wonder of her body again and again. He'd made a study of where to touch to make her laugh, to make her gasp, to make her moan.

But now his fingers stilled as the truth of his thoughts hit hard. Nothing would ever matter more than Alexa and their baby. And yet what was he supposed to do? Quit his job? Live off the Mayhew fortune? Everything inside him rebelled at the idea. Call him old-fashioned or chauvinistic, but he wanted to be a man who would support his family. And even if money wasn't an issue, he still craved the challenge and excitement his career offered. So not just a chauvinist, but a selfish one, as well.

"What do you think about Clearville?" he asked, still focused on the possibility that had followed him from the obstetrician's office.

Looking up from the book in her lap, an amused smile tipped her lips. Her face lit with laughter, the sound easing some of the pressure in his chest. "Well, I know parents who have named their children Paris or London, but I'm not sure I want to go with Clearville."

At his confused frown, she held up the book so he co~ see the title and be reminded that they were suppo̶sed ~

talking about baby names. "Sorry." He shook his head, realizing how far his mind had strayed, but he wasn't ready to let go. Taking the book from her, he set it aside on the coffee table. "We can talk baby names for the next four months, but what do you think about moving to Clearville?"

"Moving? Here?" Her eyes widened at the thought, but Chance was on a roll.

"I know Clearville doesn't have as much to offer as LA, but it's a great small town." She'd already told him that she didn't want their child raised by nannies and private tutors the way she had been. "A great place to raise a family. You'd still be able to see your grandmother when you go back for foundation events, but think about how you've already become a part of the community here. And between my sister and Evie and my parents, you'd have family nearby."

Planting her palms against the cushions, Alexa sat up straight and pulled her feet from his lap. "Your family, Chance. Not mine."

They could be.

The thought echoed in his mind. He'd blown that first proposal, but he'd been waiting for an opportunity to ask Alexa a second time to marry him. But now he wouldn't have to. She'd already given her answer.

"Oh, this looks wonderful!" Lindsay Kincaid said as she, Rory and Alexa stepped into the parlor room decorated for her sister-in-law's baby shower.

A large circle of chairs, each tied with a cluster of blue balloons and matching bows, surrounded a small love seat—the place of honor for the mom-to-be. Two tables ²overed in blue-and-white-striped tablecloths had been set against the dark walnut-paneled walls—one in anticipa-of all the baby gifts, and another holding a gorgeous

cake shaped like a cradle and an assortment of finger sandwiches, fresh cut fruits and vegetables, and a large bowl of
punch. A sign overhead proclaimed It's a Boy!, and large
boxes, mimicking a child's colorful toy blocks, spelled out
Wyatt, the name Nina and her husband, Bryce, had picked
out for their third son.

"Not that I expected anything less." Turning to Alexa,
Lindsay said, "My husband, Ryder, and I were married at
Hillcrest, and Rory did an amazing job!"

"It was so romantic," Rory agreed, "but I can't take
credit for that. You and Ryder are the ones who made the
day special. Anyone just looking could see how completely
crazy you are for each other."

Lindsay's pretty face glowed with an almost secretive
smile. The smile of a woman in love. A few months ago,
Alexa might not have recognized it for what it was. She
did now, seeing the expression every time she looked in
the mirror. But unlike Lindsay, she also saw the doubt reflected in her own eyes. She loved Chance, and while she
couldn't deny he cared for her, caring wasn't love.

Pushing the troubling thought from her mind, Alexa
waved a hand at the cluster of chairs. "It looks like you're
expecting quite a turnout. Did you invite half the town?"

"That's the thing about living in Clearville. Everybody
knows everybody." Rory rolled her eyes, but her wide
smile embraced the town. "When you have an event like
this, it's really hard to pick and choose who to invite…"

"So you end up inviting everybody," Lindsay chimed
in. "We had thought of having the party at my in-laws'.
They have a great backyard for get-togethers, but then we
worried about the weather and thought we'd be better off
playing it safe and partying here at Hillcrest.

"And just think," Lindsay added, "it won't be too long
before we're holding one of these showers for you, Ale

"I, um, yes," Alexa stuttered, taken aback by the other woman's assumption that she would still be in Clearville come spring.

But as other guests began to arrive, Alexa was surprised to realize how many of the women she had already met and how many of them she was already starting to think of as friends. Along with Rory, Lindsay and Sophia, Debbie Pirelli, Sophia's sister-in-law and the owner of the Sugar & Spice café, was also in attendance. Alexa had been back for lunch at the café several times. Having met Debbie, Alexa couldn't imagine a better name for the bubbly blonde's business. Debbie was sweet, but with a sharp sense of humor that had had Alexa laughing over her chicken salad sandwich.

These women had welcomed Alexa into their circle of friendship, making her feel at home in a way she had never felt in LA even though she'd been born and raised there. Was Chance's idea of staying in Clearville really such a crazy one?

If only he hadn't made it sound like *she* would be the only one living there. But hadn't he already told her it didn't matter where he lived? After all, Chance wasn't looking for somewhere to call home. Anywhere he chose would be little more than a way station, a brief layover between flights.

And while she did appreciate how everyone had welcomed her, she couldn't help thinking he wanted to surround her with people who would *be there* so he wouldn't feel so guilty about being gone. She didn't want to add to his guilt, but she also didn't want to be a responsibility he handed off to another relative.

Been there, grown up like that.

She'd seen the disappointment in his expression when

she'd turned him down, but it wasn't Clearville that didn't have enough to offer. It was Chance.

"How are you getting Nina here without giving away the surprise?"

"That was Rory's idea," Lindsay said. "She's asked Nina to come by to give her some ideas for floral arrangements and decorations for the hotel for Christmas."

"What can I say?" Rory asked. "I'm more devious than I look."

"She'd have to be to con me into being here."

The three women turned in unison at the sound of the deep voice behind them. Alexa's heart gave a little leap at the very sight of him, and then sucked in a quick breath as she swore she felt a second flutter of movement…this time in her belly. She didn't know if it was possible, but she didn't question how her body—how her baby—responded in recognition of this man.

He was dressed in black jeans and a matching long-sleeved T-shirt, but if he thought the muted color would help him move unobtrusively among the female guests at the shower, he'd failed miserably. The soft cotton molded to broad shoulders, and the things the worn denim did for his muscular thighs and firm backside should be illegal. He looked so masculine in the purely feminine setting of the baby shower that the sheer contrast was enough to set Alexa's head spinning.

"Ha!" Rory exclaimed. "The only guy in a room full of women? Most men would consider themselves lucky."

At the word *lucky*, Chance met Alexa's gaze with a wink. "You have no idea how lucky I feel," he said before excusing himself to set up his camera.

A few minutes later, Alexa smiled as she saw another familiar face. "Summer! I almost didn't recognize you without the cowboy boots and Wranglers."

The blonde beauty held out the skirt of the geometric-print dress she wore. "A baby shower might not be an haute couture event, but I'll take what I can get."

"Is Theresa coming to the party?"

"I'm sorry to say she's not. She's been fighting the flu and didn't want to risk getting Nina or anyone else sick."

"Oh, that's too bad."

"My brother's taking good care of her. Theresa won't be able to sneeze without Jarrett there to 'God bless you.'" Summer shifted the nylon strap on her shoulder, and Alexa realized the other woman wasn't carrying a purse. Instead, a camera bag rested against her hip.

"You brought your camera."

"Oh, yeah. I take it with me everywhere. I'd feel naked without it."

Other than working at Hillcrest events, Alexa hadn't seen Chance with his camera. Was he still trying to separate his career from their life together? Or did he fear she would one day make him choose? A sick feeling settled in her stomach even as she watched from across the room as one of the women laughed at something he said.

What was it Theresa had told her?

Jarrett loved me enough to let me go.

Alexa didn't know if she had that kind of strength, but she had to find a way to love Chance McClaren—the photojournalist—as much as she loved Chance McClaren the man.

An idea of how she might start to do that sprang to mind, and she linked her arm through Summer's. "Well, I'm glad you came. After all, there's someone here you've been dying to meet."

"Looks like you just might survive."

Chance grinned at Alexa's whispered teasing, barely

audible over the constant chatter and laughter filling the parlor. "Barely. I need to talk to Rory about hazard pay."

He'd overheard more about pregnancy pains, birthing woes and breastfeeding than he ever wanted to know. And yet as Alexa's now obvious baby bump reminded him, he needed to learn. As the only man in the group, he'd also been an easy target.

"Yes, I can see a war wound. Right about here..." She reached up with a pale blue napkin, wiped at his cheek and held up the burnt-orange lipstick smudge for him to see.

Pointing at the evidence, he said, "Okay, now that was thanks to Nina's great-aunt who's a heck of a lot faster than she looks." He leaned closer to murmur, "And if we weren't trapped in this room full of women, I would be kissing you right now."

"Hitting on a pregnant lady at a baby shower, are you?"

"Only my pregnant lady."

A blush lit her cheeks at his possessive claim, and Chance stopped his teasing to take her hands in his and lace her slender fingers through his own. "Thank you, Alexa, for suggesting that Summer take over as Hillcrest's photographer. She showed me some of the work she's done on the website for her brother's ranch. She might not have much professional experience, but she definitely has talent."

Watching Summer greet almost every guest like a long-lost friend, he gave a quick laugh. "Hell, she'll probably be better at it than I was anyway."

"That is not true. Your pictures were amazing. Any couple would be lucky to have you photograph their wedding."

"Maybe but..." His words trailed off as he realized he'd spoken them before.

Alexa's mind obviously went back to that same place

and time, standing outside the cottage that first day. "This isn't your job."

"Alexa..." He searched her expression, trying to determine if he was seeing only what he wanted to see. Had Alexa somehow made peace with his career? Could she accept him for the man he was and understand the ambition and passion that drove him?

He didn't have a chance to ask as the guest of honor called for everyone's attention. "I can't thank you all enough for this." Tears filled Nina's eyes as she gazed around the room at her friends and family. "It was such a wonderful surprise, and I—I—"

"Nina?" Concern filled Lindsay's voice as her sister-in-law stopped on a sharp gasp. "Are you okay?"

"Oh!" She sucked in a breath as she braced a hand low against her belly. "Oh, my goodness... I think—I think I'm in labor."

"Okay, Dad, are you ready for this?"

Oh, thank God! Chance glanced around the waiting room, looking for a man who might be Nina's husband. He still wasn't sure how he'd ended up at the maternity ward with a woman he barely knew, but from the moment Nina made her stunning announcement in the middle of the shower, he'd been acting on instinct.

Labor equaled the delivery room at a hospital in his world, and he'd done everything he could to get Nina there as quickly as possible. He ignored her suggestion that Lindsay drive her home first to grab the overnight bag she had packed and waiting for her scheduled delivery. He overrode Lindsay's suggestion that they try to get ahold of Bryce to pick Nina up at the hotel. He shook off Rory's quiet suggestion that they call 9-1-1 and wait for an ambulance.

His plan was clear. Labor=hospital. Do not pass go. Do not collect two hundred dollars.

Lindsay and Nina's younger sister had ridden along, Jessie sitting in the back of the SUV with Nina while Lindsay rode shotgun. At first he'd been glad to have the two other women along to keep Nina calm... Until Lindsay kept warning him to slow down and not drive like a bat out of hell when he was only doing fifty miles an hour, and Jessie and Nina were bickering over whether emailed thank-you notes for the baby gifts were appropriate or far too impersonal.

He spent the forty-five-minute drive to the hospital in Redfield with his hands clenched on the wheel, fighting the urge to remind the three of them that a baby was on its way!

And then Nina had wanted to walk into the hospital when she clearly needed a wheelchair to get her inside as soon as possible. When she slowed to breathe through a contraction, Chance had put an end to her waddling pace and scooped her into his arms.

He wanted to hand off responsibility the moment the doors swept open, but even after telling the nurse at the admittance desk *repeatedly* that a woman was in labor, said nurse repeatedly told *him* to have the patient fill out a stack of forms at least an inch thick.

Chance had been in enough hospitals over the years to know they were nothing like depicted on television, but he would have given just about anything for a white-coated physician to sweep Nina up onto a gurney and rush her down a hallway yelling "Stat!" and "Code Blue!" at the top of their lungs.

But the only doctor in sight was the one looking directly at him...

Oh, crap.

Chance glanced down at Nina, but she was breathing through another contraction and gripping his hand like a vise. And while he was glad to see she was finally taking this whole thing seriously, he needed her to throw him a lifeline here. "No! I'm not the dad. At least not her dad. I mean, her baby's dad."

Lindsay had been trying to get ahold of Bryce, but Nina's husband had been in on the surprise baby shower and had taken their two boys off on a father-son adventure to free their mom up for the afternoon. Chance's panicked gaze shot across the waiting room to where Lindsay was pacing back and forth. Judging by the cell still raised to her ear, she hadn't yet reached Nina's husband.

"That's okay. We have all kinds of relatives and friends of the family acting as a birthing coach."

Birthing coach? If not for the killer grip Nina had on his hand, Chance had the feeling he would have bolted from the waiting room, in his haste bowling over the slightly wild-eyed man coming through the automatic doors. Only what kind of man would he be if he left a pregnant woman in need? What kind of father would he be if he left the woman pregnant with his child?

"Nina, babe!"

The dark-haired man who'd rushed into the waiting room dropped to his knees in front of Nina's chair. "Hey, sweetheart. You doing okay?"

Opening her eyes, Nina smiled at her husband as if he'd been at her side the whole time. "Oh, Bryce! Lindsay threw me the most amazing baby shower. You should see all of the cute presents…" A troubled frown tightened her forehead. "Lindsay, what did you do with the presents?"

"They're still at the hotel, sweetie." Her mission accomplished, Lindsay had stuck her phone back in her purse.

"Well, we can't just leave them there. Bryce, you should go—"

"No!" Chance and Bryce shouted out in unison.

Carefully extracting his hand from Nina's, Chance transferred her bone-crushing grip to her husband. "I'll go back to the hotel and make sure the gifts are all taken care of. You stay here and...focus on having that baby."

Catching Lindsay's eye, he asked, "You'll be okay here?"

She nodded. "We have a ton of family on the way. We'll be fine. Thank you, Chance. I think this goes pretty far beyond the realm of baby shower photographer."

"Now Rory really owes me that hazard pay."

The pretty blonde laughed and patted his shoulder "You should be thanking her."

"Thanking her?" He was hoping he didn't throttle his sister the next time he saw her.

Tipping her head toward Bryce and Nina huddled together in a world of their own, she said, "You can consider it practice. For when you *are* the baby's dad."

After the exciting finish to the baby shower, Alexa stayed and helped Rory move all of the presents into a small storage room and clean up the parlor for the next event. "You do know how to throw one heck of a baby shower," Alexa told Rory once they sank into a pair of chairs to finish off the last of the cake.

"Here at Hillcrest, we aim to please."

Lindsay had called earlier to reassure them that Chance had gotten Nina to the hospital and that Bryce had shown up not long after. It would still be a while before the baby made his appearance into the world, but the doctors were confident everything would go well.

"Note to self," Alexa said as she dug into the stra

berry and cream cake. "Have baby shower well before the due date."

"Hmm, good idea. Any chance that there will be a bridal shower before that baby shower?"

Nearly choking on the bite of cake, Alexa reached for her cup of punch. Buying some time, she sipped at the sweet, berry-flavored drink. "Did Chance tell you he asked me to marry him?"

Rory nodded. "And that you turned him down."

"I know Chance wants to be a good father to our baby, but we won't have to get married for that to happen."

"Did you ever wonder if maybe what he really wants is to be a good husband?" Rory reached over and squeezed her hand. "And he does have to get married for that."

Alexa took another drink, but all the punch in the world wouldn't ease the sudden ache in her throat. She knew Chance cared about her, but could she believe that he loved her? Enough to want to marry her even if she wasn't carrying his baby?

What had Chance said about his reasons for not wanting to show his work at Roslynn St. Clare's gallery, about not trusting that the woman was interested in him for his own sake?

I'll never know for sure, will I?

Chapter Fifteen

A drizzling rain accompanied Chance and Alexa to Rory and Jamison's house on Thanksgiving Day. The couple was renting a house outside of town until their own custom home was completed, but Rory had insisted on having the meal at their place. With the windshield wipers a steady, quiet *swoosh* against the glass and the heater blowing at her feet, Alexa should have felt happy, content.

The baby fluttered in her belly, and Chance reached over to smooth his hand over her royal blue cashmere sweater. She didn't know how he seemed to know whenever the baby moved, but he did. A trained observer, Chance made his living watching people, and she probably had some slight tell that gave it away, but it seemed like more than that. Like the baby bonds tying them together were so strong that he just *knew*.

Despite that connection, Alexa couldn't help feeling like he was pulling away from her. He'd been quiet ever sir the baby shower a few days earlier. Lindsay had called to let everyone know that mother and son were doing fine. She'd told Alexa that Chance had been rock solid on the way to the hospital, then sitting at Nina's side until Bryce arrived and staying until the baby was born.

But Chance had hardly said more than a few words since.

Rory welcomed them inside with a hug, accepting the fall floral arrangement of peach roses, burgundy carnations and butterscotch daisies that Chance carried before showing them where to hang their damp coats. The house was cozy and warm, with the sound of a football game playing in the background and the scents of roasting turkey along with a mix of sage and cinnamon and cloves filling the air.

Chance introduced Alexa to Hannah, the adorable daughter of Rory's fiancé, to Evie's parents and to Evie's namesake, Evelyn.

"She's recently gone through chemo," Chance told Alexa quietly in explanation of the colorful scarf wrapped around the slender woman's head. "Her tests have come back negative, and she's cancer-free."

"Definitely something to be thankful for," she whispered back.

"So where's that other niece of mine?" Evelyn asked Rory, who rolled her eyes.

"'Hillcrest House does not take holidays,'" she said in perfect imitation of her somewhat uptight cousin. In a normal tone, she added, "You know Evie, Aunt E. She's so like you."

Evelyn fingered the end of her scarf. "Yes, that's exactly what I'm afraid of."

"If it isn't the man of the hour," Rory's fiancé, Jamison, nounced as he walked into the room, a bottle lifted in a toast. "Everyone's talking about Nina's baby shower and your wild rush to the hospital."

Though he accepted a beer from the other man, Chance shook his head. "I didn't do much, believe me, and thank God for it!"

Wrapping her arms around Jamison's waist, Rory smiled. "Well, clearly Nina and Bryce don't share your opinion. Otherwise why would they have named their baby Wyatt Chance Kincaid?"

"They named him after you?" Alexa looked up at Chance in surprise, but he only shrugged in response, having clearly already heard the news. "Why didn't you tell me?"

His attention focused on the beer in his hand, he shrugged again. "Like I said, it was no big deal. I was just..."

There.

His voice trailed off, the unspoken word a very big deal between the two of them.

He made it through dinner. He sat with his family as his father said grace. He dished up food, passed along plates and compliments as they all dived into the traditional Thanksgiving feast.

But as Rory and Jamison were clearing the dinner plates for dessert, he'd made his escape. Chance couldn't really call it anything else. Stepping out onto the front porch, he sucked in a much-needed lungful of cool, rain-scented air.

The man of the hour.

Chance knew Jamison meant the words as a teasing compliment, but he couldn't help feeling like the other man had hit the time frame right on the dot. An hour, he could do. A lifetime commitment? The kind Bryce had made to Nina? The kind Jamison had made to Rory to his daughter by walking away from a lucrative job as a corporate attorney for life in small town Clearville?

That was something Chance didn't know if he was capable of.

He swallowed hard. How had Alexa described her parents?

They were like Christmas and New Year's and the Fourth of July...

He'd been there for Thanksgiving. If he took the assignment his editor had offered, he'd be lucky to be back with Alexa by Christmas.

The screen door squeaked behind him, and Chance turned to see his father in the doorway. Matthew paused, his split-second hesitation—a hesitation Chance had caused by walking away too many times—hitting hard.

A sudden image of Alexa making pancakes flashed in his mind. She was willing to try, to work hard, not to follow in her parents' selfish, self-absorbed footsteps. Chance wanted to be a good father. Maybe his first step was in trying to be a better son.

"Hey, Dad. Wanna join me?"

Taking Chance up on the offer, Matthew stepped outside. For a moment, the two men stood silently side by side, the drip of rainwater from the eaves the only sound.

"You might want to get back in there before everyone's done fighting over that last piece of pie," Matthew said after a moment.

"I'll head back in after a minute. What about you? You've never been one to turn down dessert."

His father made a sound that might have been a laugh. "And your mother knows it. She cut me a slice so thin, it was practically see-through." He sighed. "I just needed a minute or two for myself."

They'd always had that in common, Chance realized.

A need for space. How many times as a kid had he found his father sitting by himself on their back patio? Matthew had found room to breathe in his own backyard. Chance's need had taken him a hell of a lot farther.

"You're walking better than the last time we were here," his father pointed out.

"Yes."

"I take it that means you'll be heading out on another assignment soon."

Chance opened his mouth to give another affirmative, but the words didn't come. Instead he found himself saying, "I want to explain why I've been—distant these last few months," he began before relaying the conversation he'd overheard in the hospital when they'd thought he was still asleep.

"Chance. What you heard…" His father scrubbed a hand along his jaw before clasping the back of his neck. "It wasn't what you thought you heard."

"I may have been whacked out on pain killers, but I know what I heard." Sucking in a deep breath, he added, "But I also want you to know that I…understand a little better now. When I think of anything happening to Alexa or the baby, well, I guess I can see where you were coming from in wanting to keep me safe."

"Your mother and I weren't just worried about you being safe, Chance. We were worried about you being *happy*," his father stressed.

"You thought I wasn't happy? Dad, I have the career I've always dreamed of, a job I love—"

"Do you?" his father challenged. "Do you still love it? Because over the past few years, your mother and I have both started to wonder. Not that your work has ever suffered. Your photos and the articles you've written are as inspired and as passionate as ever, but we've gotten th feeling that the demands of the job, the constant traveling, have started to take a toll."

Chance wanted to argue just—he feared—for the sake of the argument. Hadn't he started to question his commitment ever since meeting Alexa? Had his parents sensed he was burning out even earlier than that? How many times he had pushed through sheer exhaustion, times when he woke up not sure what country he was in, forget what city, by forcing himself to put one foot in front of the other?

Grabbing the railing with both hands, Chance stared out over the rain-soaked yard. "I can't go back to Medford, Dad. I know how much you love the shop but—"

Matthew interrupted with a snort of laughter. "Get a grip, son. I gave up that dream a long time ago."

"So you aren't still hoping that I'll take over?"

"Is that what I wished for when you first took an interest in photography? Sure. And I know I made the mistake of pushing too hard and ended up pushing you away. You ran off to prove that you could make it as a photographer, and you've done that. We just want you to slow down long enough to ask yourself if the life you're living is still the one you want. Or if maybe there's something more."

A rare smile softened his father's features, and Chance followed his old man's gaze to see a tiny red tricycle parked in the corner of the porch. "Your life has changed, son. You have...so much more to live for."

Chance scowled. "That makes it sound as if I didn't want to live before. Like you think I had some kind of death wish."

"Of course not. But you were reckless. You took chances other journalists wouldn't take because you only had yourself to worry about." He held up a hand before Chance could protest again. "I'm not saying you didn't care about us, but a wife and child are different. Alexa and the baby need you more."

The weight on his chest pressed harder as he admitted, "I don't know if I can just walk away. This life—being a photojournalist, it's the only job I've ever known, the only job I've ever wanted."

Matthew gave another short laugh. "You need to take a look at this." Reaching into his back pocket, he pulled out a piece of paper and unfolded it to reveal a crayon-colored picture of a lopsided, slightly turquoise Christmas tree. "As soon as Hannah saw your mother and me this morning, she wanted us to have this. It's her Christmas list, one I'm pretty sure Rory helped with since Hannah isn't old enough to write yet. But she's old enough to let her soon-to-be grandparents know that she wants a doll, a paint set and some computer game I've never heard of."

"That's great, Dad, but I'm not really sure what that has to do with anything."

After tucking the list back into his pocket, his father asked, "Do you remember what you asked for when you were five?"

"What?" His mother had always been the sentimental type, holding on to pieces of the past he'd long since forgotten, not his father. "No, Dad..."

"When you were five," he said, undeterred by his interruption, "you wanted one of those glow sword things... What were they called?"

"Lightsabers. I wanted a lightsaber."

"Right. And then when you were seven, you wanted a baseball bat and glove, and a Mariners hat."

Chance gave a short laugh, getting caught up in reminiscing despite himself. "We'd gone to a few games that past season, and I thought I was going to be the next Ken Griffey Jr."

"So you didn't always want to be a photojournalist."

"Maybe not, but, Dad, I was never going to be a Jedi warrior—lightsaber or no lightsaber."

"That is not the point." Reaching out, Matthew clapped him on the shoulder. "The point is that dreams change over the years. By the time you were a teenager, you knew you wanted to be a photographer. You followed that dream, you worked hard for that dream and you succeeded. But that was then. This is now. And walking away from that— if it's what you choose to do—that isn't quitting. You aren't giving up on your dreams, Chance. You're just... dreaming bigger."

The bedroom was still dark when Alexa woke, but she knew even before she reached across the mattress what had disturbed her. Chance was no longer lying beside her. Slipping out from beneath the blankets, she walked down the hall. She must have made some slight sound at the sight of him standing in the living room. He spun to face her—a familiar olive drab duffel bag in his hand.

"You're leaving?"

"My editor called—" Chance swore as he dropped the bag and crossed the room to catch her by the shoulders. "You're as white as a sheet."

"I'm fine. I'm just..." Her voice trailed off as he led her to the sofa. Sinking into the cushions, she closed her eyes. The image was seared on her eyelids—Chance holding that same duffel in their Santa Barbara hotel room before telling her he had to go.

"I have to do this, Lexi." Kneeling in front of her, he covered her clenched fists with his hands. "You knew I would take another assignment at some point."

She had known. But seeing him with that duffel bag... It had been her last memory of him, the one she'd carried with her for all those weeks until she read the news reports that said he'd been killed. She swallowed hard, forcing the ache in her throat to sink into a painful knot in her stomach.

"I thought we would at least discuss it first! What the assignment is, how long you'll be gone, where you'll be going…"

How dangerous it would be…

"I swear, Alexa, I won't be gone long, and when I'm back, I'll—"

"Call?" she filled in. After all, they had played this scene once before. She knew how it ended. With Chance grabbing his things and leaving her behind—hurt, angry and determined to harden her heart.

She didn't even know why she thought this time might be different, but that same toxic mix of emotions was already building inside her chest. Is that how it would always be? Chance resenting her for asking him to stay while she resented him for telling her he had to go?

"Were you even going to tell me you were leaving or were you planning to sneak out and avoid any messy farewells?"

"That's not fair, Alexa."

"Not fair?" Pulling her hand from his, she pointed at the duffel bag and demanded, "You want to talk about not fair? Your editor just called, but tell me, Chance, how long has that bag been packed and ready to go? Days? Weeks?"

His jaw tightened in response, revealing the answer he wouldn't give, and that knot inside her tripled.

Her voice thick with unshed tears, she whispered, "I can live with you being gone, Chance, but what I can't take is for you to have one foot out the door even when you're here."

Chance flinched as if she'd struck him. "That's not—do

you want to know why I had that bag packed, why I didn't stop to talk to you about the assignment before I said yes? I knew if I slowed down for even a second, that if I didn't leave now, I never would!"

He ducked his head, his voice barely audible as he confessed, "I'm afraid, Alexa."

Her heart ached at the pained admission. "Of course you are, Chance! Who wouldn't be after what happened last time?"

"I'm not afraid for me," he said as he shook his head. "What if something happens to you while I'm gone? What if something happens to the baby?"

He looked up then, and Alexa forgot how to breathe. Forgot...everything for a second, held spellbound by the vulnerability she never would have thought she'd see. Linking his fingers with hers, he held on tight as if he'd never let her go.

Faint wings of hope fluttered within her chest as she whispered, "Oh, Chance... I can't promise you that nothing will happen to me." Even as tears filled her eyes, she gave a small laugh at the reversal of roles. Wasn't she the one who was supposed to be afraid of losing him? Wasn't he the one who was supposed to reassure her?

And yet wasn't that what loving someone could do? Make you vulnerable and yet invincible? Weak and yet strong. Overjoyed and terrified, all at the same time.

"But you've shown me that some risks are worth taking and some of the best things in life are unplanned. Like meeting you, like this baby...like falling in love."

His throat moved as he swallowed, and he opened his mouth but the words didn't come. Disappointment tugged at her heart, but Alexa refused to allow the emotion to take hold. Maybe, maybe admitting how he felt would leave Chance too vulnerable. Maybe it was her turn to be strong. Strong enough to let him go and strong enough to believe he would return.

He took a step back as she stood. "Alexa—"

Reaching up, she cupped his face in her hands. "It's all right. I'll be right back."

It didn't take her long to find what she was looking for in the tiny bedroom. Chance was standing where she had left him, and Alexa didn't know if she'd ever seen him so still. As if on the edge of a crumbling precipice, not knowing which way to turn.

So different from the man she'd met in Santa Barbara, the one who'd known exactly where he was going, the one whose steps were confident and sure—even as he'd walked away from her.

That was the man she needed him to be. The man who could shut off his emotions with the single-minded purpose of getting his shot. The man who could keep his head in the game and who would survive and come back to her.

"Here." Slipping her hand into his, she pressed the butterfly hairpin into his palm. "It's your good-luck charm, remember? I want you to take it with you, and then I want—I want you to bring it back to me."

Chapter Sixteen

"So, Alexa." Seated at a table in the Hillcrest dining room, Virginia Mayhew pinned Alexa with her piercing blue gaze. "Where is this young man of yours?"

Focusing on the grilled salmon she had no desire to eat, Alexa said, "He had to leave on a business trip. I'm sorry, Grandmother. I know how you hate to travel."

Virginia sniffed as she smoothed a napkin over her silk skirt. "Well, thank goodness for private planes. Had I been forced to fly commercial, I'd be tempted to chase after him and give him a piece of my mind."

A small smile tugged at the corners of her mouth at the idea of her grandmother dressing Chance down in some middle of nowhere dot on the map.

Seeing the McClaren family together at Thanksgiving, Alexa had known she needed to call her grandmother to tell her about the baby. This was not just her child. This was Virginia's great-grandchild.

Alexa had been dreading telling her grandmother she was pregnant, fearing how her somewhat old-fashioned, austere grandmother might react. But Virginia had surprised her. After a moment of stunned silence, she had offered her genuine congratulations. And then she'd caught Alexa completely off guard with her offer to travel to Clearville to meet Chance.

Something she'd wanted to surprise him with and then completely forgot about when he told her he was leaving. But he would be back. He'd meet her grandmother some other time. Alexa held on to that belief with her whole heart.

"I'm so sorry you came all this way for nothing—"

"I came all this way for *you*, Alexa. Yes, I wanted to meet the father of your child, but I came to see you. I've missed you."

"I don't think you've ever said that before."

"You never left before." Even though a hint of reproach entered Virginia's voice, she shook her head. "And that's my fault."

"I don't understand."

"You're a grown woman, Alexa. You should have married and started your own family years ago. Instead you've spent the last two decades living— Well, not just living with an old woman, but living *like* an old woman."

"That's not—entirely true," Alexa protested, her weekend with Chance—and all that followed—the exception that proved the rule.

"You're in love with him, aren't you?" her grandmother asked.

"I do love him, but—"

"You're afraid."

"I— Yes, how did you know?"

Virginia sighed. "Because I've spent most of my life

feeling that same way. The exact same way I've taught you to live. Always afraid to trust. Always afraid to love." Her blue eyes filled with regret as she confessed, "And I am sorry for that, Alexa."

"Grandmother, no. You've taught me so much! About business, about the foundation."

Her grandmother waved a blue-veined hand. "Business, yes. I've taught you about business. But about life? About love? I'm afraid that is where I've failed miserably." Virginia signaled a server to box up the food neither of them had much interest in eating.

After the young woman swept the table clear and brought hot water for their tea, she said, "I know you don't remember your grandfather. He died while you were still a baby, but he was the love of my life. And your father was his spitting image. In ways that were both fortunate and unfortunate."

"I'm sorry I don't remember him." Alexa warmed her hands on the ceramic mug, fascinated by this side of her grandmother she had never seen before.

"They both had such energy. Lighting a room simply by stepping foot inside. I never felt as truly alive as I did when I was with your grandfather. And when he died—and then your father and mother died only a few years later... Somehow they took all that light, all that life with them."

Virginia shook her head and reached for a packet of sugar, her movement brisk and efficient as she poured the sweetener into her tea. Her voice crisp and matter-of-fact even as she admitted, "I was devastated. I didn't know how I'd go on without them, and to my shame, for a long time, I didn't want to."

As a child, Alexa had thought only of her own loss. Her mother, her father...gone. She hadn't stopped to think of Virginia's loss. It had seemed to her, at the time, as though her grandmother hadn't cared. Now, as an adult, she could better understand that Virginia had cared too much. "I'm so sorry, Grandmother."

"I wish I had been strong enough to show you how to move on, but instead I was stuck in my own sorrow. I hope someday you can forgive me for that."

"There's nothing to forgive. I loved them, too, but my parents were—unpredictable to say the least. I needed someone I could count on. Needed you."

"I hope that's true, Alexa. But it's time for you to live your own life now. Don't let your fear of losing love keep you from grabbing it with both hands and holding on tight."

Some risks are worth taking...like falling in love.

Alexa's voice echoed through his thoughts as Chance paced the waiting area at the San Francisco airport. Louder than his fellow passengers wheeling by with luggage, louder than the conversations carried on by people with cell phones all around him, louder than the distant roar of the airplane engines.

He'd made the long drive from Clearville at a record pace, not stopping to give himself time to think, only to arrive at check-in and discover the city's frequent fog had delayed the inbound plane.

Leaving him with nothing to do but wait...and think.

She loved him. Alexa had all but said the words, and in return he'd left her. Walked away from the woman carrying his child. The woman who loved him.

The woman *he* loved.

All his life he'd lived on the edge. He relished adventure and excitement. Willing to take the greatest risk for the greatest reward.

God, he was such a fraud!

Chance bent over in the chair, elbows braced on his

knees. He was brave enough to put his life on the line, but when it came to his heart? When it came to telling Alexa how he felt, he'd been a total coward.

He glanced at his watch. Damn, had his battery died? It couldn't be—but a quick look at the digital clock behind the flight attendant's station confirmed that only five minutes had passed.

After trying to sit for a few minutes with his knee jittering like a jackhammer, Chance shot to his feet. Paced. Sat. Paced some more.

"Settle down, son," the elderly man seated a few chairs away said. "No need for all this commotion. Flying's the safest way to travel."

He wasn't afraid to fly. He'd never been afraid to fly. So why was he suddenly so...terrified?

The intercom crackled, but instead of hearing the announcement, his father's voice echoed through his mind. *We just want you to slow down long enough to ask yourself if the life you're living is still the one you want.*

Slow down... The jackhammering in his leg came to a gradual stop as Chance sucked in a deep breath and asked himself if there was something he wanted more.

"I don't want to leave."

He didn't realize he'd spoken the words out loud until the old man glanced over his wire-framed reading glasses and said, "Well, then, maybe an airport isn't the best place for you to be."

The vibration of his cell phone shot Chance from the chair once more, and he scrambled to pull it from his pocket. His crazily racing heart sank when an unfamiliar number flashed across the screen. "Hello?"

"Mr. McClaren, my name is Roslynn St. Clare. You don't know me, but I own an art gallery in Beverly Hills and I saw some of your work at the Mayhew charity auction a few months ago."

"Ms. St. Clare, this is a surprise."

"A good one, I hope, once you hear what I have to say. It turns out I have an opening in the New Year and would like to showcase your work. We can finalize the details with your agent later, but I wanted to speak with you personally first. It will be a solo show, of course, as befitting your talent with a four-week run."

Listening as the woman discussed the impressive terms, Chance knew most photographers would jump at the opportunity. But he couldn't accept an offer he wasn't 100 percent certain he'd earned.

"I'm sorry, Ms. St. Clare. I don't know what Alexa told you, but I'm not interested in a gallery show."

Judging by the silence that followed, Chance figured not many people turned down a woman like Roslynn St. Clare. "I don't know what it is you *think* Alexa Mayhew told me. We discussed your work the night of the auction, but I had another engagement and had to leave before you arrived. I am sorry we didn't get to meet that night and—"

"Wait," Chance interrupted, "you spoke to Alexa that night? At the auction?"

Before he and Alexa had even met? Before she would have had any possible reason to suggest a showing of his photographs other than a real and *honest* appreciation of his work?

After another silence, the gallery owner stated, "You seem somewhat distracted, Mr. McClaren. Why don't you get with your agent and take a day or so to think about my offer and get back to me?"

But as Roslynn ended the call, Chance wasn't thinking about getting back to her. All he could think about was getting back to Alexa.

* * *

"What do you mean Alexa's gone?" Chance stalked after his cousin as she walked through the lobby, ever-present tablet in hand.

"I mean, she...left." Evie stopped to examine the display of brochures touting local businesses and upcoming Clearville events before making a note with her stylus on the glowing screen. It took every ounce of self-control he possessed not to jerk the damn thing from her hands and chuck it clear into the Pacific.

"She left."

Giving an exasperated sigh, she turned to face him. "Alexa is gone. Alexa has left. And repeating everything I say doesn't change that."

"Fine. *When* did she leave? I was only gone—"

"Oh, that's right. *You* were gone. And nope, repeating that doesn't change things either, does it?"

He should have known Evie wouldn't cut him any slack, not after her own less than stellar romantic history. After practically being left at the altar, she didn't think too highly of men who bailed.

"Her grandmother arrived and they left together."

"Her—" Chance stopped himself before he could echo Evie yet again.

"Yes, Virginia Mayhew flew in on a private jet, had a limo, and a bodyguard roughly the size of the Hulk, the whole 'crazy rich' nine yards."

"Her grandmother came to take her home?"

"No, actually, she came to meet you, the father of Alexa's baby, only..." Her voice trailed off with a pointed look as she waited for him.

"I was gone," he filled in on cue.

Years ago, he'd been in a plane that had lost altitude, plunging thousands of feet in seconds. That was nothing compared to the way his stomach dropped now. Alexa had all but said she loved him and what had he done? Walked out on her in return. And then he'd expected, what? For her to just sit around and wait for him to come back?

He swore beneath his breath. "I screwed up, Evie."

"That you did." Softening her stance slightly, she held out her tablet and said, "But you can't fix it while she's there and you're here."

Looking at the screen, Chance saw an airline website and a list of flights to LA.

"Oh, my gosh! Isn't this just…spectacular?"

Alexa managed a smile as Raquel rose on tiptoe and craned her neck to take in the glitz and glamour of the hotel ballroom. Gowns of every color gleamed beneath the golden chandelier, the light reflecting on the flash of rubies, emeralds and diamonds. Laughter and the clink of champagne flutes filled the air as the guests mingled together.

"And you look amazing! Have I told you how totally unfair it is that you look sexier pregnant than I do after dieting for the past three months?"

Alexa smoothed a hand along the skirt of her off-the-shoulder seafoam green gown. Having just hit the eighteen-week mark, the chiffon folds of the empire waist didn't quite hide her baby bump. "You don't need to diet. Most women would kill for your curves."

"I still can't believe I'm here with all these famous people!" Her grandmother's assistant looked stunning in a violet halter-style gown that complemented her dark hair and olive skin. Seeming to catch herself, Raquel sank back down on her heels and added, "And, um, it's for such a worthy cause."

"You've done a wonderful job." While Alexa had done

the initial work organizing the Giving Thanks benefit, Raquel had proved herself over the past few weeks. Alexa had no doubt that she was leaving her grandmother in good hands.

"We both know I couldn't have pulled this off without you laying the groundwork. And I can't tell you how much I appreciate all the faith you've put in me."

Alexa's heart tugged a little at the younger woman's words, but the sentimental moment ended as Raquel grabbed her arm with a gasp. "Did you see who just walked in?" A meteor shower of camera flashes announced the arrival of the latest Hollywood heartthrob. "Do you think I could go meet him? Just to, you know…"

"Welcome him on behalf of the Mayhew Foundation?" Alexa suggested wryly.

"Yes! Yes, that is exactly what I will do. I will *welcome* him." Straightening her shoulders, Raquel smoothed her hands over her skirt before giving one last half-swallowed squeal of excitement. "He is *so* hot!"

Chuckling to herself, Alexa watched Raquel cross the ballroom to meet the famous actor. Despite whatever fan-girl nerves she might have felt inside, the young woman was the epitome of professionalism as she shook the man's hand and thanked him for his support.

"She's right, you know."

Alexa glanced over her shoulder as her grandmother joined her. "I had no idea you were such an action-star fan."

"Don't be impertinent, young lady," Virginia scolded, but a small smile tugged at her grandmother's lined lips. "We couldn't have done this without you. It's a fitting farewell."

Tears scratched at the back of her throat. "It's not like I'm leaving the foundation."

On the trip back to LA, Alexa had talked to her grandmother about doing more, being more than simply the face of the foundation. How she wanted to be more hands-on, game-planning for how the money raised could be put to use and seeing at ground level the results of what all that hard work had brought to fruition.

The words had rushed out of her on a single breath of air, leaving her a little light-headed. Discussing her ideas with Lindsay and Theresa in Clearville was one thing. Bringing them up to her grandmother had been something else entirely.

But her grandmother had surprised her once more. "You're a Mayhew, Alexa. There is nothing a Mayhew can't do."

Alexa had laughed at that. After all the years of what a Mayhew didn't do...

Gazing around the ballroom, Virginia said, "I'm looking forward to seeing your efforts come to life, Alexa. But for now, I think there's a certain action movie star I would like to meet. From what I've heard, he's...hot."

Her smile faded as her grandmother walked away, leaving Alexa by herself in the ballroom. It was impossible to ignore the memories of the last time she was on her own in a gilded ballroom, surrounded by wealthy and famous people.

"Can I have this dance?"

Alexa froze, certain she was imaging things. Because the deep voice sending chills down her spine sounded just like... Slowly turning around, her breath caught in her throat. "Chance!"

He looked heart-stoppingly gorgeous in a black tuxedo, the onyx buttons marching down his chest a sharp contrast to the crisp white shirt. "This is our song, isn't it?" He stood with his hands casually tucked in his pockets, but a hint of nerves gave him away. His right hand twitched, rippling the material of his trousers.

"What—what are you doing here? What happened with your assignment?"

"I'm here because this is where you are and because I wanted to give you this." He withdrew his hand from his pocket, but instead of holding out the butterfly hairpin, he held a ring. A princess-cut diamond in a platinum art deco setting sparkled beneath the crystal chandelier, stunning in its simplicity.

"Chance…"

"If you don't like it, you can always pick out something else."

She couldn't imagine finding a ring she would like more. "It's beautiful, but I—" Her voice broke on the word, but she held her head high. She and her grandmother might have come to an understanding, but not everything had changed. There were still some things a Mayhew did not do. Including having a meltdown in the middle of a charity event. "I know how important your job is to you. How much it is a part of you—"

"You're right. It is a part of me, but only a small part. When it comes to you and our baby, I'm all in. Not just both feet, but heart and soul," he vowed. "I talked to Roslynn St. Clare. Thankfully the woman is used to dealing with temperamental artists, so even if she does think I'm a complete whack job, she's still willing to work with me on a showing."

Her heart pounded as she tried to grasp hold of what his acceptance might mean, and Chance wasn't done yet.

"I've looked at the dark side of life through my camera lens for too long. I want to focus on the good. Like the work done by the charities the Mayhew Foundation supports. The schools and clinics and shelters."

The elegant ballroom seemed to twirl in a crazy kaleidoscope as Alexa's head spun dizzily. Chance's vision of his future so perfectly matched her own that she couldn't have planned it better if she tried. "Are you sure, Chance? That you'll be happy…"

"With you? With our baby? Nothing could make me happier." He flashed her a smile that was one part cocky, one part nerves as he said, "Except maybe you saying you'll marry me."

"Oh, Chance."

"I love you, Alexa. I should have said it before…"

"You're saying it now, that's all that matters." The emotion in his eyes sparkled as brightly as the lights reflecting in the diamond ring, but one lingering doubt held her back. "What—what would you do if I wasn't pregnant?"

"If you weren't pregnant?" His expression gentled as he gazed down at her. "Is that what you're worried about? You shouldn't be because that's an easy question to answer. If you weren't pregnant, I'd do my damnedest to get you that way."

Pure pleasure rippled through her at the sensual promise. "Well, it's not like you can get me more pregnant."

His teeth flashed in a dimpled grin. "That's no reason not to keep trying. But the next time you're in my bed, I would very much like to be making love to my wife."

"I love you, Chance, and yes, I will marry you!"

After slipping the ring on her finger, Chance pulled her into his arms, and Alexa forgot all about what a Mayhew did not do as he kissed her in a ballroom filled with people. He held her tight as if they'd been apart for months, and she knew that no matter how far he might travel, he would always be with her. In the love she held in her heart. In the child they created together.

When Chance swept her into his arms beneath a sparkling chandelier all those months ago, Alexa would never have imagined he would be the man she would love, the man she would marry...

Life would never be without risks, but this was one chance she would never regret taking.

* * * * *